Wicked Altar

A Dark Irish Mafia Arranged Marriage Romance

The McCarthy Family Legacy

Jane Henry

Synopsis

I've hated Cavin McCarthy since the day he made me cry in a school closet.

He was my tormentor. My nightmare. The cruel boy who turned my name into a punchline and my life into hell.

Now? He's my fiancé.

An arranged marriage neither of us wanted, brokered by families who deal in blood and power. I'd refuse if I could. But my sister is dying, and the McCarthy's hold the key to saving her life.

So I'll walk down the aisle. I'll say the vows. I'll become Mrs. Cavin McCarthy.

But I'll never forgive him.

Except... the monster I remember isn't the man standing before me now. The boy who destroyed me has become someone who fights for me. Protects me. Touches me like I'm something precious instead of broken.

And when his hands are on my throat, his voice rough in my ear, I'm not thinking about revenge anymore.

I'm only thinking about surrender.

Chapter One

Cavin

I STAND with my hands folded in front of me, the bitter cold of a Ballyhock winter seeping through my wool coat as I stare down at what's left of Malachy.

"No one can know about this, lad." Malachy's last words. The envelope in my pocket weighs more than the coffin we carried. After the prayers, I'll deliver it. One last secret for a man buried in them.

In my peripheral vision, my brother Seamus, the eldest, stands beside our father and mother. Da looks distinguished and broken. Malachy was a second father to him.

Mam looks poised as always, her expression gentle despite the frown creasing her brow. Her hands rest on Da's forearm, folded and still—but I know better. She's always alert. My sisters stand on either side of her, dressed in formal charcoal gray—Kyla on guard and frowning, Bronwyn, the baby of the family, quietly sniffing and wiping at her eyes with a balled-up tissue.

My cousin Declan whispers something in Bronwyn's ear that makes her smile and elbow him. Garrett, a family friend, his trademark red hair stark against the cold blue sky, snorts. I shoot them all a sharp look—this isn't the fucking *time*—and they straighten up quick enough.

It's a huge turnout. I swear half of Ballyhock's come to pay their respects, which makes sense when I think about the man Malachy was, and the way our father always made sure the McCarthy men stayed within the good graces of the residents of Ballyhock. Even the best of them will overlook our... transgressions... when we toss half a million quid in the Holy Family coffers.

"Ashes to ashes," Father Gregory says in a monotone, his hand steady as he makes the sign of the cross over the coffin. My mother makes the sign of the cross and whispers what must be a prayer under her breath.

I rub my hand across my eyes. Haven't slept more than a few hours straight since prison, and it's showing.

"Mad, isn't it? Only death or marriage gets us all in the same place anymore," my cousin Daire mutters to me. He's not wrong.

I stare at the coffin. It was lighter to carry than I expected. Malachy lost weight at the end, before he lost his battle to illness and old age, and I guess the lads and I are stronger than we once were.

Movement catches my eye—someone shifting near the far

edge of the graveyard, half hidden behind a weathered angel statue.

A woman—blonde hair whipping in the wind and black coat buttoned to her throat.

She's not with the main gathering but is separate, alone, kneeling at a grave with white roses clutched in her gloved hands.

And she's staring right at *me.*

My breath catches. Is that...? It *can't* be.

Erin *fucking* Kavanagh. Perfect little Erin.

What the bloody hell is *she* doing here?

She's fifty yards away, maybe more, but I'd recognize her anywhere. That sharp little face. Those eyes that always looked at me like I was something she'd scraped off her shoe. The way she holds herself—stiff, controlled, like she's afraid she'll fly apart if she loosens her grip.

Only she's not the scrawny little bitch from St. Albert's anymore. She's filled out—tits, hips, the lot. Even in that shapeless coat, I can see the curve of her. My mouth goes dry. I want to look away, but I can't.

Christ, I'm a bastard for noticing her arse at a funeral.

She ducks her head when she realizes I've clocked her. Pretends to fuss with the flowers, but her hands are shaking now.

Good.

The Kavanaghs sent flowers yesterday, including a card with her father's signature, not hers. So why the fuck is

Padraic Kavanagh's daughter kneeling at a grave in McCarthy territory during our funeral?

My hand moves to my side, where my gun sits under my coat. Instinct. Even from this distance, I could drop her before she screams.

The thought shouldn't make my cock twitch... but it does.

My eyes narrow. Is she spying for her da? Or did she just want to watch me squirm? That'd be just like her—Little Miss Perfect, always so fucking eager to see me brought low. *Again.*

I should look away. Focus on Malachy, on the prayers, on the envelope burning a hole in my pocket.

She looks up. Our eyes lock across fifty yards of dead ground.

Her lips part, just slightly, and I see her breath catch. See the exact moment recognition hits. See fear chase hatred across her face.

My pulse kicks up, and my hands curl into fists.

She doesn't look away fast enough. Her lips part, and her pupils dilate... just for a second—a flash—before the fear slams back into place. But I saw it. That flicker of want. I've spent ten years imagining what fear looks like on Erin Kavanagh's face. I know every expression she's capable of. And that wasn't just fear.

I start walking toward her. She can answer my questions or run. I almost *hope* she runs. I hope she—

The explosion tears through the silence like a goddamn

scream of a banshee. One second, we're standing under the gray winter sky; the next, it's fire, noise, and chaos.

A blast punches through my chest like an open palm. The light is blinding, first white, then orange, devouring all color from the world. The ground jumps beneath my feet. People scream.

I hit the dirt hard, knees scraping gravel, ears ringing like a struck bell. Copper taste floods my mouth—I bit my tongue. Smoke burns my throat.

Jesus, Mary, and holy fuckin' Joseph, someone bombed the lot of us.

My first thought: *my family*. My second thought: *Erin*.

Fuck. Why her? Of all the people here, why is my brain looking for her? I don't even like the bitch.

I don't have time to question it—my body's already moving, eyes cutting through smoke and chaos before my brain catches up. Looking for that black coat, that blonde hair I've wanted to yank since we were kids. She's gone.

Fucking instinct. Fucking Malachy drilling protection into my skull since I could walk. *Protect the family. Protect the weak. Even when the weak is a stuck-up bitch.*

My hands ball into fists. My jaw locks so hard my teeth ache. Shouts blur with sobs, and the sharp, metallic scent of blood fills the air as I lurch to my feet. The gravel tears at my palms when I push myself up. Smoke chokes the air, thick and acrid. Bodies everywhere—some moving, some not. Screams. Sirens in the distance.

I should leave her. Let her family find her. Let someone else play hero.

My feet are already moving.

Fucking hell.

I vault over a toppled headstone and sprint toward the angel statue where she was kneeling.

But she's vanished. Did *she* have anything to do with this? *Goddamn.* If her father put her—

And then I see her—bent over on the ground, crumpled and unconscious, lying in the shadow of the angel statue. My rage dissipates.

"Erin." I drop to my knees beside her, my hands hovering. I don't know where to touch her. If she's hurt. If she's...

She moves. A small flinch, then her hand comes up to her head.

"Easy." My voice comes out rougher than I mean it to. "Easy, lass. Don't move yet."

Her eyes flutter open. Unfocused. Dazed.

There's blood trickling from her ear.

Fuck.

"Can you hear me?" I lean closer. "Erin. Can you hear me?"

Her lips move, but no sound comes out. Her pupils are blown wide. I can see myself reflected in them—blood on my face, dirt in my hair. I look like the monster she always thought I was.

Then recognition hits, and her eyes go wide. She tries to pull away.

"Don't." I catch her shoulders, gripping hard enough to keep her still. "You might be hurt, and I don't fancy carrying your dead weight out of here."

She's shaking, her whole body trembling under my hands.

I don't care. She's fragile, and I don't fucking care.

I scan her quickly. Blood from her ear, but nothing that'll kill her. No broken bones. Just shock, making her useless.

Typical.

"You need to get out of here," I tell her. "Can you stand, or am I fucking dragging you?"

She stares at me, then blinks slowly, like she's trying to process the words.

"Erin." I give her shoulders a shake, not gentle. "Can. You. Fucking. Stand?"

She stares at me like I've spoken a foreign language. Fuck, she's useless in a crisis.

She nods. "I think."

I slide one arm around her waist and haul her to her feet. She's light—*too* light. Breakable.

"Christ." I tighten my grip, pulling her against my side. "Hold on to me."

I need to check on my family.

"I don't—" Her voice cracks. "I don't need—"

"Shut up and hold on."

She does. Her fingers curl into my coat, gripping tight like I'm the only solid thing in the world.

And maybe I am. Right now, in this moment, with the graveyard on fire and people screaming and blood in the air —maybe I am.

I can feel every inch of her pressed against me. The soft give of her tits against my ribs. The tremble in her thighs. Her pulse hammering where my thumb digs into her side. She smells like roses and smoke and fear. My cock stirs. Sick bastard. There's a bomb site twenty yards away, and I'm getting hard.

Good. I *want* to be this fucked up. I want to be the kind of man who gets hard carrying a half-dead woman away from a bombing. At least then I'll know exactly what I am.

Damn this woman for distracting me.

I need to check on my family.

I half carry, half drag her away from the blast site, toward the low stone wall at the edge of the graveyard. Behind us, voices shout orders. Someone's crying. Smoke billows black against the gray sky.

When we reach the wall, I set her down as gently as I can. She immediately curls into herself, arms wrapped around her middle, head down.

Counting. She's counting under her breath. I can see her lips moving.

One, two, three, four. Over and over.

I remember that from school, the way she'd do it when she was overwhelmed. She'd tap her fingers, count things, anything to anchor herself.

Now I want to count with her or make her stop. Make her look at me instead.

"Stay here," I tell her. "Don't move. I'll come back for you."

Her head snaps up.

"Don't leave me here." There's panic in her voice now, raw and real. "Please. Don't—"

"I have to check on my family." I crouch down so we're eye level. "But I'll come back. I swear it."

She stares at me, those sharp eyes searching my face for a lie.

"Five minutes," I promise. "Just give me five minutes."

She doesn't answer. Just goes back to counting, rocking slightly.

Fuck.

I straighten, then turn toward the chaos—

Seamus stands ten feet away, weapons drawn, scanning the area with lethal focus. His gaze lands on me, then drops to Erin. His expression doesn't change, but I see the question in his eyes.

What the fuck?

"She was caught in the blast," I say quickly. "Kavanagh's daughter."

"I know who she is." Seamus's voice is flat. Dangerous. "What's she doing here?"

"I don't know."

"Convenient timing."

"I know." I scan the lot. "Where's Bronwyn?" I ask, changing the subject.

Seamus's face goes hard. "We don't know."

Ice floods my veins. "What do you mean *you don't know?*"

"She's gone, Cav. Mam's hysterical. Kyla found her shoe, but—" He breaks off, shaking his head. "We're searching now."

My vision tunnels. Someone's going to bleed for this. Someone's going to fucking scream. This wasn't meant to happen.

A flash of red hair catches my eye—Garrett, pushing through the smoke, his usually smirking face gone white with shock. He's got blood on his shirt, but he's moving fine, helping Lorcan herd people away from the blast site. "Garrett and Lorcan got the west side covered," Seamus adds, following my gaze. "He was near Bronwyn before it went off. Says he lost sight of her in the chaos."

Christ, I thought I had time. I swore I'd keep her safe.

The envelope. The tribute. That's what this is about.

"I'll help search," I start, but Seamus cuts me off.

"No. Get the Kavanagh girl somewhere safe and then come back. We don't need civilians in the middle of this."

He stalks away before I can argue. I turn back to Erin. She's watching me now. Some of the daze has cleared from her eyes, replaced by something sharper, more aware. Her gaze drops to my mouth, then away, quickly, like she didn't mean to look.

"Come on." I offer my hand.

"I'm fine, thank you," she says, Little Miss Perfect turning her nose up at me.

Why the fuck am I offering my hand? My mam raised me to be a gentleman, but she's no friend of mine.

 My voice comes out rougher than I intend. "Take it. You need to get the fuck out of here."

She stares at my outstretched palm like it might burn her. Her throat works as she swallows. The space between us feels charged and wrong, like we're both waiting for something to detonate again. Then, slowly, too slowly, she slides her hand into mine.

Christ.

Her palm is small and cold against mine. Delicate bones I could crush without trying. Soft skin I want to bruise. Her fingers curl around my hand, the grip tightening. She's shaking. So am I.

Electricity shoots up my arm and settles low in my belly, hot and wrong.

I could pull her close, fist my hand in that blonde hair. I feel it in my chest… in my fucking teeth. The way her pulse jumps against my thumb where it rests on her wrist. This girl who hated me, who ratted me out at every turn. Who looked at me like I was dirt. This girl whose hand fits in mine like it was made for it, but...

 What kind of woman shows up at our funeral, then takes the hand of a man she hates? Unless she's not afraid of me.

Unless... unless she *knew* this was coming. I pull her close—not gentle. Her eyes go wide.

"If you had anything to do with this," I say, low enough that only she can hear, "I'll know."

"What the *hell* are you talking about?"

I huff out a growl, then I drag her toward the car, her hand locked in mine. Not because I want to touch her. I need her out of my hair and back where she belongs... as far away from me as she can get.

Chapter Two

Erin

"WELL, THEN," I say with forced cheerfulness. "At least your lunch is sort of a game, isn't it?"

Bridget tries to smile, but it twists into something closer to pain, the kind she's gotten too good at hiding.

"Aye? What do you mean?"

I poke at the white sauce over some no-name meat and shrug. "You have to *guess* what it is."

My younger sister giggles, and my heart warms. It's a good day when I can make her smile.

"Tell you what," I say, pushing to my feet. "I'll fetch you something better than this, alright?"

Standard caretaker script. It works eighty-nine percent of the time.

"Would you?" Her eyes have gone pale blue under the latest dose of meds, and her lips are the softest blush of pink. Pupil dilation suggests the prednisone dose increased. Blue-gray sclera indicates—

Stop it, Erin.

My stomach plummets when she turns, her hospital gown falling over her shoulder. I can see her bones poking through her skin. "I'd kill for a proper sausage roll. Can you get one, for real?"

Darling, I'll give you the moon.

I reach for her too-thin hand and find it cold as ice. I tuck the blanket tighter around her. "Course I will," I say softly.

I don't want to leave her though. When she's here at St. Vincent's, I don't even like to go home to sleep because I live in deadly fear that tomorrow might be the day I get the call that she's gone.

Aplastic anemia, they call it, bone marrow failure.

I call it injustice.

Before I leave, I quickly check the color-coded notes I left for the nursing staff, double-check the locks on all her windows, and pat my pocket four times to make sure I didn't lose my mobile or keys.

I kiss her wan cheek and tuck a stray strand of hair behind her ear. "Mam'll be in soon, after her meeting," I whisper.

"Yay," Bridget deadpans. "Can't wait."

I stifle a grimace. Bridget was her golden child, the beautiful angel of a girl with auburn hair, bright blue eyes, and rosy cheeks. My mother toted her around with her like a prize, dressed her in the prettiest dresses and frilliest bonnets. I was too awkward for any parading, and we all knew it.

Then Bridget got sick, and Mam won't forgive her for it.

"Don't fret, love. I'll be back long before that."

Bridget rolls her eyes. "I'm not *fretting*. Jesus, Erin, you sound like an old lady."

I huff out a breath and roll my eyes. "There are worse things. At least men leave old ladies alone." She laughs as the door shuts behind me.

Twice. I made her laugh twice. Sometimes it happens without me even trying. My chest loosens just a fraction.

I walk to the door with my head held high, shoulders back, chin up. People don't bother you when you look like you know where you're going.

My *god*, it reeks in here. Who the fuck decided that cabbage was a good idea for dinner? In a *hospital*?

I tug my cardigan tighter, pressing my lips into a hard line.

Outside Bridget's room, leaning against the wall, arms crossed like some eternal sentinel, stands the ever-watchful shadow I can't shake.

"Evening, Miss Erin."

Darragh smiles and straightens, broad as a doorframe. He's been with us for years—long enough to know why he's really here. Not just to protect us from outside threats, but to keep Bridget hidden when she's here. To make sure no one sees her wheeled to radiation appointments, no one asks why Padraic Kavanagh's youngest daughter hasn't been seen in public for months.

Can't let people know the golden child is tarnished.

"Have you been standing here the whole time?" I arch a brow.

"Where else would I be?" he says.

I sigh and push past him toward the door.

"I don't need a watchdog, you know."

"Good thing I'm not a dog, then." His gaze flicks to the swinging hospital doors. "Your da pays me to make sure you don't end up dead. That's my job."

"What about Bridget? Aren't you gonna stay with her?"

"Her guard's enough. Your da doesn't like you out and about alone."

Don't I know it.

I roll my eyes and tuck my mobile deeper into my coat pocket, fingers tapping it four times. Just to be sure.

Keys too.

Tap, tap, tap, tap.

The motion steadies me, but I feel his eyes catch the rhythm.

"I'm fetching a sausage roll for Bridget. The food in this hospital's shite."

"Aye," he grunts. Just that.

He falls into step beside me as I stride down the hall. His boots thud, low and soft. My flats hit harder, sharper. Sounds echo in the hospital corridors.

Outside, the air is damp and cool, the kind that sneaks into your bones and stays there. I wince at the city noise—traffic, voices, that messy pulse that never stops.

Darragh scans the streets like a soldier.

The bakery on the corner smells like butter and sugar, but the moment I step inside, the heat and chatter hit me like a wall.

Too loud. Too hot. Too many fucking people.

Uncomfortable, I shift my weight, then tap my thigh. Finger-nails in threes this time. A different rhythm... a quieter one.

"Miss Erin," Darragh mutters beside me. "Want me to queue for you?"

"No," I say, sharper than I mean to. "Thank you. I'm fine. I'm not some helpless little lass who can't handle a line."

Not anymore. Not like when I was younger.

Back then, the overload would've had me curled up in a corner, rocking, crying, lost—praying my mother wouldn't lose her temper at me again for being "difficult."

A man at the counter leans back, loud enough for half the bakery to hear. His Dublin accent is rough as gravel.

"Aye, but the *McCarthys*—word is, they might not be untouchable anymore. Somebody's making them bleed."

My spine goes rigid.

I don't want to hear it. Don't want to care.

I don't go to St. Albert's anymore. The McCarthys are dead to me.

A ripple of noise rises—some curious, some pitying, some just plain nosy.

Good. Let the McCarthys fucking bleed.

I can't think about Cavin McCarthy without my pulse kicking up like a traitor.

His hand around my waist. The heat of him pressed against me, every hard plane of his body against my softness. His voice in my ear rough, commanding. The way I wanted to lean into him. Let him carry me. Let him—

Christ, what's wrong with me?

My thighs clench. Unbidden. Unwanted.

He made me cry in the school toilets more times than I can count. He called me "Little Miss Perfect," among other things. He made me feel like something broken and wrong.

One moment of forced chivalry doesn't change that.

Doesn't change how small he made me feel. Or how I apparently also shivered when he touched me.

My body doesn't seem to care that he's the enemy. Doesn't care that he hurt me. It just remembers his hands. His heat. The way my body fit against his like—

Christ, what is *wrong* with me?

He's *not* a hero. He's *not* safe. And I need to remember that.

I fix my eyes on the glass case of pastries, pretending indifference.

I can feel Darragh's unreadable stare.

"Do they know who did it yet?"

"Not that I know of. You were there." His voice is flat, knowing.

My throat tightens. "So?"

"So you're shaking."

I am. Dammit. I press my hands flat against my thighs.

"The McCarthys are no friends of yours," he says, quieter now.

"No." My voice sounds hollow. "They're not. But the residents of Ballyhock adore them, don't they?"

"Aye."

The golden ones. The untouchables.

"Can I help you, miss?"

I force a smile. My turn. A gray-haired gentleman with a bushy mustache smiles at me.

"Aye. One sausage roll, please."

"Of course. Can I get you anything else?"

"Mmm... bit of soda bread. Please."

My stomach growls. I can't even remember the last thing I ate.

"Here you are," he says, sliding them across the counter. "How are you today?"

Tears sting, fast and sharp.

My throat tightens. I swallow it down, wishing I could tell someone, but the town is full of gossips, and my parents have worked hard at keeping Bridget's illness quiet.

"I'm good," I lie, pretending to yawn to cover up my sudden surge of emotion. "You?"

"Good, good," he says with a smile, before he moves on to the next customer.

But as I turn, my mind's no longer on Bridget but on the whispers circling the room. The shiny black car that purrs by the shop, drawing every eye.

Everyone's talking about the McCarthys.

The goddamn *McCarthys*.

Darragh frowns. "They're not enemies of your family. They're just... bullies."

"They are enemies," I snap—too sharply. I make myself stop. Because if I keep talking, I'll slip. I'll become that same awkward, gangly girl I was back at St. Albert's.

The target.

The joke.

The older ones, Torin, Seamus, and Kyla graduated before me. Bronwyn was in Bridget's class.

But *Cavin*...

I inhale through my nose and shake my head.

Cavin McCarthy is a bully, and I hope he fucking suffers.

The sting in my gut still flares when I remember. Every white tile in that bathroom I memorized, hiding because I didn't want anyone to see me crying.

No one else has the power to drag me back to that helpless girl... except the McCarthys.

And I *hate* that we're in a place where everyone worships them.

"People change, you know," Darragh says, stuffing a hand into his pocket.

"Why are you suddenly best friends with the McCarthys? Because they're mafia? Torin is in prison. Cavin was just released. Only bad people doing bad things go to prison. Why would people admire them for that?" I mutter, catching a glimpse of someone nearby. Watching. I lower my voice. "They were never your mates."

"I—It's just that..." Darragh shrugs and sighs. "Things aren't always black and white, Erin. And you're not the type to hate people."

"I don't hate them," I lie.

And I know I'm lying.

I *do* hate them.

Well, not *all* of them.

But I hate Cavin McCarthy, even after I saw him at the funeral. "Pay your respects," my father told me. "It's the right thing to do." But I balked when I saw all the heads of the mafia there and pretended I was putting flowers on a grave.

He didn't try to save me, no, despite how it may've looked.

He was wondering why I was there.

I *hated* the way the girls at St. Albert's threw themselves at him just for a glance and a nod.

I hate his blue-eyed beauty and perfect body.

I hate the way he ruled everything.

I can still hear him call me a snitch, still see the curled lip and bared teeth. Still see that narrowed-eyed glare and hear his voice, low and venomous, whispering that he hated me too.

But I'm *not* that girl anymore.

"Let's get back to Bridget," I say, my head held high as I walk away from the McCarthy worshippers of Ballyhock.

I glance at the time, and my stomach sinks.

Goddamn it.

I hear my mother before I see her, on the other side of the frosted door meant to give us privacy.

"Sit *up*," she snaps. "That's a girl. Good. Now, are you going to eat this food or just play with it? You're wasting away to nothing, Bridget."

Her tone cuts. My sister's is softer. "Leave it, Mam," Bridget pleads. "If you think it's so delicious, why don't you eat it yourself?"

I step in with a pasted-on smile. "Got your sausage roll."

My mother's face twists.

"*Sausage* roll? Why would you get her that? She'll break out."

"Mam," I say, with every ounce of forced calm I've got. Darragh fades into the hallway, shadow-like, watching again. "In case you missed it, Bridget's not eating much." I glance at her frail frame. "I figured food might help. She asked for a sausage roll."

And in my head, I finish the sentence—*whatever the fuck my sister asks for, she gets.*

My mother purses her lips, then scans me from head to toe, her eyes widening in horror. Oh god. What did I do now?

"Erin, do you mean to tell me you just went *out* like that? In *public*?" When her voice gets to that high-pitched note...

I glance down.

Faded jeans. A jumper. Comfortable shoes.

"What's wrong with this?"

She lifts her chin. The queen surveying her kingdom.

Not a wrinkle on her face, even her forehead is smooth as silk. Botox. Fillers. Whatever it takes to maintain the illusion. "You're a *Kavanagh* woman. That's what's wrong."

I sigh.

Mam was beautiful when she was younger, but she's older now, and the thick makeup's beginning to wear.

"Come here," she says, as she pulls a hairbrush out of her bag.

I gawk at her. "Mom, no," I say, pulling back when she reaches for me. "Are you out of your mind?" I push her hand away.

"Just let me fix your—"

"No!" My voice rises in fury.

One. Two. Three. Four.

I tap my pocket. It doesn't help.

Fingertips to thumb. *Still doesn't help.*

I turn to Bridget, who immediately reaches for my hand and gives it a gentle squeeze. I let out a breath. It helps.

"Here," I say, handing her the sausage roll. Bridget sighs and leans back against her pillows. She takes a bite of the sausage roll and smiles. "Thanks, Erin. It's delicious."

"Of course," I say.

My mother sighs. "Did you hear about the McCarthys? Something about a bomb?"

I thought it wise not to tell them what happened when I was there. Mam's eyes are on her phone as she taps her screen with one perfectly manicured nail.

"A bomb?" ", as our family was McCarthy family adjacent.

My mother's voice is flat as she stares at the phone. "It's a shame. They're well-loved in Ballyhock. People are outraged."

A beat passes. When I don't respond, she pierces me with another look.

"Oh, for god's sake, Erin, are you still holding that high school grudge?" she says, rolling her eyes so hard they might stay that way. "Kids play. It's what they do."

Why does everyone suddenly love the McCarthys?

"Since when are you friends with the McCarthys?" I ask, giving her a curious look.

She sets the phone down like it's made of glass. Her face goes a little pale.

She clears her throat. "Since I discovered the McCarthys are friends with Dr. Rosenberg. The one in Glasgow," she says, quiet now.

I give her a sharp look.

"*The* Dr. Rosenberg? The one doing... experimental procedures. For people with..." Aplastic anemia.

"Aye."

Bridget sits up straighter, and my stomach clenches. My mother puts on a detached, impersonal front, but I know how it breaks her heart to see her daughter sick, knowing there's not a damn thing she can do about it.

No amount of motherly fussing—like brushing our hair, making us sit up straighter, or fixing what was visible so we wouldn't embarrass her—can fix what's breaking now.

"Listen..." My voice cracks. "We've talked about this. You know he's booking two years out. And he refuses to take clients now. Even for bribes. Won't even meet with Da—"

Or take his money or his bribes or anything.

Bridget's eyes hold mine. She knows what I'm not saying.

We don't have two years.

Six months, maybe eight if we're lucky. That's what the doctors said last week, the ones Mam doesn't want to know about, as if denying reality will somehow keep Bridget here longer.

"I'm just thinking, maybe... maybe if you got in their good graces, Erin—"

The words land like a punch.

My heart stutters. Races. I tap my pocket—once, twice, three times, four.

Mam grabs my wrist. "Stop that."

I can't breathe. Can't think.

She wants me to what? Seduce a McCarthy? *Befriend* them?

"Mam, what are you on about?" I ask her, trying to ignore the way my voice wobbles. "Did you actually forget how they treated me?"

She waves a hand dismissively—because *of course* she does. "Oh, Erin. You were children then. Let it *go.*"

I draw in a sharp, shuddering breath and turn back to my sister.

"You don't have to let it go, Erin," she says, her voice trembling. She takes another small bite of her sausage roll. "Not on account of me."

Then it hits—what my mother said.

That Bridget wants this too. That I just refused a choice that could actually give my sister the only thing that might save her.

The McCarthys are friends with Dr. Rosenberg. But the McCarthys...

No.

"Get in their good graces," I repeat.

Me?

"They don't like me," I tell my mother, but it feels like a last-ditch effort. Like I'm trying to convince myself.

"Maybe not," my mother says, dabbing at her eyes with a tissue. "God, it's dry in here, isn't it?"

Because even though she's mean, superficial, and sometimes cruel... it's breaking her. Watching her youngest girl disappear in slow motion.

We all know the clock's running out, and it won't slow down.

"I was just... I was just thinking," she stammers. "I could... could pay Caitlin McCarthy a visit, couldn't I?"

This isn't like her. I don't know if I've ever heard her stammer.

There's no amount of makeup, no filter sharp enough, to hide what's bleeding through her face right now—the lines, the pain, the regret.

And my heart drops like lead. If anything, my mother showed me how it's possible to both love and hate someone at the very same time.

But Bridget's sweet voice echoes: *Not on account of me.*

"They're in the news, you know. Sounds like some terrible things have happened."

"I know," my mother says quietly. "And the papers don't even cover the half of it." She would know. Make someone who's the Queen of Gossip a mafia wife, and she'll know more than anyone.

"So do *you* know what happened?" I ask, curiosity getting the best of me.

My mother swallows hard. "They say... after the bombing... Bronwyn McCarthy's gone missing."

Oh god.

Bridget's eyes go wide. "Not Bronwyn. She was kind. She was good."

She was mafia.

"What do you think they'll do, Mam?"

"I don't know," she says. "But I do know your father was talking to Seamus McCarthy just last week."

Seamus McCarthy, the acting head of the family now. I heard he got married to a Russian and they have a few kids now. I don't really know him, just a few of his younger siblings.

They call him The Undertaker though. No one calls him Seamus anymore and hasn't for quite some time.

"Right," I say. "About what?"

"Don't know that either," she says quietly. Then she pastes on a fake smile I'm all too familiar with.

"I'm meeting Caitlin later this afternoon," she says. "We're going to have tea."

Ah. So she's already made the plans.

I stare at her like she's grown a second head. Why now? Why Caitlin *McCarthy*?

"I want to see if there's anything we can do to help find Bronwyn," she says, but I already know what she's really doing.

She wants to offer up what we've got—our name, our money, our contacts—to find Bronwyn McCarthy. To curry the good favor of Caitlin McCarthy.

But why?

Is she bargaining? Trading favors? I want to ask, but I don't.

I breathe again, as deeply as I can, but it still feels shallow.

Fluorescent lights. *Goddamn* these lights.

When I look at Bridget, a thin trickle of red blood seeps from the bottom of her nose.

Oh god, oh no, not again.

I leap to my feet and grab a fistful of tissues from the bedside table. A simple nosebleed isn't what it seems when bleeding doesn't stop. We have boxes of tissues in here because, with Bridget, it starts small, before it escalates quickly.

The tissues are instantly saturated. I grab more. "Help us!" I yell into the hallway. My voice is high-pitched with a note of hysteria. "Somebody help us!"

"It's fine," Mam says, wringing her hands as she backs away from me and Bridget. "It's fine, love. It's just a nosebleed. She's fine." But Bridget's gone pale, and her lips look blue.

But Mam's backing away, her face carefully blank—the same expression she wore when the doctors first told us Bridget's diagnosis. When they said the word "terminal" and Mam stood up, smoothed her skirt, and said, "We'll get a second opinion. The Kavanaghs don't do... this."

As if illness cared about our family name.

As if Bridget could just decide to be perfect again.

"Erin," Bridget whispers. She grabs at more tissues, but they're soaked. Her words are slurred, her eyes are rolling back as a team rushes in to help, and I step back, still clutching bloodied tissues.

I watch, tears flowing freely as the nurses rush in to take over. This is happening with more and more frequency now.

My hands shake. No amount of tapping can calm me.

Bridget isn't getting better.

We're out of options.

I'd do anything to save her. Anything.

Even crawl back to Cavin McCarthy.

Even if he breaks me all over again.

Chapter Three

Cavin

By the time I make it back home, it's dark.

I've been ignoring the constant buzz of my phone for hours.

> **Seamus**
> Where the fuck are you?

> **Mam**
> Where are you, son?

I had to pay the fucking tribute.

Malachy warned me they'd come to collect. He didn't say they'd take my sister to make their point.

My hands are still shaking... from rage or fear, I don't fucking know.

He told me what the consequences would be.

And now I know something no one else knows—Bronwyn being taken was on me. A warning. A clear message.

While the others wear themselves out chasing shadows, I paid my fucking *five hundred thousand euros.*

This can't go on. I can't hide that kind of money from my family, and even if I could, I fucking *won't.*

But I have to keep Bronwyn safe. I have to find out who this is and put a decided *end* to it.

When I pull into the family estate, I don't slide in unnoticed like I'd hoped. Floodlights blaze across the driveway, burning white over gravel and stone. Seamus and Da stand in the front foyer—arms crossed, waiting.

Fuck it.

I steel myself and jog up the front steps.

The door swings open before I hit the top.

"Where the fucking hell were you?"

Seamus's fist connects with my jaw before I clear the threshold. Pain explodes white-hot. Blood floods my mouth.

He hits me again, harder. My head snaps back, skull cracking against the wall.

"Where. The. *Fuck.* Were. You?"

He grabs my throat and slams me against the wall. His thumb digs into my windpipe. I taste copper. Can't breathe.

Black spots dance at the edges of my vision.

If he were anyone else—*anyone*—I'd drop him right here, bare-knuckle, the way Malachy taught us in the barn when we were lads. Three hits: temple, throat, kidney. He'd be pissing blood for a week.

But he's my brother. My boss. The head of this family, since Da retired.

I swore an oath.

So I *let* him choke me.

"Is there an update?" I wheeze out. "Anything?"

"No," he growls. "We've got nothing. No fucking recording at the graveyard. Nothing."

"Boys."

Mam walks into the hallway, tall and regal as always.

"Let him go, Seamus," she says, cool and firm, the voice we obeyed before Da ever raised his.

Seamus drops his hand, and I drag in air that burns going down.

"Mam," he mutters. "You don't—"

"You may be the acting head, but I said *drop him.*"

There's blood on my collar... on my hands.

Then her eyes cut to me. "Where'd you go?"

I grit my teeth. "I can't tell you, but I swear to Christ, I was doing something for the family." I pause. "I've got nothing to hide. You know I don't. But if I tell you, you're all at risk. That's all I can say."

She studies me, silent. Then, finally, one sharp nod.

"Has Cavin ever lied to you, Seamus?"

Seamus steps back, his jaw ticcing. "Not that I know of."

Then all our phones buzz at once.

"Text from Bronwyn," Seamus mutters.

I pull out my phone and stare.

I'm in the garden.

Relief slams into me, and my knees buckle. I lock them before anyone notices.

It worked. It fucking *worked*. I paid the tribute, and they brought her back.

What the fuck did I just pay for? Why her? Why now?

WHO did I pay?

Silence for one blessed beat, then chaos erupts.

Mam drops her phone with a little gasp. Seamus bolts for the door, and I'm right behind him.

We tear down the front stairs, gravel crunching under boots, past the hedges, down Mam's winding path to the garden.

"Where is she?" Seamus shouts.

But none of that matters right now because, somewhere in the garden, my sister is alive.

"She's here!" Kyla falls to her knees, sobbing. "I found her! I got her!"

She scoops Bronwyn into her arms. Bronwyn is gagged and blindfolded.

"Take off her blindfold first," Seamus says, his voice softer now. "So she's not afraid." He drops to one knee beside them.

Kyla's hands shake too badly. I step in, my fingers steady, and peel the blindfold off. Bronwyn blinks up at me. I yank the gag away next in one motion. Her eyes are red-rimmed. Terrified. For half a second, I see Erin. Same fear. Same wide eyes when the bomb went off.

I shove the thought away. Not now. Not fucking *now*.

"What happened?" She gasps. "Where am I?"

She's shivering. Seamus gathers her in his arms. "Do you remember anything, love?"

Mam drops to her knees, pulling Bronwyn close, kissing her cheeks. "My baby."

"I remember... a bomb. That's all I remember."

The sun's long gone down.

Seamus and Zoya's little ones are tucked into bed upstairs. Bronwyn curls into the couch, legs folded under her, drinking tea spiked with Jack Daniels. A family favorite.

Da stands by the fireplace, arms crossed, while Seamus paces.

"You found nothing?" he asks.

Declan shakes his head. "None of the security cameras were triggered. Whoever came had access to our gates."

"So she doesn't remember anything at all about who took her," Seamus mutters. "We've got *no* footage. *No* triggered alarms. *No* signs of entry. And yet... here she is." He rakes a hand through his hair. "What the hell am I supposed to do with this? Bronwyn, you sure you don't remember anything? Nothing?"

"No." She shakes her head. "I remember the explosion. And then... blank. I just woke up, and I was here."

"How long was she gone?" Seamus asks.

"Twelve hours," Kyla answers.

"Wow." Bronwyn sips her tea. "Well, that's scary as hell."

"Tell me about it," Seamus growls. He looks at the body-guards in the hallway. "You were at the cemetery perimeter. I want a full report by eight a.m." He points at Nate, head of security. "Pick your top three. They'll be glued to Bronwyn."

"Oh, Seamus..." Bronwyn starts.

"Hush." He cuts her off.

"I agree with your brother," Da says.

"Someone showed up, took our girl, and brought her back like she's a message."

"A warning," Mam says, standing. "We *do* know it was a warning. Aye?"

"Aye." Seamus's jaw tightens. "But for what?"

I want to open my mouth and let it all spill out. Every dark, twisted bit of it. But I stay quiet. I have to.

"Well," Kyla says, thoughtful now. "It happened right at Malachy's burial, didn't it? So maybe... he had the key to something. Or he knew something none of us did."

Seamus looks at me. "Right. Something happened," he continues. "But Bronwyn came back. So we've got no leads on who the hell did this. But we do know that the stronger we solidify our clan, the less likely they are to try it again."

"Well then." Kyla rises to her feet. "Time we start making advantageous moves, isn't it? Seamus married Zoya. That gave us an alliance with the Kopolovs. But we don't need Moscow right now. We need *Ireland*. This is where we live. This is where we earn." Her eyes are bright. "This is where we set roots, gain momentum. Where we thrive."

"Yes," Seamus agrees.

"I'm not saying the alliance with the Kopolovs isn't valuable," Kyla says. "But now that it's secured... we need more. Something different." She straightens her shoulders and sighs. "Marry me off, then."

The words hit hard. Bronwyn gapes, and Mam goes still, but Kyla continues. "Marry me to someone who'll benefit the family, won't you?"

My stomach turns.

Kyla. Offering herself up like a lamb to slaughter. For us. For the family.

Because that's what we do—we sacrifice and break ourselves on the altar of the McCarthy name.

We all will, in the end.

"Kyla—" Mam gasps, stunned. "It doesn't have to come to that."

But Seamus doesn't argue. Neither does my father.

"Who?" she asks, her voice thin now. "Who can you marry me to that would make our family stronger?"

No one who deserves you, lass.

"I can't tell you how grateful we are for your sacrifice, love," my father says. "But I can't think of a single person. In fact, it's the opposite. Right now, the strongest move we can make—the *smartest*—is to expand our trade routes. Cavin, tell us the latest about your work, son, will you?"

So I tell them. As a gun runner to Belfast, my work's only increased in the past months. Doubled since this time last year.

"The East Coast is secured. Ballyhock is as strong as ever. There's talk the Boston Irish also want access, but right now, it's just that. Talk."

"Right," Seamus says, eyes narrowing. "What we *really* need is access to the West Coast and south of Ireland. Killarney. Cork. Galway."

I walk to the wall, stabbing a finger at the map. "Here. The lines. The docks. All of it." I shake my head. "If we could secure that connection, get access to the West Coast trade, we'd be..."

I stop myself.

Unstoppable. Fucking invincible.

And worth killing for.

"Did you say the West Coast?" Mum says, her voice soft. We all turn. She smiles faintly. "Funny, isn't it?"

We say nothing and just wait. It's clear she's thinking, coming to grips with what she has to say next.

"Well then. Maybe it's not one of my daughters we'll have to marry off…"

Silence.

Her eyes lock on mine.

Me.

"Maybe it's one of my sons."

My blood goes ice cold.

No. No fucking way.

"What're you on about, Mam?" Seamus asks.

"Tara Kavanagh came to me today. She heard about the bombing. Heard Bronwyn went missing. You know we've been friendly since your school days at St. Albert's, right?"

"Right," Seamus mutters.

"She said something that got my attention."

"What's that?"

"Her husband's gained access to the Western trade routes."

Seamus and I look at each other.

"Is that so?" he asks.

Declan's already pulling up his laptop, showing maps, numbers, routes. "Mmm. That would be a match made in heaven." Easy for him to say. His head isn't suddenly on the marriage block.

"Something to think about, then, isn't it?" Mam says again, sipping her tea.

"Aye," Seamus echoes. "And we need to move fast."

"The Kavanaghs have no sons, correct?" Seamus asks.

"Correct," Mam confirms. "Two daughters. Cavin, you went to school with one of them."

I nod. I did, and the girl I went to school with was at the cemetery the day of the bombing.

I was the only one who saw her though. If I were to get close to her family, I'd be able to investigate, see if her da had anything to do with the bombing.

Seamus turns to me, his expression flat. "You're the one who said you'd do anything for the family. Didn't you?"

"Yes, sir," I say, nodding.

"You meant it?"

My back goes straight. "Of *course.*"

Are they suggesting I marry Erin Kavanagh? An image flashes—her body pressed against mine in the graveyard. The way she fit against me like she was made for it. The way I got hard, carrying her to safety.

Awkward Little Miss Perfect. The girl who ratted me out, who looked at me like I was dirt.

The girl whose hand I can still feel in mine.

Christ.

"Good, then. Perhaps you'll be the one to secure this connection. Hmm?"

Secure the connection. Take vows that last a lifetime, bind myself legally to a woman I despise, and fuck her when duty demands an heir. Wake up to her hatred every goddamn morning.

Aye. That's how we secure a connection.

I blow out a breath. "Aye. Perhaps I will."

"Not Cavin," Declan snaps. "Come on, Seamus. He's done enough for the family, hasn't he?"

Done enough. *If he only fucking knew.*

"Is marrying a beautiful woman really that much of a sacrifice?" Seamus asks.

"How would you know?" Declan cuts in with a snort. "You married for *love.*"

Daire sighs. "He's not wrong."

Mam laughs quietly into her teacup, and Seamus narrows his eyes.

"You said you'd do anything for the family," Seamus pushes.

He's got me. The bastard knows it. I did say that, swore it in blood when I joined the clan's business. But this? Shackling myself to a woman who hates me? Who'll spend every day of our marriage wishing I were dead?

A woman I apparently can't stop thinking about since I touched her?

Fuck my life.

I sit up straighter. "Aye."

And I will. I remember how it felt—searching for Bronwyn, tearing the world apart just to bring her back. I remember the hours inside that godforsaken high-security prison as I paid the piper for sins I didn't commit. Torin still is... still locked away.

Of *course* I meant it.

"Then we'll arrange a marriage," Mam says, her voice final.

"Aye," Da agrees. "It's time."

My stomach drops, free fall.

Jesus fucking Christ.

"Erin Kavanagh's grown into something of a beauty, hasn't she?" Kyla says with a grim smile, though her eyes look a bit troubled. Is that relief I see as well?

"I suppose." I purse my lips.

"You don't look thrilled, Cavin," Seamus notes.

I shrug. "That girl, that *woman*, was a thorn in my side at St. Albert's. She got me into more trouble than the devil himself."

"Was ages ago," Seamus says, crossing his arms on his chest.

"Right." I won't go back on my word, but give a man a fuckin' minute.

"Honestly, Cavin," Kyla mutters. "It's not high school anymore."

Still. I remember the way she looked at me—those cold,

narrow eyes. The way she'd rat me out without flinching. She hated me. Still does. I'd bet my life on it.

"Only one problem though. She'd never agree to marry me. You do know that, right? She fuckin' *hates* me."

I made her life hell at St. Albert's. Called her names. Made her cry. She's got every reason to hate me.

But I have every fuckin' reason to hate her right back.

They stare. Declan shakes his head, but the rest look like I've just handed them the keys to the kingdom, and I know, if I marry, it'll benefit all of us.

"Fine. If marrying into the Kavanaghs is what it takes… If this is how we solidify the family… make us stronger…"

I stand, my shoulders tense.

"Fine. Do it. Tell me where and when."

And with that, I turn.

"I'm going to bed."

Erin *fuckin'* Kavanagh.

I'd rather go back to prison.

Chapter Four

Erin

To be honest, the only thing keeping me here in this car is my sister.

The last doctor's visit gave her six months. *Six months* to live—unless something drastically changes.

The beautiful thing about free healthcare is that it's free. The terrible thing about free healthcare is that it means waiting.

Waiting so long, you start forgetting what it feels like to hope, and in some cases, the treatment comes after it's already too late.

So here I am, in the back of the car.

Da is driving, with Mam next to him, her hands folded in her lap.

Me—sitting in the back, itching to count something. Anything.

I need an anchor. A number. A rhythm.

Something to stop me from focusing on the way this dress clings to my skin like a second layer of sweat. Moisture pools beneath my breasts, between my thighs, making me feel filthy and exposed.

I want to claw at my skin. Rip the fabric away. Scream.

Instead, I count.

One. Two. Three. Four.

It's too much. Way too much.

I don't know how to claw my way out of this space.

"Stop making that face," my mother snaps. "You look like you're about to have an accident or something."

"What?" My cheeks flush hot. "What are you talking about?" I shake my head.

"Your face is all scrunched up like that, and I—"

"*Tara,*" my da cuts in, placing a hand on her wrist. "Leave her alone. You know how she is."

And somehow… that hurts even more than her chiding. Like I'm broken and defective, something to be *managed*.

My throat tightens. I dig my nails into my palms until it hurts.

Better. *Pain* I can control.

I swallow hard. I can't think of that, not now.

I hope Bridget knows how much I love her.

I hope whatever negotiations they're planning tonight are worth it.

They *better* be fucking worth it.

"Oh my," Mam mutters under her breath. "It does look sort of majestic in this light, doesn't it?" She can't hide the jealousy in her tone as we pull up to the McCarthy estate. *The* McCarthy estate, famous in Ballyhock and the surrounding towns as well.

Floodlights burst across the gravel, lighting our path in harsh, golden stripes.

And for a second... I forget everything.

I forget the cologne.

The sweaty dress.

The pinched shoes.

My mother's sharp, needling voice.

Because the McCarthy estate *is* stunning.

It swallows the landscape... swallows *me* whole.

"Property's worth fifty million euros," my da mutters.

"I can see why," I say with a sigh.

My mother rolls her eyes, lips pursed tight.

"Mam, I thought you were friends with Caitlin McCarthy?"

"I am." She clears her throat. "She's a very nice person... but she didn't *build* this or anything." She waves a hand toward the house.

"No one said she did," I reply, giving her a look. "What a weird thing to say."

"She's *too* nice," my mom mutters. And I know exactly what she means.

She doesn't play games. Doesn't bluff or bite.

Good.

Caitlin and I are probably going to get along just fine.

"Fifty million euros," I say again, shaking my head.

"They say it was worth eleven when the McCarthy family bought it," Da adds. "When Keenan McCarthy became the head of the clan, they expanded it so family could stay close. Close-knit clan, they say."

Indeed.

"All of them still live here?" I ask.

"Some moved on. Some live in the nearby village. But yes, a few still have residence here. Bronwyn. Kyla. The single lads. And though Seamus has a place with his wife... Cavin's still here."

My blood goes cold.

Cavin fucking McCarthy.

The boy who made me cry in bathroom stalls.

The man who carried me out of a bombing like I weighed nothing. Like I was something precious.

My pulse kicks up just thinking about his hands on me, his voice in my ear.

Christ, what's wrong with me?

Great.

"Why is he here?" My voice tightens. "Isn't he, like, twenty-eight?"

Two years older than I am. I know that much.

"He moved back home after his release from prison," my da says quietly.

I roll my eyes so hard it almost hurts. "Right. Didn't want to keep up his property while in prison, so now he's back. Working the estate."

My lips flatten into a hard, thin line.

Well.

If Cavin McCarthy needs me to play nice for one family dinner... I can do that. For one night.

I can smile. I can nod. I can forget the way he used to look at me. The way he made me feel. The way his voice sounded like a threat, no matter how he talked to me.

Maybe he's changed.

God.

As *if.*

He was an evil son of a bitch... and there's no way in hell he's had a personality transplant.

Uniformed staff greet us as the car pulls up. One man steps forward to park it for us.

"Thank you very much," my mother says, her tone sweet, her posture stiff. I can tell she's impressed but pissed. They've got something she doesn't.

"This is gorgeous," I say, half under my breath. "Just look at it."

The gardens stretch for acres. Cut hedges. Trellises. Old trees, bent like they're praying. The greenhouse glows behind the main house like a buried lantern.

You can see how huge the place is from here—how many rooms, how many secrets.

"Stand up straight," my mother hisses from the corner of her mouth. "Stop fidgeting, for god's sake, Erin."

I inhale slowly, then let it out through tight lips.

"And maybe you," I murmur, "should stop being so phony."

"What?" she snaps, just as the door opens.

Even my father smiles at that.

"Hello, hello." Caitlin McCarthy stands framed in the doorway—tall, regal, her hair pinned in a tight silver bun. Her face is lined, but there's still a glint of youth in her eyes. A smile so warm it makes your guard slip without warning.

I like her immediately.

There's something about her, something that makes you want to be better—kinder, more human.

"Hi," I say shyly as she extends her hand.

"And you must be Erin," she says, smiling.

I swallow, then nod. "Yes. Pleased to meet you."

Did I do that right?

"Come in, come in," she says. "I'm so glad you could make it."

"Your home is absolutely breathtaking," I say sincerely. "I can only imagine how beautiful the gardens must look in daylight."

I stand there in awe, my jaw slack, and my mother shoots me one of those looks to stop gawking.

But I can't help it. It's *stunning*. I love it. It's the kind of house that makes you want to play hide-and-seek, or go set up a tripod in the front yard and take pictures or paint.

It makes me want to throw my hands in the air and spin like some idiot in a fairy tale. Just to take it all in, the majesty of it.

"Thank you so much," Caitlin says. "My mother-in-law, Maeve, God rest her soul, took such good care of the place." She smiles at me. "You know, Cavin's out in the garden. Maybe he could show you around?"

Cavin. Why Cavin? Doesn't she have like five or six other children who could do the job? Why do I have to be alone with my high school tormentor?

I can still hear the way he'd mock me, the sneer in his tone, not even bothering to hide his open disdain.

"Careful, Little Miss Perfect, you might trip on your own thoughts."

"That would be lovely," I say with a polite smile. "But you don't have to do that—I don't want to invade your privacy."

"Wouldn't be an invasion at all," she says, smiling slyly. "Especially with our arrangement."

Arrangement?

What *arrangement*?

My stomach drops. My hands go ice cold. I press them flat against my thighs to stop them from shaking.

What did they agree to without telling me?

She smiles and turns toward the door.

I give my mother a sharp look, but she won't meet my eyes.

Our *arrangement*? What the hell is she talking about?

My father clears his throat just as a distinguished man in a charcoal-gray suit rounds the corner. I can tell he was handsome once, probably a heartbreaker in his day. Silver hair now, but his face still carries the evidence: deep smile lines around his eyes, posture like an old soldier, quiet authority.

"Welcome," he says warmly. "Pleased to meet you, Erin. Keenan McCarthy."

I've heard of this family. Their history's become part of Ballyhock lore for generations. How Keenan found Caitlin, the lighthouse keeper's daughter, and took her as his own. How his father's death left him seated on the throne as leader of the clan until he retired. I wonder why.

And I wonder why the McCarthys seem so damn happy to see me?

"Pleased to meet you, sir," I say, nodding, taking his hand.

I know how to play the good girl. Don't know how to shut off the constant buzz of anxiety, but I can fake it, at least for a little while.

He escorts us into a sprawling reception room. Staff in uniform hold trays delicately in gloved hands.

There are so many *people*.

My stomach flips until I spot Bronwyn.

She has to be the youngest. She looks... approachable. Kind, even. When our eyes meet, she offers a broad smile and a little wave.

Just like that, I can breathe a little easier again.

She's standing next to another woman though. And that one? Not so friendly.

I try to piece it together.

Seamus McCarthy is easy to spot. Everyone knows him, the man they call The Undertaker.

He's got a younger woman on his arm, and she wears a wedding band. That must be his wife. Someone said he married a Russian princess. Zoya something?

I know one of their brothers is still incarcerated, though Cavin was recently released...

What arrangement?

They always tell me I get hyperfixated.

But who wouldn't?

Who wouldn't get hyperfixated when the word *arrangement* gets tossed around with families like ours?

We drove an hour, no stops, just to "discuss the possibility of some form of alliance."

I said I'd be friendly, said I'd play nice because Bridget's worth it.

After her last incident, with blood loss so bad she nearly didn't make it, they gave her an infusion and sent us home, where we have twenty-four-hour care.

The problem is, when my sister bleeds, it doesn't stop like it's supposed to.

Ironic, isn't it? That her disease is poisoned blood.

And blood is what ties us all together. My family. The McCarthys. Good blood, bad blood, and everything in between.

Before we left, my da made sure she was stable.

Of course he did. He loves Bridget.

He gives me a look now. That don't-fuck-this-up kind of look.

Play nice, Erin.

And maybe I can.

But the last person on this planet I want to be alone with?

Cavin McCarthy.

Chapter Five

Erin

"Cavin," Caitlin calls. "Come here, son."

My breath catches. Actually catches, like I've been punched.

His shoulders fill the doorway. There's ink crawling up his neck now, disappearing under his collar. His jaw is sharper, harder.

He's in a dark suit that fits him *too* well and shows every line of muscle underneath.

My mouth goes dry.

No. Absolutely *not*.

I will *not* be attracted to Cavin fucking McCarthy.

But my body doesn't seem to care what I will or won't do.

Heat floods my face. My thighs. *Lower.*

His eyes find mine across the room—they're dark, unreadable, dangerous.

For a second, just a second, his gaze drops... down my body, slow and deliberate, like he's taking inventory. Doesn't anyone else *see* this, or are they all too busy chatting?

My nipples tighten under the thin fabric of my dress.

Traitor body.

When his eyes meet mine again, something flickers in them. Or maybe I'm imagining it?

Maybe I'm losing my fucking mind.

Cavin McCarthy is *gorgeous.* Yeah, I said it.

All the McCarthys are, which is probably half the reason Ballyhock worships them so.

I try not to stare, and wish Bridget were here because I want her to *see* this guy.

Am I staring?

God, I hope I'm not staring.

But when his gaze meets mine a second time, I take an involuntary step back. There's a coldness in his eyes that wasn't there at St. Albert's, a rough edge etched into the bone of his face. I suddenly wish I could hide.

My gaze drops, too, to the powerful column of his neck and masculine collarbone. He left one tiny button undone... and still, the heat beneath his shirt pulses.

My gaze drops further. Thick arms. Tanned skin. Veins like cables.

Hands that look strong enough to crush or cradle.

I feel... small.

Oh Jesus, help me.

Even my mother's eyes widen, probably half expecting to see the boy from St. Albert's, and not this man who takes up half the room.

My father straightens, recovering fast. "Cavin. Pleased to meet you, son," he says, extending a hand.

This boy—no, *man*, takes up too much of my brain space rent-free because of how he treated me, and my own father's never even met him.

Cavin doesn't smile, just nods and shakes my father's hand. "Pleased to meet you, sir."

His voice is deeper, rougher than it was in school. We barely talked at the cemetery. I didn't notice.

Then he turns to me and takes in a deep breath again.

"Mam says you'd like a tour of the estate," he says gruffly.

His eyes find mine, and for a second, just one, something wild and feral flashes across his face.

Recognition.

Hunger.

Rage.

My breath catches. Didn't anyone else see that?

He crosses the room in three strides. Doesn't stop until he's in my space—close enough, I can feel the heat coming off him.

"Erin." He says my name like a curse. Like a promise.

I can't move. Can't breathe.

Up close, he's even *worse*. The tattoos crawling up his neck, the brutal line of his jaw, and shoulders broad enough to block out the rest of the room. And fuck, he smells good— expensive and male and *wrong* for how much I want to lean in.

My mother stares at me, silently begging, and I don't know why.

I swallow hard.

God, I *hate* playing by these rules. Of all the people in all the places in the world...

"That would be lovely," I lie.

"Excellent," he says, also lying. He looks as thrilled as I feel.

"I'll walk you through the estate." He turns and starts walking fast, without bothering to see if I'm following.

I am, of course.

"Da used to let people come through for a tour," Cavin says over his shoulder. "But he stopped. They made a mockery of it." A beat. "Thought it was some kind of circus or the like."

"Well, that's unfortunate."

Unfortunate? That's unfortunate?

He doesn't answer, just leads me down a marble corridor that looks like you could ice-skate on it.

"You've grown up," he says after a beat. "Didn't think the world'd let you."

My chest tightens. Oh, he's still the same, that lazy cruelty—half compliment, half dagger.

"And you've grown predictable," I say lightly. "Still mistaking cruelty for charm."

He glances over with a faint smirk. "Still mistaking honesty for cruelty?"

Come again?

"Well, I see you haven't lost that *scowl*," I mutter. "Charming."

"Not charming," he replies. "Familiar."

Silence... hot and sticky with history. Old wounds wrapped in heat neither of us asked for. And why is he standing so close to me?

Did I move, or did he?

I try to focus on the estate. It's beautiful, yeah. Majestic even. But none of it matters because I've never been good at pretending.

And right now? All I can think is—*I'm alone. With Cavin McCarthy.*

And I *hate* him.

I hate him so much.

I hate that his family holds more power than mine.

I hate that he's so fucking handsome.

I hate that he knows it.

And I hate that no matter how hard I try, I can't rewrite our past.

"This is the kitchen," he says, bored. I'm nervous and don't know how to reply, so the words fall out of my mouth before I can stop them.

"Right by the dungeon," I quip. "Where you keep your prisoners... or maybe it's where you train your dragons."

He throws me a look, sly and almost amused.

"I prefer the dungeon at The Craic, to be honest. But yeah... we may have one or two dragons in storage."

My cheeks flare.

The Craic.

Christ, I'd almost forgotten. The infamous McCarthy club —elite, exclusive, whispered about in the right circles. The kind of place where sin is currency.

"Very funny," I tell him, deadpan. And why do I hate the idea of him and those—those *muscles*, and those *hands*, and that *mouth* with another woman? Or three?

I don't. I don't.

He shrugs, like he doesn't care whether I believe him or not.

"I'm not joking. Behind the kitchen, there's a garden." He's got that tone now, smooth and detached, like a bored realtor showing off crown molding.

I do glance over, despite myself, and he sees it, that flicker of interest.

He turns, leading the way like he owns the damn world. "If you go this way..." His smile curves, lazy and wicked—the kind that turns my insides to ice and heat all at once. My heart jerks in my chest.

I hate myself for it.

He points to a narrow door, half hidden behind ivy and brick. "This is the one we all used to sneak through... to get to the garden." His voice drops. "It was my grandmother's favorite place."

And for a second, just one, something human ghosts across his face. A memory. A thread of something too raw to name. People speak well of Maeve McCarthy in Ballyhock. She was a bit of a legend.

"This is all well and good, Cavin," I say sharply. My tone is tight now, controlled. I'm not here to reminisce. "Are we supposed to pretend nothing happened in high school?"

His smirk is instant. Lips tilted, eyes going half lidded in that way that always made me want to slap him or kiss him or both.

"Nothing happened between us in high school, Erin, as much as you hoped it would."

My jaw drops.

And for a second, I forget how to speak. Forget how to breathe.

"You... ugh!" I clench my fists. Just like that, I'm a teen again, frustrated, buttoned-up, and always one second away from cracking. And *he*—he's still the goddamn *prince* of condescension.

"You bullied me," I snap. Because I'm not going to rewrite history to make him feel better.

"Bullied?" He shakes his head, scoffing. "We've got very different recollections of what went on, don't we?"

"For *fuck's* sake." I cross my arms over my chest and realize too late that doing so pushes my breasts up, just enough to draw his eyes.

And yes, he notices.

Of *course* he does.

He blinks, stares, then drags his gaze slowly, deliberately, back up to mine.

"I remember you always tattling on me," he says, his voice low now. "Making up shite. Getting me in trouble."

"You were always causing trouble!" I throw my hands up. "What the hell did you expect?"

He shakes his head, and a muscle twitches in his jaw. "Let's keep walking. We've only covered a small portion, and dinner will be served soon."

But I don't move.

I don't want to go. I don't want to play pretend and sit down at their perfect, gleaming dinner table, making polite small talk while acting like this isn't the same family that wrecked everything.

My phone buzzes. A text from Bridget.

Hey, how are things going?

And I immediately think of her hand in mine, that trembling grip, and her pale face as I left. "I'll never forget what you're doing for me," she whispered.

What *am* I doing, really? Just having dinner with the McCarthys, right? Smiling. Using the right fork. Pretending we were all... friends.

It wasn't that big of a deal.

Was it?

Cavin watches as I shove my phone in my little bag and sling it back over my shoulder. I would *kill* for a pair of yoga pants and an oversized jumper right now.

He shows me a little prelude to the garden first, lush, secluded, echoing with "You can walk from one room to the next, but this is a shortcut."

He shows me rooms. Too many rooms. Library. Wine cellar. Some trophy room full of his father's achievements.

I stop listening halfway through.

All I can think about is the way he stands too close. The way his hand hovers near my lower back but never quite touches, like he wants to. Like it's natural for him, but he's stopping himself.

We keep walking, and he shrugs out of his jacket, handing it to me. "Put it on. You're cold."

It's not a question.

I'm freezing, and I'm shaking, but not entirely from the cold.

"I'm fine—"

"Don't argue with me," he says, his voice low. "Just wear the fucking jacket." He drapes it over my shoulders. His hands linger for half a second, just long enough for me to feel the heat of his palms through the fabric.

The jacket smells like *him*—whiskey, woodsmoke, leather.

I want to bury my face in it.

I want to throw it off and run.

"Better?" he whispers, too close to my ear.

I nod because I don't trust myself to speak.

His hand is still on my shoulder, his thumb pressing just slightly into the hollow of my collarbone.

"Good," he says.

Then he steps back, creating distance and leaving me cold again, but... burning.

"I don't—"

"Just wear it. I promise I'm only being nice because my parents taught me to be a gentleman. It's nothing personal."

Fine, then. It's *almost* as comfy as my oversized jumper.

Cavin stands beside me, his hands jammed into his pockets. He doesn't meet my eyes. Instead, he stares through the large arch-shaped window that overlooks the ocean cliffs. Wind howls somewhere below, ripping through the trees like teeth.

I want to walk through those cliffs. Barefoot, maybe. Stand right at the edge, where the sea spits salt into your face and the rocks disappear into foam.

"It's beautiful," I say, honestly. It's really stunning.

"Thank you." Cavin gives the barest nod. He accepts the compliment with quiet gratitude, no smile. I might think it a peace offering if I were the kind of fool who believed in those.

"Is that Holy Family?" I ask, leaning just enough to see the tall steeple rising beyond the far edge of the garden.

"Aye."

"Oh." Interesting. Near Holy Family is the graveyard I've walked alone, time and time again, despite my mother's warnings.

I don't mean to laugh. It just bubbles up, bright, stupid, ill-timed. The kind of laugh my mother would slap clean out of my mouth.

Cavin whips his head toward me. His expression cuts like wire. "What's so funny?"

"It's just that..." My cheeks flush, and I hate the heat of it. "Well, nothing."

Why do I laugh when I shouldn't? Why do I always choke in the moment and spit out something inappropriate?

"Say it," he growls. His eyes narrow. "What's so funny?"

"It's just... ironic that a house like this backs right up to *Holy Family*. And... well, your family, *and mine*, to be clear, are anything *but*... holy."

He studies me for a second too long, then huffs a bitter laugh and shakes his head. Mutters something I can't make out—just enough to drag me back to childhood.

Back to that familiar sting. The kind where people laugh and you don't know why. You laugh too late, too loud— you're the butt of a joke you didn't hear.

My fingernails scrape my palms when my hands fist. I'm *not* the little Goody Two-Shoes I was back then, cowered by the likes of him.

"*Stop it,*" I tell him. "We're not at St. Albert's anymore, Cavin."

His eyes dart to mine, alert and cautious. "What the fuck are you talking about?"

"You can't bully me like you did back then. Okay?"

He blinks as if surprised. Was it my words or my willingness to talk back to him that took him off guard?

"I didn't fucking *bully* you," he says quickly. "Don't say that."

The air goes too bright and too loud. The sound of my own breathing starts to grate.

I can't look at him without my pulse kicking out of rhythm, and I hate that. So I start counting because I know how this works.

One, two, three, four, five, six, seven.

Seven light fixtures down this hallway.

One, two, three, four, five, six, seven, eight, nine, ten.

Ten stairs to the landing.

One, two, three portraits on the wall.

Tap pocket.

One, two, three, four.

Something flickers across his expression that I can't read, before he turns and walks away as if he didn't just watch me fall apart in real time.

And I can still hear it—the echoes from childhood.

Why does she count like that?

Why does her nose twitch?

Why does she have to watch everything?

"Down here," he says, like we didn't just start in this hallway, and I'm not standing here raw and stimming in front of him.

Why *Cavin?* Why did his mother send *him* to give me the tour?

It could've been Bronwyn, or Seamus, or literally anyone else.

But it's Cavin. Always fucking *Cavin.*

He tries to make small talk.

"How's your sister?"

"Alright," I say, too quickly. I'm surprised he remembered I had one.

He blows out a slow exhale.

"You still talk to anybody from St. Albert's?"

"No," I answer, too fast, too sharp, like I've rehearsed it. Like the idea of those people still clinging to me burns.

It does though. It really, really does.

He glances over his shoulder. Casual. Calculating.

"You?" I ask, trying to keep the tone light. Trying to match him beat for beat.

But truthfully? I want to know.

Does he still have the hassle of boys trailing behind him? Still worshipped like some twisted Peter Pan, leading them straight into a Neverland full of crime and consequences?

"I..." He hesitates, then shrugs. "Of course, I have to."

Right. He's mafia, isn't he?

St. Albert's wasn't just a school but a training ground. And I guess while I carved out some space for myself and stayed in the shadows, he never had that luxury.

Why does that make me feel sorry for him?

I hate that it does.

He walks faster, like he needs to outpace the conversation. Doesn't even look back to see if I'll follow.

Maybe he's just as unsettled as I am, but if he is... he hides it well.

How do people do that?

That stoic expression. That blank, untouchable calm. It

feels like a goddamn superpower, like flying or walking through fire without flinching. And I wish *I* had it.

The corridor stretches long and endless.

My eyes drop lower, taking in the way his trousers fit. The shift of muscle in his thighs as he walks.

Christ, I need to stop, but I can't.

I watch the way his shoulders move. The way his hands flex at his sides like he wants to reach for something.

Or *someone*.

Stop it, Erin. Stop.

My fingers twitch at my sides. I count the beats.

One, two, three, four… just to keep my hands from shaking.

"These portraits go back a few hundred years," Cavin mutters. His voice is flat, like he's reading rehearsed lines.

"I bet you've run out of wall space."

"Not yet."

A pause, heavy with silence.

He straightens his back every few paces, like he's under inspection. But he's not watching me; he's watching the space between us. And when he does glance over, I don't meet his eyes.

I stare at the floorboards.

Anything but his eyes.

Anything but those broad shoulders that dwarf my entire frame.

Anything but the way ink trails across his neck, or the way his hands look dangerous, masculine, and capable of both violence and tenderness.

"This way," Cavin says, dropping down a narrow staircase that opens to a side door. "Let's go outside before they ring the bell for dinner, yeah?"

I nod. Can't trust my voice. Yes, please, I want *out*.

I feel like a fish on tile, gasping, thrashing, humiliated.

But when he opens the door and steps aside, gentleman-like, letting me through first, it feels good. I take a deep breath.

I tell myself it's just how he was raised, that it has nothing to do with me.

McCarthy boys—*men*—have always known manners, even when they're cruel.

I mutter under my breath.

Whatever. You're not a child anymore, Erin. You're an adult. You're not here to make friends.

I know the rules.

Be cordial. Be polite. Don't fidget or ask too many questions. Better yet, try not to ask anything.

Do it for Bridget.

Outside, the light softens. The sun is setting behind the cliffs, casting gold over the edge of the water.

The wind carries the scent of salt and lilac. It's—god, it's *beautiful*. We walk a paved path lined with flowers.

"My god," I whisper. "Is this where you let the fairies out?" I want the words back the second they escape. My cheeks flush, but he gives me a half smile.

"The fairies and sprites, my grandmother used to say. She said they lived here in the garden."

He talks about his grandmother like she's holy. Maeve McCarthy—known in our circles. Revered.

"What would they do out here?" I ask, then almost slap my own mouth shut.

Why would I say that out loud?

"I suppose… dance down to the graves of my ancestors," he says with a dry smirk. "Because mischief gets you in trouble. Aren't sprites trouble?"

I nod, not trusting myself to speak again. But it *does* feel like a place built for fairies and sprites, as if the edge of a rainbow will touch down and turn the very ground beneath our feet enchanted.

He's looking at me differently now.

Not like the girl he tormented… but like something else. Something I don't have a name for.

His eyes drop to my mouth and stay there. My breath stutters.

"You always were… different, Erin Kavanagh," he says quietly. "But maybe that's not a bad thing."

He turns and we keep walking, his hands deep in his pockets, his too-big jacket sliding off my shoulders but still warm.

We reach a greenhouse, and the air shifts—humid, lush, alive with breath and green. Plants crawl up trellises. Flowers bloom like secrets.

"So you don't live on your own now. This where they send you when you get out of prison?" I ask.

Why did I say that?

His jaw clenches. "Better than where they send the ones who don't come out."

"I didn't mean—"

"Yes, you did." He steps closer. "You want to know if I'm the same bastard who made your life hell? If prison changed me?"

My heart hammers. "Did it?"

"No." Another step. He's close enough now that I can feel his breath. "I'm worse."

I should back away.

I don't.

"Good," I hear myself say. "At least you're honest."

His eyes darken. "Honesty's all I've got left, lass."

He laughs but barely. Just a breath. A crack in the armor. Music drifts from somewhere inside the house—soft and classical.

It hits me with the brutality of a backhand: music class.

Fucking *music* class. They put the upperclassmen in with the younger ones, and I *hated* it so damn much.

I mutter something under my breath. He catches it and gives me a sharp look.

This time, I don't bother to stop my words. "You shoved my notebook in the fountain after music class."

He doesn't respond.

"You *destroyed* my notes."

"Aye," he says, quiet and honest. I wait for an excuse or an apology, but none comes.

I look away, embarrassed by my own trauma. My fingers start their traitorous rhythm—*tap, tap, tap, tap*.

This time, I hide the twitch behind my back.

I don't want to go back inside where I don't belong. I never belong—not here, not in my family, not at St. Albert's. But especially not here.

"Let's go back inside," he says. "They'll ring the bell soon."

"I don't want to," I snap. It comes out too fast. Too loud. "I want to stay out here."

When he looks at me in surprise, my face flames.

"I'm sorry," I blurt. "I shouldn't have—"

"No." He cuts me off. "Never apologize for honesty. Jesus, lass. The least you can give me is honesty." The intensity in his voice makes my stomach flip. "Why don't you want to go inside?" he asks, quieter now.

Why does he care?

"It's—" My throat closes. "It's too much. Too loud. Too

many people. Too many..." I wave my hand, frustrated. "Everything."

Why am I telling him this?

He's watching me like he's seeing something for the first time.

"I used to find you in the library," he says slowly. "Hiding during lunch or assemblies."

I nod.

He gives me that look, curious, maybe a little confused. We step through the heavy door. The hall lights hum and crackle above us. Somewhere far off, voices, low and blurred, like we're underwater.

My senses are already on fire.

The dress scratches at my skin. The air smells like old wood and wax. The house is so cavernous I barely know where I am, and I *hate* not knowing where I am.

Cavin slows his pace, but doesn't say why. Doesn't mention the way I'm tapping at my pocket.

"Before we go inside... there's a space I want to show you." He leads me through a narrow hall to a balcony. When he opens the door, I can breathe again. It opens over the dark lawn and stone steps.

I breathe the cool, clean air in deep.

"See?" he says. "I get it." A pause. "It's not always nice inside, is it?"

I don't answer, but my shoulders relax.

"When I was…" His voice drops, rough and jagged. "When I was in prison, I used to dream about this balcony. Every night. I'd try to open the doors, but they were always locked." He shrugs. "I spend a lot of time outside."

I glance at him. Something sharp twists under my ribs. "I know what it's like," he says quietly, "to not want to be indoors."

The wind picks up, whipping my hair across my face.

Before I can move, his hand is there, his fingers brushing my temple and tucking the strand behind my ear. The touch is surprisingly gentle for a man whose family is known for violence.

Our eyes meet.

Neither of us moves.

There's something else happening here. Something neither of us is saying.

A pull. A want.

A *dare*.

Who will break first?

His thumb traces my cheekbone just as the sound of voices echo from inside. The spell breaks, and he drops his hand like I've burned him.

"We should go," he says.

As I follow him back inside, I can still feel the ghost of his touch on my skin.

And I wonder if Cavin McCarthy might be the most dangerous thing I've ever encountered.

Not just because he's cruel, but because part of me wants him to touch me again.

Chapter Six

Cavin

I LEAN against the stone railing after she steps back inside, my hands braced, head down, trying to get my breathing under control.

What the *hell* am I doing? She's Erin Kavanagh. The girl who made my life hell at St. Albert's.

The girl who's about to become *my wife*, whether either of us wants it or not.

And I just stood there on that balcony, close enough to touch, and spilled my guts like some lovesick fool.

I drag a hand through my hair, cursing under my breath. She looked at me different after that. Not with pity, thank *Christ*, but with something worse.

Understanding.

Her eyes had gone soft. Her lips parted, just slightly, like she wanted to say something but didn't know how. And for one dangerous fucking second, I wanted to close the distance between us. See if her mouth was as soft as it looked.

Christ.

I'm losing my mind. She's the girl who ratted me out at every turn. Who got me beaten more times than I can count. Who looked at me like I was dirt. But when she was counting under her breath earlier, fingers tapping that nervous rhythm against her thigh—I remembered. All those times at school when she'd do the same thing. When the other kids would mock her for it. When I'd stand there and do nothing, or worse, when I'd join in, just to keep the attention off how much I noticed her.

 How much I wanted to grab her hand and still those tapping fingers. Pull her somewhere quiet where she could breathe.

Fuck.

I wasn't kind to her... I know that, but standing on that balcony with the wind in her hair and her guard finally down, I *wanted* to be. Wanted to trace the line of her jaw. Tuck that loose strand of hair behind her ear. Feel if her pulse was racing the way mine was.

Wanted to know if she felt it too, this thing between us that I don't have a name for.

"Cavin." I turn.

Seamus is in the doorway, his arms crossed, expression unreadable. "You coming? Mam's about to ring the bell."

"Aye. Just needed some air." His eyes narrow, gaze flicking past me to the empty balcony.

"You talk to her yet?"

"About what?" I still give him shit.

"Don't fuck with me. About the marriage." I smirk but straighten. "Not yet."

"Well, you'd better before dinner. Because if she has something to say about it with both families watching, it'll be a bloodbath." He pauses, studying me too closely. "And Cav?"

"Yeah?"

"Try not to cock this up. We need this alliance."

He walks away before I can respond. I stare out at the dark garden, my jaw clenched.

Right. The alliance, family, trade routes. That's what this is about.

Not the way her hand felt in mine at the graveyard—small and cold and right. Not the way she smells like roses. Not the way something in my chest settled when I pulled her against my side, and she didn't pull away.

When her fingers curled into my coat like I was the only solid thing in the world. Not the way I wanted to keep her there. Safe. *Mine.*

How can I hate the woman and still feel murderous at the thought of her being anyone else's? How can I hate her and still feel like *mine* is the only name she should ever say?

None of that matters.

I push off the railing and head back inside, flexing my hands to get rid of the phantom feeling of her waist under my palm.

Time to face the truth. She's going to look at me with those sharp eyes and realize I'm exactly the bastard she always thought I was. That this whole thing—the tour, the vulnerability, the moment on the balcony—was just leading to a trap. She's going to hate me even more after this.

And somehow, that thought bothers me more than it should. Because part of me, the part that's still standing on that balcony in the cold with her, doesn't want her to hate me at all. Part of me wants the opposite, and that's the most dangerous thing of all.

Chapter Seven

Erin

I'm still catching my breath when Cavin comes back inside. He moves differently now—shoulders tense, jaw set, like he's steeling himself for battle. I see the shadow of his oldest brother walk down the hallway and wonder what they talked about.

"Come on," he says. His voice has lost the softer edge from earlier, when he let his guard down, probably without meaning to. "One more thing before dinner."

He doesn't wait to see if I follow. I trail after him through narrow hallways, watching the way his shoulders fill the doorway, the way his hand grips the banister as we climb the stairs.

I don't want to notice these things, but my traitorous eyes keep cataloging details: the ink that disappears under his collar. The flex of muscle in his forearms when he shoves a door open. The way his jaw tightens when he looks back to make sure I'm still there. Need to report back to Bridget, don't I?

"Is that why you used to sneak behind the school?" I ask before I can stop myself. "Because you didn't want to be indoors?"

He stops, then turns. The look he gives me could strip paint. "You don't want to admit it, do you? What you did. How you made my life hell."

Heat floods my cheeks. "What?"

His mouth curls into something cruel. "I'm not who I was at St. Albert's, Erin. And neither are you." He tilts his head, steps closer, and his tone grows sharper. "Or are you? Still gonna run tattling? Still gonna act like you're too good to breathe the same air as the rest of us?"

His voice is venom, but he's closer now. So close I can count his eyelashes. See the scar through his eyebrow. Smell the whiskey on his breath.

So close that if I leaned forward an inch, our mouths would touch.

The thought makes heat flood between my legs, even as my cheeks flame.

No. Absolutely not.

"I'm not perfect," I mutter, hating how my voice shakes. Hating how my fingers itch to tap. Hating how my body doesn't know if it wants to run from him... or toward him.

"Aye... you thought you were, back then. Didn't you?" His smile sharpens, his voice low and ragged. "Do you have any idea how much trouble you got me into?"

My heart slams against my ribs.

"How many beatings I took because of you? How many times I faced my da's belt?"

Oh god. I didn't know. Didn't think—

"How many times Malachy made me kneel on stone until my knees bled? How many times Seamus beat the shite out of me in the ring to 'teach me discipline'? All because you couldn't keep your perfect little mouth shut."

His eyes are black and furious, but then they drop to my *perfect little mouth.* Just for a second. Just long enough.

Something hot and wrong unfurls in my stomach, then lower.

My heart thunders.

He steps closer.

"I never meant to get you in trouble, Cavin," I whisper. "I—"

"Don't." His voice drops to gravel. "Don't fucking lie to me again. Not here. Not now."

His eyes bore into mine.

I let out a shaky breath.

"They'll ring the bell soon. The next floor is bedrooms." He turns and walks up the stairs without looking back.

I follow, cursing myself for everything.

For the way my eyes track his shoulders.

For the way my pulse jumps when he stops and waits.

For the damp heat between my thighs that shouldn't be there.

For wanting someone who hurt me.

For being so *fucked in the head* that his anger makes me wet.

"This one's Seamus's," he says, gesturing. "He stays here when he's working late."

Then he opens another door, stepping aside so I can see inside. The room is massive. Dark wood. A bed that could fit four people. Floor-to-ceiling windows overlooking the cliffs. "This is mine." He pauses, his eyes meeting mine in unexpected challenge. "Ours, soon, I guess."

He's watching me, gauging my reaction.

"*What?*" The word escapes before I can stop it.

"*Ours.* We'll stay here after the wedding." He pauses, running a hand across the stubble on his jaw, and his voice drops lower. Wicked. "Break it in properly."

Break it in.

Images flood my brain, unwanted and explicit.

Him. Me. That bed. Tangled sheets. His hands on my skin. His mouth on my—

Oh dear *god.*

I'm not *marrying* him.

"What are you talking about?" My voice comes out strangled. "You're takin' the piss, Cavin. What *wedding?*"

"*Jaysus.*" He drags a hand through his hair, muscles flexing.

"Why are you surprised, Erin? Don't tell me your parents didn't tell you?"

"Tell me *what*?" My voice spikes, sharp and frantic, but I can't stop staring at that bed… at the room that's apparently going to be *ours*.

"Oh, for *Christ's* sake." He mutters it under his breath, but not soft enough. "The purpose of your visit? Why do you think you're here? You think this is just a fucking estate tour?"

A bell rings somewhere behind us. "That'll be Mam," he says. "Dinner in five."

The air shifts.

"What are you talking about?"

"What did I say that confused you?" His eyes are dark. Unreadable. "I thought *you* were the one with straight A's. You knew everything back then." He steps closer. Too close.

"We're not in school anymore," he says softly. "And no one's grading us."

I grit my teeth, trying to ignore the way heat pools low in my belly.

"What the hell are you talking about, Cavin? This is ridiculous." I toss my head. "I don't believe in marriage."

Another step. He's so close I'd have to put my hands on his chest to push him back. The thought alone makes my palms tingle.

He smells good. Looks good.

And I *hate* him.

So why does my body feel like a live wire?

"Don't tell me you don't know the real reason you're here," he growls. "Your fucking parents didn't have the bollocks to say it?"

"Don't you dare—" I start, but he leans in.

His breath ghosts across my cheek. "No one told you?" he says. "You really thought this was just dinner?"

"Of course I did!" I snap, but it comes out breathless. Wrong. "We're supposed to make friends with you. That's it. We have to—" I stop myself. Too much. I've said too much.

His eyes narrow. "You were supposed to be polite to me."

Heat floods my face. "Yes."

He smirks, but there's no humor in it. "Well, if that's your goal, you're doing a terrible job." He turns to leave.

"*No.*"

My fingers hook into the front of his shirt. I drag him back toward me.

He's bigger, stronger, but I catch him off balance. He stumbles, and for one wild second, we're chest to chest. His heart pounds against my knuckles before his hand shoots up and closes around my throat.

Not squeezing. Just holding. Just there.

A threat.

A promise.

"Let. Go." His voice is raw and dangerous, but he doesn't push me away.

His thumb finds my pulse and presses... feels it hammering.

"You're terrified," he murmurs. "Or turned on. Can't tell which."

Both.

I don't respond.

His eyes flare, dark and hungry. "Fuck," he growls.

His hand tightens on my throat. Just slightly. Just enough. And I feel it everywhere... the pressure, the heat.

His erection pressed against my belly.

Oh god.

He's hard.

For me.

"What are you *talking* about, Cavin?" I demand, even though I'm shaking. Even though every nerve in my body is screaming at me to either run or close the distance. "What arrangement? What wedding?"

He stares at me for a long moment. "You're here because our families arranged a marriage." A pause. "Between you and me."

The world tilts.

He huffs out a breath without a trace of humor. "You never did have a poker face. You look like I just told you you're marrying the devil himself."

Marriage.

To Cavin McCarthy.

To the man standing in front of me right now, whose hand is still wrapped around mine, whose eyes are still burning into me like he wants to... *What?* What *does* he want?

The bell rings again—sharp and shrill, echoing down the hall like a countdown.

"I can't fucking believe they didn't tell you." He shakes his head, but his grip on my hand tightens. "We have to go. My mother gets impatient when that bell rings." His voice drops. "And you've already gotten me in enough trouble for a lifetime."

I wrench my hand free and stumble back.

I'm still wearing his fucking coat. I rip it off and throw it at his face. Hard. He catches it one-handed and doesn't even flinch.

Then he moves, fast, before I can react. His hand closes around my wrist and spins me. My chest hits the wall.

"That," he growls in my ear, "was a fucking mistake."

Oh god. I push, struggle, but can't get away from him. "Let go of—"

Smack.

His palm connects with my arse, hard, through the thin fabric of my dress. The sound echoes down the hallway, and the sting blooms hot. I gasp and try to twist away. He holds me in place with one hand pressed between my shoulder blades.

The other—*smack.*

"You want to act like a brat? In my house?" His voice is gravel. "I told you we're going to be married, Erin. You *will* learn to respect your husband."

Smack.

Oh *god.*

Heat floods through me, and not just where his hand landed. *Everywhere.*

"*Stop—*"

Smack.

"That's not your safe word." His breath is hot against my neck. "You haven't earned one yet."

My dress has ridden up, so the next smack lands on bare skin, and I bite my lip to keep from *moaning.*

"Feel that?" he asks. His hand smooths over the burning skin. Possessive. "That's what happens when you throw things at me." He leans in closer, his body pressed against my back. I can feel how hard he is.

"And Erin?" His hand slides up and grips my hip. "Next time, I won't stop at five." He releases me suddenly and steps back. I'm shaking. Burning. My arse stings, my thighs are slick, and I can't—I can't—

"Pick up my coat," he orders. "*Now.*" I turn, glaring at him through the blur of tears and rage and something else I don't want to name.

His eyes are black, his pupils blown and his jaw tight.

Cavin McCarthy is as affected as I am.

"Pick. It. *Up*." I bend down slowly, my cheeks on fire, feeling his eyes on me the whole time. It *was* petulant of me to throw it at him. I'm not a child anymore.

His fingers brush mine when I hold it out to him. "Good girl," he says softly, dangerously. "See how easy that was?" Then he drapes the coat over my shoulders again. "Keep it. You'll need it."

His thumb traces my jaw. "You're shaking."

"I *hate* you."

"I know." He leans in. His lips brush my ear. "But your body doesn't. Does it?"

I open my mouth to protest, but I've forgotten how to speak.

His voice drops to a whisper, low enough that only I can hear. "Do us both a favor tonight." It doesn't sound like a request, not the way he says it. Not with his body angled toward mine like he's caging me in without touching me, and the sting of his palm is still throbbing on my arse. "Pretend to like me."

I stop breathing. "Why the *hell* would I do that?"

He holds my gaze for one more second—long enough that I see something dangerous flash in his eyes. Long enough that I feel an answering pull low in my belly that I absolutely do not want. "Because otherwise, they might call off the arrangement. And we both need this marriage, don't we? You, for whatever reason brought you here. Me, for mine."

He walks away, leaving me trembling against the wall with my arse on fire and heat pooling between my legs.

Bastard.

I freeze. Disbelief burns to fury, then burns to something I don't have a name for. He glances back once. There's amusement in his expression, but also tension. Conflict. He doesn't like this any more than I do. But the way he looked at me, like he wanted to devour me and destroy me in equal measure. I press my palms against the cool wall and try to remember how to breathe.

Cavin McCarthy, my... husband?

What just happened?

Chapter Eight

Cavin

THE DINING ROOM feels too stuffy, too formal. All gold and noise and too bright for the hour. Light reflects off the silverware, and for a second, I wonder if this is what Erin sees.

She blinks when it's too bright and flinches at loud sounds.

And now, I feel it too.

I don't want to fucking be here.

Everyone's in place. My brothers and sisters. My cousins—Declan, Daire, Ashland, Colm, Donovan, and Lorcan. We've other men in the clan but have kept it to family tonight.

The room is full but silent, tension-packed like gunpowder. Erin's mother shoots her a warning look across the table, and I feel it, the echo of my own childhood—disciplined, polished into silence.

Behave. Remember that your presence reflects on all of us.

I love my family, I truly do, but they've been hard.

My father always said he held us to standards we'd be grateful for one day. And Seamus stepped into that role without missing a beat.

He sits to our father's right, and Declan sits next to him.

Where Seamus is bound by rules, I'm led by loyalty. My cousin Declan has neither. He's done unforgivable things for reasons we understand and doesn't do anything by halves. He's watching Erin's parents with undisguised curiosity and suspicion. Declan's the kind of man who'd drag a rival boss into the street at noon just to make a point.

Then there's Daire—the youngest, reckless. Doesn't speak unless he has something to really say.

Colm's eyes meet Erin's directly—no hesitation, no judgment in them—just steady assessment, like he's reading a ledger. Then he nods once, respectful. He's brutal in his own right, but brutality tempered with brilliance.

Cousin Ashland shifts in his seat when I say Erin's name, the barest movement, but I catch it. His eyes stay fixed on the table in front of him, his shaved head glinting in the overhead lighting, jaw taut. He's biting his tongue. Good. He learned that lesson at least.

His brothers Lorcan and Donovan sit further down. Donovan smiles when he catches my eye. His are pale and almost colorless, scary to most. But he's older and married, sort of a big brother to me.

My younger sister Kyla sits between Mam and Bronwyn. Kyla's made of iron but never bends. With her deep red curls, unruly and defiant, she's my grandmother's legacy.

Then there's Bronwyn, Kyla's opposite in every way. Delicate, almost angelic. Her face is rounder, gentler. A flush of pink blooms when she's embarrassed or emotional.

Seamus nods to the two empty chairs. One at the McCarthy end, one that bridges both sides of the table. Erin's and mine.

Great.

Excellent.

Exactly what I don't want.

I can't fuckin' believe she didn't *know.*

I can still feel the sting on my palm from the right good spanking she earned. What I'd give to take her to The Craic and punish her properly...

"Welcome," Mam says. Da's hand covers hers—larger, rougher, and protective. "Have a seat, love," she says to Erin. "Did you enjoy your tour?"

Erin looks at me before she speaks. "I did," she answers plainly. "Especially outdoors."

If there's one thing I'll give the lass, it's this—she's sincere. No poker face to save her life.

I wonder if she enjoyed the tour of her nose pressed up against the wall with my hand across her arse.

"Your house is beautiful," Erin says. "I absolutely adore it. I could stay outside for hours."

The girl's always been that way. The only time I ever saw her get in trouble at St. Albert's was for staying out too long, slipping past curfew to feel the rain on her face. Not for breaking rules but for refusing walls.

"Thank you," Mam says. "I can't take credit for the garden. My mother-in-law did it, you know. It was her little sanctuary."

"I can see why," Erin says softly.

Erin's uncomfortable, of course. Can't blame her for that. Even if she grates on me, even if she's a thorn in every conversation, she's been tossed into the lion's den without a weapon or a warning, and I don't envy her that.

I pull out her seat for her, and she nods her gratitude but doesn't meet my eyes.

Seamus raises his glass. "A toast," he says, voice steady and measured. "Tonight we let bygones be bygones, and look to the future."

Erin shoots a glance at her mother, who doesn't look at her.

"To the future," Seamus repeats, and the table echoes it back.

To the future.

The *fucking* future.

Erin's staring at me.

"Pick up your glass," I whisper, irritated that she's not playing her damn part.

She does, but she fumbles and knocks it over. Red wine spills like blood across the white tablecloth.

"Oh no—"

"It's nothing, lass, don't worry," my mother says quickly, as Erin's mother's eyes blaze, as if Erin's existence is a personal betrayal.

Even I want to slap her mother for looking at her like that.

Mam waves a hand, and in seconds, staff appear to mop up the mess.

"Could've found another way to tell them you don't drink," I quip, but it falls flat. Declan's the only one who snickers, but Erin's face flushes. She looks like she wants to disappear under the tablecloth.

Maybe she's not Miss Perfect after all.

I pour her another glass.

"No, thanks. I actually *don't* drink. I'm sorry," she whispers.

"For what?" I whisper back.

"For spilling my glass."

Great. So we're pretending that's what this is about.

"It was an accident. It's fine," I say, my voice tight.

The old men are deep in discussion now, throwing around routes and partnerships. Ports in Greece. Western harbors. Talk of linking the Belfast lanes.

Does she know she's the bridge they're using to build all of it?

While they negotiate their future, I slide a dish her way. I don't give a fuck about the routes. I know my role and play it well.

"I'm sorry," she says again.

"It's fine," I mutter. Why's she still fuckin' apologizing? "Have some bread." I pass her the bread basket.

"Oh... thank you," she says shakily.

"Don't worry," I tell her in a whisper so only she can hear. "You'll learn the rhythm soon. Smile when they drink. Laugh when they boast."

My fingers brush hers as I refill her water glass, and Christ, there it is again—that dark pull I've no business feeling.

She's here because she has to be.

Just like me.

We work through salad and appetizers while they finalize the deal. Her coast will become my roots. Our lives signed, sealed, and sold before dessert arrives.

She hates me for it. Good. That's easier. At least I know where I stand.

Her hand moves under the tablecloth. That counting thing. Tapping, always tapping.

I let her... for now.

Why does she do that? It makes me want to reach over, grab it, and squeeze until she stops. Until she's still. Until she sees me.

She makes me feel like a fucking bear, like she expects me to bite her.

I have no plans to do that.

Not yet, anyway.

I stand up from the table. "Seamus. A word."

All eyes snap to me. Good. Let me be the awkward one for once.

Seamus rises, dabs his mouth with his napkin, and folds it with military precision. Then he nods toward the exit door that leads to the hallway. We step outside together while my mother picks up the conversation.

"What is it?" Seamus asks, his voice low, calculating. He knows I wouldn't interrupt dinner unless I had a damn good reason.

"I took Erin on a tour of the estate before dinner like Mam asked, and mentioned our betrothal, like you said. The one that she knows *nothing* about, Seamus."

"I—" Seamus starts, then stops. His brow creases. "She didn't know what the fuck you were talking about?"

I nod once, watching his eyes widen as he rakes a hand through his hair.

"Jesus *fuckin'* Christ..."

"I know."

"Why does she think she's here?" he mutters, more curious than concerned. "Some kind of formal dinner? A get-to-know-you thing, maybe? Friends?" He shakes his head, exhaling sharply. "Oh my god."

"Don't bring it up at dinner," I say.

I don't know why I say it. I just know that if he does, she'll unravel, right here, in front of everyone.

"Okay," Seamus says, nodding. "I can do that. Why?"

"Because I don't think it's fair to her, putting her on the spot like that..." I trail off. My jaw tics. "I wouldn't want that done to me."

He glances at me, slow and knowing. "A soft spot for your betrothed..."

"No," I snap. Then quieter, "Yes. Whatever. I just... I don't think it's fair. I'd fucking kill you if you did that to me."

One of his brows rises, and I rein in my tone. He's the head of the family now. I don't talk back to him. Not outright.

"I'd want to kill you," I amend, which isn't much better, and he actually snorts. "If you sprung a betrothal on me at a goddamn *dinner* party."

"Aye, right. Alright then," he says. "So... after dinner, I'll take her father for a smoke. Bit of whiskey. We'll chat. Then we bring it up."

"Aye. Sounds good."

"Back inside before her mother loses her goddamn mind."

He noticed too, then.

I mutter under my breath, reentering the dining room.

Erin still looks like a deer caught in headlights—eyes wide, frozen—her knife buttering the same piece of bread for what has to be five minutes now.

"Erin," my mother says, gentle. "What'd you do for work? Remind me."

"I'm the bookkeeper for—" Erin starts, too fast. Her voice trips over the words, too eager to fill the silence.

Mam's gaze warms. "Take your time."

Erin nods too quickly. "Right. Yes. I-I manage the ledgers for the warehouses along the western coast. The imports, exports, the taxes, well, not the *real* taxes, obviously, but the collections, and the shipments. I track the whiskey barrels, and the—"

"Erin," her mother cuts in, a warning in her tone.

But Erin keeps going, momentum carrying her past sense. "There's a discrepancy in the Limerick accounts. I think someone's double invoicing, but no one listens when I—"

Tink.

The sharp tap of metal against glass freezes her mid-sentence. Tara doesn't raise her voice. Silence stretches, heavy and hot.

I lean back in my chair and watch Erin curiously, elbows resting loose on my knees.

"Interesting," I say. "Didn't know the Kavanagh books needed defending."

Erin's cheeks flare pink. "They don't. I wasn't... I only meant that I notice things, patterns and the like... they're easy to understand. Unlike human behavior," she finishes in a tiny voice.

Tara exhales, long-suffering. "She means she keeps the family's financial affairs in order. That's all." Her smile is brittle, a warning for Erin to stay in her lane.

Erin folds in on herself, her shoulders tight, mouth pressed shut, but in her eyes, there's the faintest spark of defiance.

The kind that I notice. The kind I well know doesn't stay buried for long. "I wasn't finished," she murmurs.

Mam smiles at her. "You're guileless, lass. That's rare in our stock. And I like it very much."

So do I, for reasons I don't understand. It's almost... *endearing.*

The rest of dinner passes mostly without a hitch. I take it as my personal mission to observe everything I can about my future wife.

"You sure you don't want a drink? I can get you a beer, if it's wine you don't like."

"No, thank you. I like to stay in control of myself," she replies. "I don't do anything that threatens my control."

"Right..." I mutter, then quieter, so only she can hear, "Except for formal family dinners."

She swallows and sniffs, but doesn't argue. "Aye. You're not wrong."

Why does it feel like a peace offering?

"And how's Bridget?" my mother asks politely.

Tara looks away, too quickly. "She's fine, just out of the country for a bit," she says.

"Oh, is she?" Mam says softly, while Da and Seamus discuss trade routes with Erin's father. I only half listen. My focus stays on Tara.

Unlike her daughter, who couldn't lie if her life depended on it, she's hiding everything, calculated and controlled.

Must fucking infuriate her knowing she can't get a grip on Erin.

"Where is she?"

"Oh, visiting family in Europe," Tara replies—too fast. Too rehearsed. "She'll be back in time for..." Her eyes flit to Erin's. "For the festivities and all."

She pours another glass of wine, her fourth or fifth.

Erin turns to Bronwyn, who's been quiet, watching. She gives a small smile. "I'm glad you're home again."

Tara flinches, but my mother smiles. My da too. Erin's growing on them.

Fuck. Just what I need—everyone getting soft.

"Do you know what happened?" Erin asks. "Why were you taken, Bronwyn?"

"We don't know," Bronwyn says quietly.

"You don't know anything at all?" Erin's father snaps. "What, didn't she have a guard on her?"

Seamus interjects. "Of course she did," my brother says sharply. "She's got a better one now. We don't know what happened."

"My god," my father mutters, shaking his head. "I'd lose my damn mind if one of my girls was taken."

"Tell me about it," Da murmurs. Everyone in Ballyhock knows how protective Keenan McCarthy is of his family. I served time for that damn reason.

I know the brief time Bronwyn was missing absolutely *destroyed* him.

I wonder if he blames himself for stepping down as the clan leader.

Bronwyn glances at Erin and smiles. "Thank you for asking. Erin, that dress is absolutely beautiful. Where'd you get it?"

Erin looks down. "I-I don't know. I don't like shopping much. Mam tries to buy me things, you know? She likes to dress me up..." Her cheeks turn pink.

"Oh, I love that," Bronwyn grins.

"Your mam buys you clothes?" Kyla snaps.

"I..." Erin starts, then falters. Kyla eyes her like she's something to dissect.

"I mean... I do buy my own clothes. But Mam doesn't like what I pick. Says I wear the same thing over and over, like a uniform." She laughs nervously. "Whatever. She's not wrong. I'd live in yoga pants and jumpers, but..." She shakes her head.

"Me too," I say. "Alright, maybe not the yoga pants."

Declan snorts into another glass of wine as the staff brings out trays of desserts.

"Maybe it just makes things easier. Roll out of bed. Pull on your slacks. Pull on your shirt. Who the fuck cares, right?"

I don't know why I'm taking her side, or why this even is a side.

"Right," Erin says, staring at her plate. When the staff

passes by, she eagerly takes the chocolate mousse and shortbread.

"Cavin," Mam warns me, under her breath. "*Language.*"

My cousin Ashland chuckles into his glass. But Declan watches Erin with something close to curiosity.

"Those aren't easy books to keep, Erin. Complicated work."

"I suppose for some," she says. "For me, I enjoy it. I like the challenge."

"You do?"

"Aye. It's something I'm quite good at." She lifts her chin, just slightly. "I like recognizing patterns. Numbers make sense. Unlike people, you know?" She huffs a dry laugh. And fuck me... she means it.

Black and white. That's how she sees the world.

And somehow, that honesty, the simplicity of it, makes me want to drag her into a dark corner and figure out every shade of gray in her mind. She's like a puzzle I can't quite figure out, and goddamn it, I want to.

I want to study her like a book, find what makes her smile... I want to see that light in her eyes one more time.

And then I remember something I haven't thought about in ten years or more.

The toilet. The lock.

Her screaming.

They didn't mean for it to go that far, they said afterward.

It was supposed to be a laugh, some stupid, harmless fun. That's what the lads said, anyway.

Lighten up, McCarthy. She's too bloody serious. And did you forget how she ratted you out?

We'd been partnered up in biology. She muttered something under her breath about how looks don't make up for brains. Finn thought it'd be funny to teach her a lesson. He was a right prick though.

I should've stopped them. I didn't. Part of me felt she deserved the comeuppance for her haughty attitude.

But they would've listened to me. I could've made them.

I heard her sobbing, banging on the door, pleading. Something in me snapped. Before I could think, I shoved the others aside and fumbled with the lock until it gave.

Erin was in the corner, crouched tight, her hands over her head, hair clinging to her face and neck.

"Hey. Hey, you're fine," I said. It felt like being with my father when we hunted at the Kildare estates, and he caught a deer. They'd stare, as if they knew they couldn't outrun their human predators, and it made me feel helpless and angry.

"Erin." She flinched and uncovered her eyes. I still remember the sound she made when she saw me—this broken, choked thing, like she thought I was part of it.

And maybe I was.

"Get out," she snarled. "Your stupid little joke isn't funny, and I hate you."

With a fresh sob, she grabbed her bag and ran. The boys had scattered by then, laughter fading down the hall, leaving me alone with the proof of what they'd done.

I told myself she'd be fine. She wasn't hurt. She'd just... panicked or something.

But later, when she wouldn't look at me anymore—when she'd cross the street rather than pass me in the hall—I started to understand.

I hadn't just stood by.

I'd let her believe I was the one who locked the door.

Seamus pushes to his feet. "Padraic. A word, sir."

Chapter Nine

Erin

THE CAR RIDE home is suffocating, like the air's been stolen out of the world, and I'm choking on silence.

All my tricks, all my usual anchors feel useless.

I'm tapping. Counting. Closing my eyes and trying to pretend I'm anywhere but here. But it doesn't work.

I'm trapped.

My father insisted on driving instead of having a ride. I see why now. He *knew* we'd need the privacy.

My mother's perched next to him, her back ramrod straight like the seatbelt isn't enough to keep her spine stiff. Their silence presses against my skin like a second layer—heavy, breathless, and crushing.

I'm trying to find the words to express my absolute *fury* at them, but words seem to fall short. I'm simmering, absolutely *shaking* with anger.

Because I thought I understood the bargain. *Be polite. Smile at dinner. Make friends with the McCarthys so they'd help us reach Dr. Rosenberg. So they'd use their connections to save Bridget.*

I thought I was playing nice for an evening. Maybe a few more dinners. Some tea with Caitlin McCarthy. Pleasant conversations about gardens and books.

Not this. Never *this.*

Not handing over my entire life like livestock at auction.

Finally, my mother breaks the silence.

"Well," she says tightly. "That went well, didn't it?"

"Are you absolutely out of your fucking *mind?*" My voice snaps before I can stop it, tight and shaking, rage and panic twisted together.

"*Erin,*" my father cuts sharply.

"Don't you fuckin' *Erin* me. Don't either of you talk down to me."

"Language. My *god,* to think we're marrying her off to the McCarthys," my mother mutters.

"No!" The word rips out of me. My hand trembles as I point at them. "You told me we were making friends with them! You said—" My voice cracks. "You said if I was polite, if I made a good impression, they might help us with Dr. Rosenberg. *That's* what you said, Mam. That's the only reason I agreed to go!"

"And they will help," my mother says coolly. "That's part of the arrangement."

"Part of the—" I can't breathe. "You mean the arrangement where I marry him? Where I become his wife? *That* arrangement? You let me walk into their home without telling me I was supposed to be *engaged* to Cavin McCarthy. Did you literally *forget* what he did to me at St. Albert's?" I choke, my voice breaking into something shrill and childish. I hate the sound, how small it makes me feel.

"In *school*, Erin? That was *ages* ago."

"Ages ago." I laugh, sharp and ugly. "As if time suddenly erases it. And even if he was some perfect gentleman, which he *wasn't*, you let me find out from a *stranger* that I was engaged. Engaged! To be *married*."

My vision blurs, and my fists clench at my sides. I want to tear off every pearl, shred this dress, slam a door hard enough to splinter the frame, and disappear.

"Erin," my mother snaps. "Pull yourself together. You know this is necessary for the family's survival."

"Necessary for the family's survival," I repeat. "I thought the whole point of cozying up to the McCarthys was so their doctor might help Bridget. That's why I went. You *know* that."

The realization still claws at me, the way it gutted me when I was alone with Cavin. I felt sick then. I feel sick now.

My autonomy sold like *livestock*.

Given away to a man who once tormented me.

Gift-wrapped for a stranger.

"This is an all-time low." The words slip out raw, jagged.

"Don't you *dare*." My mother twists around, her eyes venom. "Don't you *dare* make this about you."

I throw my hands up, a hollow laugh punching out of me. "Are you kidding me right now?"

The temperature in the car spikes. Disbelief curdles into fury, boiling over. "Make it about *me?* I'd give anything for Bridget. Anything."

"Would you?" my mother snarls.

My father's knuckles whiten on the steering wheel, but he doesn't speak.

"Unlike *you*," I spit. "I don't look away when she's not perfect. You lied about where she is because you can't stand the truth."

"That's not why—"

"Enough!" my father roars, like thunder cracking through the car. He stabs a finger at me through the rearview mirror. "You do *not* speak to your mother like that."

I feel seven years old again, silenced and helpless.

I bite down on my tongue until iron floods my mouth. I imagine reaching for the handle. Unlocking the door. Throwing myself out onto the highway. Concrete tearing skin. Bleeding, then… running. Far, far away, where no one knows who I am.

Silence stretches, brittle and jagged.

"When *is* the wedding?" I ask finally, defeated. "Can you tell me that much?"

"We don't have a date yet," my mother says. "But they suggested two months."

"Two months?" My voice cracks. "Two months. Oh my god."

"Well," she says coolly, "there you go again. Always about yourself. If you can't do it for yourself," she snaps, "then do it for Bridget."

Her words ignite me.

"Do it for my sister?" My tone goes deadly calm. "Where were *you* when she fainted at the sight of her own blood, and I drove her to the hospital? Where were *you* when the medicine wrecked her body, when she couldn't eat for days, and I sat beside her with a bucket and a wet cloth? Where were you when she cried that she didn't want to die, and I promised her she wouldn't, because *someone* had to?"

My throat aches, and my face is wet.

I wipe at my eyes with shaking hands.

"Stop crying," my mother snaps. "You're smearing mascara everywhere."

"I don't fucking care," I spit back. "And don't tell me to watch my language."

"Enough, Erin," she says.

I shake my head. "How dare you pretend I'm the selfish one here? When I tracked every pill, every damn side effect, while you smiled at donor galas and charmed the board of directors? Where the fuck were you then? And where are you now?"

As always, my mother doesn't soften. Doesn't yield. I'm sobbing in the back of the car, and she doesn't care.

"Then you'll do this too," she says. "You know exactly where I was. And don't you dare pretend I don't care. Who *arranged* this marriage, Erin? Who pulled everything together? Who sat with Caitlin McCarthy before anyone else dared to? Who carried it alone? *Me.* That's who."

Her voice shakes now, too, trembling on the edge of wrath. And that's when I see the trap.

"You'll do this too. Because you marrying Cavin McCarthy is the only way your sister lives."

The words slam into me, colder than any knife.

If I don't hand my life over to the only man I've ever truly hated, my baby sister dies.

Fury curdles into something colder—steel, resolve.

My eyes burn as tears spill unchecked. "The question isn't *if* I'll marry him. Of course I will. I'd bleed out on the altar if it saved her. I always do what needs to be done, don't I?"

Because that's what the eldest daughter does.

"This isn't about the marriage, Mother. This is about you *lying*. About you using me as a bargaining chip to reach Bridget. Because you—"

I choke the words back before they leave my mouth. I don't want to sound like a child, petty and unloved.

Because you love her more than you love me.

I force the thought down like poison, but the truth lingers.

I turn to the window, the glass smeared with my reflection. My face is streaked with tears, my hands clumsy and useless, as I wipe them away again.

If I have to marry Cavin McCarthy to save Bridget—*fine*. But I will not bleed myself dry for the McCarthys.

"You're acting like he's some absolute villain," my father mutters from the front seat. "And you know this is how things work in our family."

I shake my head. I don't waste my breath arguing.

They want to pretend I wasn't humiliated for years in hallways and locker rooms. Pretend I wasn't stripped down to nothing while Cavin McCarthy laughed.

They want to pretend I have a choice. Pretend I'm the selfish one here.

No. I won't let them twist me into that.

"And what does *Cavin* get out of this?" I ask.

"Were you not paying attention?" my mother snaps. She turns to me. I feel the distance between us and how different we are. Her makeup's flawless. Her hair sculpted, unmoved by the storm she's throwing me into, not a wrinkle on her clothes.

I'm a mess.

"The McCarthys get access to our trade routes."

"Why?" I press.

"Don't be stupid, Erin," she spits. "For someone so smart, you really don't see the forest for the trees."

"Tara," my father warns, chiding like a man who's already surrendered.

My mother's nostrils flare. "You both know what's at stake, and you know what we hope to gain from the McCarthys. We forfeit our trade routes, but we could save Bridget."

They forfeit trade routes, and... me. My mother folds her hands in her lap, prim and polished, as if she hasn't just sold me like another shipment in the trade route.

The car is too quiet after that. The tires hum over smooth pavement, as if the world dares to pretend my life hasn't just been detonated.

My father stares straight ahead, his jaw clamped, the silent executioner.

"I'm sorry," my mother whispers finally. The words are so thin they barely exist.

I blink because I've never heard her say them. Not once.

"It had to be done, Erin. It *had* to."

My father shifts, muttering something about timing, family needs, but I cut him off.

"You didn't even ask me. You didn't ask if I wanted to marry him." My voice breaks. "You just... gave me away."

"You said you'd do this for your sister," my mother fires back. You said you'd do anything, in the hospital, the day she collapsed."

She trembles now, and it breaks me in ways I hate.

I don't *want* to forgive her. I don't want to feel her pain. I want to hate her. I want to hate someone for the way my ribs feel like they're being crushed from the inside.

"I know you'll do this for your sister," my mother repeats, softer this time.

"Of course I will," I whisper.

Tears burn down my face. My hands shake.

And the car hums on, relentless.

From the front seat, my father finally speaks. "You'll do this for her because it's the only way she lives." He doesn't meet my eyes in the rearview mirror.

I nod once. My throat is raw.

I *know*.

And that's when it settles. The final truth. This isn't a request. It's a sentence. The decisions have already been made.

I wipe my face with the back of my hand, then breathe in once, sharp and hard.

"I will," I tell them. "But don't you dare make one more plan without me. Not *one*." My voice trembles.

The city flashes by in streaks of yellow light. How can everything outside look the same... when inside, *nothing* is.

The last leg of our journey is silent. I have nothing left to say. We pull into our drive, and I look at our house differently now. It's big enough, but nothing like the imposing majesty of the McCarthy mansion.

Inside, I step away from my parents, pull my shoes off, and walk down the long hallway, my bare feet silent against the cold wood, putting as much space between myself and them as I can.

The rule in the Kavanagh family is simple: A daughter stays with her parents until she gets married.

Old-fashioned, people would say. I'd call it fucking archaic. But fine. Whatever.

I stay. Not for them, but for my sister.

I put up with my mom. I tolerate the passive-aggressive glances, the pressure, radio silence, and judgment because I need to be near Bridget. Need to make sure she's okay.

And tonight's no different.

Every part of me wants to crawl into bed, bury my face in a pillow, and scream. But instead, my feet move down the long, dark hall to Bridget's room.

This house is old—an Irish country house passed down on my father's side. Gleaming hardwood but drafty walls. The kind of place where the cold seeps in through the baseboards. At night, the wind howls through the chimney like a ghost that never left.

The floors creak. The windows rattle.

I shiver, and... I remember Cavin.

The way he slipped his jacket over my shoulders. Not kindness, something else. Obligation, maybe? Performance?

He did it because it was expected. But still... I liked it.

I can imagine my mother now, pouring herself another glass from the sideboard in the dining room, as if she didn't drink her way through two full bottles at the McCarthys.

I knock lightly on Bridget's door. "Come in," she says so softly I can barely hear her. I open the door and brace myself for the inevitable. I just can't get used to how frail and sickly she looks these days.

"Hey," I say, my voice pitched too high. Too bright. That fake cheer I always default to with her. "How are you feeling?"

"Fine," she says too quickly. She's probably tired of the question. Sick of pretending.

"How'd it go?" she whispers.

I let out a long breath.

I open my mouth, prepare to lie, but I can't tell a lie to the person I'm closest to in the whole damn world, and I'm shite at lying anyway.

"It was... fine," I try, but my chin wobbles.

Tears threaten, pressing behind my eyes.

"Oh, Erin..." she says gently. "It wasn't fine." She reaches for my hand. "Tell me what happened."

Her room, at least, is comforting and soothing. Soft blush tones and warm white lights. Books stacked on the night-stand, spines cracked from re-reads. A candle burning in the corner, lavender and something sweet.

She's filled the room with tiny things that make her feel

human. Posters of old Audrey Hepburn films. A corkboard of photos—us, mostly.

Worn throw blankets. A faded stuffed rabbit she never let go of.

It's her sanctuary.

"Look," I mutter. "I've *got* to get out of this stupid dress." I tug at the hem like it's strangling me. "I hate it. You know how I feel about this."

"Of course," she says, smiling a little. "Wear whatever you want."

So I try to pull myself together as I strip it off and grab clothes from her dresser. I slide on a pair of her yoga pants and want to cry with relief.

They don't fit her anymore, but we used to wear the same size. We used to share everything.

I grab a jumper from her closet and peel off my bra with a loud, belabored sigh. The relief is instant.

There was a time when Bridget was so immunocompromised that we had to wear those stupid masks everywhere. I remember how they fogged up my glasses, how the elastic bit into my ears. I could barely breathe in them. And I remember the feeling when I could finally pull it off and exhale.

Taking off my bra feels *exactly* like that.

I tie my hair up, loose and messy, just as she gasps.

"Oh my goodness, Erin," she says, her eyes on my feet. "Look at your feet. Let me see."

She props herself up on the giant body pillows Dad bought her, and I glance down.

My toes are red and squeezed after my shoes dug into my skin for hours.

"Tell me about it. Why do people dress like this? I don't get it."

"Right?" she says, groaning.

"Why can't we just have dinner in yoga pants? Why is that a crime? Or leggings, if we're fancy. Take it from someone who basically lives in pajamas—these yoga pants might as well be a goddamn cocktail dress."

"I know. Seriously."

We both laugh, tired and sad, but it's real. And for a second, the cold house feels warmer.

I giggle, and so does she. That sound warms something inside me I thought had gone numb.

"So tell me everything," she says. "Were they nice? Did you guys come to an agreement?"

"Oh, we came to an agreement alright," I say. My smile fades. She's the reason I'm doing it. I can't let her know how this is killing me inside.

I exhale slow, like I can push the weight of it out with my breath. "Well... Mom and Dad didn't tell me the real reason for the trip."

"What?" Her eyes go wide—sharp with curiosity and concern. She's lost even more weight. How much weight can a person lose?

Her skin's too pale, with a sickly cast that clings to her like a shadow. But her hair is still that rich auburn, tumbling in waves down her back, curling over her forehead and along her cheek. It's lustrous and gorgeous, and I used to call her Ariel when she was little.

I sit on her bed and curl my legs underneath me. "So we get there, right?" I blow out another breath, and my voice catches on the edges. "And it's... stunning. Bridget, I can't wait for you to see it. There's this garden, all wild and elegant at the same time. Cliffs that drop off into the sea. And the house... Da says it's worth fifty million euros. It's *unbelievable*. Like a museum crossed with a palace."

"Oh..." Bridget breathes. "That sounds amazing."

"It was," I tell her. "And I made this little comment about it, just a throwaway, and the mum, Caitlin—she's like, 'Why don't you go on a tour?' And *guess* who she picks to show me around? Guess!"

I pinch the bridge of my nose.

Bridget's hands drop to her lap. "No."

"*Cavin.*"

"Are you joking?"

"Nope." I throw my hands up. "Yay me. And then—it's cold. Just a breeze, but sharp enough to make me shiver, and he puts his jacket over my shoulders."

"Wait, what?" Bridget lifts her hand. "He gave you his jacket?"

"Yeah, but not like that," I say quickly. "It wasn't romantic or anything. He's just... he's a McCarthy, isn't he? All polished up, raised to play the gentleman."

Bridget arches a brow. "Go on."

"Stop looking at me like that," I say.

She's supposed to be on my side. She's supposed to hate him with me.

"I'm not making it anything," she says, eyes wide with mock innocence. "Go on, then."

So I do.

"Cavin takes me through the estate, every inch of it done up like some ancient royal family's private playground. And then... he makes a comment about a *dungeon*. Wait. Actually, no. *I* made the comment."

I glance down, embarrassed. "I joked about it. And then *he* said he likes the dungeon at *The Craic* better."

Bridget's cheeks flush pink, and it's the first color I've seen on her all day. She slaps her hand over her mouth.

"You didn't."

"I did."

"That's amazing." She laughs, coughing mid-sentence.

And then the coughing takes over. It's harsh and rattling, and her whole body trembles with it, and I just sit there, frozen and helpless.

I wait until it passes.

"Sorry," she says, shaking her head and sipping water. But

she doesn't meet my eyes. She knows what it looks like. We both do.

"So you said dungeon, and he brought up The Craic," she says.

"Yeah. Said he liked that one better."

"Oh my god, no." Bridget groans, grinning through her disbelief.

And somehow, in the middle of this twisted mess, I'm glad I went. Just for this... this sister-to-sister *moment* with her.

"So he showed me the garden and the library. Talked about kitchens and architecture like he was some bored realtor. But then..."

Tears prick behind my eyes. I try to swallow them down, but my voice betrays me.

Bridget's brow furrows.

"What happened, Erin?" she whispers.

"He showed me the bedrooms," I whisper. "He said—*this one's mine. Soon to be ours.*"

Bridget's eyes go wide. Her jaw drops. She actually looks stunned.

"He did not."

"He *did.*" I lean closer, like if I get close enough, she'll understand what I can't say out loud.

She grabs my hand.

"But you told him that's not happening, right? You told him—"

"I didn't," I say quietly.

And just like that, the tears spill over. I didn't even feel them start. But with Bridget, I don't need to hide.

"Mom and Dad already arranged it. My wedding." My *life*. "To Cavin McCarthy."

Bridget looks like a ghost just waltzed through the window. "You're *joking*."

"No. Remember when they talked about friendship and alliances and all that bullshit?" I laugh bitterly. "They meant marriage. They meant *this*. They planned it behind my back."

"Erin..."

"I have to do it," I say, swiping at my tears.

I won't remind her why. Won't remind her what I'm trading away so she can keep fighting. "Listen..." My voice is so small, I'm not even sure she hears me. "Maybe this is the way it's supposed to go. Maybe it's not *that* bad."

Bridget stares. "Who are you right now?"

"I know. I said I'd never get married." I swipe at my eyes, and my hand comes away black with mascara.

Fancy clothes. High heels. Makeup. All of it—just another mask.

And right now? I want to rip it all off.

My phone vibrates with a text from an unknown number.

Unknown Number
This is my number. Save it. Cavin

I tap his text, hit the options, then click *Block*.

There. That ought to do it.

He's not coming into my life unannounced for another fucking second.

"You can't *marry* him, Erin," Bridget whispers, shaking her head.

I draw in a shuddering breath. "I have to."

Chapter Ten

Cavin

I'm sitting on my bed—the big, *cavernous* bed that is soon to be occupied with an enemy.

I yank at the stupid tie and tug it off, tossing it next to me.

I know the McCarthy family rules like the back of my hand. I'm not only expected to marry her, I'm expected to take care of her, and I'm expected—god—*expected* to knock her up.

I'm tense. Dammit, I want some relief.

I want to go down to the club with my brothers, grab a woman or two or three, and relieve some of this tension. But I'm an engaged man now with an invisible noose around my neck. Better than another night of shite sleep fighting my demons.

I stand up and pace the room, my hands shoved into my pockets. Voices sound at the door outside my room, and then pass. My parents have long since gone to bed. Seamus and Zoya as well. They'll probably go home tomorrow. Declan's out, and Daire is too.

I text them.

> Where are you?

Declan responds a minute later.

> **Declan**
> At the club. You?

> Home.

I scowl at the screen.

> **Declan**
> Come join us, brother. Bachelorette party tonight. The girls are in rare form. I recommend it.

I roll my eyes heavenward and respond to him in another text.

> You know I can't do that.

> **Declan**
> Can't? You're not married yet.

For fuck's sake. I toss my phone down, then pick it up again, tap out a message, and send it to Erin. I wait for her to respond.

And wait.

And wait.

But no response comes.

Perfect. Grand. Maybe she's gone to bed too.

Maybe *I* should.

Instead, I head to the shower and strip out of my clothes. I want the water scalding hot, hot enough to chasten me.

Why can't I get the woman out of my mind?

God, she looked gorgeous tonight. I was taken off guard, if I'm honest, and nothing ever fucking takes me off guard.

That dress that clung to her curves and dipped just right, revealing perfect cleavage, just enough for a goddamn handful. She'd fill my hands and my mouth, and I—

I frown.

I'm thinking about the way she looked too small, draped in my coat. The way she refused wine at dinner and sparred with me. The way her mother treated her like absolute shite.

I'll put an end to that. I might not know her family… but they will know *me*.

And for a second, I imagine taking *her* to the club. We'd get a private room. And god, the way I'd tease her, using every implement and tool at my disposal.

I'd bet she'd lose her fucking mind with a hood or a vibrator. But which one? Would she prefer sensory deprivation or overstimulation? The way she responded when I had her pressed against the wall with my hand across her arse tells me she's got a submissive streak she may not know about yet. That sharp inhale, the heat radiating off her skin, the way she didn't fight me—just took it. Her body already knows what it wants, even if her mind won't admit it.

I'd make her come, over and over again, until I'd mapped every response. Does she need it rough, or does she fall apart with gentle touches? Would she beg, or would I have to drag it out of her? How much teasing could she take before she broke?

What would make her submit completely? Restraints? My hand fisted in her hair? Orders whispered against her ear while she's trembling and desperate?

What would she *taste* like? What would she look like stripped bare—not just the clothes, but that fucking attitude? Would she still have that sharp tongue when she's tied down and needy? Or would she finally go soft and pliant?

A man can't help but wonder about his wife when he's fucking *engaged* to her. Can't help but wonder if she'd take a proper spanking—not just the quick punishment I gave her, but a real one. Slow. Deliberate. Would her arse flush that same perfect pink? Would she count for me? Would she cry? Would she get wet from it?

I want to find out. Want to bend her over and take my time, see exactly how much she can take. See if she'd break... or beg me for more.

I do a mental list of everything I know about her.

She gets nervous in crowds and in unfamiliar settings, and sometimes she flinches when the lights are too bright or the sounds are too loud.

Will she be as timid in bed?

Is she a virgin?

Two fuckin' months. Eight more weeks.

Less than sixty days until my life as I know it will be over.

I scrub shampoo through my hair, then rub a bar of soap over myself and a washcloth. Wash up.

I'm frustrated, blood's up, and I want something to relieve my pain. Feels like it did when I was in prison—too much testosterone, too little to do. Not enough freedom.

I fist my thick cock and stroke it, chasing something, anything, that'll get me out of my head. And my mind lands on... Erin.

Kneeling on her knees in front of me. There's something about that look in her eyes that makes me fucking ferocious.

I want to *ruin* her.

I want to feel that pretty, smarmy mouth of hers around my cock.

I imagine how she'd look after a good session at The Craic. Her eyes blown wide. Her body trembling. Her arousal dripping between her legs.

I want to teach her to mind her manners. How to be a good girl.

I stroke harder, faster. Imagine her sprawled on the bed, tits down, ass in the air, marked with my belt, my teeth, my hand. Imagine her slick pussy waiting for me, and I collide right into it. I imagine pumping in and out.

I fuck my hand until I come with a growl locked behind my teeth.

I'll teach her, like I'll teach her everything else—how to kneel. How to spread her legs when I eat her out. How to do what she's fucking told and respect her husband.

I clean off, and water scalds the back of my neck. Steam fogs the mirror. I turn off the water, dry off, and wrap the towel around my waist. Then I check my phone.

Still no fucking text from Erin.

Why the fuck do I care?

She's *nothing* to me, and yet... she knows how to get under my skin, and I hate that. Makes me feel young again in the worst goddamn way—back when I was some pissed-off teenager with a chip on his shoulder and something to prove.

She made me feel small. Weak. Stupid.

She'd push her glasses up that stuck-up nose and say shite like *That's not how it's done,* in that clipped, condescending voice that made me want to throw a desk across the room.

I'm gonna tell on you.

She used to clutch her books like a goddamn shield. Always watching. Always judging. The thorn in my side.

I remember that day in the hallway—my friends holding the bathroom door shut while she screamed behind it. Pounding. Crying for someone to help her—the one day I felt a spark of sympathy.

When she finally got out, red-faced and shaking, she pointed right at me.

Blamed *me.*

And I let her.

Hell, part of me *wished* it had been me.

Because I hated her.

Hated the way she made me feel, like I could bust my bollocks all day, graft myself sick, ace every bleedin' thing they threw at me, and it still wouldn't count for shite. Not when she sat there smug as fuck, hands folded on a page full of perfect answers. Perfect grades. Perfect fucking everything, teacher's little fuckin' pet.

And now?

Now I get to *marry* her.

Imagine that. A lifetime of *that* voice correcting me at dinner. Telling me I'm not doing it "the right way."

I don't drink.

Of course she doesn't. God forbid.

Saint bloody Erin. Miss Perfect lick-arse. Collectin' gold stars like rosary beads.

Everyone loves a girl who plays by the rules, don't they?

And does she?

I check my phone again, my jaw tightening.

Still nothing.

She's my *fiancée*. My goddamn betrothed. She's supposed to respond.

I drag the towel over my head, hair sticking up in all directions. I need *out*.

I need The Craic.

Not gonna fuck some nameless cunt in the back room tonight, but I *will* have a drink. I *will* see the boys. Let off some steam and remind myself who the fuck I am.

Because the nerve of her not replying?

The audacity of her parents marrying her off without even telling her? As if I'm some last-minute footnote in her story.

My phone buzzes, and I glance at it.

Not her.

Of *course* it's not her.

> Shipment moved. No details. Just a location change. Belfast.

> Fine.

> I'll go tomorrow.

Another thing for the list: check the shipment, confirm the transfer, prep the route. Once I marry her, I'll gain access to all of it.

But my house has to be in order first.

The ride to The Craic takes fifteen minutes. I know every turn and light as I ruminate over Erin Kavanagh.

I hate that.

I hate that I can't control it, control *her*.

She doesn't want to marry me.

Good. The feeling's mutual, princess.

And jerking off in the shower sure as hell didn't help. Didn't even make a dent in my frustration. Maybe it's not even sexual.

I glance at my phone again.

Nothing.

Fuck.

I drive faster, cutting through the night like it owes me something.

Christ, but I missed this—driving. Speed. Autonomy. The wind blowing through the cracked window. The hum of the engine underneath me. In prison, I damn near forgot what it meant to be free.

My phone vibrates. A flicker of hope... gone in an instant.

Declan. Seamus.

I breathe in deep, then exhale through clenched teeth. No one keeps me waiting.

No one *ignores me.*

Christ.

I think about the tribute, counting the days until the next one's due again. Another bloody reminder: The marriage isn't the only thing slipping through my fingers. I don't even know who the hell we're paying.

I park the car, and the valet steps forward.

I hand over the keys and a thick roll of notes. I like them to remember who I am and show respect.

Even if *she* doesn't.

I don't walk into The Craic—I storm in because I own the fucking place. No mask. No hesitation. Just clean, brutal purpose and my standard uniform—black on black, tailored shirt, unbuttoned just enough to show I don't give a shite. Sleeves rolled high, ink and scar tissue on display like a fucking roadmap of every bastard who thought they could take me.

And when I show? They part like the fucking Red Sea.

Heads turn, spines straighten, and eyes drop.

Respect, the only currency that matters in a place like this. You either command it or you get swallowed whole.

I'm raging inside, and every man in this room can fucking feel it. "Mr. McCarthy."

The barman—a slight dip of the head. The shadow of Rafferty behind the bar. He poured pints for my father before he poured for me. His eyes flicker once and then move on.

There's reverence in the air, or at the very least, begrudging respect.

Yeah. *This* is what I wanted tonight.

A place where I rule. A place where I can breathe without playing nice. Where control isn't just a fantasy but law.

I smile and let it bleed out slow. Because I'm not here to *play*... I'm here to burn something down.

Declan's already inside by the time I reach the front bar. The front's just the mask—a pint of Guinness and polite lies if you're on the outside. But if you're *in*, if you know the word, the look, and your background checks out, you make your way to the back.

The Craic's been ours for decades. My mother protested, thinks it's beneath us, that we shouldn't tie our names to a place where rules are broken and vices are celebrated. She's not *wrong*.

But we fucking love it. It's sacred to us, a monument of vice in Ballyhock. You don't get in unless you're a McCarthy or close enough to bleed like one.

The elevator hums as it drops us to hell. And on the other side, freedom.

My cousin Declan's there, drink in hand and leaning back like he owns the place. Lorcan is beside him, built like a goddamn weapon, his eyes brutal and assessing.

Declan looks up when I enter and smirks.

"You look terrible, mate. When's the last time you slept proper?"

Too long.

I shrug and don't bother answering, just order a Jameson neat.

My eyes scan the room. Cages, silk ropes, flesh in motion. Worship and violence so tangled they're one and the same. Moans like prayers, and whimpers like confessions.

This place doesn't just offer release. It demands truth—ugly, raw, and beautiful.

And I *love* it here.

The Craic may be elite, underground, and feral, where secrets are bought and dominance can be had for a price. Masks come off here. But what I love is not just that I'm welcome here, but that every part of me, even the ruthless, savage, scarred parts, is welcome too. Fuck, worshipped.

Everyone knows the heirs of the McCarthy name rule this place and that *this* is our playground.

I'm engaged to be married, though, goddamn it.

My phone buzzes. I check it. Still nothing from Erin.

"Why are you so pissed?" Lorcan's curious.

I lean forward and scowl. "I'm not," I growl, pissed that he's calling it out.

"Oh, come off it," he pushes. "What are you hiding?"

"I'm not hiding *anything.*"

Declan and Lorcan exchange a look.

"What?" I snap.

"He's pissed about the engagement," Declan says, too casual.

My jaw tightens. I hate the way they talk as if I'm not right here. As if I didn't just walk into the fucking room.

"Excuse me?" I say, loud enough. "Hello? I'm sitting right *fucking* here."

Lorcan shrugs. He's a big bastard, with arms like tree trunks and sandy-brown hair like his dad. His storm-gray eyes are always scanning. He's a strategist, quieter than I am.

His brother Donovan's next to him, dangerous and powerful... older. When Donovan speaks, people listen.

He's a tactician, the cleaner. The guy we call when the job's bloody and someone needs to make it disappear.

Give Donovan a command, and if he respects you, he doesn't hesitate. Just gets the job done. No flinching. No noise. Unlike his brother Ashland, he's charming, and uses it to his advantage.

His fingers tap the table, restless.

"You don't like that you're engaged?" Donovan asks, his pale blue eyes dancing before he smirks at his phone and shoots a text.

"Would be nice if I knew her," I mutter.

"Would be nice if you *let* yourself know her," Donovan corrects with his signature smile that's meant to disarm. Doesn't work on me.

"That's the fucking problem," Lorcan says. "He *does* know her, doesn't he?"

"Would you stop it," I snap. I down my drink and slam the glass on the bar. "Stop talking about me like I'm not right here."

"We *know* you're here," Declan says, grinning.

My cousin Declan's controlled chaos—adored for the way he masks violence with charm.

Declan was once the golden boy of the McCarthys. Gilded. Untouchable. But that shine dulled fast, fucked off somewhere between the pills and the power. Addiction made him chaos. Before he fell apart, everyone was drawn to him —half terrified, half mesmerized.

Where my eldest brother Seamus clings to rules like gospel, I deal in loyalty, quiet and unflinching.

Declan? He doesn't bother with either. He slides under rules, ducks around them, and fucks them sideways if he feels like it.

He's done unforgivable things, real twisted shit. He's the headline in every scandal and the center of every storm. But somehow, he always chooses whether to follow or break rank. No one decides for him.

"Tell us the truth then," Declan says, sipping his Jameson like it's holy water.

A leggy blonde drapes herself around his shoulders. She's in a silky purple number that barely clings to her tits and shows off the undercurve of her ass like a goddamn invitation.

She moans when he exhales.

"That feel good?" he murmurs, sounding almost bored.

"Would you like me to get my friend again tonight, sir?" she purrs in his ear, her eyes done up like a cat—headband, whiskers, the whole damn thing.

He nods. "Aye. Go get her."

When she turns, he gives her a parting slap to the arse like she's his favorite toy.

Declan likes his women in numbers, the McCarthy family fuck boy.

"She still holding a grudge?" Declan asks, eyeing me over the rim of his glass.

He had a different friend group back then, didn't know how deep it went or how sharp it cut. I doubt even Seamus knows.

I shake my head and try to brush it off.

"Some of my class bullied her," I mutter, but it's weak. Cowardly, really. "Fine, the truth is, I wasn't very... nice to her. She got me in so much goddamn trouble in school, which got me in trouble at home. She was one of those goody-two-shoes types. Did the right thing. Made the rest of us look worse just by existing."

"Ugh. One of those," Lorcan says, wrinkling his nose. "And you're marrying the lass, why?"

"Because Seamus fancies it'll do us good," I mutter, shrugging.

The truth? Her father made a deal we couldn't refuse. No one's been married in our family for a few years. "Guess it's my turn. Would've been Torin's if he wasn't still rotting behind fuckin' bars."

Declan sighs.

"It's just as well," I say. "Torin's got demons. Needs to fight 'em before he takes a woman."

"You get my text, brother?" he asks, changing the subject.

"Aye." I don't look up from my phone. "Told you I had it sorted."

"Couldn't read through the communication log," he mutters. "Tried."

"We had a glitch or some such."

I hate lying to my own. But I've no choice in it, have I? I had to hide it so no one would see communication about the damn tribute.

The clock is ticking before the next tribute's due, with no lead on who's demanding my goddamn bollocks in a sling, and I've got all the *wedding* festivities. *Goddamn it.*

Regulations for the tribute are clear, per Malachy. No more than twelve hours before midnight on the last day of the month. Not a second earlier. Not a second late.

"Can't bring a new wife here, can you?" Lorcan mutters.

"Hell no," I growl.

"Aye. A proper response," Declan says, smirking, just as a second girl slides up next to him. One hand for each shoulder, they knead him like he's royalty.

"A wife?" the one in purple asks, glancing at me. "You getting married, Mr. McCarthy?"

"Aye," I growl again.

"It's posted on St. Albert's page, isn't it?" the other girl says. "I saw it earlier."

"What?" I pick up my phone. "What the fuck is that?"

"Social media, you dumbass," Lorcan says.

"I hate that shite. Show me." His fingers fly over his phone, and then he does indeed show me. I narrow my eyes at the screen.

There it is. St. Albert's alumni page, with a big diamond ring announcement.

St. Albert's is pleased to announce the betrothal of Erin Kavanagh and Cavin McCarthy.

Jesus. It already has five hundred views and twenty-seven comments.

"What the hell?" I mutter.

"Well, fuck," Lorcan says, his eyebrows rising.

"What?" I growl.

"Comments aren't very nice toward Erin, are they?"

"What?" I squint at the screen. Sure enough, there are a couple of nasty comments. A few say congratulations or the like, but half of them—

Goddamn it.

"This is terrible," I say. "What the fuck? Who are these people?"

"You can't do anything about it. People are idiots on social media," Declan says. "Put it away."

"Not if people are saying nasty things about Erin."

A beautiful brunette named Katarina comes in, wearing all black. She eyes me from head to toe.

"Good evening, sir," she says quietly. "Are you in need of a submissive tonight?" She wears the subtle purple band on her forearm per club regulations, indicating she's a free submissive.

Am I in need of a submissive?

My god, I fucking am. I swallow hard and shake my head.

"Not tonight."

Declan grins. "He's engaged to be married. He won't be taking any more submissives."

I'm going to beat that boy's fuckin' arse.

Her eyes go downcast, and she walks away. "Farewell, sir. I wish you the best."

"You're not going to be a fuckin' priest," he says. "Brother, if that girl at dinner is meant to be the one you're marryin', she's not givin' you any ride."

"As if she has a choice," I say with a shrug. "We have rules in the McCarthy family, don't we?"

"Aye," Declan says. "Three days to consummate the marriage."

"Well, fuck me," Lorcan says. "You'll have to let bygones be bygones and all that."

Just like that, I'm back to being fifteen again. Standing in the corner of the room while Malachy locked the door and glared at me, prepared to deliver my punishment.

I remember how Erin looked surprised when I told her I'd gotten in trouble because of her.

Didn't mean to get you in trouble, she said. But back then, she absolutely did.

"School was a long time ago, mate," Declan says. "Wasn't it?"

"Not long enough." I hate how I feel like a child again, just being back in that headspace.

Daire walks over from the side of the pub. He's got a hickey on his neck and his eyes are blown, as if he's just had a good time of it. He's only been allowed access to The Craic for the past four years, and he's taken full advantage.

He bumps his knuckles across his lips. They're scarred with the history of his fighting—Daire, like all of us, being one of the best bare-knuckled fighters in all of Ireland. Violence isn't abstract for him. It's personal, physical, routine.

"What's the story, lads?" he asks.

"We're only after planning the wedding," Declan says with a grin like a cat that got the cream, one I'm dying to wipe clean off his gob. I lamp him one in the shoulder, and he laughs away, rubbing at it even as he's grinning like a fuckin' *eejit*.

"When is it again?" Daire asks.

"Two months," I growl. "Shut it."

"Well, I don't see why you have to be celibate until—"

"*Leave it*," I tell him.

"I'm sorry," Daire says, shaking his head. "It's right, shit luck, isn't it?"

"Could be worse," I say. "I could be back in prison, like Torin." Where I'd managed to avoid being raped, but not much else. I don't sleep at night for the memories I have of that place. And while Seamus tells me the Russians have it worse in their prisons, I can't imagine how.

My phone buzzes with another text, and I look at the screen this time.

Seamus.

> **Seamus**
> Why are you lads at The Craic tonight?

It's a simple enough question, but he's checking in—probably before he goes to bed with his wife and the kids.

> Just blowin' off a little steam

I respond, but I know what he really wants to know. *Am I taking someone home tonight? Am I being loyal now that I'm an engaged man?*

> Don't worry about me

I tell him, trying to hide the bitterness seeping into my tone.

> I'm not here for the usual reasons, Seamus.

> **Seamus**
> Aye. I understand. Staying out of your business, brother.

Like fuck he is. I blow out a breath.

Now that Torin's gone—and he won't be out for at least another year—I'm the second in command after Seamus. It's on my shoulders to take this responsibility as my own.

Lorcan mutters something under his breath, then reaches out and grabs my wrist.

On instinct, I snap.

My hand flies out. I grab his arm and throw him halfway across the table before I know what I'm doing. People scream. Glasses shatter. Lorcan sprawls across the table, his eyes wide with shock.

"Jesus fuckin' Christ, Cavin!" he shouts.

"What the hell—" I pause, breathing hard. "I'm sorry." I run a hand through my hair. God, I don't know how to tell him. People grabbing me around the wrist like that—it reminds me of being in prison.

"You don't touch his goddamn wrist," Declan snarls at Lorcan. "You ought to *know* that by now."

"Aye, I forgot," Lorcan says, inspecting the cut where glass sliced him.

"I'm sorry," I mutter again.

Thankfully, because it's The Craic, it's not out of the ordinary for people to make a commotion. A waitress comes over and quickly cleans things up. She's a pretty little lass— petite, with large brown eyes, wavy hair, and a short skirt that barely covers the curve of her arse. The type I'd take back to a room tonight with an easy word and an arm around her waist.

But no more.

Declan shakes his head. "You don't have to act like a monk. You're not taking a vow of fuckin' celibacy, you know," he says under his breath. "You're not being married for a couple months yet."

"I know," I snap at him.

Why did I come here? What the hell did I want?

Finally, I can't take it anymore, and I send another text to Erin.

Did you get my text?

Huh. The color changes, and it doesn't deliver. The message just sits there, mocking me.

"What the fuck is that?" Declan snorts and shakes his head. "Your betrothed blocked yer fuckin' number."

Fuck my life.

The door opens, and armed guards stride in. They walk straight to me.

"We have two men asking for entrance, sir," one says in a low voice. "They say they're kin, and that there was a time when their fathers frequented the pub."

"Who the hell are they?" I ask.

"Don't know, but they've got American accents, sir."

"Are they on the roster?"

"Not on the roster, sir."

"Then you know what to do," I say, my patience thinning.

"They say it's important. They want to see you directly."

Declan gives me a curious look. "What the fuck is that about?"

I frown, push to my feet, and walk to the elevator. I press the button for members only and head on up.

Two men, strong, inked, and intimidating, are waiting for me at the top when the doors open.

"You must be Cavin," one says in an American accent.

"Aye. And you are?"

"Brogan McCarthy." He extends his hand. "Pleased to meet you."

I shake his hand, firm and quick. "And you?"

"Tannen McCarthy," the other says.

They look like brothers. Dark hair, sharp eyes, the kind of build that says they know their way around a fight.

"You're cousins from America?" I say, shoving my hands in my pockets. Something about this doesn't sit right. "Strange place to meet family."

"We were told we'd get the proper welcome here," Tannen says with a smile that doesn't reach his eyes.

"Right." I study them both carefully.

But it doesn't make sense. The stance is wrong. The energy is off. They're here for something else entirely.

I turn to call for security and verify with Seamus, when Tannen moves—trying to take a swing at me. Brogan lunges for something at my side, maybe my phone, maybe a weapon.

Instinct takes over.

I duck under Tannen's fist and drive my elbow into his gut. He doubles over with a grunt, and I bring my knee up into his face. Blood spurts from his nose. Brogan grabs at my jacket, and I spin, slamming him against the wall. His head cracks against the brick, and I follow with a brutal punch to his ribs.

"Who the fuck sent you?" I snarl.

Tannen comes at me again, but he's sloppy. I catch his arm and twist it behind his back until I hear something pop. He screams. Brogan tries to get up, and I kick him square in the chest, sending him sprawling.

"You think you can come into my pub?" I grab Tannen by the collar, my fist cocked back. "You think you can—"

"She's a whore." Brogan spits blood at my feet. "Your precious little bride. Everyone knows it. She's been spreading her legs for half of—"

I don't let him finish.

My fist connects with his jaw so hard I feel the bone crack. Once. Twice. Three times. Blood sprays across the floorboards.

This, I *know*. The sharp sting across my knuckles, the way bone gives under my fist, the hot spray of blood. It's cleaner than words, more honest than any deal made over whiskey. When I'm throwing punches, there's no politics, no schemes, no questions I can't answer. Just flesh and bone and the clear, simple truth of who's stronger.

My breathing evens out. My mind clears.

Tannen tries to crawl away, and I drag him back by his ankle, calm now. Focused.

I may be pissed at Malachy for what he did, but goddamn if I'm not thankful he taught every one of us how to fight bare-knuckled. Said a man who relies on weapons is a man who doesn't trust himself. This feeling—fists connecting, blood flowing, the world narrowing down to just me and the bastard in front of me—it's the only time I feel like I'm exactly where I'm meant to be.

"Say it again," I growl, hitting him across the face. "Say one more feckin' word about her."

The guards finally appear, weapons drawn.

"Get these gobshites out of here," I order, my knuckles raw and bleeding. "If they try coming back, break their kneecaps and call me. And find out who the fuck sent them."

I don't love the lass. Hell, I don't even know if I like her most days. But she's mine. And nobody—*nobody*—talks shite about what's mine.

Chapter Eleven

Erin

"You want to go... shopping?" My mother's teacup pauses halfway to her lips. Her smile freezes in place, and I can read her thoughts as clearly as if she'd spoken them aloud.

First: You hate shopping.

Second: What if someone sees Bridget?

We don't get breaks like this anymore, rare moments when Bridget rallies and gets her strength back. So I plaster on my own fake smile and tilt my head. "Yes. Since I have all these"—I throw my hands up in the air—"events to go to, I need to be prepared."

"Oh, I've already prepared—"

"No, thank you," I say to her. "It's my turn. I'm going to take Bridget shopping because Bridget wants to go shopping, Mam."

"Alright then," my mother says, brushing her hands on her skirt. "I have an appointment at one, but I suppose I can—"

"*No,*" I tell her forcefully when Bridget's eyes grow fearful. She doesn't want to go shopping with my mother. Who would, with the constant criticism and barbed compliments? "Just the two of us this time. It's just a brief sister outing. You go to your event and, you know, we'll catch up with you later."

My mother's eyes are comically wide, and her mouth forms a perfect O.

"You have to let me go eventually, Mam," I tell her. "After all, in a couple of months' time, I'm going to be a McCarthy, aren't I?"

I don't like how it feels satisfactory to see her face pale as she lets go of control. She's got a clawlike grip on my life and my sister's, but after the way she's treated me, especially in recent weeks, I have zero interest in placating her.

I want her to hurt like I do. But that's not why we're going. Bridget asked, and I'd walk through fire for my sister. This is about her.

"Alright, make sure you have, you know, somebody with you," she says, her brows furrowed. "They have those guards the McCarthys sent, Padraic?"

My father looks up from his coffee. "Where are you two going?"

"We're going downtown to do some shopping," I tell him. "We need some clothes for the upcoming events and stuff, you know."

"You'll take the three guards with you." It's not a question.

The three?

"Three?" Bridget's eyes widen. "What happened to Nigel and Darragh?"

"Cavin McCarthy replaced them." My father doesn't look up from his paper. "His men watch you now. Anywhere you go, they go."

Bridget stares at me. "Cavin?"

"He says he texted you, but you didn't respond. In fact, he said something about how he thinks you may have blocked him?" my father says to me.

"I did."

"Erin!" Bridget gapes at me. "You can't block your own fiancé!"

"Watch me." I cross my arms. "I don't want to hear from him."

"You're marrying him," she says, as if that explains everything. "He's your fiancé!"

"Stop calling him that!"

"Oh, for god's sake," she says, taking my phone from me. "Refusing to face reality won't change it."

"Bridget, *don't*."

But it's too late. She's flipping through my contacts, and she finds where I blocked Cavin. With a flourish, she undoes it.

"Erin, I know you don't want to marry him, but you can't

block him. What if he tells you something important that you need to know?"

"Like what?"

"Like details about your engagement party, or like the fact that you have a new *guard*." She shakes her head. "You're going to have to give something up, Erin."

Only Bridget could lecture me about this without getting an earful. *Give something up?* I want to laugh. I'm giving everything up.

"Fine." I snatch my phone back. "Unblock him. Whatever."

My father's lips twitch, almost amused.

"I hate him," I announce to the room. "I want that on record."

"I know," Bridget says. "That has nothing to do with it, practically speaking. What if there's a theme for an event that you're going to? What if he's picking you up? What if he wants to buy you something?" she says coyly.

"I don't want him to buy me anything." I cross my arms over my chest to emphasize the point.

"He has to. He's going to be your future husband."

My mother mutters under her breath, throws her hands up in the air, and storms into the other room.

My father watches us with interest. "They're up front," he says. "Look like decent blokes."

I peer out the window, and when they turn to face me, I immediately hide.

"Oh my god, there *are* three of them. Jesus, how are we going to go anywhere without people knowing who we are?"

"Those days are gone, love," he says quietly.

"Haven't you seen, Erin?" Bridget says. She can't completely hide the grimace that shadows her features.

"Seen what?"

My blood runs cold when she takes my phone back because she looks like she's about to cry.

"My god, you don't even have socials on your phone, do you?"

"I hate social media."

"Fine then, look at mine." She pulls out her phone. "It's the St. Albert's account. Nobody really knows who runs it," she says, and points to a post—a sparkly post, with glitter and lights and flashing bulbs.

St. Albert's is pleased to announce the betrothal of Erin Kavanagh and Cavin McCarthy.

"Oh my god," I whisper.

There are twenty thousand views and 666 comments. "Mam would say that's bad luck. 666," Bridget says with a giggle. "But it's not, see? It's actually a good sign."

"*How* is that a *good* sign?" I ask her, throwing my hands up in the air. "It's the sign of the devil or whatever."

My father actually chuckles. I haven't heard him laugh in a couple of months.

"Oh stop. It's an *angel* number. Some say it's a wake-up call to rebalance your life. A message to refocus on relationships and inner growth. And since when are you religious?" she asks.

"Since when are *you* into New Age?"

Something flickers in her eyes that makes my stomach clench. "Since I started counting down instead of up. When you know the clock's running out, you look for signs everywhere, even the daft ones."

I swallow hard. "Well, what do the comments say?" I ask in a small voice. And I don't like that it's a small voice. I want to be proud and confident and—my *god*, I'm marrying *Cavin McCarthy*. I want to cry or break things or both. Maybe cry *while* breaking things.

"They're like, um…" Bridget frowns. She narrows her eyes at the screen. "You don't need to read these," she says. "Just ignore them, okay?"

"Ignore what?" I tell her. I snatch her phone away and scroll through the comments.

> **Siobhan_M_94:** Lol imagine being so desperate you marry a McCarthy. We all know what she had to do to land him

> **FionaKav:** Little miss perfect finally snagged the bad boy? She probably made him sign a contract. Five quid says she's already correcting his grammar in bed

> **Celtic_Rose: That frigid bitch made my brother's life hell at St. Albert's. Got him suspended twice for BREATHING wrong. She probably has a spreadsheet for their wedding night. Hope Cavin knows what he's getting into.**

I don't know these people. How do they even know who I am? Why do strangers hate me while treating Cavin like a god?

Then I scroll to the photos, and my breath catches. Oh. *Oh.*

There's Cavin in the ring, shirtless, muscles gleaming with sweat, tattoos dark against his skin. His jaw is set, fists raised, and he looks—my cheeks burn—*gorgeous*. Yes. He's handsome as all hell. But then there's only one small grainy picture of me, and it's... my *license* photo. I have glasses and braces and acne.

My cheeks instantly heat.

They're mocking me in the comments. I read, and I read until Bridget finally snatches the phone.

"Stop looking at that," she says.

"They *hate* me. Why do they hate me?"

"It doesn't matter." Bridget's voice rises. "Social media is bullshit. They're keyboard warriors who—" She sways, gripping the counter. Her knuckles go white.

"Bridge." I'm already moving, my arm around her waist. "Breathe. Just breathe."

"I'm fine, but I don't want to talk about this. And I don't care what they say about you. You're beautiful, and you're marrying him. And it's going to be a good decision. You know I feel things sometimes, and I just know... I know two things," she says.

I stare at her, my heart racing.

"Number one, I'm going to beat this, and I'm going to get better, and I'm going to be stronger than ever. And number two." She draws in a breath. "Marrying Cavin McCarthy is going to be the best thing you've ever done."

I blink and wish that I had 10 percent of her assurance of *either* of those things.

My father buries himself in his cup of coffee.

I look at my sister, and hope rises. She has good days and bad days. She's wan and thinner than ever, but no one would ever know by looking at her how ill she really is.

"Okay," I say to her, always pragmatic. "Let's go shopping."

The first saleswoman tries to tell me what to wear, all bossy hands and sharp opinions, but Bridget cuts her off with a clipped, "No, thank you."

Then another one, someone who recognizes Bridget, comes rushing over. "Oh my god, Bridget, how are you?"

"Colleen!"

Turns out she's a girl Bridget knew from school. They were close once, good friends. She takes one look at me, then at Bridget, and something shifts in her expression.

"You're here for her?" she asks, like she can't quite believe it.

Bridget nods. "Erin's getting married. To a McCarthy."

Why did she have to add on that bit?

The girl's eyes go wide. Then she smiles—not the fake customer service kind, but something real. Warm. "Right then," she says, rolling up her sleeves. "Let's make sure you look absolutely *deadly*."

And just like that, I'm in good hands.

"Here," she says, leading me toward the back. "I'm going to set you up in a private dressing room. Much better than that madness out there." She casts her eyes toward the communal changing area, then leans in conspiratorially. "Word around town is you're engaged to *Cavin* McCarthy." She grins wide. "This is brilliant. Let me help you find something that'll make him forget his own name." She gives me a thorough once-over. "Anyone ever tell you that you look like Marilyn Monroe with that platinum-blonde hair? You're *gorgeous*, Erin."

She disappears into the back and returns with an armful of options, laying them across the velvet settee in the private room.

"Right, so." She holds up the first one—a sleek black number. "This is elegant, classic, and will make your hair *glow*. High neck, but the back is completely open. Hits mid-thigh." She sets it aside. "Safe choice."

Then she pulls out a gorgeous turquoise dress, the fabric catching the light like water. "This one's got a cowl neck that drapes just so." She demonstrates with her hands. "Long sleeves, but the skirt's got a slit up to here." She gestures to her upper thigh. "Sexy but you can still move in it, and it makes your eyes *pop*."

"And this," she says, her grin widening as she holds up an ivory silk dress, "is the one I'd pick if I wanted to make a man lose his fucking mind." The neckline plunges in a deep V, the fabric so fine it would cling to every curve. "Spaghetti straps, backless, and the skirt skims your hips and arse like it was painted on. You'll need the right knickers for this one—or none at all." She winks. "It's the kind of dress that says you know exactly what you're doing to him."

"What? Right," I say, forcing on a fake smile. I've never been one to fabricate anything. How does it feel like every interaction with every human needs to be plastered on?

"Alright, okay," she says. "First of all, there are two main important things you need to know when you want to dress your best."

"Comfort and longevity," I mutter under my breath. "Will this last me long enough so I don't have to go back in the store? And are there any scratchy tags or materials I don't like?"

Bridget giggles. "You'd think she's joking," she says to Colleen.

"Of course I don't," she says. "Honestly, those would be my two choices too, but these are the two things we need to look for. Number one, what body type you have. Number two, what is your color profile? Okay?"

She's now officially speaking Greek. I have some vague idea of what color palettes are, but only because my mother's mentioned them in the past.

"Okay, so, I don't know the answer to either one of those things," I say to her, suddenly feeling like someone's just thrown me in the deep end, and I don't know how to swim. But Colleen comes in and hands me a flotation device.

"Excellent. Lucky for you, these are two things that I've studied. Alright, the first thing we need to know is that you have an hourglass figure."

"Okay," I say, nodding. "Hourglass, like those things that you tip upside down and they show you how you're running out of time?" Sounds anxiety-inducing to me.

"Yes, hourglass. Do you remember how they're shaped?" she says gently.

I nod and shrug. "I guess so, like wider at the top, narrow at the waist, wider at the bottom."

"Exactly," she says. "It means that your bust and hip proportions are larger than your waist. This is excellent. We all want hourglass figures, Erin."

"Okay."

Bridget giggles again. "You wouldn't know it, hiding it under those hoodies, but she's got great titties."

What? Why are we talking about titties with a perfect stranger?

"Oh, I believe it," Colleen says. "Alright, so we need something that shows off your cleavage and your tiny little waist. Perfect. Next, color profile." She taps her chin thoughtfully. "Show me your wrists."

My wrists?

Then she grabs my wrists and turns them over. "Ah, see, the veins right here. They're green."

"Aren't... everybody's?"

"No, they're not. If you had cool tones, your skin color would make this look blue instead of green, but you have warm undertones." She peers into my eyes. "Mmm. Brown. Oh my *god*, your eyes are gorgeous. And with that platinum-blonde hair and porcelain skin, you're a true spring."

"A true spring? Okay..."

"This is your color profile," she says as she walks up to the front desk, opens a drawer, and takes out a little index card that's hard and shaped like a credit card.

"Slide this into your wallet. These are the colors that look good on you. Okay? Now, these are the colors that *don't* look good on you. Flip it over."

I flip it over and look. Dusty colors, muted tones, black.

"Never wear these colors."

I look down at myself. I'm literally wearing a black jumper.

"These are just not your colors, girlfriend. But that's fine. Look at the ones that *are*," she says triumphantly. "They're gorgeous on you. Perfect, let's do it. Watch, I'm going to show you how it changes everything."

She walks over to a rack and pulls out two identical V-neck tops.

"Look in the mirror."

She holds a bright-white one up under my chin, and my skin looks sallow and wan, but when she holds up the second, a warm peach, my skin looks warmer, golden, and my eyes seem brighter.

"Oh, wow."

"Mm-hmm. Go now, keep your yoga pants on," she says, "and then try this on. Ready?"

"Okay," I say, nodding.

The top is a warm ivory with a deep vee, and when I put it on, it immediately makes me look slim and fit, and, as Bridget would say, my titties *do* look amazing. It brings out the color in my cheeks and in my eyes.

When I come out, Bridget claps her hands in glee.

"This looks *gorgeous*."

I bite my lip. "Okay, I like this. How much is it?"

"Doesn't matter," Bridget says in a singsong voice. "I've got Cavin's credit card he gave Da."

"What? Why did he give it to *you*?"

She sighs. "Because you blocked him, remember?"

Oh, right.

Two hours later, I'm surprised Bridget's still going. "I need something to eat," she says. "I am starving."

It actually gets me a bit emotional that she says she's hungry, since I swear she never gets hungry anymore.

"We could go to D'Agostino's," Bridget says, gesturing down the street toward the only proper Italian restaurant in this part of Ireland. "I've been craving their carbonara something fierce."

"Let's go."

D'Agostino's overlooks the harbor, all gleaming water and bobbing boats. Bridget picks at her food, which drives my mother crazy. But I, for one, like to see the fact that she took at least five generous bites of pasta.

I'm not a huge fan of going out to eat because I feel like I never know the rules, but in a family like mine, I've learned to just observe and follow.

"This looks delicious," I say. I don't even know what I ordered because I'm so overstimulated. Crowds, people, shopping.

"You're going to knock his socks off with those dresses," Bridget says, taking a sip of water. "I'm jealous." She winks. It's friendly, but it makes my heart ache a little.

A waitress comes up to us, a buxom girl with vibrant red hair pulled into a tight bun at the top of her head. "Hey," she says with a smile. "You're the Kavanagh girls, right?"

A week ago, we could have come in here, and nobody would have recognized us. Between my sister's frequent hospital stays and illness, and my hatred for all things social, we barely ventured into town. It was a rare occasion.

"Aye," I say, with a forced smile.

"You're Erin," she says.

I nod.

She shakes her head and rolls her eyes heavenward. "I can't believe they used your manky driver's license photo," she says. "You look nothing like that anymore."

"Um, thanks?" I ask with a grimace.

"No, I agree," Bridget pipes in. "Who the fuck runs that account anyway?"

"Dunno," she says. "Probably some bored eejit with nothin' better to do. It's brutal, isn't it? Don't be mindin' them, Erin."

But how am I supposed to not mind when everywhere I go, someone's there to remind me?

When we leave the restaurant, the sky is darkening, and I feel restless, anxious.

"I want a drink," I tell Bridget. "A stiff drink. An alcoholic beverage."

"You don't drink," she says to me. "Ever."

"Maybe I should start."

She gives me a curious look. "Maybe you shouldn't make rash decisions when you're stressed."

I grunt. "Are you supposed to drink? With your medication and whatnot?"

"Yes," she says with a sigh. "Not a lot, obviously, and when I'm on the blood thinners, I can't, but... What's the worst that's going to happen?"

I don't want to answer that question because I don't want to think about the worst that could happen.

"We can at least order something non-alcoholic, right?" she says, shaking her head. "I think we can manage that."

"Alright, fair enough," I tell her.

The three guards Cavin sent watch us warily as we head toward a pub.

"Why are you going in there?" one says.

"Because I want a drink," I tell him.

"Well, you shouldn't go into *that* pub. We'll go somewhere closer to home instead. It's safer."

"Safer?" That's a strange thing to say. "What if I don't want safer?" I tell him, giving him a look. I don't understand what he's going on about right now.

"Well, you shouldn't go in there. It's not for girls like you."

Girls like *me*? Well, the surest way to get me to do something is to tell me I can't.

"I don't want Cavin's bodyguard telling me what to do," I say. It feels like an extension of him. I'm not exactly going to roll over and beg. I have more self-respect than that.

His eyes narrow. "Mr. McCarthy isn't going to like you going in there."

"Well, I don't belong to Mr. McCarthy."

"You almost do," he says.

"Almost doesn't *count*." My voice is rising. Now I'm determined to go into this place he's insisting I can't go into.

"Are you out of your mind?" he says to me, tossing his hands up in the air.

I glare. "You know I have Mr. McCarthy's phone number right here."

"Call him then," he says. "Ask him." Dammit. He wasn't supposed to call my bluff.

"I'm not asking him, but I am going to tell him that you're trying to boss me around."

"Good, maybe I'll get a bonus."

"Great. Just great." I want to stomp my feet.

Instead, I look at my phone and notice that I have not one, not two, but three messages from Cavin.

I tap on the first one.

> **Cavin**
> Am I still blocked? Or do you actually see this now? You brat.

The second:

> **Cavin**
> I'm sending three of my men to watch over you.

The third:

> **Cavin**
> Put on your location tracker so that I can watch you.

I type back quickly:

> Number one: You're not blocked. Number two: I'm well aware that you sent your goons round to watch over me. Number three: Fuck off.

I toss my phone in my bag and take Bridget by the hand. "Let's go."

She wobbles a little, and one of the guards steps in as if to catch her, but she quickly steadies herself.

"I'm fine," she says with a forced smile.

When we enter, I don't understand why he protested so much. This just looks like a normal pub. There's a match on the telly—hurling, maybe, or football—playing on a massive screen. Glasses line the bar, bottles gleaming in the low light, and couples sit at round tables nursing their pints. It's actually quite nice in here, cozy even, though dimly lit.

Nothing sinister about it at all.

It isn't until my second round of soda water that I see someone questionably dressed walk past me.

"Is that... latex?" Bridget whispers, staring at the girl's black skirt. "It's an interesting clothing choice, isn't it?"

"Aye," I say, and I watch as she walks to the back of the room, whispers something to someone, and they take her down a little corridor to a separate elevator.

She doesn't come back.

"Where'd she go?" I say to Bridget. "That's odd."

Bridget gasps, covering her mouth, her eyes wide. "Oh my god. Oh my *god!*"

"What?" I whisper, alarmed, my heart racing.

"I know why he didn't want us to go in here," she says quietly.

"Well, care to fill me in?" I ask, shaking my head. "I'd like to know."

"*Erin.* This is the secret entrance to The Craic."

"Oh, right." I roll my eyes. "Cavin's little dungeon."

"Little dungeon!" Bridget giggles. "What are you talking about, Erin? You talk as if you know all about it."

"That was the whole thing, wasn't it? The McCarthys and The Craic. They own this little club. Everybody in Ballyhock worships the fucking ground they walk on because of the damn place."

"Oh god," Bridget says. "I forgot about that." She grins. "We have to find a way in."

"We?" I shake my head. "Oh no, little sister. There's no fucking way I'm taking my baby sister into a kink club. That'd be the most irresponsible thing I could possibly do."

"Oh, for once in your life, Erin!" Bridget says, shaking her head in exasperation. "Do *something* irresponsible."

I stare at her in surprise.

Her voice is passionate, raw. And there's a tone in it that I haven't heard in a while—something that arrests my attention immediately, making my chest tighten.

"I'm dying, Erin. Nobody wants to say it out loud. Nobody wants to admit it." She points to herself, her hand trembling slightly. "But I'm dying. And I don't want to die a virgin."

I don't want to tell her that I don't understand what she's talking about because I would *happily* die a virgin. Sex has never been the prize for me that it seems to be for everyone else.

And my little sister is not losing her virginity in a *club*.

"First of all, you have a life-threatening disease," I say pragmatically, falling back on logic because it's safer than emotion. "You're only dying if we don't treat it. And we're working on that. We're going to find a way to treat it. I promise you. You know I don't promise anything lightly, Bridget."

"I know." She says it so softly I almost don't hear her. "But what if we don't? What if I don't?" Her voice cracks. "I want to... I want someone to hold me. I want to be excited around a man. I want to..." She sniffs, swiping at her eyes before the tears can fall. "I want to feel like a woman. Not a girl. I want to feel like a *woman*, Erin."

She swipes at her eyes again, and even with tears threatening to spill, she's beautiful. My god, she's gorgeous.

I blow out a breath, defeated before I've even begun to fight. "You exasperating, beautiful woman." I shake my head at her. "Are you seriously trying to convince me to bring you to a sex club? *Me?*"

She taps her chin thoughtfully, a mischievous glint returning to her eyes. "I might be able to get you one of those cards that gets us in..."

"Bridget!"

She's laughing now, and god, it's good to hear.

"Well, I can't just take you in anyway, even if I did want to —which I definitely don't." I cross my arms. "You have to know how to get in. You need to know the code. There's like a secret handshake or something."

She rolls her eyes at me dramatically. "Well, that's what you're good at, isn't it?"

"What?"

"Codes. Patterns. Pattern recognition. You've never met a password you couldn't crack. You know that."

She's not wrong, but I blow out another breath. "We're not dressed for it."

She winks at me, victorious. "That's easy. I know what you have on under that sweater. And I know what I do too. Anyway, don't we have, like, bags of new clothes?"

We do. This is true.

"Oh, Bridget." I groan, rubbing my face. "What am I going to do with you?"

"Take me in?" Her grin is absolutely wicked.

"Okay, calm down." I sigh. "Great. So... we have outfits we can change into, but that doesn't solve the actual problem of getting in."

"Alright." Bridget leans forward, and there's a spark in her eye—that old fire I haven't seen in so long—and it excites me and makes my heart kick against my ribs. I want to give her anything that she wants right now. Anything at all.

"What are you thinking?" I ask.

"I think I've seen a couple of people come in here that look like they're definitely heading to the club," she says quietly, conspiratorially. "I'm thinking we head to the back of this bar, order another drink, and then we monitor everything. Just very casually look around and observe. And then, you know, maybe you work your magic and figure out how to get us in there."

"Oh, fine," I say quietly.

She grins at me—hopeful, alive, vibrant.

"Really?" Her eyes are shining now.

I look at my baby sister, at the determination written across her face, at the desperate need to feel something beyond the fear and the pain and the waiting.

"Alright. I'll figure it out." I blow out a breath. "Let's go."

Chapter Twelve

Cavin

"CAVIN," my mother calls from the dining room. "Come here for a second, love."

I let out a long exhale, stretch my neck, and reach my arms up over my head. My god, it's been a long fucking week.

"Yes," I say, stepping into the dining room where she's got glossy magazines all lined up on the table. "We're looking at options for the engagement party signage," she says with a smile. "Care to take a peek?"

I shake my head. "Honestly, Mam, no. I don't care to. I don't care what you pick. Pick anything you want. This is a transaction, you know that."

"Alright then," she says with a pained smile. She likes to think sometimes that we're normal, at least some of us. That she didn't raise criminals who live by a different code of ethics than most of the damn world.

"Do what you like, and I'll like it too," I say, turning on my heel.

As I reach the entryway, the front door bursts open. Somebody screams, and another person drops a dish with a crash.

"Jesus *fucking* Christ."

I push through and see Declan with a split lip, holding his arm at an odd angle. Ashland's behind him, supporting him, as Declan drips blood onto the foyer tiles.

"Christ, Declan. You all right?"

"Aye," he says through gritted teeth. "Fine."

"That arm doesn't look fine," I mutter under my breath. "Looks broken."

"Call the damn medic then."

"Yes. What happened?" I nod to my sister Bronwyn in the doorway and gesture for her to make the call.

"The deal's gone south," he says, wincing.

"Aye," Ashland growls. "Crowning's crew ambushed us at the docks. Three of them, armed. We handled it, but it got messy."

I sigh. Another night, another feckin' battle. Thankfully, this one won't blow back. He said he handled it, and I trust him.

Mam rushes in. "Declan!"

"I'm fine," he says again. "Seriously, don't worry about me. I've got this under control, okay?"

"Alright, but…" She shakes her head. "I thought you boys coming in the house with broken bones and blood dripping on the tile would have ended when you grew out of it. I guess not."

"I've got this," I mutter under my breath and take him into the study, where the medic quickly arrives—old Doc Sullivan, who's been patching up our family for decades, no questions asked.

"What really happened?" I ask Declan in a low voice, while Ashland's preoccupied on his phone, scowling. Declan gives me the full details. The ambush. The retaliation. The message Crowning's trying to send.

Great. Just fucking brilliant.

My phone buzzes with a text.

"Jesus. Look who's waking from the dead," I mutter under my breath.

"Who is it?" Declan asks.

"My betrothed," I say with sarcasm and an eye roll. "This little lass." I shake my head. "Might've been something with the mobile service? I swear to Christ, I don't understand why when I sent her a message, it turned all green like this. And now it's blue again."

"It's because she blocked you, lad," Declan says, chuckling to himself despite the pain. "Christ, what did you do to get yourself blocked by your own betrothed?"

"I know she fucking blocked me," I mutter, jaw clenched. "Question is why she *unblocked* me now."

He snorts. "Maybe she's finally come to her senses."

"Is *this* why she hasn't responded to any of my texts?" I glare at the screen like it's personally offended me.

"Probably," Declan says, shaking his head as I examine his arm.

I clean his wound and take a closer look. "Aye, definitely broken, lad. We're gonna have to get that set for sure." I clean up his bloody knuckles while Doc preps the splint materials.

"So what'd she say?" Declan says, wincing.

"Eh, nothing." I shake my head. "I can't believe I'm marrying this girl. She doesn't have an ounce of respect for me."

"You think it has something to do with you taking the mickey out of her in school, then?"

I scrub a hand across my brow and shrug. "Yeah."

"Hmm, interesting," Ashland says with another scowl. "You sure that's the only reason she's angry with you?"

"I don't know. Probably good enough, aye? She was the one who was Miss Perfect, always getting me in trouble."

"Uh-huh," Declan says, wincing when Doc pulls the splint tight. "Fascinating, that. What's she say?" he asks.

I read the text back to him, and he chuckles to himself.

"She is a smart one, I'll give you that."

"Aye, she is."

I glance at the clock.

Today's the fuckin' tribute day, and I haven't gotten a breath closer to figuring out who's got my bollocks in a sling. Five hundred thousand *fucking* euros a month that my family can't know about is a bitch of a thing. The fucking strings I've had to pull to make it happen could land me straight back in prison, a hell I swore I'd never revisit.

"What about you? What happened in Belfast last night?" Declan asks.

I shake my head. "Fucking catastrophe," I mutter. "Three guns jammed, shipment was light by twenty pieces, and Murphy's asking questions he shouldn't be asking."

Doc stitches him up, and I douse the wound with antiseptic.

My phone buzzes again. This time, though, it's not Erin but one of her guards.

> Sir? That Erin and her sister may have ventured into the club.

"Jesus Christ, I'm tired of this fuckin' eejit," I mutter. "What's he fucking talking about?"

I text back:

> What do you mean?

I can almost hear him quaking through the text.

Did he let my fiancée go into a dangerous situation?

Another text comes through immediately.

They went to D'Agostino's for dinner, sir.
And then after that, they decided they
wanted a drink. Someone let them in.
Someone let them know that it was the
entrance to The Craic.

"I'll hang him for this," I tell Declan before I slam my phone down on the desk.

"What happened?"

"Seems my betrothed and her sister got some wild idea, decided to go to The Craic."

"Are you takin' the piss?" Declan says. It's not often he shows surprise, but he looks fairly gobsmacked right now. "Well then, looks like I know where we need to go next."

"You're not going anywhere with that arm," I tell him. "We need to get some antibiotics, and you need to rest. Last thing you need is an infection." I don't want *anyone* catching a look at Erin at The Craic. "I've got to handle this on my own."

"Jesus, Cavin, you're as bad as your da," Declan says. "Look at me. I'm perfectly fine. I'm fit as a fiddle. You shouldn't be going alone. Plus, it seems like you're going to have to handle Erin. Who's going to handle her *sister* when you do?"

I grab him by the scruff of the shirt and pull him straight off the chair. "If you think this is a gateway to a free ride, think again, you son of a bitch."

"Ogre," Declan says, and he goes to kick me in the bollocks, but I drop him hard before he can connect.

"Cavin, you aren't supposed to upset his stitches," Doc says mildly from behind him.

"Right. My bad." I grunt. "Fine, you'll come with me, but you'll behave. I don't want you anywhere *near* her sister. Understood? All I fucking need is you and your shenanigans."

"Right," he says, nodding. "I understand."

"Good."

"Coming, Ash?"

"Not tonight. You lads go, keep each other out of mischief."

Declan snorts and I blow out a breath. I need to get changed.

I text her guard again and again, but no word.

I glare at the phone in front of me, and a part of me hopes he doesn't respond. I don't want him laying his eyes on my betrothed.

"You know," Declan says thoughtfully as we drive toward the club, "I know that you and Erin are trying to let bygones be bygones and all that." He pauses. "But this woman's going to be your wife, Cavin. Makes sense to me that you take good care of her. She hasn't had much of that in her life, has she? I mean, look at her father. She doesn't have any brothers. And her father's getting up there in age, isn't he?"

I growl under my breath and take a right turn, heading down the road toward the private entrance to The Craic.

"I'm just saying it doesn't have to be love, you know. It doesn't even have to be anything physical between you. Maybe it would be best if you could, you know, appreciate what's actually happening between the two of you."

"And what's actually happening between the two of us?" I ask him, narrowing my eyes. "What are you saying, Declan?"

He shrugs. "I'm saying you have an opportunity to make good on the bullshit that you did in the past, you know."

"I don't need a lecture from my cousin." I give him a glaring look.

"No, but you've been moaning and bitching since you became engaged to her. This is an opportunity, Cavin."

"Is it?" I ask. "Why don't you tell me, Mr. High and Mighty, what the opportunity is that I have here?"

"Put our family on the fucking map," he says, shaking his head. "Do you know what it's going to be like when we own all of the trade routes down the Eastern Seaboard and the West Coast of Ireland? My fucking *god*. It'll change everything for us."

I know.

I'm quiet for a long moment.

"She hates me," I tell him, slamming my fist in frustration on the leather steering wheel cover. "I told you. She fucking blocked my phone number. Couldn't even get through to her."

"Ah," Declan says, his eyes twinkling at me. "Do you mean

to tell me there's a lass in all of Ballyhock who doesn't fall for every whim of yours?"

I narrow my eyes at him. "What are you going on about?"

"What am I going *on* about? Ever since you were at St. Albert's, women fall at your fuckin' feet," he says, shaking his head. "Cavin McCarthy, the local fighter. 'Ooh, Cavin the ex-con.' Did you see that goddamn picture of you they posted when they announced your engagement? Half of Ballyhock's ovaries cried."

I roll my eyes.

"Cavin, do you have any idea how many women would kill to have you at the club?"

I shrug.

"You don't care because you only look at the one in front of you. You go to The Craic, you take a submissive, you have a fun night, and you go home—and you don't see the half a dozen girls who sit there weeping into their fucking handbags because you didn't pick them."

"What the hell are you talking about?"

"And now," he says, "of course you haven't realized this because you never had to. You want a woman—you snap your fingers, and you get a fucking horde ready. You're rich, you're attractive, you've got those eyes, and you're muscular and all that. Have you seen the way they fucking post about you on social media from St. Albert's? Wasn't just the engagement post."

"Post about me? What?"

"On the socials," he says, exasperated. He pulls up his phone. "Look at how many comments you have now on that fucking engagement post. Did you see the picture?"

I slow down at a red light and glance sideways at him.

It's a damn good picture of me after a fight that I won, sweat glistening on my bare chest. And I swear to Christ, somebody's touched it up because I don't normally look *that* good.

And the picture next to me...

"Oh god," I say, cringing. "What did they use for her? Her license photo? Looks like a damn mugshot."

"I think so," Declan says. "It's definitely not very becoming of her, is it?"

"Christ, not at all. My god, who runs that fucking account?" I growl.

"No idea."

"We'll find out," I say.

"Is that an order?" Declan asks quietly.

"Aye."

"Right then," he says, tapping at his phone.

"All I'm saying is this is probably the first lass in I don't know how long—since you hit fuckin' *puberty*—who doesn't throw herself at ya." He snorts. "It's puttin' a burr under your skin."

"Aye," I growl. "Perhaps."

"Not perhaps," he says, grinning.

"You're lucky you're already injured," I mutter.

I sigh again and roll my eyes heavenward.

"It's not just a woman who doesn't *like* me, Declan. It's not just that."

"Aye. It's a woman you can't *control*."

I open my mouth to protest, but the words die in my throat because—fuck—he's right. I can't control her.

And that drives me absolutely mental.

"It's not just that," I mutter, the admission scraping out rough. "It's a woman who doesn't want me. A woman I can't control, aye. But she's not just some ride I can walk away from when it suits me."

I drag a hand through my hair, gripping it hard enough to hurt.

"I'm going to marry her. She's going to be my wife. And she's out there right now, in danger, because I couldn't keep her safe. Because she'd rather risk her neck than have anything to do with me, and if she *had*, she'd know that place was off-limits ."

The words taste like acid. Like failure.

"So don't tell me it doesn't matter. Don't tell me to let it go."

"Right," Declan says with a sigh. "Seems a bit like a sentence, doesn't it?"

"Aye, a bit," I tell him, shaking my head.

"Not to be dramatic, but—"

"No, I understand," he says. "I very much do. Doesn't seem like it would be something that hard to figure out though. Does it?"

"What?" I ask him.

"How to win her over," he says, shrugging.

"I'm not trying to win her over."

"Why the fuck not? You're going to be with her for the rest of your life."

"Declan," I say, pulling to a stop, "I didn't ask for relationship advice, so shut the fuck up."

He sighs again. "Alright, alright," he says, putting his hands up in surrender. "If that's what you wish."

"That's what I fuckin' wish!" I slam my fist on the steering wheel again as a text comes through on my phone.

I think I might have found her, sir.

Good. Someone will keep breathing tonight.

I can't help but think of what Declan said as I enter the club. He's right. I am used to the looks they give me. The way their eyes follow me. Pretty women lined up at the bar, making eyes at me, smiling, hoping that I'll be the one who picks them.

At St. Albert's, I was a bit of a ringleader. I had quite a following of people. I guess I took it for granted. I haven't really thought about it until now. Not until I have one woman who doesn't want anything to do with me.

I walk through the club with my head held high, dressed in my uniform of all black, a pair of black leather gloves sticking out of my pocket.

Every woman here is looking at me the way they always do. But the only one I want to see isn't looking at me at all. And that's the fucking problem.

I'm going to find my betrothed, and I'm going to punish her for coming here unannounced. She's in a *world* of trouble.

"Welcome, sir," Griffin says at the front desk.

When I descend the private elevator for entrance to The Craic, I slide my thumb on the facial recognition software. The door opens with a soft click.

I see one of the three men I assigned to Bridget and Erin Kavanagh as guards. I snap my fingers and point to the ground in front of me.

He looks like he's about to shite himself.

"Sir?" he says nervously.

"Have you found them?" I growl.

"Believe so, sir. On this floor. Over there."

"Grand." I point my finger at him. "But that doesn't mean you're out of the woods. I'm going to kick the shite out of you for this—you and your mates. Do you understand me?"

"Yes, sir," he says, and gulps.

Declan shakes his head, cracks his knuckles, and the guard takes a step back.

"You let Cavin McCarthy's *betrothed* sneak into the fucking Craic," Declan says, his voice low and dangerous.

"I tried to keep her away, sir, but she—"

"You're trying to make an excuse now?" Declan says, furious. "That's my cousin's future wife."

"I know, sir, but I—"

"You and the other two"—Declan cuts him off—"you keep a close eye on them until we leave. Where's the younger sister?"

"They're both in the dance room, sir."

"Right." I crack my neck and head toward the back of the club, my blood running hot with anger and something else I can't quite name.

Time to collect my wayward bride.

Chapter Thirteen

Erin

I TRY NOT TO STARE, but it's hard not to. Everywhere I turn, there's another spectacle, a feast for the eyes that makes my pulse quicken and my cheeks flush.

There are different colored rooms, each named for its dominant hue. An exclusive dance floor thrums with bodies, where people are doing all sorts of mischievous things right in plain sight. Right out in the open!

Though part of me is shamefully excited about this, I've wondered how certain things work, and there are positions and acts that romance books don't quite prepare you for—not really.

I try not to stare at the threesome on the violet leather sofa. A woman is going down on a man, taking his cock deep before pulling back, her head bobbing up and down in a steady rhythm. There's a man behind her—Jesus Christ—pounding into her while she works.

Nobody else is even looking. Nobody bats an eye. I'm floored by the whole thing, heat crawling up my neck.

In the corner of the room, there's something that looks like stocks from the old ages—wooden restraints with circular holes. A woman's got her head and hands locked in place, bent forward, exposed. A man stands behind her with what looks like a leather flogger, but there's a look of absolute peace on her face. Bliss, even.

I'd managed to break the entry code to get in and quickly realized that single women without partners wore purple tags tied to their forearms. So Bridget and I acquired the purple tags so nobody would question why we didn't have somebody with us.

I'm starting to wonder if the purple tag means something else entirely, though, because I've had no less than three men approach me, trying to coax me toward one of the private rooms. Bridget's had the same problem. We do look stunning, thanks to our new spoils of war, but I was still unprepared for *this* kind of attention.

"Alright, have you seen enough now?" I whisper to her, tugging at her elbow. "If Cavin ever catches wind that I was here—"

"He'd be honored that you frequented his establishment," she says with a bold wink, cutting me off.

"Not so sure about that," I mutter under my breath. "But perhaps you're not wrong."

I looked around carefully when we first arrived, and I didn't recognize anybody. There's one man who looks vaguely familiar from dinner the other night, but I can't quite place him. A cousin, maybe? None of Cavin's family have shown up, though it's still rather early in the night. Maybe they don't come. Maybe they just own the place, rake in the profits, but don't actually frequent it themselves.

Why do I feel a twinge of disappointment that my betrothed isn't here? I think I would like to see him in his element after that provocative social media post. I think I'd like to sear the image of him into my memory.

I am so uncomfortable for so many reasons, my skin too tight, my breath too shallow. But at least it's impeccably clean here. The overhead lights aren't too bright—dim enough to offer a veil of privacy, but bright enough to see everything.

And while pulsing dance music fills this particular room, I took a peek at the vacant rooms down the hallway earlier. They were well-appointed. Quiet. Almost luxurious, if not for the metal posts screwed into the headboards and the leather straps at the foot that looked a bit like medieval torture devices.

But in one corner of this room, there's a lovely velvet settee, and on it sits a beautiful woman with long blonde hair that cascades all the way down her back and brushes the top of her arse. She's perched on a man's knee, and this man looks familiar, too, although I can't quite place him. I think he may have been at dinner at the McCarthy house as well.

He's running his hand down her back in long, slow strokes. Soothing. Possessive. And it sparks an ache in my chest I can't quite identify.

What *is* that? He... cares for her. There's a tenderness in his touch that makes me long for something like that myself—

something real beneath all the violence and posturing. I wish for a man to look at me that way, like I'm something precious. I wish for someone to rub my back that way, gentle and grounding.

I think if I had somebody willing to do that, I might not be so anti-man after all.

I sip something delicious and non-alcoholic—something Bridget suggested—and it tastes like sugared berries and cream. I'm actually kind of liking being incognito here, though I can't quite shake the strangeness of it.

For one crazy, wild second, I wonder if they slipped something alcoholic into this drink.

What would it be like being in here with him?

Would he have me caged like that woman in the corner, drinking water from the tips of her Master's fingers? Would he have me blindfolded, cuffed, tied to a bed, and spread open for his pleasure? Would he—

Oh my god. I can't believe I'm thinking about Cavin in any way sexually at all. This isn't me. This isn't what I do.

But it will be me, won't it?

What's going to be expected of me as Cavin's wife?

I don't know shite about his family's traditions yet, but I know mine well enough. When you marry someone, you're mated to them. Bound. Bonded for fucking life. Like animals—primal, permanent, with no way out.

My straw hits ice, and I slurp the last dregs of my drink.

Bridget's eyes are dancing as a handsome young man wearing a partial face mask like Batman, all sharp jawline and mystery, walks over to her. He's bare-chested, and Christ, what a gorgeous chest it is—all carved muscle and ink.

He bows, reaches for her hand, and kisses the very top of it.

"Dance," he says in a low, seductive voice.

She smiles, giggles at me, and nods.

Seconds later, she's whisked away to the dance floor, and I have no idea where she is anymore. The crowd swallows them whole.

I don't know if I like this.

We came here for a purpose... for a reason. And then I remember my sister telling me she doesn't want to die a virgin.

Well, *this* isn't where I want her to lose her virginity.

Oh my god, I need to—

Then a door opens... and the entire temperature of the room shifts.

It's like we're in the middle of a college rave and the Gardaí show up. There's one momentary pause—the eye of a storm. Heads turn, conversations drop to whispers, then silence.

Cavin. Dressed all in black, his eyes absolutely murderous, and he's staring straight at *me*.

The waitress pauses, her mouth half open as if about to ask me if I want another drink, before she thinks better of it. She quickly turns and scurries away like a scared little mouse. Even the bartender stops wiping his glass to stare at Cavin.

When I first came here, everything was too much—too bright, too dark, too loud, too crowded. Too many scents and sounds and vibrations moving through the room.

But now—now every sense I have is tuned to a single frequency: *him.*

My fiancé.

His gaze locks on mine, sharp enough to flay skin.

He looks like something untamed, his shirt stretched tight across his chest, black fabric clinging to muscle and heat. Power contained, not hidden. The air between us hums with it.

I shouldn't notice the way his throat works when he swallows. I shouldn't want to trace the ink snaking beneath his collar or feel the tension coiled in his thighs pressing against me. But my body doesn't ask for permission. Heat pools low, nerves lighting up one by one.

It's too much. Too close. Too *him.*

And all I can think is... Bridget's right. This isn't high school anymore, and he's definitely no *boy.*

Cavin cuts through the crowd like a blade. A man on a mission. The crowd parts like oil and water, scattering instantly.

I once read a description of what happens when a predator lands in a crowded flock of birds. How they squawk and scatter and flee for cover.

That's exactly what's happening now.

I should look away. Step back. Do *something* besides stand here like I'm waiting for him to pounce...

But I don't.

He reaches my table in seconds, and I forget how to breathe.

"Get up," he growls.

My heart hammers. My palms are sweaty. I hate that he has this effect on me. I feel just like I'm in school again—everyone staring, nowhere to go, nothing to say.

"I said *get up*," he says, his voice low and dangerous. "This is not a request."

Fight-or-flight kicks in, but I'm frozen to my seat.

"Excuse me?" I manage, though my voice comes out smaller and squeakier than I'd like. "I'm not a—"

His huge, calloused hand, scarred with tattoos on the knuckles like messages, wraps around my upper arm. Not rough, but firm enough that I know he's not asking twice.

"You and I will have a talk about my expectations, Erin."

His eyes drop to my arm, and something dangerous flashes across his face.

"My god," he says, his voice rising with barely contained fury. "You had the fuckin' nerve to wear *that* in here?"

"Of course I did. I'm not with anyone."

The waitress's eyes are wide as saucers.

"Mr. McCarthy, she just sat here having a drink—"

"Be quiet," he snaps without looking at her. "Say one more word and you'll be turning in your fuckin' badge."

She runs away.

"*Cavin*, you can't—"

"You too," he growls at me, his eyes never leaving mine. "Erin. Up."

Heat floods my face—part anger, part something else I don't want to name.

"You cannot just walk over here and—"

"I absolutely fuckin' can." He leans down so his face is inches from mine. His voice drops lower, meant only for me. "Do you want to have this conversation here? In front of everyone? Or do you want to walk out of here with a shred of dignity intact?"

My mouth opens and closes like a fish drowning in air.

He straightens, his hand still on my arm. His second hand slides over my other arm, and he lifts me to my feet like I weigh nothing.

I think back to that night at his house—forgetting how much bigger he is than I am. How easily he can manhandle me. How utterly powerless I am against his strength.

Is this what it's going to be? Is this how he's going to treat me?

"Cavin, I—" I try to pull back, but it's useless.

"Don't test me right now, Erin. I'm not in the damn mood." His jaw flexes, a muscle jumping beneath the skin. "You have *no* idea what you walked into. *No* fuckin' clue. So you're going to walk with me, and you're going to go into one of those private rooms where we can have a talk. Understood?"

"Is that what we're going to do? Talk?" My voice shakes. "Because it doesn't seem like people go to those rooms to *talk*."

My cheeks burn because it seems as if the entire club is looking at me now. Watching. Waiting.

I want to slap him. I want to scream.

But more than that, I need to get out of this spotlight. I need him to stop dragging me around like I'm his property.

"Fine," I hiss, yanking my arms free. "But you don't own me."

His laugh is dark... humorless and cold.

"That's something we'll discuss in private."

I look toward the dance floor, searching for Bridget. She's there, somehow miraculously oblivious to my confrontation with Cavin McCarthy, grinding against the masked man as if the world isn't watching me fall apart.

Cavin's hand moves to the small of my back—proprietary, possessive, burning through the thin fabric of my dress.

I remember the way he punished me, and heat coils low in my belly.

And for one crazy, stupid moment, I wish this *were* real. That he was mine and I was his, and he wasn't leading me away to lecture me or punish me or remind me that I'm just a fucked-up political arrangement.

That maybe, *maybe*, the proprietary, possessive part of him wanted to protect me. That he did it because he... cared.

Whispers follow in our wake like ghosts.

The second we're in the cool dimness of the hallway, I whirl on him.

"What the hell do you think you're—"

He cuts me off by caging me against the brick wall, his hands planted on either side of my head, a move that's laughably easy for him. He's not touching me, but he's close enough that I can feel the heat radiating off him—can smell the whiskey and smoke and danger clinging to his skin.

"What were you thinking?" His voice is lethal and controlled, a barely restrained snarl. "Coming here. To my club."

"*Your* club? It's not—"

"It's not *public*, Erin." He snaps the words like a whip. "It's mine. And you *don't* belong here."

"I can go wherever I fuckin' want—"

"Not anymore, you can't. Jesus," he growls, his teeth grinding together. "I had half a mind to call off the wedding for this shite."

"What?" My voice cracks, and for the first time, real conse-quences for my actions loom. I gulp hard.

No.

"*Cavin.* You can't do that."

He leans in closer, and I press back against the wall, but there's nowhere to go. "You're my fiancée. That means you don't go wandering into places like this without telling me. Without protection. Without a damn clue what you're walking into."

"I have protection," I fire back. "Your goons—"

"My *men*," he corrects sharply. "Who are supposed to keep you safe. And instead, you gave them the slip and walked straight into the one place where you should never have set foot."

"It's just a club—"

"It is *not* just a club." His eyes burn into mine, dark and furious and something else. Something that makes my stomach flip. "And you're not just some girl anymore. You're *mine*, Erin. Mine to protect. Mine to keep safe. And I will drag you out of any place I see fit if it means keeping you from harm."

"I wasn't *in* any harm," I say, but my voice is small. Uncertain.

"You're in my club," he repeats, each word deliberate. "People don't know you yet. Men come here to drink and fuck and forget the world exists. Rules don't apply here the way they do out there. Women like you, good girls, innocent girls, don't belong here unless they're being paid or they're wearing a collar."

My breath catches on *good girl.*

Wait. He thinks I'm good and innocent? Why do I... sort of like that?

"So yeah," he continues, his voice dropping to something dark and possessive, something that makes heat pool low in my belly. "I stormed in there because seeing you sitting at a table in the middle of my territory, looking like *that*, with that *fuckin'* purple band around your arm... Do you know what that means, Erin? Do you have *any* idea?"

"I didn't—" I close my mouth because I'm starting to realize that, no, I don't.

"It means you're *available*," he snarls, like the word's filthy in his mouth. "It means you're a free submissive looking for a Dom. Looking to be claimed."

The blood drains from my face.

"I didn't know," I whisper. "I'm sorry."

"Of *course* you didn't fuckin' know!" His hand slams against the wall beside my head, making me flinch. "Because you haven't been vetted. You haven't been trained. You walked into a den of wolves wearing a sign that says 'Eat me,' and you didn't even *realize* it."

He's shaking, actually shaking with barely controlled rage.

"Do you know what happened to the last person who broke into my club without permission?"

I shake my head, genuinely scared of the man looming over me.

His hand moves to my jaw, tilting my face up to his, forcing me to meet his eyes.

"I beat the fuckin' shite out of them," he says. "And I threw them out. Physically. Obviously, I won't do that to you— you're a woman. And my fiancée."

Now he's saying it too.

His face is only a breath from mine now, his mouth close to my ear.

"But there are other ways I'll have to punish you, Erin."

"You can't—" My voice shakes. "You won't—"

"I can and will." His thumb brushes over my bottom lip, and I hate how my body responds. How it melts. "Because seeing you in there with that band on your arm, looking like every man's wet dream, sitting in my club like you're up for auction—"

He pulls back just enough to look at me, and the raw possession in his eyes steals my breath.

"Makes me want to burn this fuckin' place down. Makes me want to drag you into one of those rooms and remind you exactly who you belong to. Makes me want to mark every inch of your skin so no man in this city ever forgets that you're mine."

I can't breathe. Can't think. I remember the spanking he gave me before our first dinner, the way he effortlessly dominated me and left me furious and so fucking wet I couldn't think straight.

"Now," he says softly, dangerously, his hand sliding down to wrap around my throat—not squeezing, just holding, a promise of what he could do. "Are you going to walk into that room with me? Or do I need to feckin' carry you?"

His eyes dare me to refuse.

And god help me, I don't know if I'm more terrified or aroused by the darkness I see there.

"The room, Erin," he growls. "Choose. Now."

I try to twist in his grip, but it's useless. He doesn't answer. He just lifts me, one arm under my knees, the other around my back. I'm pressed against his chest, and I can feel his heartbeat—steady, controlled—while mine's racing.

He smells good. It's a crazy thought to have right now.

"Put me down!"

"No."

Part of me wonders what he could get away with in here. He's not only the owner of the club, he's Cavin McCarthy. He walks on fucking water. He plays by a code of rules that nobody wants to know.

"No! Let me—"

He carries me further down the hallway. A bouncer takes one look at Cavin and steps aside without a word.

"Where's my sister?" I demand, panic rising in my throat. "Bridget? I need to—"

"Don't worry about your sister. My cousin Declan is watching her," he says. "You won't be leaving without her, so stop looking like a fuckin' trapped animal."

He pushes open a door with his shoulder.

I'm going to be married to this man. We are going to share a bed. And right now, I'm too afraid to be alone with him. He has ripped through every one of my boundaries and fears like they were paper.

Thank god the room's private and secluded. There's a couch, a bar in the corner, and soft music playing. It's almost... almost elegant. But there's something else too. Things I don't quite understand. Equipment that makes my stomach flip.

I've never seen anything like this.

There are... chains and things hanging from the ceiling. That looks like—oh my god. There's a bench and something with leather straps. And there's something that looks like—it can't be described as anything but a whip.

Jesus, Mary, and Joseph.

He sets me down, and I immediately step back, my eyes catching on something low to the ground. It's padded with black leather, but it doesn't look like the type of bench you... *sit* on. There are restraints attached to it. And the angle is all wrong. Too horizontal. Too... purposeful.

A cabinet stands open in the corner, and I catch a glimpse of what's inside before I can look away.

Oh god. I don't... I don't even know the names of half these things. There's something that looks like a flogger with leather tails. Something that looks like a riding crop.

My heart hammers.

On a side table, there's a neat line of items that look almost surgical. Blindfolds. Silk scarves. Something metal that glints—handcuffs? Small glass bottles I can't identify.

And then there's the couch that suddenly makes sense. It's positioned to face something wooden that looks... it looks like some kind of a cross.

This isn't just a private room. It's a *playground.*

I wonder if the walls are soundproof. I wonder if the way the door sealed when we came in means it's locked to outside intruders, and no one would hear anything that happened in here.

And then there's the mirror. A massive mirror along one wall with a gilded frame reflects everything back—shows me standing here, wide-eyed and frozen.

Is this what The Craic really is? This is why he didn't want me to come here.

My heart sinks to my toes.

This is where Cavin comes. Where he's comfortable. Where women bow to him.

I remember what I saw online. I remember the way women fawned all over him.

I may be a virgin, but he's definitely not. I don't even want to think about what he's done in here.

Is that jealousy I'm feeling?

No. I'm not... I'm not *jealous*. Why would I be jealous of a man I hate? I don't even like the man. He can have all the fucking women he wants for all I care.

I swallow hard.

There's a knock at the door. Cavin opens it, and Declan appears with Bridget at his side. He only opens the door a crack so she can't see the details in here. And my god, if he opens it even further...

"You alright, Bridget?" I ask immediately.

"I'm fine." Bridget's eyes are wide. "What's—"

"She's grand," Cavin says. Then he tells Declan, "Take her to the lounge. Get her whatever she wants. We'll be done here shortly. Take very good care of her, Declan. Don't let her out of your damn sight."

Declan nods. Before I can protest, he adds, "Wait for us in the club." Then he turns to my sister. "*Bridget.*" Not a question, a command wrapped in her name.

"Yes?" Her voice goes small, childlike. Even I gulp.

"Do you have a purple band on your arm as well?"

She swallows, then nods.

"Take it *off her*." The words come out cold and commanding—not to Bridget, but to Declan—an order that doesn't allow for debate.

Declan curses under his breath, and the door clicks shut behind them.

Now it's just us.

Why do I like the fact that Cavin is looking out for my little sister?

He isn't *protecting* her, he's just...

He turns to me, and the room shifts again. I lose all train of thought. I *never* lose my train of thought.

This time, the downshift feels heavier. Weighted.

"Do you have *any* idea what you did tonight?" His voice is controlled, but I can hear the anger simmering underneath. "You came into my club. My territory. Without permission. Without telling me. Without reading my texts. Without even understanding what you were walking into, and you told everyone that *my* fiancée was *free to take*."

Well. That does sound sort of terrible when he puts it that way...

He takes a step closer, then another, until there's hardly a fragment of space between us.

"This isn't some casual place where you grab a pint and go home. This is where I come to forget the world exists. Where normal rules don't apply. Or... I used to, anyway," he says.

"What does that mean?"

His eyes narrow on me. "You sat in my club, looking like that, with a signal on your fucking arm that you were available. That our engagement means *nothing*."

He points a finger at my chest. It doesn't hurt, but I'm hyperaware of every nerve ending it comes in contact with.

"And *you* are *anything* but available. Every fucking man in that room was wondering if you were fair game. And do you know what I would have had to do if they'd touched you? If they'd come anywhere near you?"

I shake my head, speechless. Do I want to—

"I would've had to kill them," he says. "Painfully. Publicly. Would've had to make a fuckin' spectacle in my own club because of you."

He leans in close, his breath hot against my face.

"You deserve to be punished for that." His pupils are blown.

Excitement floods me as heat colors my face.

"Cavin, I didn't know."

"*Exactly*. Of course you didn't know. Because you don't listen. You don't follow instructions. You block me on your goddamn phone. You sneak around behind my back. You give my men the slip and wander into places you have no business being."

"You don't own me," I hiss.

He's close enough now that I have to tilt my head back to meet his eyes.

"You're my fiancée, Erin. And that means something, whether you like it or not."

"It means nothing if I didn't choose it," I snap at him.

"And yet..." he says as his hand comes up, wrapping his fingers gently, so gently, around my *throat*.

Oh god.

My pulse skyrockets.

He's not squeezing. Just... holding, like a reminder.

"Yet here you are," he whispers. "In my club. In my private room. Exactly where I want you."

I should push him away. I should slap him and scream. But I don't.

Because something in me—something I don't want to acknowledge—responds to this. To him. To the way he's looking at me like I'm something he wants to devour.

"You need to learn," he says softly, his thumb brushing the side of my neck. My pulse beats rapidly under his finger.

"You need to learn what it means to be mine. And what happens when you disobey me."

I should be horrified, should be angry at his words. But something unfamiliar flares to life inside me.

"Cavin—"

"Shhh." His other hand slides to my waist and pulls me close. "You came to The Craic because you wanted to see what it was about, didn't you?"

"No. I... I came because—"

"So you're not curious, then? Hmm?"

Why is the anger seeping out of his face? Why does he look almost curious?

"I can show you. I can make it part of your punishment."

My breath catches.

His mouth hovers near my ear, and when he speaks, his voice is dark velvet.

"Do you trust me, Erin?"

"No. For *fuck's sake*, of course I don't."

He laughs, low and dangerous. I draw in a quick breath to steady myself so I don't collapse.

"Good," he says. "You shouldn't."

Then his lips brush against my jaw, and my heart flutters like the rapid beating of a hummingbird's wings.

I *hate* that my body reacts like this. That I lean into it instead of pulling away from him.

"I thought you hated me," he murmurs against my skin.

"I do." I do hate him, but... I open my mouth. "I—"

But I can't say it.

His hand tightens slightly on my throat, and a sound escapes me—something between a gasp and a whimper that I've never made before in my life. I sound desperate.

Cavin goes still.

Then he pulls back just enough to look at me, his eyes dark and searching.

"Well," he says quietly, almost to himself, "that's interesting."

"What... what is?" My voice comes out shaky, uncertain.

"You." His thumb traces my lower lip, and I feel it everywhere—my chest, my stomach, lower. "Responding to me like that."

"I'm not." But even I don't believe it.

"You are." Something shifts in his expression—satisfaction, hunger, maybe both. He leans in again, his mouth so close to mine I can feel his breath. "And I think you're as surprised by it as I am."

He's right, and I hate that he's right.

Because this—him, this moment, the way my body's gone traitor on me—shouldn't be happening. I don't even like him. I shouldn't want this. Shouldn't feel like I'm coming apart at the seams just from his hand on my face and his voice in my ear.

I've never felt anything like this. Didn't know I could.

And from the dark gleam in his eyes, he knows it too. Knows he's the first to make me feel this way.

The bastard looks delighted about it.

His hand slides from my throat down to my collarbone, lower, skimming the edge of my neckline. He's far too familiar with how to play my body. I'm vividly aware that this isn't his first time, that he's experienced because of other women, and I'm so fuckin' jealous I can't think straight.

"Do you know what your problem is?" he says.

"I'm being held against my will with a man I hate, who I'm being forced to marry," I say, my palm up in the air. "I think that about sums it up."

He gives me a half smile. "Yeah, you know, it's not much better for me."

I look away. I don't like the sadness in his eyes. It makes me feel like I want to make it better.

And I want to keep hating him. I *need* to.

"The problem is you overthink everything. Your mind races. I can see it just by looking at you. And you know what happens in a place like this?" He gestures around the room.

"I actually have no idea," I say with a grimace, even as my heart beats so fast I'm a little dizzy. "It looks kind of, um, violent and...sexual."

His low, dark chuckle is seductive, primal. Why is every nerve in my body on fire?

"This is where people let go. You need to stop thinking for once in your fuckin' life." He steps closer, his voice dropping. "I can help with that."

My breath catches. "What?"

"You heard me." His eyes drop to my mouth, then lower. "I can make that busy head of yours go quiet. Make you feel nothing but what I'm doing to you."

"Cavin—"

"That's the first time you've said my name without spitting it." He reaches out, his fingers grazing my jaw. "Say it again."

I shouldn't. This is ridiculous. But my body's already leaning into his touch. "No."

His thumb traces my bottom lip. "Your mouth says no, but everything else is screaming yes. I can see your pulse racing right here"—he touches my throat—"and feel how hot your skin is."

"You're so full of yourself—"

"And you're so wound up you're about to snap." His hand slides into my hair, gripping firmly enough to make me gasp.

"I hate you," I whisper, but it sounds weak, even to my ears.

"Grand. I wonder if you'd hate me while you came on my fingers."

Oh god.

A dull but insistent vibration comes from his pocket. With a curse, he yanks his phone out and glances at the screen. He curses, low and furious.

The moment shatters.

He drags a hand through his hair, jaw tight with frustration, and looks at the clock on the wall and curses again.

"I've got something I have to do," he says. "I have to go."

I blink at him, still trying to catch my breath. "What?"

"Go home, Erin." He's already moving toward the door. "We'll talk about this and the punishment I owe you later."

"You don't owe—"

"I do. You came here without permission, and anybody who comes in here unwelcome gets punished. That's the rule. Ask anyone who works here."

"You can't just—"

He stops and turns back, and in two strides, he's in front of me again, his hand cupping my face. "Later," he says firmly. He's so close I wonder if he'll kiss me. His gaze lingers on my lips and he swallows hard.

I draw in another breath when his thumb brushes my bottom lip. "You listen to me, lass. Are you listening, Erin?"

I nod.

"Don't you *ever* come here again without me. I'm having you sent home."

He doesn't wait for an answer but turns and marches away.

He leaves me aching, my heart racing, and my body trembling, trying to figure out what the hell just happened.

Chapter Fourteen

Cavin

"Y'ALRIGHT, BROTHER?" My cousin Donovan eyes me curiously.

I shake my head. "Need to get the fuck out of here."

"Right, then. I'll notify the front," he says with a chin lift.

I slam my office door hard enough to rattle the frame. My hands are shaking—not with fear, never with fear. It's something far more dangerous coursing through me, something that needs blood and violence to settle.

That girl. That *fuckin'* girl.

That beautiful, exhausting, infuriating fucking *woman*.

I stalk down the back corridor, and my crew melts out of my way like they can smell what's coming off me. Good lads. They know better than to get in my path when I'm like this.

The bass thrums through the walls, but it's not enough—not enough to burn off whatever the fuck burns inside me. My skin feels too tight, my blood too hot.

"Sir, do you need anything?" one of the bouncers asks, but I shake my head.

Need anything? Like fuck, I need something.

Her.

But I can't have her, not yet.

I need the ring.

The thought comes to me so quickly, so naturally, it surprises me. But not now. I *can't*. I haven't been in a ring since before my time in prison.

I shove through the doors into the main club. The crowd's thick tonight, bodies pressed together, the air hazy with smoke and sweat and spilled drink. But it's beautiful, and it's mine. I love it here. It's my second home.

My feet carry me with purpose, straight toward the exit that takes me to my car so I can pay the *fucking* tribute. Not only do I hate being strung by the bollocks, but I could still be *here*, still have more time with Erin. I owe her a punishment for coming here, and goddamn it, I'm *aching* to fuckin' administer it.

But here we go again. The goddamn monthly tribute, and I'm not even one step closer to discovering who demands it.

I get to my car, my hand on the door handle, then pause. A prickle of awareness skates across my neck.

Something's out of place. Something's wrong...

Is this where I parked?

I frown, pulling out my phone. "Declan," I say when he answers. "Check the security footage, will ye? I know where I parked my car, and it looks like it's been moved."

"It's been moved?" he says. "*Jaysus.*"

I gesture to a valet who's nearby.

"Here, I want you to take my car, pull it up to the front," I tell him, handing over the keys. "I want to go through security footage first."

"Yes, sir."

I go back to the phone and head to the entrance of the club. "What do you see on the footage?"

"Nothing," Declan says. "It's too dark. What the hell? It looks as if—"

BOOM!

I fall to the ground on instinct as glass splinters. The car goes up in flames.

"Christ!" I gasp, staring at the inferno.

Someone bombed my goddamn car.

The door to the club flies open, and Declan runs toward me, his face pale in the orange glow of the flames.

"The valet—" I start, but I can already see him. Or what's left of him. He was at the other end of the lot, standing by my car when it went up. He's fucking toast now—dead. Burned to a crisp.

The acrid smell of burning fuel and flesh hits me, and my stomach turns. That could've been me. I was seconds away from getting in that fuckin' car.

I look at my watch. Ten goddamn minutes. I have ten goddamn minutes to pay this tribute.

Of *course*. This is what they do. Every single fuckin' month, something comes up. Something stops me from paying it.

This was no accident.

"Goddamn it!" I slam my fist on the hood of another car. "You have to take care of this. I parked it myself tonight. Who was the valet?" The one whose family we need to visit and pay our respects to now that he's gone.

"I don't know his name," Declan says, shaking his head, his voice trembling as security pours out of the club. "He just got here, and I—"

His eyes are glassy as he scrubs a hand across his face. That was one of ours. One of *my men*, and it should've been me. And he died because I parked there.

Because someone wants me dead bad enough to kill innocents. If I'd been the one to go up in flames... there'd be no wedding, and that tribute would sit unpaid.

My cousins pour out of the club, taking in the smoking car, with curses and promises of revenge.

"*I* sent him over," Donovan says, walking up with his hands in his pockets. His face is stricken, pale eyes wide. "Jaysus, Cavin, I sent him to get your car. I didn't realize you had parked it yourself. I told him you'd be wanting to leave soon. *Fuck!*"

He runs his hands through his hair. "That should've been—I almost went myself, but I thought—"

"It's not your fault," I tell him, even as my mind races.

"Aye, well, when we find out, they'll wish they didn't," Declan says darkly.

Donovan laughs, but it doesn't quite reach his eyes. "Just saying—whoever it is, they know our movements. Know our people. Has to be someone close, doesn't it?"

I look at the time.

"Jesus Christ." My mind races. "I have to go."

"Cavin," Declan snaps, "where the fuck are you going *now?*"

"I can't tell you," I tell him. "Not now. You have to trust me."

"Don't I trust ye?" he says, shaking his head. "*Fuck.* Go now. Go."

"I've got to go. I need to take one of the cars—" We've got backups used for escorts and the like.

"Goddamn it, you're gonna tell me what this is," he growls under his breath, even as he tosses me a fob on a ring.

"I promise. As soon as I know there won't be blowback, I'll tell you."

I get in the car and drive like the devil. *Five hundred thousand euros. Every fucking month.* The numbers burn through my mind. *And I don't even know who the bastard is bleeding us dry.*

I pay the goddamn tribute at 11:58 p.m. I slam the fucking envelope in the fucking slot, with two minutes to spare, and scream into the night, "*MILLIONS!*" like a goddamn were-wolf fighting a full moon.

My family's safe for another month.

My bollocks are in a sling for another month.

I'm draining us dry, bit by bit. Making moves I never wanted to make. Getting into bed with people I shouldn't have. All to keep the cash flowing to some faceless fuck who's got us by the throat.

Christ, but I'd have loved to take it out on Erin's disobedient, willful little arse.

When it's done, I call Declan. "Okay," I say. "I'm sorted."

"Right," he says. "I instructed the guards to take Erin and her sister home and closed the club for the night."

"I owe you. Thank you."

I get back in the car, call Seamus, and drive—my mind racing the entire time.

Seamus answers right away. "What the hell happened?"

I fill him in.

"Somebody bombed your car. We have nothing recorded. This is insanity, these random attacks once a month. Seems like clockwork."

Yes, yes, it does.

I know exactly why. There's someone who doesn't want me to pay that goddamn tribute.

"Is everybody else safe?" I ask Seamus.

"Aye," he says.

He doesn't know that Erin was there tonight. I don't want him to know. I don't want anybody to know yet.

"Good," I say. "We need to up the security at the club."

"Agreed," he says.

All the more reason for my betrothed to be nowhere fucking near it.

I find myself taking a route I haven't driven in goddamn years. My hands turn the wheel without conscious thought, guiding me with purpose toward the one place that's always made sense.

The ring.

I can't get it out of my mind. I need to get in the ring. I crave it like a man craves drink.

I park Declan's car and send a quick message to the group chat. I'll be back. They'll know where I am by now.

I need to be here.

This used to be my second home, before the club became that. When I was a lad, barely tall enough to see over the ropes, Malachy brought me to the gym to train. Taught me how to fight properly, not the scrappy street brawling every kid from Ballyhock knew, but real fighting. Technique. Discipline. How to read a man's body before he even knows what he's going to do himself.

It always felt perfectly right, being here. More right than school ever did, more right than sitting in a pew at Mass, listening to Father O'Brien drone on about sin and redemption.

In the ring, everything made sense. There were rules, but they were simple. Hit harder. Move faster. Don't go down.

The rest of life was complicated. This never was.

Conversations die as I pass through the crowd. I hear the whispers, feel the eyes tracking me.

"Is that—?"

"No fucking way."

"Cavin McCarthy."

"Thought he was done with all that."

"Look at him. Does he look done?"

"He hasn't fought since—"

I don't acknowledge any of it. My focus narrows to a single point: the ring.

It smells familiar—sweat, blood, desperation, victory. A ref sits by the bar, drinking. The bartender materializes at my elbow with a shot glass. Jameson, neat.

I take it without looking, throw it back, and slam the glass down on the nearest table. The whiskey fucking burns, but it's not enough.

I reach the ring's edge and grab the top rope, vaulting myself up and through. The crowd goes quiet.

The canvas is stained with old blood, some of it probably mine. My boots hit solid, and I straighten, then roll my shoulders.

I begin to unbutton my shirt, one button at a time, and the crowd falls to a whisper.

I shrug it off, grab a fistful of my undershirt, and yank it over my head.

The roar is instantaneous.

The entire fuckin' club goes *wild*. The sound hits me like a physical thing—screaming, stamping, fists pounding on tables.

I toss my shirt outside the ropes, and it disappears into grasping hands.

I turn in a slow circle, bouncing on the balls of my feet to warm up. They can all see it now with the overhead lighting, the scars mapping my ribs, my back. Evidence of who I am, what I've done, what I've survived.

Prison didn't soften me—it honed me into something sharper, meaner.

I crack my knuckles and roll my neck. The familiar pre-fight ritual settles over me like a second skin.

"Well, fuck me."

A low growl of a voice, familiar and unwelcome, cuts through the noise. I know it before I look.

Tommy "The Butcher" O'Sullivan shoulders his way through the crowd, that ugly grin splitting his fuckin' face. He's thicker now, running to fat around the middle, but his hands are still the size of goddamn dinner plates.

We've got history, Tommy and me. Bad blood that never got properly settled.

Excellent.

"Heard you've gone soft inside, McCarthy," he says, climbing into the ring and stripping off his own shirt. "Heard prison feckin' broke ye."

"Do I *look* broken?" I say to him, then wink. "Come find out, ye thick bastard. Let's see if your fists work better than your brain."

The spectators are losing their minds now. They know what this is—old grudges, old violence, coming home to roost.

I don't respond beyond that. I watch him, let him run his mouth while I measure the way he's moving. He's favoring his left side. Knee's probably shot.

Noted.

"Nothing to say?" Tommy spreads his arms wide, playing to the crowd. "Cat got your—"

I hit him.

No warning, no preamble. My right fist crashes into his jaw, and his head snaps back. Blood sprays from his mouth. I've split his lip.

Good.

The bell rings a second too late, and nobody cares.

Tommy roars and charges at me like a bull. The referee's behind us shouting, but he knows better than to come between an O'Sullivan and a McCarthy.

Tommy always fought like this, all power, no finesse. He swings wild, and I duck under, driving my fist into his kidney once, twice. He grunts but doesn't go down.

His elbow catches me in the temple, and stars explode across my vision. The taste of copper floods my mouth.

There it is.

Yes.

God, that's what I needed. I feel like a shark tasting blood as adrenaline surges through me.

We trade blows in the center of the ring, neither of us backing down. My knuckles split open on his teeth. His fist connects with my ribs, and something cracks—not broken, but close.

The pain is clarifying. Pure. I goddamn *welcome* it.

I'm not thinking about Erin anymore. Not thinking about those defiant eyes, that smart mouth, the way her pulse felt under my—

Tommy's fist crashes into my jaw, and I stumble back against the ropes.

Focus. Fucking *focus*.

He charges in for the kill, and I let him come. At the last second, I drop low, grab him around the middle, and use his own momentum to flip him. One swift move and his back hits the canvas hard enough to bounce. The air goes out of him in a whoosh.

I'm on him before he can take a breath. Knees pinning his arms, fists raining down. It feels like a symphony.

Left, right, left, right. Methodical. Brutal.

His face becomes a mask of blood, and he's trying to buck me off, but I'm locked on. Immovable.

Erin's face swims in my vision for a moment. In this ring, I don't have to pretend.

This is what I am. This is what I've always been.

Strip it all away and I'm just a bare-knuckled fuckin' McCarthy from Ballyhock who knows how to hurt people.

"Yield," I growl, my fist cocked back for another strike.

Tommy's eyes roll, unfocused. He's done.

"He yields!" the ref shouts. "He yields, McCarthy!" He grabs my shoulder. "He's done!"

I stare down at Tommy's ruined face for another long moment, my chest heaving, blood dripping from my knuckles. Every muscle in my body is screaming. My hands are destroyed, and I can already feel tomorrow's bruises forming.

But the fire's burned down to a low ember.

Finally.

Finally, I can breathe.

I climb off him and let the ref raise my arm. The crowd's absolutely mental, chanting my name like I'm some kind of god, some kind of savior. "McCARthy! McCARthy! McCARthy!" Money's changing hands everywhere—bets being settled, new ones being made for my next fight. I don't fuckin' care. I didn't come here to be worshipped like a goddamn hero.

I spit blood onto the canvas and turn toward the ropes, ready to climb out, ready to disappear back into the night—

And I freeze.

Because *she's* there.

How? She isn't supposed to be here.

Erin is standing at the edge of the crowd, partially hidden in the shadow of a support beam. Her face is pale in the strobing lights, making her look almost ghostly. Still wearing that same outfit she wore to the club, minus the purple band. Her eyes are wide, locked on me—on my bloodied knuckles, my split lip, my bare chest, and all the scars I carry like medals of dishonor.

She's seeing exactly who I am. No polish, no pretense, no expensive suits or charming smiles. Just violence in its purest form. Just the beast she's being forced to marry.

Our eyes meet across the chaos, and I watch something flicker across her face—something I wish I could see closer, something I need to understand. Is it fear? Disgust? The horror of realizing what she's trapped herself into?

Or is it something else? Something that looks almost like...

Arousal?

No. Can't be. Not for this. Not for the monster standing in a ring, covered in another man's blood.

But I remember the way her eyes danced in the club, the way her body practically screamed at me to be dominated... *Christ.* If Erin likes what I think she does...

I can't tell in the dim light, but she doesn't look away.

Neither do I.

The moment stretches between us like a taut wire, vibrating with tension. Everything else fades—the crowd, the noise,

Tommy groaning on the canvas behind me. It's just her and me and the question hanging in the air: Can she be with a man like this?

With a man who needs violence the way other men need air?

The crowd surges between us, drunk men stumbling, pushing to get closer to the ring, and when they clear, all I see is the back of the fuckin' guard I hired for her—Declan's man, escorting her out, protecting her like I asked him to.

But I felt it, that connection, that pull.

And I wonder if her presence was good luck or something darker.

I wonder if she came here looking for me, or if fate's just cruel enough to keep throwing us together.

I wonder if she's running from me or running toward something she doesn't understand yet.

I climb through the ropes, and someone hands me my shirt and a towel. I wipe blood from my face, can't tell if it's mine or Tommy's, and shrug into my shirt, not bothering to button it.

"McCarthy." O'Grady flags me down. "Yer winnings, son."

I frown. I don't need the damn money. Still, I take the thick envelope and nod my thanks.

I walk to the exit, staring at my purse.

I didn't do this for money. I think about what to do with it, and finally decide to call Bronwyn. I can trust her.

"Hello?" she says, sleepy.

"Bronwyn," I say when she answers, even though it's two a.m.

She sounds instantly alert. "Cav? Are you okay? Where are you?"

"I need a favor. A private one."

A pause. Then, "Go on."

"I'm sending you money. I need you to give it to Erin. Tell her it's from you. Tell her it's... I don't know, wedding gift money, or shopping money, or whatever."

"How much money?" I glance at the envelope. "Eighteen thousand euros."

"*Jesus, Mary, and Joseph.* What did you do, rob a bank?"

"I fought."

Another pause, longer this time. "You went back to the ring."

"Aye."

"Does Seamus know?"

"No." Not yet. Won't take long. "This is from you, Bronwyn. Can you do that for me?"

"Of course."

"Thank you."

I step out into the cold night air, and it hits my overheated skin. Steam rises from my body. My breath comes in clouds.

I lean against the car for a moment, letting my heart rate slow, letting the adrenaline drain away.

But before I go home, I need answers. I send Erin a text.

How the fuck did you get here? You were supposed to be going home

I hope she hears the implied raised eyebrow there.

Erin
Overheard your cousin say you'd be there, so I told the guard to bring me after we dropped Bridget off at home

I go to respond when another message pops up.

Erin
Also. You're a monster.

And I grin at the words. Is that right, darlin'? Am I such a monster that you ran from me? Or did you have to come see for yourself?

But then three dots appear. She's typing again.

Erin
But I'm…

beginning to see the appeal of the villain.

I close my eyes and lean my head back against the car.

Christ.

This girl is going to destroy me.

Or save me.

Maybe both.

Chapter Fifteen

Erin

I CANNOT GET Cavin out of my mind. But it probably has something to do with the fact that the bastard texts like a *thousand* times a day.

> **Cavin**
> Is your location on?

> **Cavin**
> My mother would like to talk to you about favors for the party.

> **Cavin**
> My sisters want to know what color dress you're wearing.

And on and on the list goes.

> **Cavin**
> What are your plans today?

Questions that would actually be quite welcome and even make a lot of sense if we had any type of relationship or ounce of care between us. If we were *actually* two people in love, planning a wedding.

I'm not someone to fall for fairy-tale stories, so I never even dreamed of marrying my Prince Charming. I always assumed that I would somehow get away with being single for the rest of my life, even being born into the Irish mob.

Now? *Definitely* not interested in marriage.

The day of shopping and going to the club was borrowed time. The next day, Bridget paid for it. She fell ill with a fever, and she's been in the hospital ever since.

So while a part of me is kicking and screaming and resisting the idea of going all the way to the McCarthy house and becoming one of them, my conviction that this is the right thing to do is stronger than ever.

I guess most women who are engaged look forward to the engagement party. But me? It's a looming date on my calendar, just like any formal event has always been and probably always will be.

> Like something that's supposed to guide
> me to the right colors?

Cavin
Ah. Rules and regulations and the like.
That's very you

For some reason, that makes me smile. It is very me—over-thinking to the point of paralysis, while the world moves on without asking my permission.

The bell rings, and my mother calls for me. "Erin? Some-one's here to see you."

No one ever comes here to see me. My heart beats faster. It can't be... I pad downstairs in my yoga pants and oversized jumper, hair still damp from the shower. I'm not expecting anyone. The last forty-eight hours have been a blur of restless sleep and replaying that night at the club over and over. The way Cavin's hand felt on my throat. The way his eyes looked when he—

I stop at the bottom of the stairs.

Why am I disappointed it isn't... him?

Am I *falling* for him?

Bronwyn McCarthy stands in our foyer like a beam of light in a dark room. She's wearing a soft-pink coat and cream-colored trousers, her light brown hair perfectly styled in loose waves. She looks like she stepped out of a magazine, effortlessly elegant in that way I've never managed.

"Hiya," she says softly, offering a gentle smile.

"Hiya," I echo, suddenly aware of how disheveled I must look.

My mother hovers nearby, clearly uncomfortable. The McCarthys don't just drop by. This isn't how our families operate.

"I'll leave you girls to it," my mother says, though her tone suggests she'd rather stay and spy. She disappears into the kitchen, but I know she's listening.

"Would you like to come up to my room?" I ask quietly. Is that what people do?

Bronwyn nods, relief flashing across her face.

I lead her upstairs and close the door behind us. My room is exactly as I left it this morning—books stacked on every surface, my laptop open on the bed, a half-drunk cup of tea gone cold on the nightstand.

"Sorry about the mess," I mutter, shoving a pile of clothes off the chair so she can sit.

"Don't apologize. This is lovely." She settles into the chair with the kind of grace that seems innate to her. "Your room suits you."

I perch on the edge of my bed, tucking my feet under me. "Not like yours, I imagine."

"Mine's all white and gold. Looks like a hotel room." She wrinkles her nose slightly. "This actually feels lived in. I like it."

She sighs and smiles, then asks the last thing I expect her to.

"How are you? After... everything?"

My cheeks flush. Does she know I went to The Craic? Does the whole family know?

"I'm fine," I say automatically.

"Erin." Her voice is kind but firm. "You don't have to pretend with me." She smiles in a way that makes me feel weirdly emotional. "We're going to be sisters."

Why haven't I thought of that before now? She's right, of course. I'm not just marrying Cavin. I'm marrying into the whole *family*. I'll have sisters and, for the first time in my life... brothers.

Oh god.

"I don't know if I'm fine," I admit quietly. "I don't know what I am. It's just a bit much."

She nods slowly. "That's fair. This is... a lot. All of it."

"Did Cavin send you?" The question comes out sharper than I intended.

"No." She reaches into her handbag and pulls out an envelope—a thick manila envelope that looks stuffed full. "Well, yes and no. He asked me to bring you this."

She hands me the envelope.

It's heavy. Substantial.

"What is it?" I ask, though something in my gut already knows.

"Open it."

My fingers fumble with the clasp. I pull out the contents, and my breath catches.

Money. Stacks of it. Euros, neatly bundled in groups of five hundred.

"What—" I can't finish the sentence.

"It's eighteen thousand euros," Bronwyn says quietly. "He wanted you to have it."

I stare at the money in my lap like it might bite me. "Why?"

"He said to tell you it's wedding money. For shopping, or whatever you need. But Erin…" She leans forward, her blue eyes intense. "That's not what this is."

"Then what is it?"

"It's his fight purse. From the other night."

The room tilts slightly. "His what?"

"He went to the ring… after whatever happened at the club. He fought Tommy O'Sullivan and won. This is what he earned."

My mind races. I saw him. I saw him in that ring, bare-chested and bloody, fighting like something feral and beautiful and terrifying. I left quickly because I couldn't process what I was feeling.

But I could've watched Cavin fight *forever*.

"He gave me his fight money?" My voice sounds small.

"All of it. Every cent." Bronwyn's expression is soft. "He made me promise to tell you it was from me. That it was family money or wedding money or whatever would make you take it."

"But you're telling me the truth."

"Because you deserve the truth." She reaches out and touches my hand. "Erin, my brother is… complicated. He's rough and violent, and he's done things that would horrify you. But he's also..." She pauses, choosing her words carefully. "He's trying. In his own broken way, he's trying. And soon, you'll be his. His to protect. I think this is one way of him doing that. He probably knows that even though your family has money, it isn't necessarily *yours*. But this is."

She rises. "Have some fun with it, Erin. Do some shopping."

"Buy some of the fancy yarn and the *nice* puzzles, hmm?" I say, then quickly wish I could take the words back. Was that too awkward? But she only laughs, kisses my cheeks, and heads to the door.

"I'm sorry, I need to go. Just wanted to give this to you in person."

I stare at the money. I know *exactly* what I'm going to do with it. And I smile to myself.

I may have a little hobby I've kept all to myself.

Later that night, he texts.

Cavin
I want to take you to dinner

I freak *out* and quickly text him back.

No. I'm busy.

It's a lie though.

He tries again the next day, and I feel guilty as fuck. Maybe it *is* a good idea. Maybe we *can* at least find a way to pretend that we like each other for something like this.

Cavin
I'm not asking, Erin

I can still see him standing in the ring, sweaty and scarred—the first time I've seen my future husband bare-chested after a fight. I knew when he was in school, he fought, but I never witnessed it. I didn't like violence.

But now—now, it affects me in a way I never anticipated.

He was magnificent. Terrifying. Beautiful in the most dangerous way possible.

The scars mapped across his torso told stories I'd never heard—white lines across his ribs, a puckered mark near his collarbone that looked like a stab wound, the evidence of broken bones healed wrong. His body was a history of violence, and under the lights, slick with sweat and spattered with blood, he looked like some ancient warrior marked with tribal ink.

But it wasn't just his *appearance*. It was the way he… moved.

I've never seen anything like it. Every punch was calculated, precise. He read his opponent three moves ahead, slipping strikes that should have connected, countering with devastating accuracy. There was an intelligence to his violence, a genius to the brutality that made it almost an art form.

He didn't just overpower his opponent. He dismantled him. Systematically. Beautifully. Ruthlessly.

And I couldn't look away.

My heart pounded in my chest, my breath coming short. When his fist connected, that sickening thud of knuckles on flesh should have made me flinch. Should have made me turn away.

Instead, I leaned forward.

Heat flooded through me, pooling low in my belly. My breasts felt heavier, my pulse racing. My skin felt too tight. Every brutal hit, every display of raw power, sent electricity skittering down my spine. I was afraid of him in that moment —truly afraid of what he was capable of—and somehow, that fear tangled with desire until I couldn't separate them.

This was who Cavin really was beneath the expensive suits and measured words. This violence, this power, this absolute dominance wasn't a side of him. It was his foundation.

And god help me, I wanted it. I wanted *him*. But here's what truly undid me: I realized, watching him in that ring, that when he's with me, he cages all of that.

Every touch has been controlled. Every kiss measured. Even when he's angry with me, even when I went into the club and he was furious, he held himself back. That massive, devastating force that could break a man in half, and nearly did, treats me... differently.

Maybe Cavin *isn't* the boy I knew in school.

He fights like a demon but doesn't unleash himself on me.

Or hasn't yet.

The restraint that must take... the control.

Standing there in the crowd, watching him raise his bloodied fists in victory, I felt something shift inside me. Fear, yes. Awe, absolutely. Arousal that made my knees weak.

But also... pride.

He's mine.

This dangerous, violent man has chosen to be gentle with me. And that choice, that constant caging of his nature, is somehow more intimate than anything else between us.

When his eyes found mine across the crowd, dark and predatory and hungry, I felt it like a physical touch.

Maybe he won't always cage it with me. Not forever.

And the most terrifying part?

I *want* him to let it loose. Excitement and arousal twist together. I've replayed the fight and his hand around my neck, replayed those moments a thousand times since, trying to understand why it didn't terrify me but did the opposite.

And I want to feel it again.

But this time, I want to see how it ends.

So finally, I say yes.

> Okay, fine. Alright I'll go out to dinner with you.
>
> When?

> **Cavin**
> Tonight. I'll pick you up at six o'clock. Wear something pretty.

My heart flutters in my chest.

I wish Bridget wasn't back in the hospital for treatments because I want someone to complain to and then squeal with. I want someone who will help me pick out the clothes I should wear. I want to talk about what I'm going to do tonight.

I may be marrying a man I hate, but at least he's a man and not a boy. He's picking me up. He told me what time. He told me what to wear.

I like black and white. I like expectations and dependability. So if anything, Cavin is competent. That has to count for something, doesn't it?

I don't tell my mother—I have at least an ounce of self-preservation left. But I do go to my da.

"Listen," I tell my father over breakfast. "Would you agree that I'm making a sacrifice for this family?"

"Of course," he says, pushing his cup of tea away. "What's this about?"

"I'm going out to dinner with Cavin tonight, and I do not want Mam breathing down my neck."

"So you want me to occupy your mother?" he says with a nod. "Fair enough. What time do you need?"

"I guess I need... I don't know, an hour to get ready? He's picking me up at six."

"I'll have her out of the house by half four," he says with a nod.

I get up from the table, and he reaches for my hand. "You do what you have to, Erin. Make that man fall in love with you."

He lets me go and leaves the table. I'm reeling, staring after him.

Make that man fall in love with you.

Since when was *that* the goal? Isn't it enough to marry him?

And how exactly does one do that? I don't know how to *make* him fall in love with me.

Love me? Sure, no problem, Da. I'll just figure out which parts of myself to bury so Cavin doesn't rip the piss out of me like he did in school. Grand.

In the afternoon, I go to my room and set up my tablet with the YouTube tutorials Bridget showed me before she went back to the hospital. Then I get a brilliant idea.

I click video call, and she picks up on the first ring.

But Bridget looks pale. She has dark circles under her eyes. And is that a fleck of blood at the corner of her mouth? I gasp when I look at her.

I *need* to make it work tonight.

"Hey," Bridget says with a watery smile. "What's up? I know, I know, I look terrible. It was a rough night, but I'm feeling a little better."

Bridget's a terrible liar.

"Cavin's taking me out to dinner," I say with a grimace. "And I need to... Oh god, I don't know. I need to be ready soon."

"Where's he taking you?"

"He just said"—my voice lowers to a deep pitch—'I'll pick you up at six. Wear something nice.'"

Bridget smiles, and I swear her eyes have hearts in them like a little emoji. "He *did*?"

"Yes," I say, blowing out a breath. "I'm not that impressed, so relax. What should I wear?"

"It's cute though."

"It's not cute, it's bossy."

Is there anything about the McCarthy family men that isn't bossy?

I sigh.

"Okay, you definitely need to wear the ivory dress that dips all the way down in front. The backless one."

"Bridget!" I scold her.

"I know," she says with a grin. "But don't you want this man to be attracted to you?"

I remember the way he looked at me in the club—hungry, like a wolf circling its prey. And somehow... I don't think that's a problem.

I didn't see a purple band on *his* arm.

Wait a minute. Do the men there wear bands too? I need to find out.

I shrug. "I suppose."

"Yes! Of course. But wear something beautiful, maybe that emerald dress. Make him jealous. Make him want to protect you."

I remember the way he snarled in my ear: *You come into this club... Men here come with one purpose.*

I remember exactly how that felt.

"Alright," I say. "Sure."

"Well, your *makeup* looks beautiful," she says.

I nod. "It does. Thank you."

Bridget smiles and giggles, and I'm not sure why, but it's not that complicated. She showed me a video, and now I know how to do it.

I like to keep it natural. My eyes are brighter. My cheeks are slightly flushed. My lips are full from a lip plumper and stained with something that doesn't come off when I eat or drink. I've had my eyebrows waxed, and I used a little filler brush. She showed me this really amazing mascara that does something called "tubing" that just washes off with warm water. Kind of miraculous.

I look pretty good.

"Alright," she says. "Go put that dress on. And what did you do with your hair?"

"Well, I just washed it," I tell her. "And did a little with the stuff you bought me and did a bit of a blowout or some such. It's pretty easy once you get the hang of it."

All through secondary school, I had frizz-ball hair. But up until recently, she showed me some kind of method. And I'm not going to argue—it's nice being able to wake up to luxurious, silky waves.

And when I put that dress on? It's stunning.

I look at the time. Five fifty.

"What am I going to do for the next ten minutes?" I say nervously.

Bridget giggles and starts coughing. She coughs louder and louder until I feel my own ribs begin to rattle in sympathy.

"You know what?" I say. "I don't have to go out to dinner tonight. I need to—"

"No," Bridget says firmly. "You do. You're doing this for our family. And honestly, Erin, after I hang up the phone, I'm just going to sleep. I just need sleep."

She needs *so* much more than sleep.

I draw in a deep breath.

"So before he arrives, maybe mentally rehearse a couple of conversations you'll have with him in your head before you have them in person. You know how that helps you. Okay? Can you do that?"

"Rehearse conversations?" I grimace. "What do you mean?"

"Oh my god, you're so cute," she says, coughing again. "I wish I were there. Like this—let's practice."

I wait again until the coughing subsides.

Fuck aplastic anemia. Why did *she* get the faulty bone marrow? She's the pretty one, the one who would've done really well playing this part in our world.

I should be the one in that hospital bed.

Bridget sinks back against a bed of pillows. A nurse comes in and adjusts her IV. Then another one comes in and checks her medication.

We go on as if this is normal because this has become our new normal.

"Tell me a little bit about yourself, Erin," she says in a deep, masculine voice, and I can't help but giggle.

"Don't ask me that," I tell her, shaking my head.

"Why not?"

"Because I can't tell him that I'm into knitting and puzzles, Bridget. He'll think he's marrying an old lady."

"Who do you think he wants to marry?" she says. "He wants to marry *you*. You're not an old lady. You don't have shriveled up titties and ovaries."

I roll my eyes but snort.

"Listen, Erin." She leans forward into the camera, and I wish that she didn't, because when she does, the harsh fluorescent lighting makes her eyes look bright and highlights the dark circles underneath. It scares me.

"You need to be honest. Honesty is still the best policy. You have to understand," she says vehemently. "In our world, everything is cloaked in lies, right? It's all about who you know, how you play the game, who the power players are, who's rising, who's falling. Who's next." She swallows hard. "*You* don't play by those rules. Honestly, babe," she says with a soft smile, "it's one of the things I love best about you. You are who you are, no matter what anybody else thinks." She gives me a half smile and lowers her voice again. "So tell me, Erin. Tell me a little bit about yourself."

Hmm. "I...don't like to drink? I don't like loud music. I don't like..."

Me pushed up against the wall, his hand on my throat, his voice right up against my ear, and the way my heart fluttered in excitement. I liked that. But I quickly move on, pushing the thought away.

I swallow hard. "What about you?"

Bridget grins. "I like guns, fast cars, and fighting," she says in this comically gruff, masculine voice. "And the plans I have for the beautiful woman I'm marrying."

"Oh my god, Bridget," I say with a giggle.

"Erin?" My father's voice calls from downstairs, and there's a soft knock at the door.

"Yes?"

I open it to find our housekeeper on the other side. "Your ride's here, ma'am," she says, her eyes wide. "And what a ride it is," she adds with a little smile as she quickly scurries away.

"Oh god. Oh god, Bridget. I have to go. He's... he's here."

"Relax," she says with a big smile. "Remember, this is the man you're marrying, okay?"

"I know," I say with a grimace.

"It's not like it's a blind date," she says. "Just *go*. Have fun. Eat good food."

"How do I look?"

Bridget clasps her hands over her heart, sighs, and leans back against the pillows. "You look absolutely, stunningly, amazingly beautiful. And if you weren't my sister, and he wasn't marrying you, I would ask to marry you myself."

That makes me smile. "You're crazy."

"But you love me," she says.

"I do. So much."

I can't cry, not now, because even though this mascara is supposedly waterproof, I don't want to risk fate.

"Bye." I kiss the tips of my fingers and waggle them at her. "I love you so much too."

There was a time when my sister and I didn't tell each other that we loved one another, but now we realize there's no way to know when the last goodbye will be.

I square my shoulders and walk downstairs.

I don't know what to expect when I go downstairs, but I definitely don't expect to see Cavin McCarthy sitting in one of the camel-colored chairs in my living room, having a drink with my father.

Oh my god. Why can't he be outside, waiting in the car, so I can just run out to him? I don't want to prolong this torture.

Cavin rises when I enter the room. And again, I think: *gentleman*. His mama raised him well.

"Erin," Cavin says with a bow, and his eyes linger on me a second too long. He takes it all in—my dress, my makeup. "You look…" He clears his throat. "You look gorgeous."

And it may be the first honest thing he's ever said to me.

Will I ever be able to look at my future husband again and not remember the Dom in his sex club, the man who ruled that dark world, the lion in his lair? Because even now, with that look in his eyes—appreciative, a little stunned—I can feel his hand around my neck again.

And a part of me thinks, for one crazy, wild moment, that when his eyes meet mine, he's thinking of that too.

"Thank you," he says politely to my father. "That's excellent whiskey."

"I'll have a case sent to you," my father says with a nod. I'll hand it to my dad—he knows how to play the part well.

"I'd appreciate that," Cavin says with a loud, firm slap of hands and a handshake. And then we're headed to the door, and he's opening it for me. I have a little shawl draped over my elbow because Bridget told me to, and it all feels surreal. Why am I looking forward to going on a date with a man I hate?

His car is absolutely gorgeous. It smells like leather and luxury, it's spacious, and it's immaculately clean.

"This car is gorgeous," I tell him.

"Thank you," he says. "It's a loaner."

"Oh, right. What happened the other night?"

"We don't know yet."

There's a pause, and I wonder if he thinks it's awkward. What exactly qualifies as an awkward pause? Three seconds? Five? Is there a scientific measurement? How do people know these things?

"Well, it's a very nice car for my first date." I instantly press my lips together. *Why* did I just confess to that?

He shrugs. "Aye. What do you mean?"

"I mean, well, you know, it's my first date. I might as well go in style."

"Your first date with me," he asks quietly, "or your first date, period?"

Oh no. Was I not supposed to tell him that? I bite my lip and look out the window. It's probably unusual for someone who's twenty-six years old to be on her first date, but I've never wanted to date before.

"Um, no, just... just first date in general."

"Alright. No pressure or anything," he says with a smile that's almost boyish. "Though I'm honored to be your first."

He can't look at me that way. When he looks at me that way, I forget that I'm supposed to hate him.

My phone buzzes with a text.

Bridget
How are you doing?

I text her back. We text for a few minutes, and Cavin gives me a side glance. I realize this is probably rude and put the phone down in my lap.

"Erin, tell me a little bit about yourself," he says quietly.

And I actually laugh out loud.

"What?" he says, a little sheepish.

"Nothing. I..." *Be honest*, she said. *Be brutally honest.* "I was a little nervous about tonight, and I may have practiced a little bit with my sister. This sounds so awkward right now." Oh god, maybe I wasn't supposed to be *this* honest. I wring my hands and look out the window again.

"And the question that she asked me was, 'Tell me a little bit about yourself.' And I didn't expect that that would actually be the question you'd ask."

"No way," he says with a chuckle. "Didn't need to be that predictable, did I?"

Why is he so... disarming when he's smiling?

"Right," I say with a smile. "Alright. So, honestly—"

Be honest, you're marrying this man.

"I don't live a very exciting life." I sigh, shaking my head. "I like to be home. And when I'm home, I like to wear comfortable, familiar clothing. I don't like..." I sigh and blow out a breath. "Getting dressed up and going to places. I don't like crowds or noise or anything like that. When I'm home, I like to do puzzles. Intricate ones with lots of pieces. My mind works very quickly when it comes to patterns, and I piece things together. It needs to be a challenge for me to find it enjoyable."

A challenge. Just like him.

"And I knit for pretty much the same reason," I tell him quietly. "I like to listen to audiobooks while I knit. And thanks to my job, I may be a tad obsessed with finances and investing and whatnot. So there you go. I'm sorry, it's...not exciting."

"There's no need to apologize for—"

The phone rings. The screen reads "Daire."

Cavin curses and punches the screen.

"Hey. There's an incident at St. Albert's. Seamus needs you to go."

Oh no.

No. Please no.

"Fuck," Cavin mutters, already making a U-turn. "I'm sorry, I have to—"

"Don't." The word comes out sharp, panicked. "Don't take me there."

He glances at me, his brow furrowed. "What?"

"St. Albert's. I can't—" My chest tightens. I can't breathe properly. "Just take me home. Please."

I grip the door handle like I might jump out of the moving car. He pulls over to the side of the road and turns to face me fully.

"What's wrong?"

Everything. Everything is wrong.

That place. Those hallways. The lockers where they'd corner me. The classrooms where he'd laugh. The bathroom where they—

"Erin." His voice is gentle, confused. "Talk to me."

"That's where…" I can't finish. My throat closes up.

Understanding dawns across his face, followed immediately by something that looks like horror. "Christ," he breathes out. "That's where we… where I…"

"Where you tormented me," I finish in a whisper. "Where I spent every day terrified and hid in the library during lunch because it was the only place your friends wouldn't find me."

Where I learned what it felt like to be both invisible and hypervisible at the same time.

His hands grip the steering wheel so hard his knuckles go white. "Where they locked me in that bathroom," I continue, the words spilling out now. I can't stop them. "And you opened the door, and I thought for one stupid second that you were saving me. But you just stood there. And then you left. And I heard you laughing with them in the hallway while I was still shaking in the dark."

"I didn't—" He stops. Swallows hard. "Fuck. Erin, I *didn't* laugh. I swear to Christ, I didn't—"

"It doesn't matter." I wipe at my eyes angrily. "You didn't stop them. You never stopped them."

His phone rings again. Daire. Again. "I have to go," he says quietly. "Seamus needs—"

"I know." I force myself to breathe. "I know you have to go. But I can't go there. I can't walk through those halls with you like nothing happened. Like you didn't make my life hell."

He stares at me for a long moment, and something works in his jaw.

I draw in a breath and think. I don't want to cower. I don't want to hide. I need to face my fears.

"I can leave you in the car," he says quietly.

"Alright."

"For what it's worth, I'm sorry. For all of it. For what I did. For what I let happen. For making you afraid."

I don't know what to say to that. Sorry doesn't undo years of hell. But it's something, and it's what I need.

I nod. "Thank you. Let's go."

"Are you sure?"

I nod. "Aye. Just don't make me go inside."

"I won't." He gives me a curious look and drives to St. Albert's.

Chapter Sixteen

Cavin

St. Albert's looks the same as it always has—brick facade, the painted sign barely visible in the streetlight, the narrow alley beside it where we used to smoke after training. I can see lights on inside, hear raised voices, even from the car park.

I park and turn to her. She looks stunning in that dress—some emerald color that makes her skin glow, her hair done up in a way that makes me want to pull it down. "Stay here. I'll be quick."

"No." Her voice is tight. "I changed my mind. I'll... I'll come in."

"You don't have to—"

"I said I'll come in." There's that stubborn set to her jaw I'm starting to recognize. "Let's just get this over with."

Something in her tone makes my chest tight. But I nod and open my door. "Stay close to me, aye?"

Inside the school's gym, it's controlled chaos. Declan and Lorcan are holding two lads apart, both of them bloodied and still swearing at each other. There's blood on the canvas, on the ropes.

"Cavin, thank Christ," Declan says when he sees me. "This Quinn kid won't—"

But I'm not listening. I'm watching Erin.

She's frozen just inside the doorway, her eyes wide, scanning the space like she's seeing ghosts. Her chest is rising and falling too fast.

"Erin?" I move toward her, instinctively putting myself between her and the others.

She blinks, then seems to come back to herself. "I'm fine."

"You're not."

"I said I'm fine." But she's trembling.

I turn to Declan. "Give me five minutes."

"Cavin, the Quinn boy—"

"Five. Minutes."

He reads something in my face and nods, hauling the fighters toward the back office.

I guide Erin to the side, away from the ring, away from prying eyes. My hand is on her lower back, and I can feel her shaking.

And suddenly I remember.

Fuck.

A memory surfaces—her, maybe fifteen years old, coming here to meet a friend after training. And me, showing off for the lads, seventeen and stupid and cruel.

What had I said? Something about her hair being a bird's nest. Her clothes looking like her granny's. The way she stood apart from everyone else, like she thought she was too good for the rest of us. Stupid comments I never thought about again and didn't mean.

She heard them though.

I'd made the lads laugh. Made her face go red.

Made her cry.

And then there was the other time—the worst time—when she tried to tell one of the trainers that I was bullying younger kids for protection money, and I...

Christ, I'd humiliated her. Called her a snitch. Said no one would ever want her because she was too fucking perfect. That she should do everyone a favor and stay home where she belonged.

The lads had laughed and laughed. She'd run out, tears streaming down her face.

I remember feeling powerful in that moment. Like I'd won something.

Looking at her now, seeing the way she's holding herself together by sheer will, seeing her standing in this place that clearly terrifies her—

I realize what I actually won. Her hatred. Her fear. The right to make her feel small.

"Erin—" My voice comes out rough.

"It's fine." She's blinking rapidly, trying not to cry. "It was a long time ago. I'm over it."

"You're not."

"I am." But a tear escapes, tracking down her cheek, and she swipes at it angrily. "God, I'm so stupid. It doesn't even matter anymore. We were kids, and you were just—"

"Just what? Just cruel?" I catch her hand before she can turn away. "Just a bastard who made you feel like shite for no reason except that I could?"

She finally looks at me, and the pain in her eyes nearly breaks me.

"You made me feel like nothing," she whispers. "Like I was wrong. Like everything about me was wrong and everyone could see it, and I was just—just this pathetic girl who didn't know how to be normal. Who tattled to make herself feel better or bigger, when I just—I just didn't know any better. I was... a rule follower." She takes a deep breath. "I like rules. They make me feel safe."

Each word is a knife between my ribs.

"I was terrified to come here," she continues, the words spilling out now like she's been holding them in for years. "Terrified you'd see me and find some new way to—to prove I didn't belong. And you always did. Every single time." Her voice breaks. "You'd look at me like I was this, this *thing* you'd found under a rock, and you'd make sure everyone else saw it too."

"Erin..."

"And the worst part?" Tears are streaming down her face now. "The worst part is, I started to believe you. Started to think maybe you were right. Maybe I really was too weird, too different, too much and not enough all at once. Maybe I deserved it."

"*Stop.*"

The word comes out harder than I intended, but I can't listen to another second of her believing the poison I put in her head.

I cup her face in my hands, forcing her to look at me.

"I was wrong," I say roughly. "I was a cruel, stupid bastard, and I was wrong."

"Cavin—"

"No, listen to me." My thumbs brush away her tears. "Everything I said to you, everything I did—it wasn't about you. It was never about you."

"Then what was it about?" Her voice is small, broken.

I close my eyes. This is the part I've never admitted to anyone. The part I've barely admitted to myself.

"I didn't hate *you*," I say quietly. "I hated what you had that I didn't."

I can still see her, still feel the rage boiling up inside me at her self-satisfied grin, still feel the rough hand of the headmaster grabbing me by the collar before he called my father.

Her eyes widen. "What?"

"You made me so *angry*. Everything came easy to you."

"Everything?" she repeats, shaking her head. "Are you mad?"

"Everything academic." I force myself to meet her gaze. "And I'd get the belt if I didn't pull good marks, because failing at St. Albert's meant I wasn't fit for my family. Because here... this is where we were forged. Where boys became men. Where you proved you were McCarthy enough."

"Don't I know it," she whispers and looks away.

I go on. She needs to know. I'll give her the truth because, goddamn, the lass deserves it. "And you were so—you didn't care what anyone thought. You didn't try to fit in or play the games everyone else played. You just showed up as yourself, completely yourself, and I—"

I break off, but she's waiting.

"I couldn't do that," I continue, the words coming harder now. "I had to be what my family needed. What the life demanded. Hard, mean, dangerous. I had to prove myself every fucking day, prove I was tough enough, ruthless enough, that I belonged in this world."

"So you proved it by tormenting me."

"Aye." The admission tastes bitter. "You'd walk in here with your books and your quiet voice and your complete disinterest in impressing anyone, and it made me feel—"

"What?"

"Jealous." The word comes out barely above a whisper. "And ashamed. Because I wanted that freedom to just exist without performing, but I couldn't have it. So I made you pay for it."

I force myself to keep going, even though every word feels like pulling out my own teeth.

"You were brave in a way I couldn't be," I tell her. "And I hated you for it. Hated that you could be yourself when I had to be what everyone else needed me to be. So I did what a dumbass with too much testosterone and too little common sense does. Tried to make you as miserable as I was."

The silence stretches between us, heavy and suffocating.

"That's not an excuse," I add quickly. "There's no excuse for what I did. I was a coward and a bully, and you deserved none of it. But it's the truth. You were everything I wanted to be and couldn't, and I punished you for it."

Another tear slides down her cheek. I catch it with my thumb.

"I'm sorry," I say, and my voice breaks on the words. "I'm so fucking sorry, Erin. For every cruel word. Every time I made you feel small. Every time I—"

She kisses me.

It's sudden, desperate, and for a second, I'm too stunned to respond. Her hands cup my face, and her lips meet mine, silencing me.

Then my hands tighten on her face, and I'm kissing her

back, pouring every apology I don't have words for into the press of my mouth against hers.

She tastes like salty tears. Her hands fist in my shirt, and I pull her closer, carefully, like she might break or disappear if I hold too tight.

When we finally break apart, we're both breathing hard.

"I don't forgive you," she whispers against my mouth.

"I know."

"But I want to." Her eyes search mine, vulnerable and fierce all at once. "I want to believe you mean it."

"I do." I rest my forehead against hers. "I swear to you, Erin, I mean every word."

She nods slowly. "Then prove it."

I press another kiss to her forehead, then her temple, then her lips again, softer this time, a vow.

"Cavin!" Declan's voice cuts through the moment. "The Quinn boy's asking for you!"

Garrett appears behind Declan, that perpetual smirk back in place. "Jaysus, brother, you should see your face. All moony-eyed over the lass." He winks at me. "Never thought I'd see the day Cavin McCarthy went soft."

"Piss off, Garrett."

"Can't. Seamus has me running messages tonight. Speaking of—" He pulls out his phone, frowning at the screen. "Got a text from an unknown number. Probably nothing, but..." He shows it to me. It's an address, nothing else.

"Shite, that's near the docks," Declan mutters. Garrett shrugs. "Probably a wrong number. I'll delete it."

"Forward it to me first," I tell him. I pull back reluctantly. "I need to—"

"I know." She straightens, wiping her eyes. The eye makeup is smudged, but she's still so fucking beautiful, all curves and dimples and flushed pink cheeks. "Go *handle* it."

"You sure?"

She nods. "I'll wait here."

"No." I take her hand. "Come with me. I want you to see—" I stop, trying to find the words. "I want you to see me handle this right. Not like before. Not like the bastard I was."

Her eyes soften. "Okay."

Twenty minutes later, the situation's sorted. The Quinn boy's calmed down, his da's been called, and everyone's shaken hands. I handled it the way Seamus taught me—firm but fair, no ego, just problem-solving.

The whole time, Erin stood to the side, watching.

Maybe she's starting to see I'm not just the cruel boy I was. That I can be better.

That I am better... with her.

Before we leave, I pull Declan aside. "You get a chance to figure this out?" I ask quietly. I show him the one with Erin's license picture and the nasty comments.

He shakes his head. "Not yet, Cav."

I blow out a frustrated breath. "Fine, then. Work with Kyla. She's good at this. Find out the real identity of every nasty arsehole in the comments. I'm going to pay them a visit. And make bloody sure we find out who's posting these."

Declan grins. "On it."

When we're back in the car, the atmosphere's different—lighter somehow. Like something heavy has been lifted, even if just a little.

"You were good in there," she says quietly.

I glance at her. "Yeah?"

"Yeah. You could have been harsh. But you weren't."

"Trying to prove I'm not a complete bastard." I reach over and lace my fingers through hers.

She squeezes my hand. "It's working."

My chest does something warm and uncomfortable.

"So," I say, needing to lighten the mood. "About that date."

She glances at me, a small smile playing at her lips. "The one that's been thoroughly derailed?"

"Aye, that one." I grin. "What if we skip the fancy restaurant, get those comfortable clothes, and order that takeaway?"

"*Really?*"

"Really." I bring her hand to my lips, pressing a kiss to her knuckles. "You said you like simple things. Let's keep it simple."

Her smile widens, genuine this time. "Okay. Yeah. I'd like that."

"Good." I pull back onto the road. "Because I'd like to actually get to know you, Erin. The real you. Not the version I made up in my head when I was a cruel little shite. So I'm asking you, love. What do you want?"

Her cheeks flush pink, spreading down her neck. "I—" She bites her lip. "I want to be comfortable. I want to not worry about saying the wrong thing or using the wrong fork or—"

"Done." I squeeze her hand. "Let's get you some comfortable clothes. What would you wear right now if you could?"

"Besides taking off this damn bra?" she says, then immediately looks mortified. "Oh god, I shouldn't have said that."

I nearly swerve the car. My grip tightens on the wheel as blood rushes south. Christ, the image of her stripping out of that dress, reaching back to unhook—I have to shift in my seat. "Don't worry about that, lass," I manage, my voice rougher than I intended. "I'll be taking it off soon enough."

The little squeal she couldn't quite stifle sends heat straight to my cock. I want to hear what other sounds I can pull from her.

I can't help but tease her. It's so easy. "*Slowly*. With my teeth, maybe." I watch her pupils dilate.

"*Cavin.*"

"My sisters say they're torture devices anyway," I add, trying to sound casual when I'm imagining sliding the straps down her shoulders, watching that emerald fabric pool at her feet. "Among other things that need removing," I add, trying to sound casual when my blood's currently on fire.

"They are," she agrees, then sighs. She gives me a sidelong look. "And I don't want to wear these shoes anymore either, and if you make *that* sexual—"

I laugh out loud and shake my head.

"What would you wish you were wearing right now?"

"My comfy stretchy pants and a jumper," she says with a genuine smile that lights up her whole face. "The soft kind that feels like a hug."

Christ, she's going to kill me.

"Where'd you buy them?"

"Oh, I don't know," she says. "Online usually. I don't like going into stores. Too many people, too much noise."

"Wait, hold on a sec." I pull up a shopping app on my phone at a red light, then hand it to her. "Pick whatever you want. I'll have it delivered to my place within the hour."

She blinks at me. "You can do that?"

"Aye."

When I hang up, Erin's on her phone, smiling at a text. Jealousy bubbles up. Who's she chatting with now?

"That's sorted," I tell her. "What kind of takeaway would you like?"

"Oh," she says, her eyes wide. "I get to pick that too?"

"Aye. Tonight's about what you want, love."

Her smile could light up the whole of Dublin.

"I'd half kill for some chicken curry and vegetable samosas," she says with a grin.

"Me too," I say, "but only if they season it with garam masala."

She blinks at me. "You like Indian food?"

"Love it. Had a mate in prison who was from Mumbai. He'd go on about his ma's cooking for hours. Made me crave it something awful."

"Prison," she says quietly. "That's where you were. In prison."

"Aye." I glance at her, waiting for the judgment, the fear.

But she just nods, processing. "What for?"

"Aggravated assault. Put a man in the hospital who deserved it." I don't tell her I wasn't the one who did it, but I took the hit for my da.

"Oh."

That's it. Just "Oh." Like I told her I'd been on holiday.

"Does that bother you?" I ask.

"Well... yeah. 'Course it does. But it's not exactly shocking, is it?"

I reach over and squeeze her hand again. "You're something else."

She ducks her head, but I catch her smile.

And for the first time since this engagement started, I think maybe, just maybe, this could actually work.

Maybe we could actually be... happy.

The thought should terrify me.

It doesn't.

Chapter Seventeen

Erin

I CAN'T STOP LOOKING at his hands on the steering wheel.

It's ridiculous, really. They're just hands. Large, scarred knuckles, a thin white line across his left thumb that looks like an old knife wound. The way his fingers grip the leather, confident and controlled.

But all I can think about is the way those hands felt cupping my face. The gentleness of his thumbs brushing away my tears. The restraint in his touch when I know, I *know*, what those hands are capable of.

I saw him fight. Saw him destroy a man with methodical precision.

And then he touched me like I was something precious.

The contradiction is doing things to me that I don't fully understand.

"You all right over there?" His voice breaks through my thoughts, quiet and a bit amused.

I realize I've been staring. Heat floods my cheeks. "Fine. I'm fine."

"You sure? You've gone all quiet."

Because I'm imagining what it would feel like if you touched me everywhere else the way you touched my face.

I clear my throat. "Just thinking."

"About?"

You. Your hands. The way you looked at me when you apologized. The way your voice went rough when you said you'd be taking off my bra.

"Nothing important," I manage.

He glances at me, and there's something in his eyes that makes my breath catch.

"Liar," he says softly. "I'll add lying to your punishment."

My pulse kicks up. "I'm *not*."

"You're a terrible liar, Erin." His voice drops lower. "Your cheeks go pink. You bite your lip. And you won't look at me."

I force myself to meet his eyes, even though it feels dangerous. "Maybe I just don't want to tell you what I'm thinking."

"Why not?"

Because it's inappropriate. Because we're not even married yet. Because I shouldn't be thinking about the way his shirt stretched across his shoulders when he handled those fighters, or the way his voice sounds when he calls me "*love*," or what it would feel like to have his hands on my bare skin instead of just my face.

"Because," I say primly, folding my hands in my lap.

He laughs, a real laugh, rich and warm. "That's not an answer."

"It's the only one you're getting."

We pull up outside the McCarthy house, and he parks, but doesn't immediately get out. Instead, he turns to face me fully, his arm draped over the steering wheel.

"Tell me something," he says.

"What?"

"When I said I'd be taking off your bra soon enough—" His eyes are locked on mine, intense. "Did that scare you?"

My mouth goes dry. "No."

"No?" He leans slightly closer. "Then what did it do?"

I should look away… should deflect. Should do literally anything except tell him the truth. I start mentally counting in my head, but pull myself back to the present. I *want* to answer him.

"It made me wonder when," I whisper.

The air between us goes electric.

His eyes darken, his jaw tightens. I watch his Adam's apple bob as he swallows hard.

"Erin," he says, and my name sounds like a warning.

"Yes?"

"We're sitting in a car outside my family's house, and if you keep looking at me like that, I'm going to—" He cuts himself off and closes his eyes. "*Christ.*"

"You asked! And you're going to... what?" My heart's pounding so hard I can hear it.

When he opens his eyes again, the look in them makes my stomach flip.

"I'm going to forget that you deserve to be courted properly. That this is your first date. That I promised myself I'd take things slow with you." His voice is rough, strained. "That I've been raised to be a gentleman. I'm going to reach over there and—"

"And what?"

He makes a sound low in his throat. "You're killing me, lass."

"I'm just asking questions."

"You're playing with fire." He shifts in his seat, and I notice his knuckles are white where he's gripping the steering wheel again. "And you don't even know it."

"Maybe I *do* know it."

His head snaps toward me. "What?"

I'm not sure where this bravery is coming from. Maybe it's the way he apologized. Maybe it's seeing him be gentle and fierce all at once. Maybe it's just that I'm tired of being afraid.

"Maybe I know exactly what I'm doing," I say, and I'm shocked by how steady my voice sounds.

For a long moment, he just stares at me. Then he reaches over, so slowly I could stop him if I wanted, and cups my jaw with one hand.

And the buzzing in my head comes to a full, delicious *stop.* My eyelids flutter closed as he whispers, "You have no idea what you're asking for," he murmurs, his thumb tracing my lower lip.

I look up at him and swallow hard. "Then *tell* me."

His eyes drop to my mouth. "I want to kiss you properly. Not because you're upset or because I'm apologizing. I want to kiss you because I can't stop thinking about it. About *you.*"

My breath hitches. "So do it."

"If I start—" His thumb stills. "If I start, I won't want to stop at just kissing."

"Good."

"*Erin.*"

"I'm not a child, Cavin. I know what I want. And we're going to be married."

His hand slides around to the back of my neck, his fingers tangling gently in my hair. "You seemed scared back at St. Albert's. Now you're looking at me like you want me to ruin you."

The words should shock me, should make me pull back. Instead, they send heat pooling low in my belly.

. . .

"Maybe I do," I whisper.

He makes that sound again—half groan, half growl. "You're going to be the death of me."

"Is that a yes or a no?"

Instead of answering, he pulls me toward him. The center console is between us, awkward and in the way, but I don't care because his mouth is on mine.

This kiss is nothing like the one at the school.

That one was apology, desperation, promise.

This one is *hunger*. This one is *heat*.

His lips are firm, demanding, and when I gasp against his mouth, he takes advantage, deepening the kiss. His hand tightens in my hair.

My hands find his shirt, fisting in the fabric, pulling him closer, even though we can't get much closer with the stupid console between us.

He pulls back just enough to mutter, "Fuck this," before opening his door.

Before I can process what's happening, he's around to my side, pulling open my door and reaching for me.

"Come here," he says, and it's not a request.

I let him pull me out of the car, and then my back is against the side of it, and he's crowding into my space, one hand on the car beside my head, the other still tangled in my hair.

"This," he says roughly, his forehead against mine, "is what happens when you look at me like that."

"Like what?"

"Like you trust me. Like you want me. Like you're not afraid of what I am, and marrying me isn't the worst."

"I'm not afraid, and that's still to be determined."

He chuckles, but his mouth is on mine again, and any response I might have had dissolves.

He kisses like he fights—with precision, control, and devastating effectiveness. His teeth catch my lower lip, and I make a sound I've never made before, something between a gasp and a whimper.

He pulls back immediately. "Did I hurt you?"

"No." I grab his shirt and pull him back. "Don't stop. *Please* don't stop."

The please does something to him. I feel it in the way his body goes taut, the way his breathing gets rougher.

"You're going to kill me," he mutters against my mouth. "Absolutely fucking kill me."

His hand slides from my hair down my neck, my shoulder, coming to rest on my waist. Even through the fabric of my dress, I can feel the heat of his palm, the slight pressure of his fingers.

I want those hands everywhere.

The thought should embarrass me. Instead, it makes me arch into him, pressing closer.

He groans. "We need to stop."

"Why?"

"Because we're in a driveway. Because if we don't stop now, I'm going to forget every good intention I have." He pulls back enough to look at me, and his eyes are nearly black with desire. "I'll put you in the back of this car and make you come apart until you can't remember your own name."

The image that creates—his hands, his mouth, the leather seats—makes my knees actually weak. My pulse flutters.

"And that would be bad because...?" My voice comes out breathy, barely recognizable.

He laughs, but it sounds pained. "Because you deserve better than a quick fuck in a car, lass. We may have met when we were teens, but we don't have to act like them."

Now I'm the one giggling through my disappointment.

"You deserve..." He cups my face again, gentle despite the hunger in his eyes. "You deserve everything. Slow, sweet, proper. Not me losing control like some teenager."

"What if I don't want slow and sweet?"

His eyes close. "*Jesus, Mary, and Joseph.* You really are trying to kill me."

"I'm being honest."

"I know." He opens his eyes. "And that's exactly the problem. Because when you're honest like that, when you look at me like you're looking at me right now, all I want to do is give you everything you're asking for."

"So give it to me."

"Not tonight." His thumb brushes across my cheek. "Tonight, we're going to get you into comfortable clothes, eat some curry, and I'm going to learn everything about you that I should have learned years ago, instead of being a cruel bastard."

"And then?"

"And then, when the time's right, I'm going to make good on every single thing I've promised you tonight."

I shiver.

"Cold?" he asks.

"No."

"Then why are you trembling?"

Because you're looking at me like you want to devour me. Because I can still feel where your hands were. Because I've never wanted anything as much as I want you right now, and I don't know what to do with that.

"Just excited," I manage. "About the curry."

He laughs, and the tension breaks just enough. "About the curry. Right."

But he doesn't move away. His hand stays on my face, his body still close enough that I can feel the heat of him.

"For the record," he says quietly, "I've never wanted anyone the way I want you right now."

My breath catches. "Really?"

"Really." He leans in, presses one more soft kiss to my lips. "And that terrifies me almost as much as it excites me."

"Why does it terrify you?"

"Because wanting someone this much gives them power over you. And in my world, that's dangerous."

I reach up, covering his hand with mine. "I won't hurt you." I don't want to. Only cruel people desire pain for others, and I'm not cruel.

My phone buzzes with a text, loud and insistent. I watch his eyes flick to it then back to me again.

"It's nothing," I whisper. If I tell him it's Bridget, he might start to ask questions. And if he knows something's wrong...

Something shifts in his expression, leaning into vulnerability I've never seen before.

He nods slowly, then steps back, breaking the contact between us.

The loss of his warmth makes me want to pull him back.

"Come on," he says, his voice still rough. "Let's get those clothes before I change my mind about being good."

He offers me his hand, and I take it, letting him lead me toward the house.

But I can still feel the imprint of his body against mine. Can still taste him on my lips.

And I absolutely *know* that this is just the beginning.

Whatever's building between us isn't going to stay controlled for long.

And I can't wait for it to break.

Chapter Eighteen

Cavin

IT'S BEEN two days since that kiss, and I've replayed it in my head approximately eight thousand times. The soft sounds she made. The way she grabbed my shirt like she needed something to hold onto.

I'm sitting in my office at The Craic, supposedly reviewing the quarterly reports, but the numbers blur together. All I can see is her face, flushed and wanting, telling me she knows exactly what she's doing.

All I can think about is having her alone in here, with me.

Christ, my focus is all over the place.

My phone buzzes. A text from her guard—the one I assigned to shadow her during the day.

Sir, Miss Kavanagh is at the bookshop on Grafton Street. She's been here forty minutes. Should I be concerned about the duration?

I type back quickly:

No. She likes books. Let her browse.

Then I add:

But keep eyes on her. Report anyone who approaches.

Because that's not obsessive at all, McCarthy.

There's a knock at my door.

"Come in."

Declan enters, followed by Daire. They both look like they've been up to something, wearing matching grins that spell trouble.

"What?" I ask, not looking up from the reports I'm pretending to read.

"Heard you've been texting your betrothed approximately ninety times a day," Declan says, dropping into the chair across from me. "Very romantic, that."

"Piss off."

"And that you had her guards file hourly reports on her whereabouts," Daire adds, leaning against the doorframe. "Very normal behavior."

"It's for her safety."

"Right." Declan grins. "Safety. Not because you're completely gone on the lass."

I flip him off, which only makes him laugh.

"So when's the wedding again?" Daire asks.

"Five weeks."

"And you're already this whipped? Jesus, Cavin. What are you going to be like after you marry her?"

"Shut it."

But they're not wrong. I *am* whipped. Completely fucking whipped for a woman who, not long ago, blocked my number and looked at me like I was something she'd scraped off her shoe.

My phone buzzes again. This time it's Erin.

> **Erin**
> Just bought nine books. Don't judge me.

I smile, despite myself, and type back.

> What kind? Are there pictures?

> **Erin**
> Ha! No. Mystery. Puzzle-based ones. I like solving them before the detective does.

> Of course you do.

> **Erin**
> What's that supposed to mean??

Means you can't resist a challenge, lass. Including me.

Three dots appear, disappear, then appear again. Finally:

Erin
You're not a challenge. I can read you like a book. Get it?

I actually laugh out loud.

That must mean you like me.

Erin
I tolerate you.

You kissed me.

Erin
That was a moment of weakness.

I'm ignoring you now.

No you're not. You can't. You're gone on me.

Erin
Mm. Aye. Perhaps.

Then stop texting back.

I don't want her to though.

Another long pause. Then:

I'm still grinning when I look up and realize they're both staring at me like I've grown a second head.

"What?" I ask.

"You're smiling at your phone like a feckin' eejit," Declan says. "Never thought I'd see the day."

"Oh piss off."

"No, seriously." He leans forward, genuinely curious now. "What's she like? The real her, not the version from school."

I consider not answering. But they're my family, and if I can't talk to them about this, who can I talk to?

"She's..." I search for the right words. "Brilliant. Funny when she's not overthinking. Honest to a fault. She knits, for fuck's sake. Sits there with these intricate patterns and makes jumpers while listening to audiobooks."

"That's kind of adorable," Daire says.

"It is, isn't it?" I realize I'm smiling again and force my face into neutrality. "She's also stubborn as hell. Doesn't back down when she thinks she's right. And she's terrified of crowds, but she went into The Craic anyway because her sister wanted to."

"Sounds like you're actually into her," Declan observes.

I grunt and rub my chin. "Suppose I am."

"Good." He stands, then claps me on the shoulder. "You deserve someone good, Cav. Someone who's not in this life by choice. Someone who can remind you there's more to the world than blood and business."

After they leave, I try to focus on work, I really do.

But my mind keeps drifting back to her. The way she smelled—something floral and clean. I bet it's just her soap. She isn't the perfume or body-spray type.

The way she fit against me in that driveway. The way she looked at me when I apologized at St. Albert's, like she was seeing me for the first time.

There's another knock at my door. Ashland, looking uncomfortable.

"What?" I ask.

"Need to talk to you about something." He closes the door behind him, which immediately puts me on edge. Ashland doesn't do private conversations unless it's serious.

"Spit it out."

He shifts his weight. "Look, I don't like being the bearer of bad news, but I heard something at the club last night. About your girl."

My blood goes cold. "What about her?"

"Couple of drunk eejits talking shite, probably nothing—"

"*Ashland.* What did they say?"

He meets my eyes. "They said she's been seen around town with some lad. Someone who's not you. They were... laughing about it. Saying things."

"What things?"

"The usual bollocks. That maybe she's not as innocent as she seems." He stops, clearly uncomfortable.

I'm out of my chair so fast it nearly tips over. "Who said this?"

"I don't know. Bar talk. I shut it down, told them they were full of shite. But, Cavin..." He pauses. "I thought you should know. In case there's truth to it."

"There's not."

"But you don't really know her, do you? I mean, you knew her in school, but that was years ago. People change. And she's been forced into this marriage. Maybe she's got someone she actually wanted, someone—"

"Get out."

"Cavin—"

"I said *get out*."

It's not true. It *can't* be true.

She told me she'd never had a boyfriend. That her first date was with me.

I remember those men at the club, the ones who attacked me. One of them said something before I broke his jaw. Something about her being a whore, about her spreading her legs for half of—

I'd shut him up before he could finish. Assumed it was just an attempt to get under my skin, to make me lose focus.

They knew it would get to me. There's nothing more to it.

I pull up my messages with Erin and stare at our conversation from earlier. Her telling me about the books. Me being smug. Her saying I was a catastrophe.

It felt real.

What if every smile, every kiss, every moment in that driveway was just her playing the part she's been forced to play?

No.

I shake my head, trying to clear my thoughts.

This is absurd. Erin doesn't lie. She can't. The lass is too honest for her own good. Hell, that's what I like about her.

But people lie when they have to, don't they? When they're trapped.

And she's definitely trapped. Fuck, she didn't even know she was getting married to me until a few weeks ago.

I call my guard. "Where is she right now?"

"Still at the bookshop, sir."

"Alone?"

A pause. "Yes, sir. Alone."

"Has anyone approached her? Talked to her?"

"Just the shop clerk. Why? Is something wrong?"

"No. Nothing. Keep watching."

I hang up and sit back in my chair, my mind racing. This is stupid. I'm being mental.

By the time my phone rings again, I'm wound so tight I nearly break the damn thing answering it.

"What?"

"Christ, who pissed in your cornflakes?" Declan. "I'm just calling to see if you want to grab dinner tonight."

"Can't. I have plans."

"With Erin?"

"No. She's... busy."

"Busy?" He sounds suspicious. "Doing what?"

"I don't know. Reading. Whatever she does."

"And you're okay with that? Not joining her?"

"She didn't invite me."

"So invite yourself. You're engaged, not strangers."

"Maybe she wants space."

"Or maybe you're being an eejit." He sighs. "What's going on, Cavin? You sound off, mate."

I want to tell him. Want to ask if I'm being irrational, if the doubts eating at me are justified or just my own damage manifesting.

"Nothing. I'm fine."

"You're a shite liar."

"Runs in the family."

He's quiet for a moment. "You know what? Forget dinner. Come to the gym. Beat the fuck out of a bag or something.

You need to work off whatever this is before you do something stupid."

How does he always know?

"I'll think about it."

"Don't think. Just come. Seven o'clock."

He hangs up before I can argue.

I sit there, staring at my phone, at the last message from Erin about the books and the challenges.

Am I just so damaged, so convinced that good things don't happen to men like me, that I'm inventing problems where there aren't any?

The next day, I want to see her.

I get an idea, so I send her a text on a whim.

> Need you in the garden? The wee sprites are running wild on me.

And her responding text that came shortly thereafter:

> **Erin**
> Can't you just sort them like you did the lads at St. Albert's?

And I can almost *see* that cute little smirk she gets when she's being cheeky.

Cheeky little thing. Those lads had it
coming. Your plants are innocent, mostly.
Now shift your arse,

Erin
Lucky for you it's good timing, Mam's on
the rampage today and I need to get out of
the line of fire. See you half past?

I'm as nervous as a fuckin' schoolboy, and it takes me off guard. I haven't been this nervous since I *was* a fuckin' schoolboy.

I'm leaning against the fence when she arrives, right on time. Course she is. The lass probably color-codes her fucking calendar.

Why's that so goddamn adorable?

She's wearing leggings today and a jumper that's too big for her. Why do I want to see her in *my* jumper?

Her hair's pulled back in a plait, and she's got her arms wrapped round herself, like she's bracing for impact.

And Christ, she's a fucking sight for sore eyes, this unbe-guiling woman. Part of me is half glad I didn't know the real Erin in school. I needed to grow the fuck up before I could meet her match.

"You came," I say.

"You told me to." She stops a few feet away, her head cocked to the side. The garden beds and vines, the stone path. Cata-loging everything. "This is where you keep the sprites? And what's the story with them?" Her eyes twinkle at me.

"Aye. Your wee sprites and fae. They're taking over the whole garden. Come on." I push off the fence and gesture toward the wildest section, where the plants have gone mental. "Let me show you what your magical friends have been up to."

"I'm surprised. You've got siblings and cousins younger than you, and you let a few wayward sprites get to you?"

"Aye. After I texted, I sent the lot of them to time-out in the shed."

She smirks. "Did you, now? Or did you use their misbehavior to get my attention, Cavin?"

I shrug. "Might've done."

Her gaze finally lands on me. "You wanted to talk."

I push off the fence and gesture toward the barn. "Let's walk."

She hesitates, then follows. Inside, the smell of hay and horse and leather fills the space. It's quiet here. Bronwyn's a horse lover, and Da liked to put the barn on the property to good use.

"Horses," she breathes out. "You have horses."

"Aye. They're Bronwyn's."

Here, it's peaceful... almost. I lead her past the stalls— Midnight, Banshee, Finn—until we reach the tack room in the back.

I grab two stools, then set them facing each other. "Sit." When she quirks a brow at me, I tack on a "Please."

She does, perching on the edge like she might bolt. Her hands rest on her knees, fingers tapping. One, two, three, four. Over and over.

"You do that a lot," I say, nodding at her hands.

She stills them immediately, clasping them together. "Do what?" Her pretty cheeks flush pink.

"The tapping. Counting."

Her jaw tightens. "It helps me think."

"Helps you think, or helps you cope?"

Her eyes narrow, but her voice drops. "What's the difference?"

"One's about problem-solving. The other's about surviving." I lean back, arms crossed. "Which is it?"

She doesn't answer right away. Just stares at me, weighing whether I'm taking the piss or if I actually give a fuck.

"Both," she says finally. "It's both."

Fair enough.

"Look," I say, "we're doing this thing. Getting married. And I know you didn't sign up for it willingly, but neither did I, so we're even there."

"Even." She repeats the word like she's testing it. "You think this is even."

"No. But I think we're both stuck, and we can either make it hell or we can try not to kill each other. Your choice."

She considers this, her head tilting slightly. "You're surprisingly pragmatic for someone who locked me in a bathroom."

Jesus Christ. Straight for the throat.

Are her eyes dancin' a bit?

"Erin, *I* didn't lock you in," I say, keeping my voice level. "The lads did."

She holds my gaze for a moment. "But you were there."

"Aye."

"And you didn't stop them."

I shake my head. "I didn't."

She nods once, like I've just confirmed something she already knew. "At least you're honest about it."

"Would lyin' make you feel better?"

"No." Her fingers start tapping again. "But an apology might. It felt... good when you apologized at St. Albert's."

I exhale slowly, scrubbing a hand over my jaw. "I'm sorry. For that, and for every other shite thing I did to you back then. I'm sorry, Erin. You didn't deserve it."

She blinks—once, twice—like she's processing.

"Okay," she says.

"Okay?"

"Yes. Okay. You apologized. And this time, I... I accept." She shifts on the stool. "Can we move on now?"

Christ, she's a different sort.

"Right. Moving on." I lean forward, elbows on my knees. "Figured we needed some time, just the two of us, without crowds or family pressin' in. And every time we're together, we've got a damn audience, so..." I rub a hand across the back of my neck. "Now that the sprites and fae are momentarily quiet..."

Her lips twitch, and she nods. "You want to get to know each other a bit more? Cavin McCarthy, if I didn't know any better, I'd think that was downright *civilized*."

I snort. "Let's not get carried away. I do have a reputation to keep."

She smiles softly. "So I can ask questions?"

"Aye."

"Are there... limits to the questions?" Her brow rises.

"You can ask anything you want. I'll tell you as much as I'm able."

Nodding, she leans back a bit. "That's fair. Alright." She studies me for a long moment. I could get lost in those earthy brown eyes and be happy for it. "Can you tell me more about why you were in prison?"

Of course that's her first question. Likely been holdin' back.

"Assault. But it... wasn't me. It was my da. But I took the hit. At the time, he was acting head." I sigh. "And it would've killed Mam. He nearly killed a man."

"Nearly." Her tone is clinical, detached. "Not quite."

"No. Not quite."

She blinks. "Why?"

"Bloke hurt my sister, Bronwyn. Not the kidnapping—this was before that. He... touched her. At a party."

Erin's expression doesn't change, but her fingers stop tapping. "And your da found out."

"Aye. Beat him bloody. Broke his jaw, three ribs, and fractured his skull. Would've kept going if Seamus and I hadn't intervened. When the police arrived, I was the one standing over him. And that was on purpose."

She blinks. "How long were you in?"

"Six months. Got out early for good behavior." I snort. "Barely."

She nods, filing the information away like she's adding it to a spreadsheet in her mind. "Your brother Torin. He's in prison too?"

"Aye. He's got time to serve, still."

"I'm sorry," she says. And the thing is, she sounds like she means it. Not performative. Just... factual.

We sit in silence for a moment, the only sound the soft snorting of horses in their stalls.

"Your cousins," she says eventually. "And your uncles. Tell me about them."

I settle back, glad for the change in subject.

"Ashland's older than me. Uncle Nolan's son. He's..." I search for the words. "Dangerous. Quiet about it though. You'd never know unless you saw him work. He's Seamus's enforcer. When someone needs to disappear, Ashland handles it."

"Disappear as in leave town, or disappear as in die?"

"Both, depending."

She nods like I've just told her he's an accountant.

"And Lorcan?"

"Uncle Nolan's boy, Ashland and Donovan's brother. He was at the dinner? Built like a tank. Does security, mostly. Studied engineering at Trinity before he dropped out to work for the family."

"Why did he drop out?"

"His da got shot. Nearly died. Lorcan came home to help run things with Donovan while Nolan recovered."

"That's loyal."

"That's family."

She absorbs this, filing it away. "And your uncles? Cormac and Nolan?"

"Aye. Da's younger brothers. Once ran the clan, but they're older now, with families of their own, so they don't hold the weight in the clan they once did, and now their sons are of age. Still, they're well respected and hold heavy clout in Bally-hock. You don't fuck with the McCarthys because of them."

"And your father?"

"Head of the family. Was, anyway, until he handed it to Seamus. He retired after the... incident." The one that sent me and Torin to prison. "But he's still the most dangerous man in Ireland when he wants to be."

Erin's quiet for a moment, processing. Then, "Your family operates in a clear hierarchical structure. Patriarchal, mili-taristic. Roles are defined by skill set and reinforced through loyalty and violence." She gives me a curious glance. "And your family's... prolific, one could say."

I smile. The lass is bloody brilliant, if a bit quirky.

"You writin' an essay, lass? That's one way to put it."

"It's the most accurate way." She tilts her head. "My family is different."

"How so?"

"We're more... distributed. Less hierarchical. My father's the head, technically, but my mother controls the money, the alliances, the social networks. My father handles the violent side—the enforcement, the intimidation. But he doesn't make decisions without her."

"A partnership, then."

"No. A codependency." Her voice is flat, clinical. "He needs her intelligence. She needs his brutality. Together, they're formidable. Apart, they'd crumble."

"And where do you fit?"

"I don't." She says it simply, without self-pity. "I'm useful, but not valued. I manage the books because I'm good at it and because no one else wants to. But I'm not part of the inner circle. I never have been."

"And your sister? Bridget?"

Her expression shifts—just barely, but I catch it. Pain, there and gone.

"Mam doesn't like to talk about it, but it's useless hiding it. Bridget's sick right now."

She twists her hair as if she's uncomfortable. It takes me by surprise. Sometimes, she seems so poised and detached. Then others...

"I'm sorry."

"It isn't your fault."

I smile. "I know."

I study her for a long moment. The way she holds herself—rigid, controlled. The way her mind works—data and patterns and brutal honesty. She's not like anyone I've ever met.

"You really don't care what people think of you, do you?" I ask.

She shifts and sighs, tucking a stray strand of hair out of her face, back into the plait that's come loose. "I care. I just can't change how my brain works, so I stopped trying." She shrugs. "People think I'm rude, or cold, or strange. Maybe I am. But I'm also right most of the time, and I'd rather be right than be liked."

God, I fuckin' love that. She tilts her head to the side.

"You're not what I expected," she says suddenly.

"Aye? How so?"

"You're not..." She pauses, searching. "You're not performing. Most people perform. They say what they think you want to hear, or what makes them look good. You don't do that."

"Neither do you."

"No. I don't." She almost smiles. Almost. "Sort of a pair, then? Maybe that's why this... might work."

"This being...?"

"The marriage. The arrangement. Whatever this is." She stands, brushing hay off her leggings. "I should go. I have work."

"Erin."

She stops, then turns back.

"For what it's worth," I say, "I'll try not to make this hell for you."

She considers this, her head tilting again. "That's surprisingly kind."

I smirk. "Don't get used to it."

"I won't." She heads for the door, then pauses. "Cavin?"

"Aye?"

"Thank you. I'm putting this behind us. I'm... not the girl I was in school anymore, and... you're not who you were either."

I reach for her. I don't want her to go.

"Stay." The word comes out rougher than I meant. Her eyes flick to where my fingers wrap around her wrist, then back to my face.

"Why?"

"Because I'm not done with you yet."

Her breath catches... just barely, but I hear it.

"Cavin—"

I pull her closer, slow enough she could pull away if she wanted. She doesn't. "Your plait's loose. Let me... fix it."

"Is it?" she says with a soft smile, patting her hair. "You know how to plait hair?"

"I've two sisters, don't I?"

She nods, a little flushed. And then she turns around and stands primly in front of me. With an arm wrapped around her waist, I tug her onto my lap. She giggles, actually giggles, and a surge of something like pride swells through my chest.

I made Erin Kavanagh giggle.

I loosen her hair and let it tumble over her shoulders. I can't help myself. I brush it off her neck, bend, and kiss her just there. She lets out a half sigh, half moan and leans further back against me.

I run my fingers through her hair. It's soft and fragrant and a little damp, like she tossed it up after a shower. I exhale. Touching her like this loosens something in my chest.

I move her hair further and kiss her neck again. When she sighs and leans back into me, I turn her around, tip her head back, and kiss along the column of her neck to her collarbone.

Her eyes flutter closed.

"Tell me to stop."

"You're not going to," she whispers.

"Not unless you tell me to."

Her hand comes up, fingers grazing the scar along my jaw. Tentative. Testing. "I don't want you to stop."

That's all I need.

I pull her closer to me, one hand sliding into her hair, the other gripping her hip as she straddles me. Her lips part in surprise, and I take full advantage, kissing her hard— claiming her mouth like I've wanted to since she walked into this garden, looking soft and rumpled in that oversized jumper.

She makes a sound in the back of her throat, and Christ, it goes straight through me.

For a second, she's frozen. Then her hands fist in my shirt, pulling me closer, and she's kissing me back like she's been thinking about this too. Like she's been holding back just as much as I have.

I lift her jumper and slide my palm higher up, over the soft swell of her belly. She gasps against my mouth. I take advantage, deepening the kiss, tasting her. Her nails dig into my shoulders through the fabric of my shirt, anchoring herself.

"Cavin," she breathes out when I break away to kiss along her jaw, down the side of her neck. Her head tips back, giving me access, and fuck me, the trust in that gesture alone nearly undoes me.

"Say it again," I murmur against her throat.

"Cavin." It's barely a whisper this time, and I feel it more than hear it.

My second hand slides under the hem of her jumper, fingers splaying across the bare skin of her waist. She's soft there, warm. She shivers under my touch, and I grin against her neck.

"Cold?"

"No." Her voice is breathless. "Definitely not cold."

I pull back just enough to look at her—flushed cheeks, kiss-swollen lips, eyes dark and dilated. She looks thoroughly ravaged, and we've barely started.

"Thought you were a good girl," I whisper.

"Only for you."

She pulls me back down, kissing me again—slower this time, exploring. Her tongue traces my bottom lip, and I groan. My hand slides higher under her jumper, my thumb brushing the underside of her ribs, and she arches into the touch.

Christ, I could do this all day. Just kiss her. Touch her. Learn every sound she makes, every curve of her body, every secret place that makes her melt.

But then she pulls back, breathing hard, resting her forehead against mine. "Cavin..."

"What?"

"I really do have work."

I close my eyes, trying to get my breathing under control. "Right. Work."

"And I..."

"We should wait," I whisper. "Wait to go further."

Why does the wedding that seemed too fuckin' close suddenly feel like it's years away?

She nods against me, but her fingers are still twisted in my shirt. Neither of us moves.

"You're making it very hard to be good," she says finally.

"That's rich, coming from you." I press one more kiss to her temple and set her on her feet, forcing myself to step back. "You taste like honey."

She blinks up at me, lips still swollen, cheeks flushed. "I had honey on toast."

"Course you did." I can't help smiling. I brush a thumb across her bottom lip, and she shivers. "Come on, then. Before I change my mind about being honorable."

"Honorable?" She raises an eyebrow as I take her hand, leading her toward the gate. "Is that what we're calling it?"

"Would you prefer 'desperate'? Because that's the other option."

She laughs—actually laughs—and the sound does something dangerous to my chest. "I'll bring you home," I say, lacing my fingers through hers. "But you're sitting close in the truck."

"How close?"

"Close enough I can still smell honey."

She ducks her head, but I catch the smile. "You're flirting, Cavin McCarthy."

"Aye." I open the gate for her, then pull her against my side as we walk. "But you like it."

"Aye," she murmurs, leaning into me. "I really do."

Chapter Nineteen

Erin

"Alright," my mother says, clapping her hands like she's trying to get a classroom of unruly children to attention, even though it's literally just me and my father, dressed once again in formal, torturous clothing. "We need to go."

"Yes, I know," I tell her.

I wish that Bridget could come, but even if she were feeling better, I don't think my mom would allow it. She'd come up with some excuse. She's in her room, for now anyway, and the night nurse is here—a woman who's grumpy and irritable and doesn't crack a smile from the minute she arrives to the minute she leaves.

Lovely.

I wish I could stay. I wish I could take care of Bridget, though the truth is getting harder to ignore—she's getting worse. The bruises that used to fade in days now linger for weeks. The nosebleeds are more frequent. And last night, when I helped her to the bathroom, there was blood in places there shouldn't be. She tried to hide it from me, but I saw.

The scent of antiseptic makes my stomach turn, and my heart somersaults in my chest anytime there's blood, but I want to take care of her. And in some strange way, by being here, by going through with all of this, I am.

I wish that the second envelope Bronwyn slipped me last night could buy something that would make my sister happy. Something that would make her better.

And I wish I knew why my future husband doesn't want me to know he's sending me his winnings.

Why did he go again? I want to know the next time. I want to see him again.

"Remember," my mother says, prepping me for the McCarthy engagement party. "Everyone is your enemy, but treat them all as your friends." She begins her lecture. "Smile. Put your hand out. Shake their hand. Make sure that you—"

"Mam!" I tell her, my voice stern. "I know what my role is. Smile. Hold on to Cavin McCarthy's arm, pretend I like him, and act like I don't hate being there. I get it."

Is it really pretend, though, now?

The McCarthy estate is lit up like a castle, every window blazing. Cars line the circular driveway—expensive ones that purr like kittens and glint under a full moon.

My stomach twists.

Inside, Keenan's holding court with a few other men in the massive entryway, with Caitlin beside him in an elegant silvery gown that drapes to the floor.

"Ah, the Kavanaghs," Keenan says, voice booming like he's greeting old. "Come in, come in."

Caitlin's smile is warm and genuine, and it puts me a little at ease.

Keenan gestures to the man on his right, a bit younger than he is, with silver threading through sandy-blond hair, his suit immaculate. There's something calculating but likable in his eyes, sharper than Keenan's blunt force.

"My brother Nolan," Keenan says. "And this old man here is Cormac."

I remember to laugh, but too late, and I finish awkwardly. But thankfully, they don't seem to notice.

Cormac's got a scar cutting through his eyebrow and hands that look like they've broken more bones than a butcher's cleaver. He smiles, though, and it feels genuine.

Note to self: Stay on their *good* side.

"So this is the Kavanagh girl," Nolan says, his voice smooth as expensive whiskey. "I've heard so much about you, Erin. Welcome."

My mother's grip tightens on her clutch. I want to tell her to relax—I'm sure they're not talking about which fork I used at dinner.

I meet Cormac's stare and don't look away.

"Pleased to meet you," I say, congratulating myself on remembering.

It's hard to keep tabs on everyone, but thankfully, I have a veritable spreadsheet in my mind, with people lined up like little wooden pegs on a board.

Cormac —-Da to Declan and Colm

Nolan—Da to Ashland, Lorcan, and Donovan

Those are the ones I've met, anyway.

"Oh my gosh! Erin, is that you?"

I turn and look toward the voice to find a stunningly beautiful woman in stilettos, wearing all black and clutching a silver sequined handbag. She waves her hand.

"Erin, you don't remember me? Naomi? You sat next to me in biology?" She says it as if that's supposed to trigger a memory.

I remember lots of things, but I forget people quickly. Sadly, it's because I find most people forgettable.

"Sorry, I don't," I say.

"Look at you!" she says, eyeing me up and down. "You've had quite the glow-up, huh? Come here." She gestures for me to lean forward.

My stomach clenches into a tight ball.

"But you have a little..." She reaches out and brushes her thumb across my face.

Everything in me recoils. I don't like people I know touching me, never mind strangers.

"You just had a little smear of makeup on you. But you look beautiful. And lucky you," she says, winking at me. "Cavin McCarthy? Wonder what kind of strings you had to pull for that, huh?"

Then she laughs and leaves.

And I'm reeling. I knew some of my cousins would be here, the ones I know and the ones I don't. I knew my uncles and aunts and all the power players in my father's family, like Darragh and his mates, would be here too. So why did it not occur to me that the people from St. Albert's were going to be here? My tormentors. The people I hated. *Of course* they are. It was a finishing school for families just like us.

And then I hear a warm voice behind me. "You *do* look gorgeous, love."

I turn to see Cavin and breathe out a sigh of relief. I reach for his arm to steady me and swallow hard. "Thank you," I say with a little bow.

Cameras flash. A photographer, a tall, lanky lad of about twenty, stands blinking. There's something familiar about his profile when he turns, like I've seen him somewhere before. But half of Ballyhock probably looks familiar at this point.

"Put that away," Cavin snarls.

"Your mother told me—"

"And I told you to put it away," he says. "Do not take pictures of my fiancée without permission."

"Yes, sir. Yes, sir." The nervous photographer nods quickly.

Before he can say anything else, one of the cousins I remember from our first dinner approaches. He claps Cavin on the shoulder, firm enough that it's not entirely friendly and smiles. Ah, yes. I remember that smile. Ashland and Lorcan's older brother, Donovan.

"Ah, ease up there, cuz," he says, his voice low and steady. "Lad's just doing his job, yeah? Your ma hired him special for tonight."

"Fuck off, Donovan." Cavin's jaw tics, but he doesn't shake off Donovan's hand.

Donovan only chuckles.

The photographer shifts his weight, looking between them nervously. Then he glances at me, manages a shaky smile. "May I take your picture, miss?" he asks. Polite. Deferential. "Just yourself, like. For the family album?"

I look at Cavin, who's still glaring at the man like he's considering breaking his camera. Or his face. Maybe both.

He nods to me, terse. "It's up to you, Erin."

I can't remember the last time someone said that something was actually up to me.

"Um, sure," I say. "Okay."

"You too, sir?" the photographer asks cautiously.

"Fine," Cavin growls.

Donovan steps back, still watching, something unreadable in his expression. "There ye go. Everyone's happy, yeah?" He shoots Cavin a reproachful look, as if Cavin's being unreasonable. "No need to terrorize the help on your engagement night." He winks at me. He's as charming as his brother Ashland's terrifying.

I giggle and shake my head. Cavin looks at me for an explanation, as if I could possibly explain that I'm wondering why a professional photographer asking to do his literal job has him this wound up.

"You alright?" I ask quietly.

"Grand," he mutters.

He comes up next to me, taller than I am, even with my heels on. Broad. And he smells so good as he casually wraps his arm around my shoulder, takes my hand in his, and we pose... like a couple in love. And it feels almost natural.

"Smile, Erin," he whispers in my ear.

I smile. I wonder if it looks fake.

"Why did I say yes? And how many times do we have to do this?" I whisper to him.

"Oh, about a thousand," he says, and then he chuckles.

And I remember the way his voice felt in my ear. I remember the way it felt being pressed up against the wall. I remember... *all* of it.

"Come, let's get you a drink," he says, then winks at me. My stomach flips again. But this time, this time it feels nice.

"I know, I know. Soda water or whatever for you."

I nod. "Thank you."

"Are you hungry? Have you eaten today?" He asks me two questions at the same time. Why do people do that?

"I can't remember if I've eaten... I was all nervous, but I don't feel hungry."

"We need to get something in you," he says protectively. "Come on, let's go this way."

And somehow, miraculously, he escorts me through the throng of people into a little quiet area, right outside on the balcony, without an interruption.

I let out a breath again.

"Bet you'd give anything for some yoga pants and a jumper right now," he says. "And I'm sorry, this isn't a vegetable samosa, but my mother did order some good food."

I smile. "Is there anything *you* don't like to eat?" I ask him because I feel like if we're going to be married and we're going to be sharing space, I need to start knowing things about him.

"I'll eat literally anything," he says. "But the past few years, I've been busy traveling. You know, lots of restaurants and takeout and the like. And prison food will make you yearn for something good. I miss homemade food." He pauses when I stare. "But we can get a chef or something, I don't need—"

"I know how to cook," I tell him, nodding. "I like to cook. It's soothing. Calming. And maybe stems from a little paranoia because when you cook for yourself, you know what's going into your food."

"Yes." For him, he might wonder if someone's poisoning it or whatever. For me, it's an entirely different reason. "I respect that," he says quietly.

Of course he does.

But then something shifts in his expression. His eyes scan the crowd behind me, sharp and assessing, and his jaw tightens almost imperceptibly. It's subtle—most people probably wouldn't notice—but I do. There's a hardness there, a wariness that doesn't match the easy conversation we were just having.

"What is it?" I ask.

His gaze snaps back to me, and he forces a smile. "Nothing. Just keeping an eye out."

"For what?"

"Everyone," he says simply, but the way he says it makes my skin prickle. "Everything." Like he's expecting something, and he doesn't trust anyone here.

Before I can ask more, a crowd of younger girls eyes him with nothing short of adoration. I remember how, back in St. Albert's, the girls there would have worshipped him like he was some kind of hero.

"Put that away," one of them hisses quietly, looking nervously over her shoulder at Cavin. "He's right there."

I give him a curious look. "Are they hiding something from you? They're shite at doing it if they are."

"I don't know," he says, and there's that edge again in his voice. He stalks over, hands in his pockets. "What are we looking at over here?"

Their eyes go wide, and they step back.

"Nothing," one says.

"Hand it over." His voice brooks no argument.

Someone hands him the phone, and he scans it, his eyes quickly going dark, actually dark—like something twisted and violent just woke up inside him.

"Who the *fuck* posted that?" he growls.

Oh no. Not another one.

"Don't know. Whoever manages the St. Albert's account—"

"What is it?" I ask him. "Another stupid post? Not worth getting upset about, Cavin."

Now at the doorway, his cousin Declan walks over. "Right. Find out who the fuck is running the St. Albert's account. We need to have a word with them," Cavin growls.

"Come here, Erin."

He gestures to the girl with the phone. "Take *this* picture."

He puts his mouth to my ear, and it feels intimate and warm despite the tension radiating off him. I feel a flush creep over my cheeks.

"Smile for me, yeah?" he murmurs. "Let's show them all you're not bothered."

I do. I smile. And he turns and kisses me like I'm the only person in his world as she takes a picture of us together.

"*There,*" he says. The girl shows us the picture. "That's better, isn't it?"

It is. It's actually beautiful. Moving, even. We look... we look like we're in love.

"Post *that*," he tells Declan. "Make sure everyone sees it, and tell them Erin Kavanagh is *mine*."

"Aye."

"Well done, McCarthy." My cousin Shane approaches and shakes Cavin's hand with a hard slap to the back that seems customary for men, but makes me flinch. He smiles at me and gives me a quick hug and a peck on the cheek. "Congrats, Erin."

"Y'alright?" Cavin asks in my ear.

"Aye," I whisper, but my throat feels tight, my breathing ragged. "There are just so many *people*. Why are there so many people?"

"Aye," he says with a sigh. "McCarthys plus Kavanaghs could field a right good football team, if we were of a mind."

That makes me smile. "We could, but the ref would have his cards out before kickoff, knowing this lot."

When we're alone again, or as alone as we can be in a crowd like this, I study him. Really look at him. The way his eyes never stop moving. The way he positions himself so that his back is never to the room. The way his hand rests on the small of my back, but his body is coiled tight, ready to move.

"You're always watching, aren't you?" I say softly.

His eyes meet mine, and for a moment, I see something raw there. Something that looks almost like fear, though I'm not sure Cavin McCarthy is capable of that emotion.

"Have to," he says simply. "It's how you stay alive."

The words send a chill through me because he's not being dramatic. He means it. He's lived in a world where one moment of inattention could mean death. Maybe he still does.

"Is that what it was like?" I ask carefully. "In prison?"

His jaw tightens, and for a second, I think he won't answer. But then he nods, just once. "Every fucking day, Erin. Every day you wake up, wondering if it's the day someone decides you're more useful dead than alive. And you learn quick that the only person you can trust is yourself."

"That sounds... lonely."

"It was." His eyes soften slightly. "But maybe it doesn't have to be anymore."

I know. I understand.

I'm lonely, too.

Before I can respond, a voice calls out. "Cavin! There you are."

We both turn to see an older man approaching, maybe in his early fifties, with graying hair and kind eyes behind wire-rimmed glasses. He's wearing an expensive suit, but there's something about the way he carries himself that seems less predatory than most of the people here. More... genuine, somehow.

"Dr. Rosenberg," Cavin says, and I hear genuine warmth in his voice. "Good to see you, mate."

My heart stops.

Dr. Rosenberg.

Oh my god. That's him. That's the doctor who could save Bridget.

And he's here. Right here.

Mam was right.

"And this must be your fiancée," Dr. Rosenberg says, extending his hand to me with a smile. "I've heard quite a bit about you, Miss Kavanagh."

I take his hand, trying not to let my shock show. "It's lovely to meet you, Dr. Rosenberg," I manage, my voice steadier than I feel. "Cavin's told me about you as well."

I'm stretching the truth, but I know who this man is. I know what he could mean for Bridget.

"Liam's one of the best doctors in the UK," Cavin says, his hand warm on my lower back. "Saved my uncle's life a few years back when no one else could figure out what was wrong with him."

"Oh, I just did my job," Dr. Rosenberg says modestly, but there's pride in his eyes. "Though I must say, it was a challenging case. Took nearly six months to get the diagnosis right."

Six months. The thought hits me like a punch to the gut, but I force myself to smile.

"Your work must be fascinating," I say, and I hear the slight tremor in my voice. "I've read about some of your research. The work you're doing with patients who have complex hematological conditions—it's really remarkable. Groundbreaking, even."

Dr. Rosenberg's eyebrows rise, and I see genuine surprise—and interest—flash across his face. I'm guessing most people don't know the details about the work he does. "You've done your homework. Most people's eyes glaze over when I start talking about blood disorders."

"I know someone," I start, then stop myself. Not here. Not now. Not in front of all these people.

But Dr. Rosenberg is watching me with those kind, intelligent eyes.

"Well," he says carefully, "if you ever want to discuss my work further, Miss Kavanagh, I'd be happy to. Cavin has my number." He glances at Cavin. "You'll pass it along?"

"Of course," Cavin says, but there's a question in his eyes when he looks at me. Have I said too much?

"Thank you," I tell Dr. Rosenberg, and I mean it more than he could possibly know. "That would be wonderful."

He gives me a warm smile, shakes Cavin's hand again, and melts back into the crowd.

The moment he's gone, Cavin turns to me. "Alright. What was that about?"

"What do you mean?"

"Erin." His voice is gentle but firm. "You looked like you'd seen a ghost when I introduced him. And that bit about reading his research? You weren't just being polite."

I swallow hard, debating how much to tell him. But he's going to be my husband. And if there's anyone who might actually be able to help me get Bridget in to see Dr. Rosenberg...

The bruising and bleeding aren't getting any better. My sister's running out of time.

We're interrupted by someone calling Cavin's name—some business associate wanting to talk about investments or politics or whatever it is these people discuss when they're not busy destroying lives.

"Mr. McCarthy!" The man is tall and barrel-chested, with a red face that suggests too much whiskey and too many rich meals. "Been wanting to catch you. Need to discuss the developments in—"

"Not now, Finnegan," Cavin says smoothly, but there's steel underneath the politeness.

"But it's important—"

"I said not now." Cavin's voice drops lower, more dangerous. "I'm with my fiancée. Whatever you need can wait until Monday."

Finnegan's face gets redder, but he backs off with a mumbled apology.

"Christ," Cavin mutters once he's gone. "This is exactly why I fucking hate these things."

"Because people want to talk business?"

"Because everyone wants something from you, and they don't care if you're in the middle of a conversation or eating dinner or taking a piss. They just want, want, want." He runs a hand through his hair, disrupting the carefully styled look. "It's exhausting."

I understand that feeling more than he knows.

"Come on," he says, taking my hand again. "Let's get you out of here for a minute."

"We just got here."

"And I'm already done with it." His mouth quirks. "Perks of being the groom—I can leave whenever the fuck I want."

He's lying, of course. We both know we can't actually leave, but I appreciate the sentiment.

He leads me through the crowd, and I notice the way people part for him. The way they watch him with a mixture of respect and fear. The way even the most powerful men here give him a wide berth.

And somehow, that makes me feel safer than I have in years.

I like being with the scary one.

We end up in a hallway that's blessedly quiet, away from the main party.

"Better?" he asks.

"Much." I lean against the wall, suddenly exhausted. "I don't know how you do this all the time."

"Practice," he says. "And a healthy amount of not giving a fuck what people think. This way," he says, leading me down a long corridor, past a bunch of flittering faces. "If you want to get out of the crowd and you don't want them to stop you, you have to act like you're walking with purpose." He says it with a smile. "Hold your head up, Erin," he says, guiding me toward the exit. "This way. Left."

A couple of people are bold enough to try to stop us, but he only gives them a little smile and a shake of his head, gesturing toward where we're going. We have somewhere to be, somewhere important, and nobody's going to interrupt us. Not now. That's very clear.

Finally, we find ourselves in the kitchen.

"Why are we in the kitchen?" I say with a smile, shaking my head.

The staff is busy, but we're at the far end near the refrigerator, and they're all clustered by the industrial ovens. Trays are clacking, overhead lights bright, but here in the corner, it's quiet. Private.

"Christ." He loosens his tie, and I watch his throat work as he swallows. "It's worse than I expected."

"What is?"

"Anxiety," he says, and the admission seems to cost him. "Didn't used to be like this before." He shakes his head, rubbing a hand over his face.

"Christ, Cavin. We're supposed to be married, remember? You're supposed to be able to tell me these things. Before what?"

He looks at me for a long moment, something dark and haunted crossing his features. "Before I went to prison."

The words hang between us.

He exhales roughly. "Didn't mind the crowds before. I could, you know, play along with it all. But now? I can't fuckin' stand it. I don't like that people disrespect personal space at events like this, you know? And I get why we have to do it—it's part of the game, right? But I hate it. Don't like being around people I can't trust. Don't like not knowing who's planning something."

"You think someone's planning something?" I ask carefully.

His eyes meet mine, and there's no humor in them now. Only cold, hard certainty. "Someone's always planning something, Erin. That's how this world works."

A chill runs down my spine—because he's not wrong. And because I'm realizing that whatever happened to him in prison, whatever he saw or did or had done to him—it's changed him. Made him harder. More paranoid.

More dangerous.

"Well, it's one thing we have in common," I say softly.

He lets out a breath and laughs, but it's not a happy sound. "Aye. I think it's two, actually."

"What would be the first?"

"I don't know," he says, and his eyes drop to my mouth. "I think we need to go back to The Craic to find that out. But I have my suspicions."

Heat floods through me. "Oh dear god. Don't tell me we're going now, are we?"

"No," he says with a laugh, and some of the darkness lifts from his expression. "No. You think I don't have enough self-respect for that? I may not be a good man, Erin, but my parents raised me right. I'm a gentleman, and I'll not take advantage of you before—" He shrugs. "Before I need to."

"What is that supposed to mean?"

My heart is thundering, and why do I feel this crazy need to tell him that it's okay, that I *want* him to, that maybe I don't want to have to dread our wedding night? Maybe I want this to be natural and not forced. Maybe I don't want to feel like every choice in my life is being made for me.

But I don't. I don't tell him any of that.

Instead, I just nod, and he reaches out, tucking a strand of hair behind my ear. The gesture is surprisingly tender.

"Come on," he says. "Let's get back out there before they send a search party. But stay close to me, yeah? Don't let anyone pull you aside."

"Why not?"

His jaw tightens. "Because I don't trust any of these fuckers, and I'll not have you alone with them." He blows out a breath. "And to think we have to do this all over again in a matter of *weeks*."

It should bother me, the way he's being so controlling. But instead, all I feel is... safe. Protected. Like maybe, just maybe, I can trust him.

Even if I'm not entirely sure he trusts himself.

And something he said... makes a lightbulb go off in my head.

My mind spins and circles and puts pieces of the puzzle into place. The final one clicks.

"Cavin," I say, resting my hand on his arm. "The absolute *last* thing I want to do is go home tonight, with my mother breathing down my neck planning this damn wedding. What if... what if we *don't* have to wait for the wedding?"

Chapter Twenty

Cavin

I STARE AT HER. The woman's brilliant and reckless, and I think I might... I think I might love her.

I take her by both arms and look her straight in the eyes. "Say that again."

"Tonight. Right now." Her eyes are bright with something wild, something that matches the chaos in my own head. "Everything's in place. I know our families filed paperwork already, as soon as the wedding was agreed on, right?"

I blink and nod. "Right."

"Even the priest is here, Cavin. We could... we could do it."

"Your family will lose their shite." I'm studying her face, trying to work out if she's serious.

Her smile is wicked, sharp as broken glass. "They'll absolutely lose their minds. My mother especially. Even better."

"But your sister's not here."

A shadow crosses her face, and she nods. "She wasn't going to be able to make the original date either, Cavin. Let's do this. No excuses."

Christ, she's serious. And the idea of it, walking out of here with her legally mine, with none of the pomp and circumstance, without having to worry about keeping her safe for the next few weeks under another person's roof... it's *perfect*.

It's completely fucking crazy, and it's *perfect*.

I grin, probably looking half mad. "Let's do it."

Bronwyn's expression when we corner her by the bar is priceless—somewhere between shocked and delighted.

"You're having me on," she says, eyes darting between us.

"We're dead serious," Erin says. "I need a witness. You in?"

"Are you absolutely mental?" Bronwyn hisses, but she's already grinning. "Of *course* I'm fucking in. This is the best craic I've seen in years."

Erin's cheeks flush at the word *craic*, but I only wink at her.

The three of us slip through the crowd like thieves. No one's paying attention, as they're all too busy drinking Da's expensive whiskey and kissing his arse. We find Father Gregory in the back corner of the room, looking half asleep in a velvet chair, with a tumbler of whiskey in his hand.

"Father," Erin says, sweet as honey. "We were thinking..."

The priest's eyes sharpen. He looks between us, taking in

Erin's formal dress, my suit, and the determination on both our faces as we tell him the plan.

He sighs, long and heavy, but he's already setting down his glass and pushing himself up. "Your fathers will have my head for this."

"More like our mothers," I say with a shrug. "But I'll take the hit. Don't worry about that."

"You're supposed to go through pre-Cana at the church," he says, then he shakes his head. "To discuss things like finances, children, conflict resolution... That's just a formality though. I know as well as you do that any wedding between a McCarthy and a Kavanagh is set in stone."

Erin looks up at me, her eyes wide. Pride swells my chest. I can't believe she's willing to do something so outrageous, so crazy and wild.

"Finances?" I say to her. "You'll have all your needs met and more."

"Aye," she says. "I come into the marriage with a hefty dowry, so no worries there as well. And children? Do you want them?"

"Of course I do," I say with a nod.

"Same," she says. "Eventually."

"Aye. Conflict resolution... I suggest we discuss that in private."

"Alright," she says, her cheeks flushing, and I hope she remembers the way I solved the *conflict* of her whipping my coat at my face.

Conflict resolution could actually *lead* to children, if we do it right.

"There," I say to Father Gregory. "We've done it, then. Sorted."

He blinks.

"Sorted."

"Aye. We have the paperwork, witnesses, and a priest. What more do we need?"

"Rings, son," he says, his eyes wide. "Did you buy a ring for your betrothed?"

I swallow hard, the thick gold bands that were my grandparents' sit in a black velvet case in my father's study. "Aye. Bronwyn," I gesture for her to come closer. "Do you remember the ring I showed you?"

"Aye," she says, clapping her hands with glee. "I'll be right back!"

She runs to fetch them.

"I can't believe we're doing this," Erin says, her voice thin and reedy, not her usual tone.

Something's off. Her eyes are too wide, the pupils blown, and her breathing's coming in short, quick bursts through her nose. She's trying to hide it, of course she is, but I've been watching her long enough to know when she's struggling.

Her fingers start tapping against her thigh, rapid and rhythmic, the movement barely visible. She catches herself after a few seconds and stops abruptly, tucking her hand under her leg like she's been scolded for it before. Probably has been, knowing how people are.

"Erin." I keep my voice low, steady.

She doesn't answer. Her gaze darts around the room, and her jaw's clenched tight. There's a fine tremor running through her shoulders.

Fuck. She's losing it.

I shift closer, angling my body to block her from the rest of the room. Give her some privacy from the nosy fuckers who'd stare. "Erin, look at me."

Her eyes snap to mine, but they're unfocused, glassy. Her breathing's getting worse—faster, shallower. She's not getting enough air.

"Too much," she whispers, so quiet I almost miss it. "It's too much. The—the lights are too bright, and that woman won't stop talking, and everyone's looking at us, and I can't—I can't—breathe—"

"Hey, hey." I reach out slowly, telegraphing the movement so I don't startle her. My hand hovers near hers. "Can I touch you?"

She nods frantically, and the second my palm covers hers, some of the panic in her face eases. Just a fraction, but it's there.

"That's it, lass. You're alright." I lace our fingers together, squeezing firm enough that she can feel the pressure. Grounding. "What else helps? Tell me what you need."

"I—" Her breath hitches. "I don't know. I can't think. My head's too loud."

"Is it the noise? The people?"

"Everything. All of it." Her free hand comes up to clutch at her chest, nails digging into the fabric of her dress. "I need— I need it to stop. Make it stop."

Christ. I hate seeing her like this. Hate that I can't just punch whatever's hurting her.

I lean in close, pressing my forehead to hers, our noses nearly touching. "Breathe with me, Erin. Match me, yeah?"

I take a slow, deliberate breath in through my nose—four counts—and let it out through my mouth. She tries to follow, but it's choppy, uneven. Her whole body's shaking now.

"You're doing grand," I murmur. "Again. In through your nose. That's it."

It takes a few tries, but gradually, her breathing starts to sync with mine. In. Hold. Out. Her grip on my hand is tight enough to hurt, but I don't care.

"You're safe," I whisper. "I've got you. Nothing's going to hurt you here."

"Everyone's staring," she chokes out.

"Let them fucking stare. Focus on me. Just me."

Her eyes flutter closed, lashes damp. "You. Just you."

"That's my girl." I bring our joined hands up between us, pressing them against my chest so she can feel the steady thump of my heartbeat. "Feel that? I'm right here. Not going anywhere."

She nods against my forehead, her breathing still unsteady but slower now, less frantic. The tremors start to ease.

"This," she whispers after a long moment. "This helps. You touching me. Matching my breathing. Just like… just like that."

"Then that's what we'll do." I press a kiss to her temple, lingering. "For as long as you need, lass. I'm not letting go."

"When you—when you touch me," she whispers. "It stops the chatter in my head."

I lace my fingers around the small of her back and hold her to me. "Like that?" I whisper.

"Aye," she says, our foreheads touching again. "Just like that."

"I've got them!" Bronwyn stands triumphantly with the black velvet box, Declan next to her, presenting us with the rings. But then she notices Erin's wide eyes, the way she's breathing a bit fast, and that I'm holding her. She takes a step back. "Right, yeah. Take your time."

"I'm good now," Erin says. "Thank you, Cavin."

"Right, then," Father Gregory says in a quiet voice. "Cavin, assemble your witnesses, and we'll make the announcement."

Witnesses are an easy matter. Bronwyn and Declan's eyes shine with excitement as Declan holds the rings and Bronwyn quickly pulls together floral arrangements in front of the fireplace.

"What are you doing, lass?" Mam asks her. Bronwyn turns to me.

"We have an announcement to make."

I watch Erin begin to tap again, her lips moving in a quiet rhythm as if whispering something to herself.

"Are we *mad?*" she whispers to me.

"Absolutely. Do we care?" I whisper back. I slide my hand across her lower back and tug her to me.

She looks up at me and smiles. "Not in the slightest. But promise me one thing." I lean over and tuck a strand of hair behind her ear.

"My god, you're beautiful. And aye, love. Anything."

She grimaces. "You'll handle my mother this time?"

I release a low chuckle. "Sweet lass, I thought you'd never ask."

And then we're laughing, both of us, as if we're in on a secret just meant for us. "Let's do this, then. Please, Cavin, before I lose my mind."

This was the best idea she's ever had. Can't imagine the poor lass fretting over the next few weeks, her mam breathing down her neck.

I gesture for one of the staff to come over, and order several bottles of champagne. I take an empty glass and a spoon, then click the metal on the glass while I clear my throat.

All eyes in the room come to us.

"We have an announcement to make," I say, my voice loud and clear in the large expanse of the room.

The chatter dies down, and all heads turn.

My mother watches me thoughtfully, that calculating look in her eye like she already knows what's coming. My father cants his head, jaw tight. Seamus and Zoya share a look—curious, maybe a bit concerned. Someone escorts Tara and Padraic Kavanagh into the room, and I watch as confusion flickers across their faces when they clock the setup.

All eyes are on me now—the weight of expectation, curiosity, judgment. I couldn't give less of a fuck.

I reach for Erin's hand and tuck it firmly into my side, anchoring her there. She's tense, I can feel it, but she doesn't pull away. *Good girl.*

"Erin and I have something to tell you all." I pause, letting the silence stretch just long enough to make them uncomfortable. "As some of you know, we're here to celebrate and announce our engagement."

My mother's eyes narrow slightly. She's connecting the dots.

"What you don't know," I continue, my thumb brushing over Erin's knuckles, "is that we're not waiting until next month. Or next week."

I feel Erin shift beside me, her fingers tightening around mine.

"We're getting married today. Right now, actually. In about two minutes."

The room erupts.

My mother's mouth falls open—an actual rare sight. My father straightens, his eyebrows shooting up. Seamus barks out a laugh that sounds half disbelieving, half impressed.

Tara Kavanagh gasps, her hand flying to her chest, and Padraic looks like he might have a stroke.

"Today?" Tara's voice is shrill. "Cavin, what are you—you can't just—there's no time to—"

"It's already done, Mrs. Kavanagh." I cut her off smoothly. "Venue's sorted. Priest's sorted. Witnesses are here. The only thing left is for you lot to shut up, sit down, and watch me marry your daughter."

I look down at Erin then, and the corner of my mouth lifts. "Unless you've changed your mind in the last ten minutes, lass?"

Her cheeks are flushed, but there's a fire in her eyes now, that spark I love. "Not a chance in hell."

"Grand." I press a kiss to her temple, then look back at the stunned faces around us. "So. You can all either get on board, or you can fuck off. Either way, this is happening."

My mother recovers first, naturally. She stands, smoothing down her dress, and there's the faintest hint of a smile tugging at her lips. "Well then. I suppose we'd better not keep Father Gregory waiting."

"Erin." Tara walks over to us, beside herself. "You can't—can't just—"

"She can and will," I tell her firmly.

"Are you deciding this for her?" Tara's eyes flash at me. My god, the woman really does need putting in her place.

Erin snorts. "You wouldn't know anything about that, would you?"

Her mother's jaw drops open.

"Actually, it was my idea," Erin says. "I didn't want to wait. It makes me so nervous. I didn't want to go through all of this again, all the pomp and circumstance." She turns to me, and I hold both her hands in mine. "Shall we?"

Chapter Twenty-One

Erin

THE LIVING ROOM has been hastily transformed into
something resembling a chapel, though "chapel" might be
generous. Someone—probably Bronwyn—shoved the furniture against the walls and lined up chairs in uneven rows.
Candles flicker on every available surface, their flames
dancing in the draft from the windows someone cracked open
because it got too stuffy with everyone crammed in here.

I'm standing in the middle of the room in the dress I wore to
what I thought was just an engagement party, my hands
twisting together at my waist. My heart's hammering so
hard I'm sure everyone can hear it.

Cavin's beside me in his crisp white shirt and dark trousers,
sleeves rolled up his forearms like he couldn't be bothered
with the jacket anymore. His hair's mussed—probably from
running his hands through it when he made the announcement that sent everyone into a tailspin.

Father Gregory looks mildly scandalized but game, prayer book clutched in his hands. He keeps glancing around like he's not entirely sure this is liturgically sound, but he's here, and that's what matters.

"Wait," I say suddenly, my voice cracking. "Wait, I need—can we call my sister?"

My mother's eyes go wide. She doesn't want anyone to see her gaunt face or skeletal frame, but I can't imagine Bridget not being here, at least in some part.

Cavin doesn't even blink. He's already pulling his phone from his pocket. "Course we can, lass. Not doing this without your sister. You want to call her?"

My throat tightens. God, I may love him.

It rings twice before Bridget's face fills the screen, and I immediately burst out laughing because she's wearing enormous sunglasses, a flower crown, and what appears to be a coconut bra. Behind her, there's impossibly blue water and swaying palm trees—I know it to be a filter, but she's committed to the bit, and from a distance you definitely can't tell.

"Erin? What's—" She shoves the sunglasses up, squinting at the screen. Her eyes go wide. "Are you—is that Father Gregory? Are you in a living room? What the hell is happening?"

"I'm getting married," I blurt out. "Right now. In Cavin's living room. Surprise?"

"You're getting married?" She shrieks so loud that half the room flinches. "Right now? Oh, you absolute bitch—"

She's laughing, though, tears already filling her eyes. "Oh my god. And you called *me*? Oh, Erin. Is Cavin there? I mean, he must be. You're not marrying without him." At one point, she coughs, but she mutes it, and only I see the way her shoulders shake, and she covers her mouth before she recovers as I hand the phone to Cavin.

"Right here." Cavin waves at the screen.

"Cavin McCarthy, before you say I do, I want you to know that I love my sister with my whole heart, and if you ever do anything to hurt her, I will know." She makes the "eyes on you" gesture with her fingers, and Cavin actually laughs out loud before he sobers. "You may be mafia, but she's my ride or die."

The room erupts in nervous giggles. My mother looks as if she's about to pass out.

"Listen, Bridget." He squeezes my hand. "I promise you. You have nothing to worry about."

Cavin angles the phone so she can see everything, propping it on a makeshift stand someone rigged up on the mantle. Bridget's face beams out at us, tropical paradise and all, and somehow it makes this chaotic, imperfect moment even more perfect.

Father Gregory clears his throat. "Well then. Shall we begin?"

Cavin takes my hand, his grip warm and steady, and I nod.

"Right, so." Father Gregory's voice carries that thick Cork accent, the kind that rounds every word. "We're gathered here, in this... living room, to witness the... fairly impromptu joining of Cavin and Erin in holy matrimony. With all witnesses present, we'll proceed." Father Gregory looks between us. "The vows, then. Cavin?"

Cavin turns to face me fully, and the room seems to fall away. His eyes—those impossible blue eyes—lock onto mine, and suddenly, I can breathe again.

He doesn't have notes... doesn't look away.

"Erin." His voice is rough, gravelly. "I'm not good with words, yeah? Not the flowery shite. But I'll tell you this, and I'll mean every fucking word of it."

Someone gasps—probably my mother—but Father Gregory just sighs like he expected nothing less.

"I promise to stand by you. Not just when it's easy, but when it's brutal and messy and you want to throttle me. I promise to protect you—from everyone else, and from yourself when you need it. I promise to learn you. Every piece. The bits you show the world and the bits you hide."

His thumb brushes over my knuckles, and my vision blurs.

"I promise to be your safe place. Your home. Your person. And I promise that every day, for the rest of my life, I'll choose you. Over everything. Over everyone. Because you're mine, Erin. And I'm yours. Simple as that."

My breath catches. I'm crying now. I can feel the tears sliding down my cheeks, but I don't care.

Father Gregory nods, satisfied, then looks at me. "Erin?"

I swallow hard, trying to find my voice. When I speak, it's steadier than I expected.

"Cavin." I squeeze his hands, holding on like he's the only solid thing in the world. "I promise to stand by you too. In the chaos and the quiet. When you're perfect and when you're impossible—which, let's be honest, is most of the time."

He huffs out a laugh, and I watch his eyes go glassy.

"I promise to let you protect me, even when I want to do everything myself. I promise to learn you back—all the rough edges and soft places you don't let anyone else see. I promise to be your safe place too. Your home. Your person."

My voice cracks, but I push through.

"And I promise that every day, for the rest of my life, I'll choose you. Over my fears. Over what anyone else thinks. Because you're mine, Cavin, and I'm yours." My voice is just above a whisper now. "Simple as... that."

The room is dead silent except for someone sniffling—I think it's Seamus, actually.

From the phone, Bridget's voice rings out: *"I'm not crying, you're crying."*

Father Gregory smiles, soft and genuine. "By the power vested in me by the Holy Catholic Church and the Republic of Ireland, I now pronounce you husband and wife." He looks at Cavin. "You may kiss your bride. And mind yourself—we're still in the presence of God and family."

Cavin doesn't wait. He cups my face in both hands, his thumbs brushing away my tears, and kisses me.

It's not gentle. Not polite. It's claiming and desperate and ours, and I kiss him back just as fiercely, my fingers curling into his shirt. I relish the quiet contentment that floods me.

The room erupts. Cheering, clapping, Bridget screaming through the phone, Declan whistling loud enough to wake the dead, Seamus popping open a bottle of champagne.

When we finally break apart, Cavin presses his forehead to mine, his breath warm against my lips.

"Mine," he murmurs, just for me.

"Yours," I whisper back.

The next half hour is a blur. Hugs and congratulations, and my mother crying into my father's shoulder while he looks equal parts bewildered and resigned. I can't believe that I... won't be going home with them tonight.

Seamus claps Cavin on the back so hard he nearly knocks him over.

I'm tucked into Cavin's side, his arm a solid weight around my waist, when he leans down to murmur in my ear.

"We're not going upstairs. Not tonight."

I blink up at him. "What?"

His mouth curves into that wicked smile I know too well. "I've a surprise for you, Mrs. McCarthy."

Chapter Twenty-Two

Erin

MY STOMACH FLIPS at the name.

Mrs. McCarthy.

"What kind of surprise?"

"The kind you'll like." He presses a kiss to my temple. "Come on, lass. Let's go."

I've never seen Cavin this... happy. I've seen him smile and look boyish—I've seen fleeting moments of joy, but now it looks like he's practically vibrating with excitement.

And I like it. He's excited about something he wants to show *me*.

The drive is short—twenty minutes, maybe—and Cavin won't tell me where we're going, no matter how many times I ask. His hand stays on my thigh the whole way, warm and possessive, his thumb tracing absent circles that make it hard to think.

I'm excited and nervous, and I can't believe we just did that. I text Bridget the whole way. She's out of her mind excited that we're married and that Mam doesn't get to control this for another bloody second.

> **Bridget**
> He sounds like he isn't the boy who tormented you anymore

I swallow hard and look up at my... at my husband before I reply.

> He's not

When we finally pull up, I don't recognize the house at first. It's set back from the road, surrounded by trees, with a long gravel drive that crunches under the tires. It's not huge, not ostentatious, just a beautiful stone cottage with ivy climbing up one side and warm light glowing from the windows. The kind of place that welcomes you, apart from the rest.

"Cavin," I whisper. "What is this?"

He cuts the engine and turns to me, his expression unreadable. "Ours."

My heart stops. "What?"

"I bought it when I got released, before I knew you'd... be mine," he says, running his hand through his hair. I love when he looks boyish like this. "Been fixing it up." He reaches over, tucking a strand of hair behind my ear. "Wanted it to be perfect for you. For us."

I stare at him, then at the house, then back at him. "You— you bought us a house?"

"Aye. At first, I had every intention of staying in my family's home, as this wasn't ready yet. But then... I thought of you and your family and figured the last thing you'd want is to be married to me and sharing space with a crowd."

He's not wrong.

"So I tabled the plans for renovation and did a quick fix of the place instead. Thought you might like having a place that's just ours. No family. No business. Just... us." His jaw tightens slightly, like he's nervous. "If you don't like it, we can—"

I kiss him... hard, pouring everything I can't say into it—the overwhelming gratitude, the tentative love.

When I pull back, he's grinning. "I'll take that as a yes, then?"

"Show me," I whisper. "Show me everything."

He carries me over the threshold—literally sweeps me up like I weigh nothing, and I'm laughing and almost crying at the same time because it's ridiculous and perfect and him.

The inside is stunning. Warm wood floors, exposed beams, a stone fireplace that's already crackling with a fire someone must have lit for us. The furniture is simple but beautiful, all soft fabrics, and warm colors, like he chose a palette that said *calm* and filled it with perfection.

There's a kitchen that opens into the living space, all clean lines and modern touches, balanced with rustic charm.

"Cavin," I whisper, spinning slowly to take it all in. "It's perfect."

"There's more." He takes my hand, leading me down a hallway lined with framed photographs—landscapes mostly, rolling green hills and dramatic coastlines. "Three bedrooms. Main one's ours, obviously."

He pushes open the first door, revealing a spacious room with a massive bed that looks like it could sleep four. The furniture is dark wood, masculine but not oppressive, and there's a wall of windows overlooking what I can only assume is the back garden.

"This one's just a spare for now," he says, moving to the next door. "Thought maybe... if family ever needed a place to stay..."

I blink. I *love* it.

The third door opens to a smaller room, and I suck in a breath.

There's a comfortable armchair positioned near a window with the best light, a small table already set up beside it. Shelves line one wall—empty now, but clearly waiting to be filled. The walls are painted a soft, warm cream, and there's a reading lamp, the expensive kind that doesn't strain your eyes.

"There's a little room for you," he says, and I can hear the uncertainty creeping into his voice. "Set up a little table for puzzles and the like. Thought you could... knit or some such."

I turn to look at him, and he's rubbing the back of his neck, not quite meeting my eyes.

"Figured you'd need a space that's just yours. To think, or read, or whatever it is you do. Maybe retreat or whatever."

My throat tightens. "Cavin..."

"If it's shite, we can change it," he says quickly. "Paint it different, move things around. Whatever you want."

"It's not shite," I manage. "It's... you made me a *space*. For *me*."

"Aye, well." He shifts his weight and winks. "Can't have you cluttering up the whole house with your bits and bobs, can I?"

But I can see through the gruffness. He's given me a room of my own in a house that's supposed to be ours. A place to retreat, to breathe, to be myself.

I step into him, wrapping my arms around his waist. "Thank you."

His arms come around me, solid and warm. "It's nothing."

"It's not nothing," I insist, pulling back to look at him. "It's everything."

He *didn't*.

"And this..." He opens a door, and I gasp. "This is ours."

Chapter Twenty-Three

Erin

"So after all your carrying on about your bedroom being *mine*," I say, which earns me a teasing smack to the arse.

The primary bedroom is breathtaking. A massive four-poster bed dominates the space, piled with soft linens and thick pillows. There are candles everywhere, lit and glowing softly, and the windows overlook the dark expanse of trees outside. It's intimate and romantic and exactly what I didn't know I needed.

"Cavin." I turn to him, my eyes stinging again.

He brushes his lips against mine and kisses me. "Do you have any idea how hard I've been holding myself back?" he says, his eyes growing heated and possessive. "Any idea?"

The kiss deepens, then turns hungry.

"Cavin." I breathe against his mouth.

"Aye?"

"I want this. I want you."

He pulls back just enough to look at me, his eyes dark and searching. "You're sure?"

"I've never been more sure of anything."

His control snaps. He kisses me like he's starving, and I'm fumbling with the buttons of his shirt, desperate to feel his skin against mine. His hands are everywhere—tangling in my hair, gripping my waist, sliding up my ribs, over my breasts with reverence.

"Fuck this," he growls and rips his shirt open. Buttons scatter across the floor.

I gasp, staring at the expanse of golden skin, the hard planes of muscle, the black ink winding over his shoulder and down his ribs. The scars that map out his history.

He's gorgeous. Dangerous. *Mine.*

His hands find the zipper of my dress. The sound of it sliding down is obscenely loud in the quiet room. Cool air hits my heated skin as the fabric pools at my feet.

I'm standing there in my white lace bra and knickers, and the way he looks at me—

"Christ, Erin." He sighs. "Look at you. You're gorgeous."

I reach for him and pull him close, then kiss the small tattoo of a rose on his shoulder. "Thank you."

My hands stroke down the length of his chest. His abs contract under my touch. His cock is a hard, thick ridge against my hip, straining against his trousers.

"My fuckin' god," he growls. "Keep touching me like that and this'll be over before it starts."

I do it again. Deliberately. My thumbs graze over his nipples.

He makes a rough sound—something between a curse and a prayer—and his hips jerk forward involuntarily.

Power surges through me. *I* did that. *I* made him lose control.

He lifts me effortlessly and lays me on the bed like I'm something precious and breakable, even though his eyes are wild and hungry.

"You're so beautiful," he murmurs, crawling over me. His mouth finds my throat. My collarbone. Lower. "So fucking beautiful, Erin."

He unclasps my bra, slides it off my shoulders, then tosses it aside. Cool air hits my nipples, and they tighten into hard peaks.

His eyes darken. "Fuck me, lass, you're perfect."

I arch into his touch, every nerve ending on fire. He's maddeningly patient, taking his time, and I want to urge him to hurry, but I can't form words because his mouth is doing things that make my brain shut down entirely.

He kisses my shoulder. "Mine," he whispers, and the constant chatter of anxiety in my mind—the voices that never stop—becomes blissfully, deliciously *quiet*. "Mine."

His rough fingers skate down the length of my arm, then back up, tracing my collarbone. They come to rest on my hip, his thumb stroking the sensitive skin there.

"Do you like that, Erin? Does that feel good?"

I close my eyes, then breathe out on an exhale. "Yes. I love it when you touch me. Don't stop, please."

"Good lass." He wraps his hand in my hair and claims my mouth. His tongue sweeps against mine. Demanding. Possessive.

My thighs are slick with arousal. My brain is blissfully content. Quiet. Focused only on us.

He breaks the kiss, resting his forehead against mine. "Are you nervous?"

I nod.

"Don't be." His hand slides down and cups me through my knickers. I gasp. "Let me make this body sing for me. Mine now, yeah? Every fuckin' sound you make belongs to me." And when I let myself go, relaxing into him, he makes a deep, masculine sound of approval. "That's my good girl. That's it, love. I'll take my time until you're ready and panting for me. We have all night."

My body turns pliant and warm under his touch. My breasts feel heavy, aching.

The pad of his thumb grazes one nipple. His mouth closes over the other, the flat of his tongue lapping at the peak.

My body arches on instinct. I let out a soft gasp, needing pressure, needing something.

"That's it," he murmurs against my skin. "Let me hear you."

The scent of our bodies and arousal fills the air around us. It's intoxicating. When he releases my nipples to kiss my cheek, I pull his body close to mine and stroke his chest, my thumbs skating over his nipples too.

"My fuckin' *god.*" He releases a short growl of approval. His hardened cock throbs against my thigh. "*Christ,* you're perfect. *Mine.* Say it—tell me you're mine while I'm touchin' what belongs to me."

"I'm yours."

"Jesus, love, I love it when you touch me. You're gonna kill me, but I'll die a happy man buried between these thighs." His voice is strained, barely controlled.

He claims my mouth again, before his hand wraps around my arse and pulls me to him until we're flush. The hard length of him presses against my core, only thin lace separating us.

Oh god. I love the feel of his hand on my arse. The possessive grip. The way he manhandles me like I'm his to do with as he pleases.

He hooks his fingers in my knickers, then drags them down my legs and tosses them aside.

I'm completely naked, exposed, and vulnerable.

He strips off his trousers and boxers, and his cock springs free—thick and heavy, flushed dark at the tip. A bead of moisture glistens there.

My mouth goes dry. He's bigger than I expected. Fear flickers through me.

"Hey." He cups my face and makes me look at him. "We'll go slow. I promise."

"Okay."

He spreads my thighs with his big hands and lowers himself to the floor. I realize what he's going to do, and it feels too much, too intimate. I press them closer together when his eyes darken on me.

"I want to taste you, love. Can you trust me?"

"That's too much," I whisper.

"If you let me do this, it'll be easier to take me," he whispers back.

He settles between my thighs, spreading them wider. His eyes find mine and hold them. And I find my courage. I'm so eager to see what it feels like... what he feels like.

He kisses my inner thigh, then stretches the tip of his tongue to lick the slick arousal painted on the sensitive skin. Heat floods me. He presses his nose lower still, and I gasp. My mind again goes quiet, like my whole body is nothing but one big pulse of expectation.

"Tell me if it's too much," he says softly. "Tell me if you need me to stop."

"Okay," I whisper back. His responding growl makes my pussy clench with need. I spread my thighs, feeling power-ful. I watch his eyes grow dark and heated as he breathes me in and releases a shuddering groan. My grip on the sheets relaxes, and instead, my fingers weave into his hair, anchoring me.

And then he drags the flat of his tongue to my throbbing, aching core. I cry out, my back arching off the bed, gripping his hair. Oh my god, this feels amazing. With every stroke of his tongue, heat blooms inside me, the pressure building. My resistance melts, and I whimper when he suckles my clit between his full lips.

His groan of approval tells me he likes this too.

"Right there," I whisper when he strokes just right, and I whimper in need. I press the back of his head to keep him in place. "My god, don't stop."

"That's my girl," he says, his voice muffled between my thighs. "So fucking sweet. So fucking perfect. Let yourself go, love. Come on my tongue."

My body grows boneless, and I sigh—the delicious feeling of his tongue, his rough hands gripping my thighs, the way pleasure is building, growing—it's unlike anything I've ever felt before.

My fear dissolves into trust, and I let myself just… melt. "That's it, love," he whispers, before he scratches the stubble on his chin across my thighs. "You're doing so well. Come on my tongue, love."

I cry out in pleasure when my orgasm suddenly claims me. Bliss floods me, my hips rise, and he holds my thighs and continues to lick me through every spasm of ecstasy.

"Good girl." And I'm still coming, still in the throes of bliss, when he kisses his way back up my body.

"See? I told you I'd take care of you. Now you're so damn wet for me, aren't you?" He slides his fingers through my wet heat just to prove his point, before he laps them clean, inches from me.

I whimper wordlessly, suddenly overcome with an unexpected need to be filled by him, to draw closer, to feel him *inside* me.

"Tell me if it's too much," he whispers in my ear, trembling with the effort of holding himself back.

"No. Don't stop," I whisper. "Please don't stop, Cavin."

He reaches down and positions himself. The broad head of his cock presses against my entrance.

"Breathe, love."

I try. He pushes forward. Just the tip.

The stretch is immediate. Intense. My body resists.

"Fuck, you're tight." His jaw is clenched, the muscles corded with the effort of holding still. "Relax for me, Erin. Let me in."

I breathe... try to relax. He pushes deeper.

There's pressure, then a sharp sting that makes me tense.

"Shh, shh." He kisses me, murmuring against my lips—soft reassurances in that rough brogue that grounds me. "That's it, love. I've got you. You're doing so well. Taking me so fucking well."

He bottoms out, then stays completely still, letting me adjust. I feel so full, stretched, connected to him in the most intimate way possible.

"How do you feel?" His voice is strained.

"Full." I shift my hips experimentally. "So full."

"Christ." His hips jerk involuntarily. "Don't—don't move like that unless you want this over fast."

"I want—" I don't know what I want. I just know I need more. "*Move*. Please move."

He pulls back slowly, then pushes in again, watching my face for any sign of pain.

The sting fades, replaced by something else entirely. Pleasure builds gradually, a rising tide.

"More," I breathe out. "Faster."

"Greedy girl," he says with a light slap to my arse that sends heat blooming between my legs. But he gives me what I want and picks up the pace. Each thrust hits something inside me that makes stars burst behind my eyelids.

His forehead presses to mine. We move together, finding a rhythm. His hand slides between us and circles my clit.

"Oh god—Cavin—"

"That's it. Let go for me, love. I want to feel you come on my cock."

My body clamps down on him as pleasure crashes over me in waves. I cry out his name, my nails digging into his shoulders. I shatter, lost to the echo of the first orgasm, eclipsed by the second.

"Fuck—Erin—" He loses his rhythm. His thrusts become erratic, desperate. "I'm—fuck—"

He buries himself deep and comes with a groan that sounds like it's torn from his chest. I feel him pulse inside me. Feel the warmth of him spilling into me.

It's messy and overwhelming and utterly perfect.

For a long time, we just breathe together, tangled up in each other and the sheets. His weight is heavy on top of me, comforting rather than crushing.

Slowly, he pulls out. I wince at the sensitivity.

"Alright?" His eyes search mine, worried.

"More than alright."

He rolls to the side, pulling me with him, and tucks me against his chest. His hand strokes up and down my spine in a soothing rhythm.

"Mine," he murmurs eventually, pressing a kiss to my shoulder. "My wife."

"Yours," I whisper back, running my fingers through his hair. "Always yours."

And in this house—our house—with the candles flickering and the fire crackling and the world locked safely outside, I've never felt more at home. Never felt safer. Never felt more seen.

The voices in my head are quiet. The anxiety that usually thrums through my veins like a second heartbeat is gone.

There's only him. Only us. Only this.

He pulls the sheet over us, and his arms tighten around me.

"Sleep, love," he murmurs into my hair. "I've got you."

I believe him.

For the first time in my life, I actually believe someone when they say that.

Chapter Twenty-Four

Cavin

I DON'T KNOW how I got back here. I'm behind bars, the dank smell of my fucking prison flooding my senses.

"Where is she?" I growl into the dark. What did they do with my wife, and why am I here? I can't talk to anyone in this condition because I'm pacing, my hands fisted by my sides. There are men in the cells behind me and around me, crowding me in.

"Where is who?" one taunts.

"My *wife*!" I roar. I punch one and then round out and punch the second.

When someone grabs me from behind and touches my wrist, I lift them, just about vaulting them across the room.

"Cavin!" It's Erin's voice in my ear. "Cavin, Cavin, wake *up*."

I blink. When I come to, I have Erin pinned in my grasp beneath me, with the sheets tangled around my legs.

Holy *fucking* shit. Oh my *god*.

Erin.

I release her like she's a hot coal and shake my head, trying to blink it all away. The desperation, trying to find her. The coldness of the cell. The way I knew I was going to be attacked and beaten by a gang.

Oh my god.

I cage myself over her and run my hands over every inch of her skin, looking at her eyes, her arms. "Did I hurt you? Are you alright?" The last time Lorcan grabbed me, I tossed him across the fucking table at the bar.

"I'm fine. You were just—you were sleeping, and you were tangled in the sheets, and you were very upset," she says softly. "Are you alright now?"

She rests her hand on my cheek, and for the first time, I feel what she says I do for her. *I'm* quieting. My voice—the one in my head that constantly berates and judges me—falls silent.

"I'm fine."

Jesus, Mary, and Joseph. My voice is hoarse with worry. "You'll have to sleep in another room."

"Cavin," she says, giving me a long look. "I'm *not* sleeping in another room."

"You need to," I snap, too harsh, too firm. "I'm sorry." I run a hand through my hair. "I didn't mean that. I just—my god,

Erin." I shake my head and look heavenward. "I'm sorry. I just don't want to hurt you."

She sits up in bed, my beautiful bride, and eyes me curiously. "You didn't hurt me, and I'm not sleeping alone." She crosses her arms over her chest. Stubborn lass. I push out of bed and pace the room.

"I don't want you to either. After that first night together, I thought we'd be fine. I thought that I'd been cured of my nightmares with my wife next to me. The second night was the same. But now..." I shake my head.

"Come here, Cavin," she says, "please." She pats the bed beside her, and I walk over. I sit on the bed, and she crawls over and curls up in my arms.

"It's okay. You had a nightmare. Of course you did. After everything you've seen and you've done—especially that time in prison—of course you had a nightmare. It's okay," she says quietly.

I run my hands over her again, reassuring myself that she's alright. "Thank you."

"Of course," she says. "Now let's get up. I made some overnight oats. You have to soak them for exactly eight hours. The clock says it's been precisely eight hours and fifteen minutes."

When she tries to slip out of bed, I reach for her, wrapping my arm around her waist to pull her back. But she doesn't just let me—she turns in my grip, her hands already sliding up my chest as she presses against me.

"Going somewhere?" I murmur against her mouth.

"The oats"—she bites my bottom lip, hard enough to sting— "can wait."

Her kiss is hungry, demanding, and suddenly, I'm the one being pushed back against the mattress. She straddles me, her hair falling around us like a curtain as she grinds down, making me groan.

"Thought you were worried about your fuckin' breakfast," I manage, gripping her hips.

"I changed my mind." Her nails rake down my chest. "You can make it worth my while, can't you?"

"Is that a *challenge, Mrs. McCarthy*?"

She rocks against me, slow and deliberate, watching my face. "Maybe. You up for it, *Mr. McCarthy*?"

I flip her in one quick movement, but she's already wrapping her legs around my waist, pulling me closer. Christ, but I love it when I make her giggle.

"Overnight oats. What's the fuck is that?" I say against her throat.

"It's—" Her breath catches when I thrust into her. "Fuck— it's good for you."

"So is *this*." I move harder, deeper, and she meets me stroke for stroke, her hands fisted in my hair.

"Then give me a very good reason"—she gasps, her body arching beneath mine—"to let those oats soak for a little while longer."

When she finally pushes out of bed, she's flushed, her hair an absolute mess. "Now do you want breakfast, champion?" she says, sliding onto my lap, kissing my cheek.

I love her.

"Let's go." When she turns to go, I give her a teasing slap to the arse.

I've never been happier. Erin is everything to me. The house feels alive with her in it. I don't miss being alone because I have... her.

I go down to breakfast and eat her overnight damn oats, and they're not half bad. When I look at my calendar—*Christ.* Panic grips my chest when I realize I almost forgot, which would be fuckin' *disastrous.*

It's tribute night.

How will I explain my absence to my wife, who curls herself up beside me in bed? I can't take her, no. And once again, I'm no closer to finding out who's demanding the tribute.

"I have somewhere to be tonight, after I go to the club," I tell her quietly.

"Oh, where?"

I look away. "Ah, I can't say much about it. I'm sorry."

Her eyebrows rise. "You can't tell me? Why not? That makes no sense, Cavin."

I blow out a breath. "I'm Irish mafia, Erin, you know that.

"Aye," she says.

"And you know I have business to handle, right?"

"Right."

"Well, it's not safe for you to come with me, so you'll stay here, right?"

"Well, aren't I safest with *you*?"

Well played.

"I said no." My words come out sharper than I intended, and she takes a little step back.

"Well, it didn't take long for the honeymoon to be over," she says, wrapping her arms around herself.

She's wearing my shirt, and it rides up, showing the little dimple right at her thigh. I want to kiss it. I want to lay her back in bed and help her forget anything that's ever troubled her, but I can't.

"I have to go to the club first, but I'll be late tonight."

"Are you going back to the ring?" she says, her eyes meeting mine. She knows that Seamus and Da don't approve of me going to the ring.

But I only shrug. "Maybe," I tell her. "Maybe one more fight."

"Well, I can't see why I can't go with you to that," she says.

"No back talk," I snap. "It's dangerous business, Erin, and I don't want you to worry about it. I'll be back later tonight."

But her eyes are on me with suspicion. "Why won't you tell me where you're going? I've seen you fight in the ring before. Are you trying to keep something else from your family?"

"No," I say, but it's a lie. I shrug. "Maybe. I can't tell them either. I hope someday I can, but not now."

She bites her lower lip, and I can see that moment when her insecurity comes into play again.

"What kind of business is it?" she says, insistent.

"You don't show me everything on your phone."

"That's different. That's private."

"Aye, and so is this."

We stand at odds with each other.

"So we're keeping secrets now?" she says. "That's how marriage works in your family?"

Fuck this. I need to go handle this before it gets worse. I check the time. I've got hours before I need to pay the tribute, but I need to clear my head.

"Fine. Go. Do whatever you're doing. Or *whoever* you're doing."

I stop at the door and spin around. "That's not fair, and you fucking know it."

"Then tell me where you're going!"

I can't, but she won't back down, so I leave angry—leaving her behind, hurt and suspicious—and I don't like it.

I slam the car door harder than necessary. My hands grip the steering wheel tight enough that my knuckles go white.

Or whoever.

Her words echo in my head, making my jaw clench, as if I'd ever—as if there's anyone else I'd even look at, now that I have her. Didn't even fucking touch her until we were married.

But she won't tell me who she's texting, and I can't tell her where I'm going.

Grand. Just fucking grand. Our first real fight, and we're both too stubborn to back down now.

I start the engine, and my car purrs to life. The club is calling, and I need to bury myself in work to get my mind off this mess.

The hours at the club crawl by. I've been going through the books, meeting the lads about collections, making sure everything's running smooth. But my mind keeps wandering back to Erin. The hurt in her eyes.

I check my watch. Two hours until I have to pay the tribute. Two hours before I need to be at the neutral ground, or they'll use my tardiness as an excuse to start shite with Bronwyn.

My phone rings, and Lorcan's name flashes across the screen.

"What?" I answer, too sharp.

"Boss, we've got a situation."

My blood goes cold. "What kind of situation?"

"It's Mrs. McCarthy." He still sounds awkward calling her that, like he can't quite believe Erin's my wife. "She left the house about twenty minutes ago and told Ciarán she was just going for a walk, but—"

"But what?" My voice comes out deadly quiet.

"She got in a car, boss. A black sedan that wasn't one of ours."

Everything in me goes still. That cold, calculating part of my brain that handles threats kicks into gear. "Where?"

"Ciarán's following at a distance. Boss, she's heading to the hospital."

The hospital.

My mind flashes to the phone and the texts she doesn't explain.

And now she's at the hospital. Something's...wrong.

No. I'm not doing this. I'm not sitting here wondering, imagining, driving myself mad while she's out there doing—what?

"Boss," Lorcan says. "What do you want us to do?"

I check the time again.

Fuck them. Erin's my wife. She's out there, visiting a hospital, and every instinct I have is screaming that something's wrong.

"Send me the location," I say.

Even as my heart pounds, I can't miss the fuckin' tribute. My sister's face flashes in my mind—the reason I pay tribute in the first place and the leverage they hold.

I grit my teeth. I have time. I can get there, see what she's doing, and still make the payment.

I hang up the phone, and a second later, my phone pings with a notification. It's a location pin. Erin's location.

I park a good distance away, enough that I can see her shadowy form and see that nobody's out here to hurt her. But who is she going to see? Where is she going?

I watch her walk with purpose. I shut the door quietly and follow her.

Is she meeting an old high school friend? The words that have been whispered behind my back come to roost. *Your wife's been around.*

No.

That was a fucking lie they knew would get under my skin.

But she's texting someone, I know that for a fact.

She walks up a winding staircase. I follow. But she doesn't take the left into the main hospital entrance. No, she heads somewhere else.

Is she sick? Is she hiding something from me?

I take the stairs two at a time, my heart pounding in my chest. The fluorescent lights of the hospital corridor burn my eyes, but I don't slow down. I saw which way she went.

I round the corner and spot her through a window in a door. She's standing beside a hospital bed, her hand covering her mouth, her shoulders shaking.

That... doesn't look like...

What the *hell?*

I shove the door open, ready to—

And stop dead.

The person in the bed is a young woman. A girl, really. Maybe nineteen, twenty at most. And she looks vaguely familiar.

Is that her... sister?

Jesus Christ.

She's pale as death, hooked up to more machines than I can count—an IV drip and beeping monitors. Her hair is thin, patchy, like it's been falling out. She's so small under those blankets that she barely makes a dent in the mattress. She's asleep, or...

I feel vaguely sick. I'm a right fuckin' arsehole.

Erin spins around at the sound of the door, her eyes red-rimmed and wet. When she sees me, her face crumples completely.

"Cavin," she whispers, and it sounds like a broken thing. My heart. My goddamn heart. She reaches for me, and I envelop her on instinct, holding her as she breaks down and cries.

All that rage, all that jealousy, all that fuckin' stupidity, drains out of me in a single breath.

"Erin." I feel her whole body shaking with silent sobs.

I hold her tight, one hand cradling the back of her head, the other wrapped around her waist. "I'm sorry," I murmur into her hair. "I'm so fuckin' sorry, love."

She cries harder, and I just hold her, letting her break apart in my arms because I can feel that she's been holding this in for too long.

After a few minutes, she pulls back slightly, wiping at her face with shaking hands. "I'm sorry," she says. "I didn't mean to—I just—I should've told you the whole truth."

"Don't," I tell her firmly. "Don't apologize."

We're not just apologizing for this, but for our stupid damn fight, and we both know it.

She takes a shuddering breath and looks back at the girl in the bed. The girl's eyes are closed, her breathing shallow.

My chest tightens. "This is your sister."

Erin's voice cracks. "She's sick, and she's getting worse. Aplastic anemia—it's rare. Her bone marrow's fucked. She can't make blood cells properly anymore."

The words hit me like a fist to the gut.

"She was diagnosed two years ago," Erin continues, her voice barely above a whisper. "We thought—we thought the treatment was working. But it came back, worse this time. The doctors say..." She can't finish the sentence.

I pull her back against me, tucking her head under my chin. Over her shoulder, I look at Bridget. Really look at her. And I can see the resemblance. She has Erin's nose. The same shape to her face, though it's gaunt now, hollowed out by illness. She'd be a beauty, like her sister.

"That's who you've been texting," I say. It's not a question.

Erin nods against my chest. "Her. And the doctors. And... sometimes I'm just checking her charts online. They give family access to the medical portal. I check it constantly. Looking for any changes, any updates, any—" Her voice breaks again. "Any hope."

"Erin." I tilt her face up to look at me, brushing away her tears with my thumbs.

"I should have told you the whole truth," she whispers. "I just—" She squeezes her eyes shut. "I've been so scared, Cavin. I'm terrified I'm going to lose her."

I pull her close again, and this time I press a kiss to the top of her head. "You're not alone anymore," I tell her. "You hear me? Whatever happens, you're not facing this alone."

She makes a small sound, something between a sob and a laugh. "You must think I'm such a mess."

"I think you're the strongest woman I've ever met." And I mean it. Carrying this weight, keeping it hidden, trying to be normal while her sister fights for her life—that takes a kind of strength I'm not sure I have.

Movement from the bed draws our attention. Bridget's eyes flutter open, unfocused at first, then land on us.

I'm not scared of fucking anything, but somehow, facing her sister and her illness has me shaking.

"Erin?" Her voice is barely a whisper, rough and weak.

Erin pulls away from me and goes to her sister's side immediately, taking her hand. "I'm here, love. I'm right here."

Bridget's gaze shifts to me, confused and hazy. She blinks

slowly, like she's trying to focus. "You brought the husband?"

"Aye," Erin says softly, glancing back at me. Her eyes are still wet, but there's something else there now. Something like hope and definite pride. "You remember Cavin."

"Mmm. You're right, sis, he's well fit," Bridget mumbles with a lopsided smile, her eyes drifting closed again before opening. Erin giggles in spite of herself. I squeeze her hand. "You're brave. Braver than me." She's clearly delirious, the fever or the meds making her thoughts scattered.

I step closer to the bed, keeping my movements slow and gentle. "Hello again, Bridget."

Her eyes find me again, struggling to stay open. "You're real big," she says, almost childlike. "Erin said you were big. Like a... a mountain."

Despite everything, I feel the corner of my mouth twitch. "Did she now?"

"Don't listen to her," Erin says quickly, her cheeks flushing. "She's on a lot of medication."

"Mountains are good," Bridget continues, her voice fading. "Safe. You keep Erin safe?" Her eyes try to focus on me, and there's something fierce there despite how weak she is.

"I will," I tell her, and I mean it with everything I have. "I promise."

"Good." Bridget's hand twitches in Erin's grasp. "She deserves... deserves to be happy. Even if I'm..." She trails off, her eyes closing.

"Hey, none of that," Erin says, her voice thick with tears. "You're going to be fine. You're going to get better."

"Liar," Bridget whispers, but she's smiling slightly. "Love you though."

"Love you too," Erin chokes out.

I watch them together, and something in my chest cracks open. This is what Erin's been carrying. This is the weight she's been shouldering alone. While I was busy being jealous about her fuckin' phone, she was watching her baby sister die.

Bridget drifts off again, her breathing evening out into sleep. Erin sits on the edge of the bed, holding her hand, reluctant to let go.

"She's been like this for a few days now," Erin whispers. "Some days she's more lucid. Other days, she doesn't even know where she is."

I'm quiet for a moment, processing. "Your mam wasn't honest with us."

Erin stiffens under my hands. "I know. I'm sorry." She sighs. "My mom has reasons for joining our family to yours, and I didn't want you to think we were using you, or—"

"Erin." I turn her to face me. "Before? We *were* using each other. But that doesn't matter now because what we have has *nothing* to do with our families. I'm going to help because you're my wife. Because Bridget is my family now too. You understand?"

Her eyes fill with fresh tears. "You don't have to—"

"I want to." I cup her face in my hands. "Whatever she needs. Whatever you need. We'll figure it out."

She breaks down completely then, sobbing into my chest while I hold her. I let her cry it out, all the fear and stress and exhaustion she's been holding in. My god, if this were one of my sisters—if Bronwyn or Kyla—I can't complete the thought, but my throat is tight, and my eyes are blurry.

I let out a shuddering breath of my own.

Bridget's my sister now.

Eventually, she calms, hiccupping slightly. "I need to stay a bit longer."

"I know." I check my watch.

Fuck.

Thirty-three minutes until the tribute.

I look at Erin—exhausted, heartbroken, finally trusting me with the truth. I look at Bridget, so small and fragile in that bed.

I walk over to the bed and tuck a blanket closer around Bridget. She looks up at me and smiles. "You're sweet," she says, before she turns her head back to the pillow and falls back asleep.

Erin snorts softly behind me. "She's definitely delirious."

I tug a lock of her blonde curls and shake my head at her, then sigh. I do have to go. I don't want to but...

She's my *wife.*

I make a decision then.

"I have somewhere I have to go."

I hate the way her face crumples, squaring herself to face her sister's situation alone, and nods.

And I make a decision, right then. It's time to take the fucking risk.

"I want to tell you what this is, and why I need to go. Tonight... I'll be home after midnight. And I'm going to tell you everything."

She nods. "Okay. And I'll... tell you everything too."

I kiss her forehead fiercely. "Stay strong, love." I hold her to me. "I love you."

Chapter Twenty-Five

Erin

HE SAID... *I love you.* It made me cry all over again.

I didn't say it back.

When I tell him I love him, I want him to *know* that I do. That when I tell him I love him, I'll give everything I have for him. It isn't something I can say lightly.

But I'm getting there. I know I am. I can't even believe that a few months ago, I hated him, but now...

I will replay the image of him gently tucking the blanket in around Bridget on repeat, over and over, because I like the way I softened watching him with her.

Money doesn't mean shite if I can't use it to help the people I love.

I love you.

I love you.

I drive home with those thoughts circling through my mind. The city lights blur past my windows. Ciarán's driving, and I barely register the route we're taking while my brain replays everything. His confession. His tenderness with Bridget. The way he looked at me like I was the only solid thing in his collapsing world.

I send him a text because I'm curious.

> What brought you to the hospital?

I can see he's texting when the little dots appear, but they start and stop a few times. Finally, a brief message comes through.

> **Cavin**
> Let's talk about that in person

> Okay

I must have drifted off. Noises from downstairs wake me. When I reach the landing, he's in the sitting room, standing by the window with a glass of whiskey in his hand, staring out at nothing. When I step through the doorway, he turns, and the raw vulnerability on his face makes my chest tighten.

He's stripped to just a white tee that stretches across his back, but is still wearing the fitted trousers that hug his arse. Bridget wasn't kidding. He *is* easy on the eyes.

"You woke up," he says, voice rough.

He sets the glass down and runs both hands through his hair, a gesture I've come to recognize as his tell when he's about to say something difficult. I love how it makes his hair stand up on end a bit, all boyish and disheveled. "We need to talk, love. Properly this time. No more keeping you in the dark."

I settle onto the sofa, tucking one leg under me. "I'm listening."

He paces for a moment, then stops, facing me fully. "Every month, on the nose, I'm tasked to pay a fuckin' tribute. The money I've been hemorrhaging every month isn't some business arrangement gone sideways. It's extortion. Pure and simple."

My stomach drops. "How long?"

"Since Malachy died." His jaw works. "Five hundred thousand euros. Every month. Like clockwork."

"*Jaysus.*" The numbers make my head spin. "That's—"

"Millions. Aye." He laughs, but there's no humor in it. "Been draining us dry, bit by bit. I've had to make moves I never wanted to make, get into bed with people I shouldn't have, just to keep the cash flowing."

I cross my arms over my chest. "Why? Who's demanding it?"

"That's the fuckin' problem, Erin. I don't bloody *know*." He drops onto the sofa. I can't help it—I crawl into his lap, facing him. "The instructions come through burner phones. Different numbers every time. Drop-off locations change.

I've tried tracing the money—it gets laundered through so many accounts it's impossible to track. Malachy wouldn't tell me who, and I know it's because he suspected that I'd refuse or get my brothers involved and cause a fuckin' war."

I reach for his hand, threading our fingers together. "So he just wanted you to keep paying a ridiculous sum of money to a stranger? You, one of the most powerful and feared men this side of Ireland? That's *gobshite*."

He holds my chin, tips my face toward his, and kisses me. "That's my girl," he says softly.

"Cavin, there has to be *something*. Some clue about who—"

"I know. And if I don't pay it, my family pays. Bronwyn's kidnapping was a warning."

"My god," I mutter. "That's terrible."

His grip on my hand tightens almost painfully. "I can't... Erin, I can't let anything happen to them. Christ. I don't want someone innocent hurt."

The anguish in his voice breaks something open in me. This dangerous, violent, complicated man would do anything for his family.

"I still don't get why Malachy didn't tell you who it was?" I ask. "He *had* to know."

Cavin's expression darkens. "That's what's been eating at me. He knew, Erin. I know he did. Right before he died, he told me about the tribute—said I had to pay it, no questions asked. Said I couldn't tell anyone, couldn't try to find out who was behind it. He made me swear."

"That doesn't make sense. Why would he—"

"I don't know!" The frustration in his voice makes me flinch. He immediately gentles, his thumb brushing over my knuckles. "Sorry. It's just... he was terrified. Whatever this was, whoever this is... He said if I tried to investigate, if I told anyone, they'd know."

"So you've been dealing with this alone."

"Aye. Couldn't risk telling anyone. Every month, I make the drop and pray it's enough to keep her safe. Family's caught on some, but I've kept them in the dark. Malachy said if I told my brothers or cousins, they'd find out."

I shake my head. "Then there's someone on the inside."

"Of course not," he scoffs. "We're all fucking loyal to the core."

"Then why not tell them? Why not use the resources your family has to find out who this is?"

He sighs. "I can't risk it. Malachy made that abundantly clear."

"Then we *find* them," I say firmly. "Whoever's doing this, we find them, and we *end* it."

He looks at me like I've lost my mind. "We?" He snorts. "Erin—"

"You think I'm going to sit back and do nothing? After everything?" I shift in his lap. "I'm not some fragile thing that needs protecting. I grew up in this world, too, remember? My da wasn't exactly running a *charity*." I tug a lock of *his* hair. "You should know that."

"This is different. This is—"

"This is the bastard who's been bleeding you dry and threatening your sister." My voice turns hard. "I want every detail about the tribute. Every single one. Dates, times, locations, amounts, instructions—everything. And I want a list of every enemy your family has. Everyone who might have a grudge, everyone who'd benefit from bringing you down."

He stares at me. "That's a long fuckin' list, love."

"Then we better get started." I lean closer. "I'm not walking away from this. From you. So either we do this together, or I do it on my own, and you can spend your energy worrying about both me *and* Bronwyn... *and* Bridget."

A muscle tics in his jaw.

I stand, suddenly restless. "I need to change. I've been in these clothes all day and fell asleep in them."

"Go on, then. I'll start making that list."

I head upstairs to the bedroom, stripping off my jeans and jumper. I completely forgot I was wearing the periwinkle-blue top underneath. It came just before Bridget's nurse called me, so I just pulled a jumper over it. It's backless, the fabric draping elegantly but leaving my entire back exposed. Sophisticated but sexy as hell.

I stare in the mirror. The color brings out my eyes, and the way it skims my curves while showing off my back makes me feel powerful. Dangerous.

I'm still admiring it when I hear Cavin's footsteps on the stairs. He appears in the doorway, and the moment his eyes land on me, he goes completely still.

"What's this, then?" His voice has dropped an octave.

"Something I ordered online. Just trying it on." I turn, giving him the full view. "It's called *periwinkle*. Isn't that cute? I thought maybe when you take me back to The Craic—"

"*No.*" He crosses the room in three strides, his hand sliding possessively across my bare back. "Absolutely fuckin' not."

I raise an eyebrow. "Excuse me?"

His eyes have gone dark, pupils blown wide. "If you wear that in public, Erin, I swear to Christ, I will bend you over my knee and spank your arse until you can't sit."

Heat floods through me at the promise in his voice. "Is that supposed to discourage me?"

He makes a sound low in his throat—half growl, half groan. "You're going to be the death of me."

"Good thing you love me, then."

His hand slides up my spine, fingers tracing the exposed skin. "Aye. Good thing."

Then he's kissing me, and it's hungry and desperate and everything we both need after the day we've had. His hands map every inch of bare skin, and I arch into his touch.

"The list can wait," he murmurs against my mouth. "We need make-up sex."

"Aye," I breathe out. "It can wait. I like the sound of make-up sex."

He backs me toward the bed, and I forget about tributes and

enemies and everything else except the way he makes me feel—wanted, needed, *his*.

When my legs hit the mattress, he eases me down, following me onto it. His hands slide under the fabric, pushing it up and over my head in one fluid motion. Then I'm bare from the waist up, and he looks at me like I'm something precious. My breath catches.

"You're so fuckin' beautiful," he whispers, and then his mouth is on my breast, his tongue circling my nipple before he takes it between his teeth, just enough bite to make me arch into him with a cry.

My fingers tangle in his hair, holding him to me as he lavishes attention on first one breast, then the other. Every touch feels electric, like my skin has been sensitized to him specifically.

I tug at his shirt impatiently, and he helps me pull it off, baring the sculpted muscle and scattered scars beneath. I trace one with my finger—a long, thin line across his ribs.

"Belfast job gone wrong," he murmurs. "Four years ago."

I lean up and press my lips to it. Then another scar, and another... mapping his history with my mouth until he groans and captures my lips again.

His hands make quick work of the rest of my clothes, dragging them down my legs along with my knickers. Then I'm bare beneath him, and the hunger in his eyes makes me feel powerful.

"You're overdressed," I tell him, my voice husky.

"Aye. Can't have my girl lookin' at me with all that hunger and not give her what she wants, can I, *mo chroi?*" He smirks and stands to shed the rest of his clothes. When he's finally naked, I let myself look. Really look. He's all lean muscle and coiled strength, and his thick erection tells me he *wants* me.

He prowls back onto the bed, settling between my thighs. His fingers trace up the inside of my leg, teasing, until I'm squirming beneath him.

"Mmm, yes. Please."

"Please what?" His finger circles where I need him most but doesn't quite touch. "Use your words, love."

"Touch me. Please."

He rewards me by sliding one finger inside, and I cry out at the sensation. He adds another, curling them just right while his thumb finds my clit. The combination makes stars burst behind my eyelids.

"Mmm, look at you, already trembling. You've missed my hands, haven't you? Sweet fuckin' *Jaysus*, you're tight as a drum, love," he murmurs appreciatively. "So perfect."

He works me with devastating precision, building the pleasure higher and higher until I'm right on the edge. Then he withdraws, ignoring my whimper of protest, and replaces his fingers with his mouth.

The first stroke of his tongue makes me arch off the bed. He grips my hips, holding me in place, while he devours me like a man starving.

Every nerve ending feels like it's on fire, pleasure coiling tighter and tighter in my core.

"Cavin, I'm going to—"

"That's it, love. Let go for me. I want to feel you fall apart on my tongue," he commands against me. "Come for me, Erin."

I shatter, crying out his name as waves of pleasure crash through me. He doesn't stop, working me through it until I'm trembling and oversensitive.

When he finally pulls back, his lips are glistening, and his eyes are dark with need. He crawls up my body, kissing me deeply so I can taste myself on his tongue.

"I need to be inside you," he growls.

"Yes. God, yes."

He positions himself at my entrance, then pushes inside in one slow, devastating thrust. We both groan at the sensation —the perfect stretch, the overwhelming fullness.

"Fuck," he groans. "You feel incredible."

He starts to move, finding a rhythm that has me clinging to his shoulders. Each thrust hits deeper than the last, stoking the fire building in my core all over again.

"Harder," I demand, raking my nails down his back.

"Aye, my lass wants it rough, does she? Take it then, Erin McCarthy. Take what's yours."

He complies with a growl, snapping his hips faster, rougher. The headboard bangs against the wall with the force of it, and I don't care. I just need *more*—more of him, more of this, more of us.

"You're mine," he says fiercely. "Say it."

"*Yours.*" I gasp. "I'm yours."

He buries his face in my neck, his teeth finding that spot that makes me see stars. I can feel another orgasm building, bigger than the first. He knows *exactly* how to play me, and I am savoring every second.

"Come with me," I manage. "I want to feel you—"

"Aye, love," he whispers.

His hand slides between us, fingers finding my clit, and that's all it takes. I come apart with a cry, clenching around him, and he follows with a guttural moan. I feel him pulse inside me as he empties himself, and the intimacy of it makes emotion swell in my chest.

We stay locked together for long moments, both of us breathing hard. Finally, he pulls out carefully and rolls onto his back, dragging me with him so I'm sprawled across his chest.

His fingers trace idle patterns on my spine. "You're amazing, you know that?"

I press a kiss to his collarbone. "You're not so bad yourself."

He huffs a laugh, and I feel it rumble through his chest. We lie there in comfortable silence, our heartbeats slowly returning to normal.

"We'll figure it out," I finally say. "The tribute, whoever's behind it. We'll find them. We'll do it."

His arms tighten around me. "Together?"

"Together," I promise. "There's an answer somewhere."

"Aye. There is." His voice is determined now, not defeated. "And we'll find the bastard."

And in this moment, tangled up in him, with the weight of the world waiting outside, I almost believe it.

Chapter Twenty-Six

Erin

Cavin's fighting tonight, and I'm fucking thrilled
about it. The guy's a ticking time bomb of energy, and
nothing settles him like a brutal brawl. And let me tell you,
watching him in the ring? It's fucking *hot*.

There's something incredibly validating about seeing my
man dominate like that. He takes every hit and gives it right
back, tenfold. And the raw, primal energy? It's a fucking
aphrodisiac.

So when I slip into that blue top, I know *exactly* what I'm
doing.

It's backless, held up by the thinnest straps, and it shows off
way too much skin. Cavin ordered me not to wear it to the
fights or in public. Which, of course, is exactly why I'm
wearing it.

I check myself in the mirror one last time. My hair's wild,
falling in messy blonde waves around my shoulders. The

fabric clings to all the right places, and the color makes my skin glow under the dim lights.

He's going to be pissed, and that thought sends a thrill straight through me.

Ciarán gives me a knowing look when I emerge from the back room, but he keeps his mouth shut. Smart man. He's learned not to get between Cavin and me when we're playing these games.

Because that's what this is. A dangerous game.

The ring's packed, the energy electric. There's a big fight tonight, some arsehole from Dublin thinks he can take Cavin down. Ha! *Eejit*.

I position myself near the bar where I know Cavin will see me—close enough to the ring that there's no missing me, but far enough back that I'm "safe" in the crowd.

I should not be here, and I well know it. I put safety precautions in place, of course. All my guards and a few extra.

The lights dim. The crowd *roars*.

And then... *he* appears.

Cavin walks through the crowd like he owns the place. Every person here is part of his world, playing by his rules. He's shirtless, his skin gleaming under the lights, scars and muscles on full display.

My mouth goes dry.

He's mine.

He's almost to the ring when his eyes find me.

I watch it happen in slow motion. His gaze sweeps the crowd, lands on me, and stops. I see the exact moment he registers that I'm there. That he sees what I'm wearing, sees the bare expanse of my back, the way the fabric drapes.

His jaw clenches, and his eyes go dark, dangerous.

He points at me, one finger, direct and unmistakable. Then he drags that finger across his throat in a gesture that's crystal clear: *I'm proper fucked now.*

I smile at him—it's slow, deliberate, and defiant.

His nostrils flare, and for a second, I think he might actually climb back down, come over here, and drag me out by my hair in front of everyone.

But the ref's calling him, and the crowd's chanting his name. He shoots me one last look of pure promise and climbs into the ring. I stifle a giggle, but the laughter soon dies in my throat when the first punch is thrown.

The fight is *brutal.*

Cavin's always controlled in the ring, methodical, but tonight there's an edge to him, an aggression that goes beyond strategy. He's punishing his opponent, every punch harder than it needs to be, faster.

Uh-oh.

He's fighting angry... because of me.

The knowledge does something to me. Heat pools low in my belly, and my skin feels too tight, too hot. I watch the way his body moves—the flex of his shoulders, the blood on his knuckles. The way he dominates the space, the other man, *everything.*

And my fuckin' *god*, I want him.

It's wrong, probably. He's dangerous and violent, and he's definitely going to punish me for this. But watching him like this, all powerful and primal and *mine* in some possessive way I don't fully understand... I've never been more turned on in my life.

The crowd presses close around me, and I'm grateful for it, grateful they can't see the way I'm breathing too fast and the flush creeping up my chest. I clench my thighs together, but I'm aroused out of my *mind*.

I replay the spanking he gave me in the hallway before our first dinner. I remember how hot and bothered I was after, even when I hated him.

How I'd play it over and over in my mind when I touched myself.

Cavin lands a devastating combination, and his opponent goes down hard. The ref counts *eight, nine, ten...* and it's over.

Shite.

Cavin's won. Of course he's won.

He doesn't celebrate. Doesn't play to the crowd. Instead, his eyes find me immediately, laser-focused through the chaos.

He crooks one finger at me, then points toward the back hallway and his private changing room, and mouths one word:

Now.

Oh god, oh god, oh god.

I am not prepared for this.

I'm not ready.

What have I done?

I have to face my husband and can't even call Bridget. "*Hey, so, I did this thing I knew would piss him off, and he's mentioned a few times that he was going to punish me, and because I'm fucked in the head, I maybe want him to, but now that it's time, I'm thinking I'm crazy, so...*"

My heart kicks into overdrive.

I push through the crowd on shaking legs. My guard moves to follow, but Cavin must signal him off because he stops, letting me go alone.

The hallway is dimmer, quieter. The sounds of the ring fade behind me as I walk toward the changing room door. My hand trembles when I reach for the handle.

I'm scared.

I'm excited.

I'm so far gone for this man.

The changing room is small, sparse. Just a bench, some lockers, and a shower in the corner. It smells like sweat and leather and violence.

I wait.

Every second feels like an hour. I pace, then force myself to stand still. Sit on the bench, then stand again. My pulse is racing, my skin hypersensitive.

What's he going to do?

The door opens.

Cavin fills the doorway, backlit by the hallway. He's still shirtless, still streaked with sweat and blood. His chest heaves with exertion, and his eyes are absolutely feral.

He steps inside and closes the door behind him.

Locks it.

The click of the lock is the loudest sound I've ever heard.

"Hey, handsome."

"I told you," he says, low and rough, "not to wear that."

"I know." My voice comes out breathier than I intended.

"You knew damn well what you were doing and wore it anyway, didn't you?" He stalks toward me slowly, predatory. "You wore it to provoke me. To get a reaction. You deliberately *disobeyed* me."

I lift my chin. "Might've done."

"Might've done," he repeats. "You wanted my attention, Erin? Well, you have it now."

He's close enough now that I can see the way his pupils are wide, see the muscle flexing in his jaw.

"Turn around," he says quietly.

My breath catches. "Cavin—"

His hand claps against my arse, hard, the hardest spank he's ever given me. Oh *shit*. "This is not the time to sass me, woman. I said, *turn around*."

I turn slowly, and I hear his sharp intake of breath when he sees my bare back fully exposed. Can feel the heat of his gaze like a physical touch trailing down my spine.

"You have any idea what you do to me?" He's closer now, right behind me. "Walking around in this, knowing every man in that club is looking at what's mine?"

His hand touches my lower back, just his fingertips, featherlight, and I shiver.

"You wanted to taunt me. To push me." His hand slides up my spine, slowly, possessively. "Well done, then."

Before I can respond, his hand closes around my upper arm, and he guides me toward a thick wooden chair.

He sits.

And then he pulls me down across his lap.

Oh god.

"Cavin—" I gasp, suddenly very aware of my position, of his thighs beneath me, solid and unyielding, how much bigger he is, and how strong. I just saw him beat a full-grown monster of a man to a pulp, and he barely broke a sweat.

"You want to act like a bold girl?" His hand rests on my lower back, holding me in place. "Then you get treated like one."

My heart's pounding so hard I'm sure he can feel it. I'm draped across his lap, my hands braced on the floor on one side, my toes barely touching on the other. Completely at his mercy.

"This is what happens," he says, his hand sliding down to rest on the curve of my ass through the thin fabric of my skirt, "when you disobey me."

I should protest. Should tell him to let me up.

But I don't want to.

"Do you understand?" His hand flexes, possessive.

"Yes," I whisper.

"Good girl."

His hand disappears, and I have just enough time to tense before—

Smack.

The first spank lands hard, and I gasp, more from shock than pain. The sound echoes in the small room. It's much harder than the spanking he gave me before. And much... hotter, now that I know what he can do with those hands.

"*That's* for wearing the top."

Smack. The other side.

"That's for disobeying me."

The sting builds, spreads, and god help me, but it's not just pain. It's heat, need, and something electric sparking under my skin.

But he's holding himself back—I know he is. Why did I expect him to really lay into me?

Why do I want that?

His hand slides up and finds the zipper of my skirt.

"And this," he says, with barely controlled restraint, "is so you really learn your lesson."

He pulls the zipper down slowly. His hand slides under the fabric, tracing the curve of my ass, teasing the edge of my thong. I shiver, anticipation building with each touch.

"Cavin," I whisper, my voice trembling with a mix of fear and desire.

"Shh," he murmurs, his breath hot against my ear. "I'm not done with you yet."

His fingers hook into the waistband of my thong, pulling it down slowly, agonizingly. I lift my hips to help him, my body aching with need.

The cool air hits my bare skin, and I feel exposed, vulnerable. But there's something thrilling about it too, knowing that I'm completely at his mercy.

"Spread your legs," he commands.

I do as he says, my heart pounding in my chest. His hand slides between my thighs, his fingers finding my most sensitive spot with ease.

I gasp, my body arching at his touch. He's gentle at first, teasing, but then his fingers become more insistent, more demanding.

"Cavin," I moan, my hips moving in time with his touch.

"Quiet," he growls, his other hand coming down hard on my arse, the sting mixing with the pleasure.

I cry out, the sound muffled by the bench. His fingers

continue their relentless assault, pushing me closer and closer to the edge.

Just when I think I can't take it anymore, he stops, his hand resting possessively on my ass.

"Please," I beg, my body aching for release.

"Please what?" he asks in a low growl.

"Please let me come," I whisper, my cheeks flushing with embarrassment.

He chuckles, a dark, dangerous sound. "Not yet. You don't get to come until I say so. Not bad girls like you."

His fingers slide back inside me, and I moan, my body clenching around him. He starts to move them in and out, slowly at first, then faster, harder.

I can feel my orgasm building, my body tensing with each stroke. But just as I'm about to tip over the edge, he pulls his fingers out, leaving me gasping and desperate.

"No," I whimper, my body aching for release.

"Patience," he murmurs, his hand coming down hard on my ass again. "I'll let you come when I'm ready. When I'm convinced you'll be a good girl again."

His fingers find my clit again, rubbing in slow, deliberate circles. I moan, my hips moving against his hand, seeking more friction.

"Cavin, please," I beg, my body trembling with need.

"Are you going to behave? Obey your husband?"

"*Yes*. Yes, I promise."

"Are you sorry for being a naughty little lass?"

"Yes, so sorry!"

"Come for me, Erin," he commands.

And I do, my body exploding with pleasure, waves of ecstasy crashing over me. I cry out, my voice echoing in the small room.

He continues to rub, drawing out my orgasm until I'm a trembling, boneless mess across his lap. Only then does he pull his hand away, leaving me gasping and spent.

"There's a good lass," he murmurs, his hand stroking my back soothingly.

I take a deep, shuddering breath, my body still tingling with the aftershocks of my orgasm.

"Cavin," I whisper.

He leans down, his lips capturing mine in a fierce, possessive kiss. I melt into him, my body molding to his, completely and utterly his.

When he finally pulls away, I'm breathless, my heart racing. I look up at him, my eyes filled with love and desire.

"Yours," I say, the words a promise.

He smiles, a slow, dangerous smile. "Mine," he agrees, his hand cupping my face tenderly. "You're always fuckin' mine, woman, and don't you forget it. Now, the night is still young, lass, isn't it?"

I turn around and give him a curious look.

"That wasn't proper punishment, was it? That was a warning."

Ahh.

He spins me around to sit in his lap, and I start tapping my pocket. One, two, three, four.

"You've been to The Craic before, but not as *my* guest."

My eyes go wide.

"You know it's a private family club. Exclusive. But if you want to be my wife, you need to understand what this means."

Oh, okay.

"And I want to deal with my wife properly. You disobeyed me twice tonight, on purpose. You wore that top, and you came to the fight. You think a few smacks on the arse is enough for that?"

I giggle nervously. "Um, what are we going to do?"

He leans in and gives me a wicked smile. His pupils look nearly black. "Take you somewhere where you can scream as loud as you want, and no one will come running to save you."

My jaw drops open.

"And we're going to start right now, love. I don't want you to see anything on the way. I want you to rely on your other senses."

I feel him reach down and take something—I can't quite see what it is. A T-shirt? He slides it over my eyes and ties it at the back.

"You wear my fucking coat so nobody sees you like this too."

And then, just like that first night by the cliffs, he drapes his jacket over my shoulders.

"Let's go."

Just like usual, he lifts me and slides me over his shoulder. My bag is back with my bodyguards.

"Cavin, I have to—"

His hand claps across my arse. "You have to obey your husband. That's what you have to do, love."

My heart beats a frantic rhythm in my chest. How can someone feel both scared and utterly safe at the very same time?

I know The Craic and the ring are within walking distance. Is he... walking with me, over his shoulder, blindfolded?

I believe he is.

Cavin!

How did he just beat the shite out of the man in the ring and still have the stamina to *carry me* to the club?

I feel a rush of warm air and hear a hush come over the crowd. And they go wild—clapping, screaming. They must see me over his shoulder like *I'm* his purse of winnings tonight.

Oh my *god*. I feel a bit dizzy.

"Mr. McCarthy, sir." Someone says. "Can I help you, sir?"

"Bring my car around," he says. "Have my cousin park it at

The Craic. And as per usual, have my purse sent to the same place as always."

He doesn't know yet what I've been doing with his winnings. He will soon. Makes me feel like I have a bit of control here, even when I'm being hauled to my doom by my modern-day caveman, who's two steps away from banging his chest with a damn club.

I've got my own secrets. And mine actually make money.

"Right away, sir."

I can hear the sounds of music, laughter, people drinking, and glasses clinking. But his hand is possessive on my lower back, and everybody who speaks to him speaks with respect.

"Mr. McCarthy, well done, sir. Proud of you."

"Fuckin' honor to see you back in the ring, sir."

And then we're outside. The weather shifts, but I'm not cold because I'm still wearing his coat.

"Are you still half naked?" I yell out, and he pinches my arse.

"Of course not," he growls, but I can hear the laughter in his voice. "Pulled on a tee."

"Aye, it's got to be near freezing, and you're wearin' naught but a tee?"

"I'm hot," he says. "Be a good girl and be quiet before I take away your permission to speak."

"Oh my goodness, you can't—"

"Watch me," he says, right before his hand claps down on my arse again, and this time we have an audience.

We're walking down the street. People talk to him, and he keeps up the conversation, not even winded, as if it's totally normal to carry your blindfolded wife over your shoulder. The next thing I know, he comes to a stop and slides me down.

"Right, now. Walk with me. Hold my hand. I promise I'll take care of you."

I can hear the sounds—people talking, everyone speaking to him, still with respect.

"Yes, sir. No, sir. Right away, sir."

And it isn't until we get inside the club that the sounds change. I recognize something that sounds remarkably similar to Cavin's hand across my arse—a thud that makes heat flood through my body. Hushed voices of couples. The clink of chains. The sound of reverence.

"Daire. Lorcan." He greets his cousins.

"Evening, lads." I recognize Declan's voice. "Thought you weren't bringing her back here?"

"A bloke can change his mind," Cavin says.

"Anything I can get you, sir?"

"The private room."

This is where he comes. This is what he needs. This is the man I've married.

"Aye, McCarthy. You've got the Kavanagh girl."

"She's mine," Cavin says in a warning growl. "Eyes off. And she's no fuckin' girl—she's a woman who wears my ring and bears my name."

"So sorry, sir. Didn't know you got married."

"Learn it. Spread it. Pass it on."

We're walking down a hallway now—I can tell because the voices are quieter. I want to ask him more questions, but I don't want to lose the privilege of speaking.

"That's my girl. Keep walking. I won't let you trip. Head held high, Mrs. McCarthy, shoulders back." His voice dips low, rough with command, and every muscle in my body tightens in answer. He doesn't even have to touch me. The air between us feels taut, charged. My breath, traitorous, betrays the thrill that curls low in my belly.

"Here we are, love. Take off your blindfold."

I obey and blink in the bright light. Cavin reaches for the blindfold and rolls it in his hand. "Did the mask make it easier for you? Didn't want you to be overstimulated coming in here. It can be a bit much."

Oh my gosh. He was looking out for me, watching me to make sure I didn't get overwhelmed? That is so damn sweet.

"It did. Thank you," I whisper, and my eyes start scanning the room.

There's a flogger. Leather restraints. Mirrors and dim lighting.

He walks purposefully to the door and throws the lock. There's a shift in his energy now. This is Cavin's domain. Cavin's rules.

He circles me slowly, his eyes predatory. "You're going to take what I give you, love, aren't you?"

I swallow, nod, and lick my lips.

"Good. That's my good girl." He runs his knuckle across my jaw, down to my chin, and lower to my neck. "My very good girl. Now I want to watch you strip. Make a show of it, love. Everything but your knickers." He holds my face in his hand and kisses my forehead. I melt a little. "Leave those for *me*."

"Strip?" I repeat in a whisper.

"Aye," he says, his eyes going dark. "I'm going to show you exactly what happens when you don't listen to me. And you're going to thank me for it."

I'm breathless, aroused, and a tiny bit scared. "Cavin—"

His eyes darken. He leans in closer, his forehead pressed to mine, his thick, warm fingers encircling the back of my neck. "That's *sir* when we're in this room."

Oh god. Oh god, oh god, oh god.

"I'm a little nervous," I say quietly.

"Good," he says, turning to face me. "You should be. You were a naughty little thing, weren't you? Testing me, right before I went into the ring."

My heart pounds. I'm not prepared. Nothing could have prepared me for this.

This room is bathed in a deep red light, shadows dancing across the leather furniture and exposed brick walls. Beyond the door, the music thrums low and hypnotic—

something dark and primal. The room is larger than I remembered, with a massive bed that dominates one wall, covered in charcoal gray. There's a wooden sideways cross, mirrors on two walls, along with one full wall of... things. Leather straps, whips, things I don't recognize.

"Eyes on me, love," Cavin growls.

He's watching me as his fingers travel to his waist and he unbuckles his belt, sliding the leather free. It's a sound that makes me shiver. I watch as he coils it and places it deliberately on a little table.

"The last thing I want to do is control you," he says quietly. "This is for both of us. You and me. This only happens if you like it. If you're into this. If you want this."

I swallow hard and lick my lips. Part of me wants this, and part of me is scared as hell.

"So there's a safeword. A system," he says. "You say the word '*purl*' and this stops immediately."

"Purl? As in knit and purl?" I bite my lip so I don't giggle. He was listening, then.

"Mm-hmm," he says. "But unless you say that word, you take what I give you. You obey. You submit. And this is not the time to sass me, woman. This is not the time to test me."

I swallow hard. He's giving me an out, but I'm not sure I want to use it. I want to see where he can take me.

He circles me, and I feel his gaze like a physical touch, trailing over my skin.

"You wanted to provoke me tonight," he says. "You wore that top, knowing full well what it would do to me. And you did it, knowing I didn't want you there. You pushed and pushed, and here we are."

He stops behind me, so close I can feel his heat, and his mouth goes to my ear. "Congratulations, love. You have my full attention now, don't you?"

I do.

His hand slides up my spine, his fingers finding the zipper of my skirt. He drags it down slowly, deliberately. "Now strip. Don't make me say it again."

My hands shake as I comply. The damned backless top that started all this comes off first, followed by the skirt that pools at my feet. I step out of my heels and stand there in just my black lace thong—vulnerable and exposed—while he drinks me in.

"You're fucking beautiful. And all mine," he murmurs, circling back around to face me. His hand comes up, fingers gripping my jaw firmly. "Look at me."

My eyes meet his.

"Good girl. Now, who do you belong to?"

"You?" I whisper.

"That a question?"

I shake my head. "No. No, sir. *You.* I belong to you, Cavin."

His grip tightens. "Louder."

"*You.* I belong to you."

"That's right." He releases my jaw only to fist his hand in my hair, tilting my head back. "You've been racking them up, haven't you, love? Your punishments. Every little act of defiance."

I move toward him on trembling legs, but he stops me with a hand on my chest.

"Did I say you could move?" His eyes darken. "Stay right there."

He releases me, lifts the coiled belt, and pulls out the chair so he can sit in it, legs spread, belt folded in his thick hand. He doesn't speak, just lets me stare at it, lets the anticipation wind tighter in my belly.

"Now, over."

This is it. He's been dying to give me a proper punishment, and now here I am.

I drape myself across his lap, feeling the hard muscle of his thighs beneath me, the thick length of his arousal pressing against my hip. His hand smooths over my arse, almost gentle, before he hooks his fingers in the waistband of my thong and drags it down to my thighs.

"There we go," he says, his voice rough with approval. "Fucking gorgeous."

His belt connects with my bare skin—sharp, stinging. I gasp.

"Count them. And thank me for each one."

"One. Thank you."

Another spank, harder this time. "Louder, love."

"Two! Thank you!"

He doesn't rush. Between each strike, his hand roams—possessive, teasing, never giving me what I'm truly desperate for. His fingers trail between my thighs, barely grazing where I need him most, before pulling away.

"Jesus, you're *drenched*," he growls. "You like being punished, don't you, lass?"

"Yes," I whimper.

"Yes, what?"

"Yes, sir. Yes, I like it."

His belt comes down again, and I cry out the count. By ten, I'm shaking, grinding against his thigh, shameless and needy.

He fists my hair again, pulling my head back so I have to arch. "Greedy little thing. You think you've earned it?"

"Please—"

"Please, what?"

"Please, I need—"

He cuts me off with another spank, then his fingers finally, *finally* slide where I'm aching. But just as quickly, they're gone.

"Not yet. You'll come when I say you can, and not before. Understand?"

I nod desperately.

"Say it."

"I understand. I'll come when you say."

"Good girl." He pulls me up by my hair, positioning me so I'm straddling his thigh, the rough fabric of his trousers against my bare, sensitive skin. His hand wraps around my throat—not choking, but possessive, controlling. "Now ride my thigh. Show me how fucking desperate you are."

His other hand guides my hip, setting a torturous rhythm while his grip on my throat keeps me exactly where he wants me. Every time I get close, he stops me, holds me still, and watches me tremble and beg.

"Who do you belong to?" he asks again.

"You. Only you."

"And who decides when you come?"

"You do."

His thumb strokes my jaw, almost tender, while his eyes burn into mine. "That's my good girl. Now let me hear you beg for it properly."

Again, he lands the belt across my arse until I feel a strange sort of floating sensation begin to take over.

"Sir," I say, but my words come out slurred, and I can't speak right.

"Good girl," he says, cradling me in his lap. "Oh, that's my lovely girl. Now, I'd love to have my way with you, but I want you totally sober and awake for that. It's not right to take advantage when you're drunk."

"Not drunk," I say, but my words are slurred, and I can't open my eyes.

"You're a good girl," he whispers in my ear. "You took that so well, lass."

"Thank you."

I try to get to my feet, but I can't. I'm jello, floating, when the sound of an alarm blaring breaks the silence.

"Fuck," Cavin says. "Erin, can you stand? Can you walk, love?"

I open my bleary eyes and get to my feet, shaking. "I think… I think so." But I'm feeling woozy.

"Christ," he growls. "You stay right here and let me see what's happened. Don't come out. Do you hear me? Are you aware of what I'm saying right now?"

"Yes," I whisper, but the word feels far away, floating somewhere outside my body. Everything's soft around the edges, warm and distant. I'm cold, but I don't care. Nothing matters except the sound of his voice anchoring me.

He reaches for a thick, warm blanket and drapes it around my shoulders. The weight of it makes me sink deeper into whatever this floating feeling is.

Safe. I'm safe here.

His phone vibrates with a message. I'm vaguely aware of him scowling at it. I feel like I'm half asleep. My eyes are fluttering closed.

"Well," he says softly. "We'll see what she does with *this.*"

Chapter Twenty-Seven

Cavin

Of fucking *course* Erin's tripped out on a scene. The lass is ripe for it, primed and ready, but I need her lucid.

"Tell Declan to wait," I mutter. "He can send whatever he needs to me. I'll be sure she sees it."

Then I wrap her tighter in the blanket while she shivers, holding her close to me. If she wasn't half asleep, the lass would be asking me a million questions, but she's practically floating. I kiss the top of her head. She's half giggling, half asleep, high on what just happened. Christ, but she's perfect.

I hold her in my arms, pliant and quiet. I've heard that if you hold somebody chest-to-chest, after four minutes, your heartbeats sync.

I like to think ours already have.

"What do they need?" she whispers, even as she looks up at me with her eyes blown wide, her cheeks flushed pink— even the top of her chest is pink. She's naked under the blanket I've wrapped around her.

"They've got information you asked for," I say. "We have three more weeks to find out who the fuck is demanding this tribute."

"Mmm. Been mulling that over," she says quietly as her head lolls to the side, and I make a decision right then. Whatever information Declan has to send me, he can send us right here at The Craic. It's not that I don't want to take her home tonight, but I don't want to move her.

I want her right here with me until the morning light filters through the windows.

So I draw a bath. I squint at the little bottle next to the tub with pearly green-tinted beads and read "bath salts." Okay, that's supposed to be nice, I guess. So I shake some in, and soon the bath is lightly fragranced like eucalyptus and mint, and it makes the whole space feel clean and green.

We're secure here. Her guards are at the door, as well as mine, and no one gets into the club without permission.

Maybe we'll spend a few days here.

Maybe we'll enjoy ourselves, have a little honeymoon. What better place to have a honeymoon than a kink club? I smirk to myself, unwrap her blanket, and lift her.

"I was thinking," she says. "You know how sometimes thoughts come to you in the middle of the night when you're turning them over?"

"I've heard that happens, but it's not what happens to me when I dream. Yeah? What were you thinking?"

She swallows as I lower her into the water. "Oh *god*, you have to make sure I don't drown."

I grumble under my breath. That's not a laughing matter.

"Why would you drown?"

She opens one eye. "Because this is so relaxing, and I feel like I'm going to fall asleep."

Fair.

"I was thinking about the word 'tribute.' That's not something used here very often, is it? We don't pay tribute. There was a tradition years ago where one family would pay tribute to the next with a bride, right? My dad told me about it."

I nod. "Aye, my Uncle Cormac was the last one who fulfilled that tradition, but it was a one-time deal and not one we continued."

"But it's sort of an *American* term, isn't it? *Tribute*."

My eyes narrow. "Aye."

She nods, thoughtfully tapping her chin. "Who do you know in America?"

"We have some friends in New York," I say quietly. "They're Russian Bratva, but American Russian Bratva. The Romanovs. Mikhail Romanov's the head. Zoya's related."

She nods. "Yes. What about Boston?"

"Why do you ask about Boston?"

"Because there's a long history of Boston Irish."

"True. The Rossis. We know the Rossi family, but they're Italian mafia."

"Right. That was the man with blonde-gray hair who was there the day of the bombing, wasn't it? His sister's Marialena Rossi. She's a friend of a friend of Bridget's."

I nod. "Aye."

"Okay." She submerges lower in the bath once again so the warm water laps up to her chin. "Oh, this feels good. Have you seen anyone from America recently?"

"Aye, lads who came by and tried to lie their way into The Craic."

"Hmm. Interesting. Why would Americans even know this place existed?"

Erin's piecing things together. I can see it in her eyes—the way they dart back and forth, calculating. She's connecting dots I hadn't even realized were there. The American terminology, the Boston connection, the timing of it all. Her mind works like a fucking machine, cataloging every detail, cross-referencing information I didn't know she had stored away.

It's brilliant, terrifying, and sexy as hell.

My phone dings with a text, and I immediately tap it, assuming it's Declan.

It isn't.

The terms and conditions have been laid out in our initial contract. As per our agreement, the tribute payments will now increase to every two weeks. Your next is due in six days

I blink at the screen and scowl. "Jesus Christ, I swear—"

Her eyes open wide. "What?" She takes a little washcloth from a shelf and starts washing her face and her arms, eyeing me thoughtfully. "What is it?" she asks warily.

I notice the way her fingers tap, even on the water's surface. *One, two, three, four.*

I show her the text.

"How can they *do* that?" She shakes her head. "It's almost as if they want you to find out."

"Aye," I say. "Or almost as if they want me to not pay."

"And if you don't pay, they'll find a way to take your sister." She squeezes the bridge of her nose and exhales.

"Aye. And there's something I haven't told you." I sit on the commode, still clothed. I feel like I need to be ready, though for what, I don't know.

She props herself up on her forearms at the edge of the tub, studying me as I tell her what a bollocks situation we're in.

"Every time payment's due, something terrible happens. Something—it's almost as if they're trying to sabotage me."

"Of course they are," she says. "Who wants millions of dollars when they can have an actual kingdom? Makes total sense."

God, I love the way she thinks. I love watching the way her mind works, the way she doesn't try to sugarcoat or trivialize anything.

My phone dings with another text. And this time it actually is Declan, with file upon file of information.

"Okay, alright," she says, nodding. "Show it to me. Give me some time. I want to take a look at it and see what I can find."

I hand her the phone, watching as her eyes scan the information with laser focus.

This was the lass who aced every exam in school, got torn apart by the others for being too clever, and always handed in five pages when three were required.

Her brain is a fucking weapon, sharp and deadly, and I'm goddamn hard again just watching her.

She scrolls through documents, her fingers tapping that rhythm again. One, two, three, four. Financial records, shipping manifests, communication logs. Since Declan doesn't know about the tribute, I kept neutral and only asked to see information that dealt with our adversaries and alliances.

Now Erin's absorbing it all, filing it away in that magnificent mind of hers.

"Jesus, no wonder you got perfect marks in school," I mutter. "You're so fucking brilliant."

She smiles. "Yes, this makes a lot of sense," she says to me, not even looking up.

"What does?"

"It's not someone here in Ireland, no... You have rivals, yes, but they're too wise to how powerful you are here. And they know that if you found them out, you would destroy them. Right?"

"*Right.*"

"And then there are people like my da, who want to fortify themselves with your connections."

"It's a strange thing about connections with your da," I say to her, shaking my head. "I'm not quite sure how he benefits."

She gets a distant look and bites her lip.

"Erin," I say warningly. She gets that look when she's hiding something from me. It's almost childish, vulnerable in a way that makes my chest tighten. "What is it?"

"You met Bridget," she says haltingly. "Do you remember, at our engagement party turned wedding... when I met Dr. Rosenberg?"

"Aye." I cross my arms over my chest and nod. "Of course I do."

"I knew about him and his treatments because Dr. Rosenberg is one of the few people... maybe the only one... who can help my sister."

"*What?*" I stand up straighter.

"Yes," she says. She sighs and blows out a breath. "I didn't want you to think I was using you."

I narrow my eyes at her. "Okay?"

"He wouldn't have anything to do with my family. We tried. My father tried to send him money. Tried to bribe him to treat my sister. But he said that there are rules and regulations and whatnot, you know, with the free healthcare system. He has a two-year waiting list."

Her eyes water, and she blinks. A fat tear rolls down her cheek.

"And we don't..." She clears her throat and swallows hard. "We don't have two years. Right. So my hope was that you would talk to him. Maybe use the connection that you have. Pull some strings, Cavin, and have Bridget seen by Dr. Rosenberg."

She pauses, meeting my eyes with a fierce determination that's wet with tears. "And I don't know what else I can offer you, but I do have..." She clears her throat. "Seventy-two thousand quid that I've turned into two million."

She eyes me, defiant and desperate all at once. She's taken my purses, my winnings, and gambled with them.

"Is that how your brain works, Erin?" I ask, stunned.

"Aye," she says. "It's something my parents don't know. Because if they knew I had the ability to gamble and make money, they would have used me as a bargaining chip much sooner than they did."

"Holy Christ." I shake my head. "That's bloody brilliant."

She shrugs. "I may not have been the popular one in secondary school," she says quietly, "but I would definitely be the popular one in our circles now."

I grin at her. She's full of surprises. "You beautiful, frustrating thief. Of course we'll call Dr. Rosenberg. You save that money. Save it for Bridget. Invest it. Do whatever. We'll pay him. He owes us a favor. anyhow."

"He does?" More tears. I know that I tore her wide open emotionally. That she's vulnerable and susceptible to this, but I didn't expect—

"Aye," I say, kneeling down beside her. I cup her face in my hands, thumbs brushing away the tears. "This is going to work out. You'll look over the information that Declan sent. You'll find out who's behind this. Right? And then we'll *destroy* them. Together."

"Cavin." Her voice breaks.

"Right. And I'll make sure—can we save her, d'you think?"

She blinks, her lower lip trembling. "I don't know, but if there's anyone who could, it's him."

"Excellent."

Now it's her phone ringing.

"Why doesn't anyone give us a moment's peace? Honest to fucking Christ," I say, rolling my eyes skyward. Then her brow furrows, and she stares at the phone.

"It's Mam. She never calls me, especially this late."

Dread pools in my stomach. "Answer it, lass," I say. "Wait, I'll answer it. I know your hands are wet. Hold it up. Put it on speaker?"

She nods. I answer the phone and put it on speaker.

"Erin?" Her mother's voice is tight, strained. *Wrong.*

"I'm here, Mam." Erin's is steady, but I can see her knuckles going white where she grips the edge of the tub.

"It's Bridget." A pause, and I hear Tara Kavanagh draw a shaky breath. "She's collapsed. We're at the hospital now. They've got her in ICU, and the doctors are saying—" Her voice breaks. "They're saying it's worse than before. Much worse."

"*No.*" The word comes out of Erin like she's been punched.

"Can you come? Please? She's asking for you."

Erin's already trying to stand, water sloshing everywhere. I grab a towel and wrap it around her, holding her steady because she's shaking so badly I'm afraid she'll fall.

"I'm coming," Erin says.

The line goes dead.

Erin stares at the phone in my hand like it's a weapon. Then she makes this sound—this horrible, broken sound that tears something in my chest.

"I need to—I have to—" She's trying to move, but she can't seem to make her body work properly.

"Easy, love. Easy." I guide her out of the bath, keeping the towel wrapped around her. "I've got you. We'll get you dressed, and I'll drive you there."

"The tribute—" She gasps. "We were supposed to find—"

"Fuck the tribute." The words come out hard, fierce. "Your sister comes first. Always."

She looks up at me then, and Christ, the devastation in her eyes nearly brings me to my knees.

"She can't die, Cavin. She's twenty-two. She's my baby sister. She can't—" A sob cuts her off.

I pull her against my chest, not giving a shite that she's soaking through my shirt. "We're going to get there. And we're going to figure this out. I promise you. Whatever it takes."

I dry her off quickly, efficiently, then help her dress. She's moving on autopilot now, the shock setting in. I grab my coat and keys, and we're out the door in under five minutes.

The drive to St. Vincent's feels like it takes a lifetime and no time at all. Erin sits rigid in the passenger seat, staring straight ahead, her hands twisted together in her lap so tightly I'm worried she'll break her own fingers.

"Breathe, love," I murmur, reaching over to take one of her hands. "Just breathe."

"I should have visited her yesterday. I was going to, but then we got caught up with the files, and I thought—I thought I had time." Her voice cracks. "What if I don't get to say goodbye?"

"You'll get to say goodbye. Or better yet, you'll get to tell her to stop being dramatic and get well."

She lets out a sound that's half laugh, half sob. "She is dramatic. Always has been. Mam says she got all the personality, and I got all the brains."

"You've got plenty of personality, lass. *Trust* me."

That makes her giggle, which feels like a huge win right now.

She squeezes my hand. "Will you come in with me?"

I squeeze her hand back. "Try and stop me."

We pull up to the hospital, and I find a spot near the emergency entrance. Erin's out of the car before I've even turned off the engine, running toward the doors. I follow close behind, catching up to her in the lobby.

Her mother is there, looking a decade older than she did at our wedding. Her eyes are red-rimmed, her hair disheveled.

"Erin, thank god." She pulls Erin into her arms. "She's stable for now, but the doctors want to talk to us. Your father's already in with them."

Erin nods, swallowing hard. She glances back at me.

"Go," I say quietly. "I'll be right here."

She hesitates for just a second, then follows her mother down the corridor.

I sink into one of those uncomfortable plastic chairs and pull out my phone. Dr. Rosenberg answers on the second ring.

"McCarthy. Bit early for a social call."

"I need a favor," I say without preamble. "A big one."

"I'm listening."

"I'm told you know about aplastic anemia, and you're renowned for the treatments you provide."

"Aye," he says hesitantly. "It's my specialty."

"Name your price."

Another pause, longer this time. "This have anything to do with the Kavanagh girl?"

"Aye. And her sister is dying."

"Ah." I can hear the understanding in his voice. "I've got surgeries booked until... that's a full month out, but let me see—"

"We don't have a month."

He sighs. "Right. Alright, let me see. I can... I'll have to cancel the trip with my wife. You'll have to pay for the divorce, McCarthy." He laughs dryly.

"I'll pay for an all-inclusive, anywhere in the world."

"I may take you up on that. Alright. I can come to Ballyhock next weekend."

"That's bloody brilliant. Thank you."

"Don't thank me yet. Sometimes things are too far gone, and even I can't do anything to help. But I'll do my best. In the meantime, have her on continuous transfusion support and keep her in isolation. No visitors except immediate family— her immune system can't fight off a cold right now, never mind something worse."

"On it."

I hang up and lean back in the chair, closing my eyes. The tribute deadline is in six days. I can't pay before or after.

But when I think about Erin's face in the club, the way she looked when her mother called—

There's no choice at all.

Chapter Twenty-Eight

Erin

WHEN WE WALK in the room, Mam scowls at Cavin, and then at me. Turns out Cavin had a backup bag in the car with my signature uniform—yoga pants and an oversized jumper with "Cork City FC" on it. It's Cavin's.

"You're a respectable member of the McCarthy family now," my mother says. "Cavin, for Christ's sake, you let her walk around like *that*."

Cavin draws himself up to his full height. "That's my wife you're talking about. She married me for *you lot*, and she's beautiful in whatever she chooses to wear. Now, you'll bite your tongue about what she says and how she looks, or you'll find yourself not welcome in her presence. We clear on that?"

My mother stares, and her jaw drops a little bit.

"You wouldn't dare—"

"Try me," he says, hard. "I know what you're going through is difficult, Mrs. Kavanagh." His nostrils flare, and his knuckles turn white with the fist he's holding. "But you'll not be taking out your temper on Erin, never again, ma'am. Do you understand?"

She purses her lips at him and stares. "*Fine.* Wear whatever you want. I'm getting a cup of coffee."

"Go then," he says. "Text me before you come back in the room, will you?"

"Excuse me?" She turns on her heel.

"I'm with Erin. And you wind her up," he says. "Unless you learn to treat her properly, you'll be needing my say-so before you're allowed near her again."

"I have never in my entire life—I'm calling your mother," she says, pointing an irate finger at Cavin before she slams the door behind her.

"Good thing she didn't see what you wore *before*," he says in my ear.

Cavin's deep, masculine laugh fills the room, followed quickly by Bridget's tinkling one.

"That was bloody brilliant," Bridget says. "Well done, you."

She leans back on the pillow. There's a bloodstain from her last nosebleed.

"Let me get you fresh sheets and a pillowcase, Bridget."

"Thank you," she says with a grimace. "This is the bloody pits, isn't it?"

"Ugh, it is," I tell her. "But I have news. I wanted to tell you when Mam wasn't in the room."

"What's that?" she asks.

"There's a doctor, Dr. Rosenberg. He does experimental procedures for aplastic anemia. Do you remember we spoke to Mam about it?"

"Aye," she says. "This is the one who knows the McCarthys, right?"

I share a look with Cavin and nod.

"I've been in touch with him," he says quietly. "And he says he's going to see you in six more days."

My heart feels like it's soaring. "Six days, Bridget. You have to hold out. Can you?"

She laughs, brushing at the air. "Hold out? What are you on about? I've got years left. Thank you, Cavin," she says quietly. "I do very much appreciate it."

"Aye, of course," he says, reaching for my fingertips and kissing each one.

"Oh, you two lovebirds are the cutest. Who said that you'd want to spend your newlywed days *here*?" She shakes her head. "That isn't right, I tell you."

"We haven't just spent it here," I tell her with a shrug. "We've gone to Cavin's club a few times." Her eyes dance. "He's taken me to D'Agostino's for dinner. You know, I do like a good Italian dinner. And you know I don't want to *travel*."

Bridget grins. "I do."

"And you have to see the room he had fashioned for me."

I pull up the picture on my phone to show her. "Look how cute that little electric kettle is."

Bridget smiles. "You've got backup jumpers in the closet. I *love* that." She sighs. "I haven't seen you this relaxed in god knows how long. What spell have you cast on her?" she asks Cavin.

"The better question is, what spell has she cast on me?" He takes my hand. "Do you know I love her?" He pulls me onto his lap and kisses the apple of my cheek.

"Look at you two," she says. "You should at least have a proper honeymoon."

"Dunno, I'd say we've gotten a proper honeymoon," Cavin says.

Bridget rolls her eyes heavenward. "Oh, just like a man, isn't it?" she says, but she's giggling.

And I'm rolling mine too. Cavin smiles and gets a wicked gleam in his eyes. "Just got a text from your mam. She's asking for permission to come back in the room."

Bridget giggles. "Oh my, is she then?"

"Aye," he says.

"Well, did you give her permission to enter?" Bridget says, grinning at Cavin.

"Should I?" he asks my baby sister.

"Oh, I suppose," she says, with a dramatic sigh. "I mean, she is my mam after all. Honestly, Cavin, she can be abrasive, but she's harmless. She's not going to hurt anybody."

He says nothing, obviously disbelieving her. I'm yawning, exhausted. I don't know if I agree with Bridget. Cavin definitely doesn't.

"Got a text from Dr. Rosenberg," he says. "Gave him access to Bridget's labs, and this is what he says.

> **Dr. Rosenberg**
> The labs are concerning, but I see a way
> forward. We'll do what we can.

"I..." My lower lip wobbles.

"C'mere," he says, holding me to his chest. "Y'are alright."

There's something incredibly therapeutic about soaking a man's tee with your tears when he loves you. I finally slow my crying, as he rubs soothing circles on my back, and I take a deep breath.

"Cavin. She's asleep. Let's go back to the house," I say to him. "I'd like to look through those files that you and I were discussing."

We're quiet on the elevator, and he holds my hand.

"She'll be better, lass. I promise you."

"You can't promise me that."

"Well, I promise you I won't let your mother bully you anymore."

I smile at him softly. "I'll take you up on that. Did you see the look on her face?"

The elevator cruises to a stop at the bottom.

"We have six days," I whisper.

"Aye," he says. "But I'll have more for you to... invest soon."

"You don't mean—?" I ask him curiously.

"We're set to prepare for another fight tomorrow."

I blow out a breath. "Are you sure you want to keep doing this?"

He sighs and leans back. "I *love* fighting."

"But maybe... there's another way to do it that doesn't involve you and another man's fists, potential injuries, broken bones, and your blood spilled?"

He laughs. "Well, this time, I know I'm going to win and give you my purse. Mackey doesn't stand a bloody chance. And I'd like to see what you can invest in and do with it. Right?"

"Right," I say, smiling sheepishly. "I do know how to turn a dollar."

"Yeah, absolutely you do. You've got the Midas touch."

That makes me giggle. "You can fight, but only under one condition."

"I didn't ask you for permission," he says with an almost petulant look like a little toddler.

"I'm your wife. It only makes sense that you get permission to fight."

He gives me a lazy grin and tugs a lock of hair. "Alright, fine then. What's the condition?"

"The condition is that I *am* allowed to go. I don't want to be separated from you. I don't like it. But after the fight, maybe... you can take me to The Craic again."

"Alright," he says. "Deal."

We have six more days—the clock ticking like a time bomb, and death knocking at our door.

Six more days before my sister sees Dr. Rosenberg.

Before the tribute's due again.

Six more days... that we hope and pray Bridget can hold out.

Chapter Twenty-Nine

Cavin

Erin likes to keep herself busy. She's sat in the corner of my study, needles clicking away, while I pretend to focus on ledgers for hours. The truth is, I've been watching her more than the numbers.

The way the firelight catches on her soft golden hair. The little furrow between her brows when she counts stitches. Domestic, that's what this is.

And I'm fucking terrified of how much I love it.

I didn't know how much I needed it, wanted it, or how it grounds me. I grew up in a stable family, for all our flaws. And my time in prison showed me there's nothing I wouldn't trade for more of this domestic peace and comfort.

"What're you makin', then?" I ask her.

"Wouldn't you like to know," she says with a little wink. "This yarn's gorgeous, Cavin."

"Bridget might've texted me some tips."

"Oh, really? You and my sister are besties, now, is it?"

I chuckle. "Someone needs to tell me your secrets. You sure bloody won't." Truth is, I text her because I like to keep tabs on Erin's mam, and I like to know if there's anything Bridget needs. She's my sister now too. "Now are you going to tell me what you're makin'?"

"It's a surprise," she says, her lips tipping up at the edges.

Erin smiles a lot more lately, especially now that we know we have a chance with her sister. My pen stalls over the ledgers.

"Is it for me?"

"Don't be getting the big head about it," she says with a wink. But she's grinning like she just won something, and god, I'd give her the world to keep that smile on her face.

"Cavin, I've been getting these... apologies? People from St. Albert's."

"Aye," I say, not meeting her eyes.

"Cavin... what'd you *do*?"

"We're still trying to locate who's running the damn account, but I paid a few people a visit, didn't I? I didn't rough them up, not these nasty bitches in the comments. But I made it damn clear you're mine, and I won't tolerate another second of their bullshit."

Her eyes shine at me. "Thank you."

I wink at her. "You can thank me later."

Smiling at me, she ties off the last stitch and holds up a knit cap. I can't believe I didn't know this is what she was knitting right there in front of me. But now that she places her hands underneath it and stretches it around them, I can see it's simple but well-made. The kind that'll actually keep the cold out, not the shite fashion ones. The kind that people pay big money for.

"Come here," she says, crooking a finger at me.

I love when she looks at me like she wants me to fucking devour her. Or she wants to fucking devour *me*.

I cross to her, and she stands on her toes to reach the top of my head, adjusting it with careful fingers. Then she steps back, and her eyes go wide. Her lips part.

"*Jaysus*, Cavin," she whispers.

"What?" I touch the cap, wondering if I look like an eejit.

"I need you to chop wood. In that hat and no shirt. Like right now. Immediately."

Heat floods straight to my cock. "Is that right?"

"Yes," she says, fanning herself. "It's a medical emergency. I'll perish if you don't."

"Can't have that." I span her waist with my hands, lifting her like she weighs nothing. "What kind of husband would I be, letting my wife perish?"

I carry her to the desk and sweep the papers away with one arm. Files scatter across the floor. Projections, accounts, things that seemed vital five seconds ago now mean fuck all.

"Keep the hat on," she manages, right before I take her mouth.

I kiss her like I'm starving for it, like she's air and I've been drowning. Her lips part against mine, and I take full advantage, sliding my tongue against hers, swallowing the little moan that she makes.

Erin and I fit together like two pieces of a puzzle, and I crave the connection.

"Cavin." She breathes against my mouth. "Christ."

I love the way she says my name, like she can't quite believe this is happening. When she's in my arms like this, I can see the stillness on her face. And I know the constant noise in her head begins to quiet. Makes me feel ten feet tall, that.

I laugh and pull back just enough to look at her. Her lips are gently parted and cheeks flushed pink, eyes dark with want.

"Hat," she whispers, "stays on."

I grin at her, reaching up to adjust it on my head. "Doctor's orders, remember? Medical emergency."

"But you were supposed to go chop wood," she says with a wink.

"Then we need to take a trip. I don't think I have an axe or wood to chop."

She giggles, and the sound does something to my chest, making it tight and warm and full. This woman will be the death of me, and I'll die fucking grateful for it. Nobody makes me feel the way she does. I'm absolutely bolloxed when it comes to her—didn't know I needed it, didn't know I craved it like my next breath.

Her hands are already working at the buttons of my shirt. "Well, we can imagine, can't we?"

"Are you *objectifyin'* me?" I ask with a teasing swat to her arse.

"I—" She flushes, biting her lip. She loves when I spank her. "I am. And you love it."

I lean in, trailing kisses down her neck, finding that spot just below her ear that makes her shiver. "Behave yourself, Mrs. McCarthy," I whisper in her ear, and she stifles a moan. She loves hearing me call her that. Tells me everything I need to know.

"Say it again."

"Mrs. McCarthy..." I slide my hands up her thighs, pushing her skirt up. I reach the top of those damn leggings she wears every day and slide them down, over the curve of her hips, over the swell of her arse, down her thighs. "My wife. Mine."

She kisses me, harder this time, desperate. Her fingers fumble with the last button on my shirt, and then she pushes it off my shoulders, her palms flat against my chest.

"My god, you're..." She breaks off and flushes.

"What's that?" I cup the back of her head, kissing the apple of her cheek, her nose, her lips.

"Jaysus, Cavin," she whispers, almost reverent. "You're fucking gorgeous. Like something out of a dream, you are." Her fingers trace the tattoos on my ribs, the scars from fights and wars. "I love looking at you."

Her fingertips trace the scar right above the sternum, where I got shanked in prison. Should've killed me, but I'll never fuckin' go down without a fight.

"I know you don't believe me," she says, meeting my eyes. "But every part of you, even the parts that you think are broken, is beautiful."

Something in my chest tears open, raw and bleeding. No one's ever called me that. Dangerous, aye. Brutal, a right bastard—but beautiful?

Her hands span my chest. "I love you," she says, her eyes meeting mine. "I love you." She says it like she's just discovered it, and I love the way her smile lights up her whole face.

I kiss her again, softer this time—kissing her like I can claim her with the press of my mouth against hers. My hands find the hem of the worn jumper of mine she wears—too big, roomy, but she loves it. I pull it over her head and toss it aside.

She wears a simple white bra, nothing fancy, but she's the sexiest fucking thing I've ever seen.

"You're the beautiful one," I tell her, trailing my fingers along the edge of the lace. "Just look at you. Bloody perfect."

"I'm not—"

"You are." I silence her protest with another kiss, my hands working the clasp of her bra before I lower it and cup her arse. "Go way outta that talk," I warn her, my voice dropping low. "Don't let me hear you say otherwise again." She knows she'll go over my lap for a good, hard spanking, the *real* kind, if she does.

She bites her lip and nods. "Okay."

I laugh, then pull back to look at her properly. Erin and her "okays" will never not make me laugh.

Christ, but she's stunning. All soft curves and flushed skin, her nipples tight and begging for my mouth.

"Cavin." She tries to cover herself, suddenly shy.

"Don't you fucking dare." I catch her wrists and pin them to her sides. "Let me look at you. Let me see what's mine."

She shivers, but doesn't fight. Just watches me with those big eyes as I take my time, memorizing every inch of her.

"I like what I see. So fucking beautiful," I murmur, leaning down to take one nipple in my mouth.

She gasps, her back arching, hands flying into my hair, knocking that hat askew. I pull back with a grin. "Careful, love. You made that for me. You wouldn't want to ruin it now, would you?"

She smiles and reaches up to straighten the hat on my head, giving me full access to her breasts. I cup them, running my fingers along the sides and my thumbs over each hardened pink peak. She shivers as her fingers linger.

"Tell me you love me again."

"I love you, Cavin McCarthy."

I capture her mouth again, one hand sliding between her thighs. I find her already wet through her knickers, and when I press my thumb against the damp fabric, she moans.

"Please," she whimpers, grinding against my hand.

"Please what?" I tease, rubbing slow circles that make her squirm.

"Touch me properly. Pull the damn knickers aside."

"I know what you need, love." I hook my fingers and pull them down, helping her lift her hips. "I always know what you need, don't I?"

I slide one finger inside her tight, wet heat, then two, curling them just right. She cries out, her hands gripping my shoulders hard enough to leave marks, and Christ, I hope they bruise. I want her marks on me.

"Oh, sweet *Jaysus*," she curses.

"Let yourself go, darlin'. Mmm, that's my lass. That's my good girl," I murmur against her neck. "Let me hear you enjoy yourself."

She's so tight, so warm, clenching around my fingers as I work her slowly. My thumb finds her clit, and she lets out a half sob, her body trembling. "Oh, that feels so fucking good."

Her pussy clenches around my fingers, so wet I can feel it dripping down my hand. "That's it, love. You're soaked for me, aren't you? Absolutely dripping. Good girl," I say approvingly. "But not yet."

I slow my movements, keeping her right on the edge. "You'll not come till I'm inside you."

"Please, Cavin."

She begs, and Christ, I love hearing her beg. Love that she trusts me enough to fall apart like this. I withdraw my fingers, and she whimpers at the loss.

"You want me to touch you? You want me to finger you?"

"Yes, please." She grabs me and pulls me to her, as if somehow that would make the friction come quicker.

I chuckle and slide two fingers in and out of her, before I circle her clit again, until her mouth parts, her back arches, and I know she's on the edge.

"You come before my cock's inside you, I'll take my belt to your pretty arse," I whisper in her ear, harsh, making her shiver. I know she loves when I threaten her. "Hold on, love. Just hold on."

I make quick work of my belt and jeans. I grab the belt, loop it, and crack it against my palm. The sound makes her jump, eyes going half-lidded.

"Roll over," I tell her. "Arse up."

"*Cavin—*"

She fuckin' loves my belt, goes wet and languid at the mere mention of it, the sweet little pain slut.

"You wanted the hat and no shirt, didn't you? Well, now you get the belt too." I give her arse a proper smack with the leather—not hard enough to truly hurt, but enough to leave a red mark blooming across that perfect pale skin. She gasps, then moans.

"Again?" I ask, my voice rough.

"Yes," she whimpers. "Please."

I give her two more, watching the marks appear, watching her squirm and push back for more. "That's my good girl. Taking it so well."

"Lie back," I tell her, and she does, turning over and lying back on my desk, offering herself to me.

I position myself between her thighs, the head of my cock pressing against her entrance. "Are you ready for me, love?"

"Yes," she breathes out. "Yes, please, Cavin."

I push inside her slow, savoring every fucking inch, every little gasp and moan she makes. When I'm fully seated, buried to the hilt, I pause. "Alright?" I ask her, smoothing her hair back from her face.

"Perfect," she whispers, wrapping her legs around my waist. "I love you inside me."

I start to move, slow and deep, watching her face as I do—the way her eyes flutter closed, the way her lips part, the way she says my name like it's the only fuckin' word she knows.

"Look at me," I say roughly. "I want to see you when you come."

Her eyes open, locking onto mine, and the connection is so intense it nearly undoes me.

"Erin fucking McCarthy." I angle my hips and hit that spot inside her that makes her cry out. I feel her tighten around me.

I bury my face in her neck, biting down on the soft skin where her shoulder meets her throat—hard enough to brand. She cries out, her nails raking down my back, scratching lines of fire across my skin.

"Mark me," I growl against her throat. "I want everyone to

see your scratches on me in the ring. Want them to know I'm yours."

She digs her nails in harder, drawing blood probably, and I fuckin' love it. "That's it," I encourage, speeding up my thrusts. "Come for me, Erin. Come on my cock. Let go, lass."

She shatters, her body arching clean off the desk as she comes with a cry that's nearly a scream. Her cunt clenches around me, rhythmic and tight, milking my cock.

"That's it, that's fucking it, Erin—" I can barely get the words out. "Christ, I can feel you coming—"

The sight of her, the feel of her, sends me over the edge, and I follow her into bliss, burying my face in her neck as I groan and come.

For a while we stay like that, breathing hard, connected.

"The hat," she says, her voice sleepy, amused but satisfied.

I reach up. It's still on my head. "Told you it was staying on."

"Who knew a little navy cap would turn you on like that, love?"

She giggles, and the sound makes me smile against her skin. She didn't giggle once in my presence at school. Now she giggles every damn day.

"Come on," I say. "Let's move to the sofa before your arse gets a splinter from this damn desk."

"Romantic," she teases, but she lets me carry her to the sofa, settling her on my lap. I grab a throw blanket from the back and drape it over us, tucking her against my chest. The fire's burnt low, casting warm shadows around the room.

"Cavin," she says after a while, "I'm glad you kept the hat on."

"That's grand with me," I say, running my fingers through her hair.

We're tangled on the sofa, her head on my chest, the fire burning low. I feel half asleep, content in a way I've never been. And somehow the contentment sets me on edge.

"You keeping that hat?" she murmurs.

"I'll wear it every day if this is the reaction I get."

My phone buzzes on the side table.

"Cavin," she whispers against my mouth, "leave it."

It keeps buzzing, insistent.

"You know I can't," I murmur. Between Bridget, the tribute, the damn intel from Declan...

It's Declan. The message on the screen stops me cold.

Declan
West Coast contact is pissed. The trade route doesn't fucking exist. Padraic played us. Call me now.

Her da.

Goddamn fucking traitor. If he were anyone else—

But Christ. It's her *father*. I can't bloody well murder the traitorous bastard. But there *will* be repercussions.

I can't let her know. No. She'll worry about Bridget and Dr. Rosenberg. About *us*. She'll worry about her parents. And to be honest, she ought to. She's in trouble—but she's *mine*.

"I've been working on something, Cavin," she says.

I turn my phone over so she can't see the message.

"The tribute payments. I've been tracking them like you asked me to. And I found something more."

My hand stills in her hair. "What'd you find?"

"I think I'm getting closer to figuring out who's collecting them." She sits up a bit, pulling the blanket around her shoulders. "But there's something that doesn't make sense."

"What doesn't make sense?"

"The timing, the amounts..." She chews her lip, thinking. "It's like someone knows exactly when you're vulnerable, when to catch you off guard, when you're stretched thin."

Ice slides down my spine. "Go on."

She faces me, her eyes worried. "I think there's someone on the... on the inside. Someone feeding information to whoever's behind this. Possibly even—"

"*No*." The word comes out harder than I mean it. "Look again, Erin. I told you before, that's not possible. I know my men. That's my family you're talking about."

"Cavin, I—"

"I said *no*. Every single one of them. They're loyal."

"I'm not saying it's one of your crew, per *se*," she says carefully.

I stand, dislodging her. "You're taking the piss now, seeing patterns that aren't fucking there."

"You're some thick if you think I'm droppin' this." She's on her feet now, clutching the blanket. "The numbers don't lie. Someone's leaking information, and if we can't figure out who—"

"Drop it, Erin."

"Don't tell me to drop it." Her cheeks flush with anger. "You asked me to help with this, and now that I've found something, you're just going to dismiss it because you don't want to face the truth?"

"You don't know my family, Erin. You don't know shite about how we operate." My hands curl into fists at my sides.

She pulls the blanket tighter, her eyes flashing. "Then explain it to me! Why was there no record at the funeral? Why couldn't you figure out who bombed your car? Explain how else someone would know exactly when to hit you, exactly where you are, exactly how much you can afford—"

"I said *drop* it." My voice cracks through the room like a whip.

Silence falls between us, heavy and sharp.

Her eyes go hard. "You asked me to help. You put me on this. And now that I'm actually getting somewhere, you want to pretend there's no problem because you can't handle the idea that someone you trust might be—"

My phone buzzes again. Another message from Declan.

> **Declan**
> Did you get my text?

"What is it?" Erin says, her anger fading into concern.

"Nothing." I shove the phone back down. "Just Declan."

But I don't like lying to her. My mind is racing. If the West Coast connection falls through, if Padraic's played us... *fuck.* I can't lose her. I won't lose her. Not over this. Not over anything.

"Cavin," she says, "you're scaring me. What's going on?"

"Nothing, love." I force myself to meet her eyes. "I just—I'm sorry for dismissing you like that. You're right to be careful."

She studies my face. The woman's too smart for her own damn good. "You're lying to me."

"I'm not."

"You are." Her voice softens. "But I'm guessing it's something you can't tell me yet."

I know then she's come to trust me. I sigh. "Don't mention... what you said to me to anyone else. Not until we're sure."

"Right," she says, "because if there is someone, obviously we don't want to tip them off."

"Exactly."

She nods and crosses to me, letting the blanket drop. She's bare in the firelight, and I love her so.

"We're in this together, yeah?" she says. "Whatever it is you're not telling me, whatever it is—"

"Aye." The lie sits bitter on my tongue, but I kiss her instead of speaking. "Together," I whisper.

She smiles at me, adjusting the hat on my head. "You really do look obscenely good in this."

"Keep talking like that and I'll miss the fight tonight," I murmur against her ear, my eyes closing as I smell her, hold her, feel her, ground myself in the woman I love... my wife.

"The fight." Her eyes widen. "Shite. What time is it?"

I glance at my watch. "I've got an hour."

"Then you'd better get moving," she says, kissing me again, this time quick and sweet. "Go. Win me some money so I can buy some yarn."

"Five days till the fucking tribute's due," I say, shaking my head. "This purse will help."

"Or maybe we won't pay it this time."

She pulls her clothes on, efficient, unselfconscious. "Remember, you said I could come with you this time?"

"Aye. But I don't know about that."

"Cavin," she says, warningly. "Someone needs to tend to your inevitable bruises."

"Inevitable?"

"You're fighting Mackey. Rumor has it he's a dirty bastard."

"Aye, but I'm dirtier."

She crosses to me, standing on her toes to kiss me properly. "I love you, you know that."

The words still feel foreign on my tongue, but they're so fucking true it terrifies me. "I do know it. And you know I love you too."

"Now go."

Another message from Declan.

> **Declan**
> We need to talk about Padraic. Now.

I delete it. I'll deal with it after the fight, after things settle.

After I've figured out how to keep her.

Because losing Erin is *not* a fucking option.

I look back at her one more time. She's curled up on the sofa again, her knitting needles clicking away. Home—that's what she's made this place.

"Cavin," she says without looking up, "you're staring."

"Just appreciating the view."

"You're a sap." But she's smiling.

I force myself to get ready, the weight of Declan's messages heavy in my pocket.

Five days until the tribute's due.

Five days to find a way to keep everything from falling apart.

I'm still wearing the hat she made. Won't fucking take it off, even though we just had a what bordered on another row.

Five days to fix this with Erin before she realizes just how bolloxed we really are.

Another buzz. I check it at the door.

> **Declan**
> Don't ignore me, Cavin. We sort this tonight
> or I'm going to Seamus.

I delete it and pocket the phone. I head out into the night, my knuckles already itching for the fight. Maybe Mackey will give me an excuse to go truly brutal tonight.

Maybe I need to bleed a little before I can face her again.

The hat stays on.

Chapter Thirty

Erin

I CHECK in with Bridget before the fight, but she's not answering. Neither's Mam. The mobile reception can be shite at the hospital. I know Cavin got a text that rattled him before he stepped in the ring. He doesn't want to admit it, but I can see it in him.

I probably shouldn't have brought it up, but I'm not very good at timing and knowing social cues or anything like that, so fuck it. I shouldn't have brought it up before he fought though.

I know he needs to focus, but sometimes rage fuels his energy unlike anything else. I probably shouldn't be here. But I made Cavin promise I could.

That's what Ciarán keeps telling me with his eyes every time I glance at my assigned bodyguard. He's positioned himself between me and the ring like his body can shield me from what's happening in there, but I can see through the gaps in the crowd. I can see Cavin.

He moves like violence personified—controlled, precise, and brutal. I can still feel him inside me.

I hope he can still feel me too. I hope his back stings where I scratched him and wrecked him. He likes that; I know he does.

He's fighting some young lad from Cork tonight, scrappy little Mackey with more heart than brains. Mackey's outmatched, and everyone knows it. You can see it in the way the crowd leans forward, hungry for blood, certain of the outcome.

Tonight's purse is heavy with bets placed. I should look away. I should go upstairs like a good girl and pretend I don't care, but I can't stop watching him.

The way his muscles coil with each punch, the ink on his ribs shifting with every breath. Blood on his knuckles—not his. Never his. The cold focus in his eyes, like he's somewhere else entirely—somewhere dark and distant.

This is who Cavin McCarthy is, and I know it better than anyone else in this fucking ring. Stripped of the suits and smooth words and the gentle way he touches me when we're alone. Just raw, dangerous man. *Mine.*

The navy cap I knitted him is pulled tight on his head. He's fighting bare-chested, bare-knuckled, wearin' the fuckin' hat.

Something in my chest clenches at the sight of it. I wish we hadn't argued before the fight.

I wish—

Then something in the crowd shifts. I feel it before I see it, and I wonder if it's my connection to Cavin. There's a wrongness in the energy, like the air pressure drop before a storm. Bodies move with purpose instead of excitement, and the roar changes pitch, goes from bloodlust to something sharper.

Ciarán feels it too. I watch his eyes flicker to mine, and then his hand goes to his weapon, his body tense.

"What the fuck—" I start, but then I see him.

A big bastard in a bandana pushes through the crowd on the far side of the ring. Not a fighter. Something worse. His eyes are cold and focused, and he moves too deliberately.

I grab at Ciarán. "Stop him—Ciarán, fucking stop him! What's he—" The man climbs into the ring behind Cavin.

"No. No. Cavin!" I scream. "*Cavin!*"

My voice hurts from the effort of screaming and pushing through the crowd. Ciarán grabs me and hauls me back, but I shove at him, batting his hands away..

"Cavin, *behind you!*"

But my voice is lost in the sudden surge of noise. This isn't right. This isn't how it works. There are rules, even here in this world of blood and broken bones—there are fucking *rules.*

The big man crashes into Cavin from behind. Mackey just stands there, stunned and useless. Cavin staggers forward, caught completely off guard, and the young, stupid Cork kid, out of desperation, sees his chance and lunges.

"Cavin!" I scream. "*No!*"

The word rips out of me, but it's drowned in the sudden roar of the crowd—half of them screaming in outrage, the other half howling in savage glee.

He spins and gets an elbow into the man's face. Blood sprays across the canvas, and I can see Cavin knows something's wrong. For a second, I think he's survived things that would kill normal men... but he's not a bloody *immortal*.

The big man's boot catches him in the kidney.

Cavin's face goes white, and his body seizes. And then he's falling, crumpling to his knees.

And my whole world collapses.

"Cavin!"

I'm screaming his name now, proper screaming, and I don't care who hears. Don't care that I'm supposed to be calm and collected.

"Ciarán! Do something!"

He's moving, trying to shove through the crowd, but it's too thick. I reach for my phone, my hands trembling, and text every bloody one of his cousins and brother:

> Get to the ring NOW! It's an ambush.

They're pushing in from all sides now—some trying to get away, others pushing closer to see. We're stuck in a crush of flesh and sweat and rage.

I grab Ciarán's arm. "Move! We have to—"

The big man pulls something from his jacket, and time slows. I see the pipe before it's fully out. It's metal and heavy, the kind that could cave in a skull, that could kill a man with one good hit. My knees buckle.

Cavin's on his knees, shaking his head like he's trying to clear it. The Cork kid stares and finally forgets his fight.

"McCarthy!" he yells. "Watch out!"

"No! No! Cavin!" I'm screaming. It's a prayer. A plea. It's useless.

Because the pipe is rising. Because Cavin's not getting up fast enough. Because I'm too far away and there are too many bodies between us.

The pipe comes down... and hits him.

The sound is wet and hollow and terrible, a sound I'll hear in my nightmares for the rest of my fucking life.

And Cavin goes limp. Just stops. Collapses boneless onto the canvas. Blood starts immediately, dark and wet, pooling beneath his head.

Everything in me stops. The crowd is screaming, wild.

My heart. My breath. *My world.*

The man moves, raising the pipe again.

I'm not thinking. I have to do something.

My hand closes around the grip of Ciarán's gun. He's still focused on the ring, trying to shove through, and his holster isn't secured properly. Thank fucking god.

The weight of the gun surprises me. It's heavier than it looks. For a split second, I think I can't.

I fucking have to.

My hands shake so badly. Is there a safety? I don't fucking know.

I raise it toward the ceiling and pull the damn trigger.

The recoil slams through my arm like lightning, up through my fingers, into my shoulder. I feel like they shatter. My shoulder screams in protest, and the gun nearly flies from my grip. The sound's so loud it feels like my skull cracks open.

But it works.

It fucking works.

Every single person in the ring goes still, and the pipe misses its mark.

Heads swivel toward me—toward the gun in my hand— toward the girl in the nice dress who just fired a weapon into the ceiling of an illegal fighting ring.

The big man looks up, and for one perfect moment, our eyes meet.

I cock the gun and point it straight between his eyes.

His eyes are flat. Dead. The eyes of a man who kills for money and sleeps like a baby afterward.

He runs. Drops the pipe with a clatter and bolts for the exit, the Cork kid right behind him, the fucking coward.

The spell breaks, and panic erupts like a bomb went off. People stampede toward the exits. Strong arms are around me—I step on the foot of an unknown man who screams behind me. Everyone's trampling to get away from the girl with the gun.

There's another gunshot, but I don't care. I don't care about anything except—

Cavin.

Cavin.

My heels catch on something—broken glass, something slippery, a wallet, a person, I don't fucking know. I kick off my shoes, feeling the sting of glass biting into my foot, but it doesn't matter. Nothing matters except getting to him.

They part for me, too busy trying to save their own arses to block my path. The ones who aren't running just stare at me as I shove them aside.

Ciarán screams at me from behind. My phone is buzzing and ringing in my pocket.

I vault over the ropes, don't even feel my knees hit the canvas. Just scramble forward on my knees toward where Cavin collapsed in a pool of blood.

Ciarán falls beside me. I snap at him. "Grab the pipe. Stick that into a fucking shirt. We need fingerprints."

There's so much blood. Too much. It's soaking into the canvas and dripping through the ropes. Up close, the smell hits me—copper and salt—and my stomach heaves.

"Cavin. Cavin, *please.*"

My hands find his face, his neck, searching for a pulse with shaking fingers.

It's there, faint but steady, beating against my fingertips like a promise.

The cap I knit helped cushion the blow.

Relief hits me so hard I nearly collapse on top of him. "Oh thank god. Fuck."

His eyes flutter open, unfocused and glassy. There's a gash across his temple, deep and ragged, blood matting his hair and running down the side of his face.

"What are you doing here? Go home, lass." Then he blinks, and his face goes livid. "Jesus *fucking* Christ, Ciarán, I'll fucking tear every single goddamn limb off whoever did this and beat you with it. Someone shot a fucking gun. Get her out of here—"

"*No*. I'm not going anywhere. You're hurt. Cavin," I say, my voice steady and calm. "And... well, *I* shot the gun."

"You cleared the fuckin' room, lass." Despite the blood and the violence, I almost smile.

"I shot it into the ceiling. I'm not here killing anybody." My hands move over him. "Unlike that bloody sod who came after you with a fucking pipe." I keep pressure on the wound, my cardigan already soaked through. Thirty seconds. Sixty. The bleeding has to slow.

"Fuck. Okay. Okay." Possible internal bleeding. Concussion for certain. And the head wound is still pumping blood under my hands. "Okay, we need to move you. Can you—"

I touch his shoulder, and he makes a sound low in his throat, agonized, and I have to swallow the bile that rises in my chest. Shoulders shouldn't look like *this*.

I turn to Ciarán. "Call the medic. Cavin, can you stand?"

He tries—because even half conscious, bleeding and broken, he's too stubborn to stay down. He tries to lever himself up with his good arm, wobbles, and falls heavy like a shot elephant.

"Easy. *Easy*." I get under his good shoulder, taking as much of the weight as I can. Christ, he's heavy, all muscle and bone and dead weight.

Ciarán's face is white. "Ciarán, help me."

He takes Cavin's other side, carefully avoiding the shoulder. Between us, we haul him to his feet. Cavin's legs barely hold him. His head lolls against my shoulder, and I can feel him shaking.

"Declan's come," Ciarán says. "Got yer text."

"Right. Get him to the office."

Declan barrels toward us and helps me carry Cavin.

"Some man came at him with a pipe," I tell Declan when he appears, grateful he can help carry him. "Hit him right in the head."

"Ciarán says you shot the gun." Declan's eyes flicker to me, then back to Cavin.

"Aye."

We drag him through pure carnage. The place is wrecked— overturned tables, broken glass crunching underfoot, abandoned drinks scattered across the floor. My bare feet slip, and I don't even think about what it might be. Someone's phone is ringing. The telly's still playing, showing a football match like nothing happened.

We lower him onto the couch in the office, and his face goes gray.

"Get the first aid kit," I tell Ciarán. "This is a fucking fight ring. They've got to have something."

Ciarán looks at Cavin, who manages a slight nod, then disappears.

I grab the whiskey off the shelf—the good stuff—and pour it over my hands. They're shaking now, the delayed reaction setting in and the adrenaline fading, leaving me hollow and nauseous.

The whiskey stings the cuts on my palms, but I watch it turn pink and think, distantly, *this might stain.*

Can't fall apart. Not yet.

I turn back to Cavin, and in the office light, I see the full extent of it. The gash on his head is deep, at least ten centimeters long, and bleeding profusely. His left shoulder sits wrong, the joint visibly displaced beneath the skin. Bruises are already blooming across his ribs like dark flowers. And when he breathes, I can see how he favors one side.

Definitely a concussion. Or worse.

He could have... died.

That hits me like a physical blow. I stifle a sob. My knees go weak, and my stomach rolls. I'm going to be sick.

He could have died right there in front of me.

"Erin." His voice is rough. "You're alright, lass."

Even half dead, he's worried about me.

"And you're not, and I'm sorry. This is going to hurt."

He grunts, rolling his eyes. "Not my first time."

I've seen the scars marking his body, the evidence of the beatings he's taken. Fights. Every time, he survived something that should have killed him. My fucking husband with nine lives. The knife wounds and bullet grazes and marks from fists and boots and god knows what else.

But this time I was there. This time I watched it happen and tried to stop it—but couldn't.

Ciarán comes back with a proper first aid kit, military-grade supplies in a little case. Good. Illegal fighting rings have people who don't go to hospitals. They're prepared for someone to sew them up and send them out.

Tonight, *I'm* that person.

I take the kit with shaking hands and open it. Gauze, antiseptic, surgical thread.

"Ciarán, I need a lighter or matches. And something clean he can... that he can bite down on."

He produces a leather belt. Cavin eyes it. "Don't bloody need it."

"Scalp wounds are different. You're going to feel every stitch."

I take a deep breath and steady myself. The gash needs to be closed.

"If it's an ambush, they'll be back," Declan says. "Patch him up fast. We'll get him back to our house."

"Right. Sew me up, Erin," Cavin says, his eyes already half closed.

"Declan says—"

"*Sew me up*, lass. Can you do it? Could bleed out if you fucking don't."

Jesus. Up close, the wound is worse than I thought. Deep enough, I can see the pale gleam of skull beneath bone and torn skin. It'll take at least six, maybe eight stitches. I don't know. I *knit*, I don't fucking sew human flesh.

I press a towel to his head to staunch the bleeding, my belly roiling.

"I've never done this before. Not on someone I—" My hands start to shake.

"Erin," he says, his voice slurred. "You can do this."

"I'm not a... not a doctor."

"You're smart as fuck. Figure it out." His good hand reaches up and catches my wrist. "Bravest fucking lass I know. You can do it. Trust yourself."

Then he closes his eyes, and my pulse spikes.

"Cavin?"

"I'm still here. Just need to close my eyes a minute, okay?"

"*No* closing your eyes. If you fuckin' die on me, you bloody bastard—"

"Not dying tonight, love," he says, but his voice is weak.

"Hold his head still," I say to Declan.

I thread the needle with surgical thread, my hands steadier now. Mam did this years ago. I saw her when my father came home from a fight outside a pub. I *know* I can do this.

I peel back the towel. Fresh blood wells up immediately. I dab at it with gauze, trying to see the edges clearly.

"This is going to hurt. One. Two—"

I don't wait for three.

The first stitch goes in, and Cavin's jaw clenches, but he doesn't make a sound.

"You're doing grand," he says through gritted teeth. "Grand, lass."

The fact that he's trying to reassure me right now while I'm literally sewing his head shut—

"You're delirious," I say to him, but I can feel myself smile in the midst of it all. My voice wobbles. "Hush, love, and hold still."

I lean down and kiss his sweaty cheek, brushing my free hand to wipe away tears, and go back to sewing. "I love you," I whisper.

My hands steady. Another stitch. And another.

I tie it off and cut the thread. Blood is still oozing around the stitches, seeping through. "Ciarán, hand me that gauze. All of it."

Another stitch. The needle punches through skin, and I feel it in my teeth. Nausea rumbles. The wound closes slowly, the work rough but functional. It just needs to hold.

Everything just needs to hold.

My hands are shaking so badly that the next stitch goes crooked. I need to move, need to do *something* with this energy crawling under my skin, but I can't because my hands are covered in his blood, and... and... if I stop stitching... what if he dies?

I try to bounce my knee, but it makes my hands shake worse. *Fuck.*

The next stitch goes in, and my vision blurs again. Tears or shock or both, I don't know, don't care. I'm humming without meaning to, some tuneless anxious sound, trying to self-soothe while my brain screams at me that this isn't working, nothing's working, I need to move—

"Erin," Cavin says, his voice soft and slurred. "Look at me, love."

"I'm busy saving your life, will you *please* shut the fuck up." My voice cracks. I can taste bile in the back of my throat. I'm rocking now without meaning to, tiny movements while I work. "Jesus Christ, there's so much blood—"

"Erin."

"I can't—if I don't get this closed—" Another stitch. My fingers are slick and red, and I can't tap them, can't flutter them, can't release any of this pressure building in my chest because I have to hold the needle steady, have to keep going.

"Look. At. Me."

I meet his eyes, and the intensity there nearly breaks me. He's the one bleeding, the one with his head split open, and he's looking at me like I'm the one who needs saving.

But I do.

"You're doing perfect, love. Just keep going, my brave lass." His hand finds mine and gives it a weak squeeze. "I love you. I'll never forget this."

The words hit me hard. I choke on a sob, still rocking slightly, and force myself to keep stitching. I can fall apart after. After he's safe. After he's breathing steady and his eyes stay open.

Just hold on. Both of us just need to hold on.

I realize I've been holding my breath. My lungs burn as I take in air.

"Relax," I tell him. "Just relax now, okay?"

But Cavin tries to sit up and immediately goes white. He's trembling. *Fuck.* Shock is setting in properly now. His skin is gray and clammy, and his lips are starting to lose color.

His left arm hangs at an odd angle. The goddamn shoulder.

"Shoulder's dislocated," Ciarán says. "Help hold him steady. Grab his hand, Erin."

"*Christ.*" I exhale. "What are you—"

"I need to put his arm back in the socket. We've done this before. On three," he says. "One... two... three."

He pulls, twists, and pushes with his whole body weight.

The pop is audible and horrible, loud enough that even Ciarán flinches. The joint slots back into place with a wet grinding sound that makes my stomach heave.

Cavin makes a sound low in his throat—not quite a scream, more like a growl dragged up from somewhere deep and primal. His eyes roll back, and I fear he's going to pass out.

"He's a big man. I can't hold him if he—"

"Fuck!" He gasps. "*Jesus, Mary, and Joseph.*"

"Done. It's done. It's back in."

"Good," he says, breathing hard.

This time, I can't help it. I fall to my knees, grab the wastebasket just in time, and heave up the contents of my dinner. I wipe my mouth with the back of my hand and take a deep breath. Got that sorted. I don't have time to be sick again.

When I stand back up, Ciarán's draped someone's jacket over Cavin's chest. He's still shaking, teeth chattering now.

"He's in shock," I say. "We need to keep him warm."

We're not done.

For once in my life, I'm grateful that the many trips with Bridget to the hospital have taught me a thing or two.

I check his pupils again, clean the smaller cuts on his face and hands. He needs a CAT scan and X-rays and proper care.

I think to myself… of all the fucking things in the world, he's going to end up at the same hospital as my sister.

But I already suspect he won't go, that he'd rather die on this couch than answer the questions that come with walking into an emergency room like this.

So I do what I can with what I have.

"You saved me," he says quietly, catching my hands.

"You'd have done the same."

"Course I would." His good hand comes up, cups my face.

And I burst into tears.

"Oh, Cavin." I collapse against him, careful of his injuries.

"Shh," he says, holding me against his bloody, sweaty chest. "I know, love. I know."

"Good. Then live. Don't die, okay?"

Declan clears his throat from somewhere near the door. "I'll give you two a minute. You alright?"

"Alright," I whisper.

The door clicks shut. We're alone in the wreckage—blood on the floor, torn gauze and scattered supplies everywhere.

"Fuck," Cavin mutters.

His forehead is still pressed to mine, and I can feel his breath, shallow and uneven.

"You could have got yourself killed, Erin. The gun." His voice cracks. "You could have—it could have gone off while you were running. If someone had grabbed you, if that shot had gone wide—"

"It didn't."

"You don't know—"

His good hand slides to the back of my neck, fingers tangling in my sticky hair. "Don't ever fucking do that again."

"I promise, as long as *you* promise you don't get yourself beaten half to death again."

He shakes his head, then winces. "Can't promise that, love."

The words hang between us, a promise neither one of us can keep. Because next time, it might be too late. Next time, there might not be a gun. Next time, we might not both get up.

We stay like that, bloody and exhausted, until Declan finally knocks on the door.

"They're here. Let's get him home."

Chapter Thirty-One

Cavin

Everything's fuckin' sideways. Voices drift in and out, familiar but distorted, like I'm drowning underwater. Hands on me—too many hands. I try to shove them off, but my body won't cooperate.

One arm's dead weight and useless, and the other swings wild, connecting with something solid.

"Easy, Cav, fuck off!"

"Where's Erin?" I try to talk, but the words come out wrong and thick and mangled.

"She's fine, lad. Knock it off."

And then Seamus's voice, authoritative and angry. "Stop fuckin' fighting us."

"Hold him down," says somebody else.

No. Nobody's holding me down. Never again.

Somebody grabs my arm, and I thrash harder. Pain explodes through my fuckin' skull like a bullet—white-hot and blinding. I might scream. I can't tell.

Then her voice cuts through the chaos. "Cavin? Cavin, it's alright. You're home. You're safe."

I feel her tiny hand slide into mine. "No," she says to somebody, not me. "Don't hold me back. He won't hurt me."

"Erin?" I force an eye open. Everything's blurry and doubled.

Faces lean over me—Seamus, Declan, Daire—too close, too many.

"Where's Erin?"

"I'm here, love." My tongue feels too big for my mouth.

"I'm here." Her small hands are on my face now, gentle and warm. "I'm right here. Please, do what you're told for once in your fuckin' life, will you?"

Somebody laughs behind her, but she's serious. Her hair's a mess, and she's streaked with blood.

"Oh my god, are you alright?" My vision swims.

"I'm fine," she says quickly. "It's your blood on me, love. Please."

When she blinks, a fat tear rolls down her cheek. She's crying.

I blink hard, trying to focus. She's pale as death, her clothes covered in my blood. But she's standing. Breathing. Thank Christ.

I can't remember what happened, but I remember her.

"Are you sure you're not hurt?" I ask, the words scraped out of me.

"No, I'm the one who's fine. *You're* hurt, Cavin," she says, and then she's crying freely now.

"You're a liar." I see the cuts on her feet, the shake in her hands. "You're—"

"Cavin, stop," she says, her voice sharp and commanding. "You need to settle. The medic's here. I promise, I'm fine. Somebody tell him I'm fuckin' fine."

"She's fine, lad," Seamus says, his firm hand on my shoulder. "Lie down. You want to be here to see tomorrow, don't you?"

I blink at him. There are two Seamuses floating in front of me.

Then I remember. The fight. The kid from Cork. Mackey.

Something wrong. Somebody behind me.

Fuck. Who was it?

I try to sit up, but hands push me back down. Probably Seamus, the big bastard.

"Get the fuck off—"

"Easy, brother. You're grand. Just stay down."

"Did you get him?" I growl. "The big fucker with the—" Another wave of pain crashes through my skull, and I lose the words... lose everything for a second. The world swims in front of me.

Erin starts crying harder.

"Stop it," she says firmly. She pushes Seamus off and takes my hand, gripping it tight. She lets me squeeze. "Let *me* handle him. I'm the only one he listens to." She bends her face to mine again. "Cavin. Lie down. This is what happened. You fought the Cork lad, Mackey. Do you remember that?"

I nod, just barely.

"During the fight, somebody ambushed you with a pipe. Cracked you over the skull." She swallows hard. "Tried to get you a second time, but I stopped him."

"That she did with Ciarán's gun."

"You've got to teach me how to fuckin' shoot when you're better," she says under her breath. "I would have shot him if I could have, but I wasn't sure I wouldn't hurt somebody accidentally in the crowd."

I let out a breath. "Right. We'll talk about that later, I promise."

"Right. But we got the pipe. Declan, you still have it?" she says over her shoulder.

"Aye," he says, brandishing it.

Erin winces when she sees blood dripping down the side. "Take it. Scan it for prints. Find out who the fuck he is."

And then Seamus is barking out orders to Declan and Lorcan. "We have to go see if there's any footage in the club."

"You know there's no fuckin' footage in the ring," they say.

But Erin ushers them out.

And then I blink and see the doc leaning over me. Where's Erin?

"Concussion," he's saying. "Could be worse. Of all things, the little knit cap took some of the impact."

The cap? But there it is—Erin's holding it.

"A little knit cap like that. Who'd have known?"

"Maybe I knew," she says with a wink. But of course she didn't. She's just taking the mickey out of me, trying to lighten the mood.

Then she's gone again, and it's dark outside.

"Erin. Erin, where are you?"

"I'm right here, love," she says. "Please, Cavin. Just let them take care of you, will you? For me. Do it for me."

She's beside me now, her hand in mine.

The memory surfaces, jagged and surreal. The crack of the shot. The crowd scattering.

"We need to know," I force out. "Who sent them. The big bastard with the fucking pipe."

"Of course we need to know. What do you think we're doing?" Declan says from somewhere distant. "We're working on it. We'll find him."

"What is it?" I turn to Erin. "You've got that look."

"Shh. Don't worry about that now," she says too quickly.

I can't say anything about the fuckin' tribute in front of my family, but I'm worried. There's something there—something scratching at the edges of my consciousness. The text that came before the fight. The one that made me see red. The one I haven't told her about.

"I need to talk to Declan."

"You will," she says. "Right now, we're taking a look at you. Okay?"

First, the tribute. Somebody thinking they can squeeze me. Her da, not trusted. And now this—the ambush, the attack.

Has to be connected.

"How long—" I start, but the medic sticks something in my arm—painkiller, probably—and the world starts to blur.

I try to fight. I can't pass out. I need to stay awake. I need to protect Erin. I need to—

"Let it take you," Doc Sullivan says. "Relax."

"Please, Cavin. Just for a little bit," Erin says. "I'll be right here."

Her voice follows me down into the dark. "I promise."

The dream comes in fragments—distorted and wrong.

I'm in a warehouse, one that Da used to use for storage. But it's different now. Darker. Colder.

Is it a warehouse or a cell? It's a cell in a fuckin' warehouse.

Bronwyn's supposed to be here. That's what the note said. But it's not Bronwyn tied to the chair in the center of the room.

It's—

No.

Erin.

Her head's down, blonde hair falling over her face. And there's blood. Blood on her dress. So much fuckin' blood.

My feet won't move. I'm rooted to the spot, watching as a figure emerges from the shadows.

The big bastard with the bandana, the same one from the ring. And he's got a fuckin' pipe in his hand.

"No." I'm running now, but as I run, the warehouse stretches impossibly long. Every step takes me nowhere.

"Get the fuck away from her, you fuckin'—"

The pipe rises.

"Erin!"

It comes down.

I wake gasping, pain lancing through my skull. For a second, I don't know if I got hit or she did. If I'm awake or asleep.

The room's wrong. Dark. Quiet.

But it all comes crashing back. The fight a few days ago. The attack. Home.

Erin.

The tribute.

Betrayal.

I try to sit up, and my body screams in protest. Everything fuckin' hurts. But I force myself upright anyway, breathing hard, sweat soaking through the tee that somebody put on me.

There's light coming from under the door, voices low and urgent.

What time is it?

I find my phone plugged in on the nightstand. It's nearly midnight.

And there's a text waiting... from an unknown number.

> Twenty-four hours. You know what happens
> if you don't pay.

The tribute's due tomorrow night, and I still don't know who the fuck's demanding it.

But I know one thing: Whoever sent that big bastard with the pipe made the biggest mistake of their fuckin' life—because Cavin McCarthy doesn't play.

And I'm done fuckin' paying tribute.

I'm ready to *collect* it.

Chapter Thirty-Two

Erin

THE KITCHEN SMELLS like coffee and something burnt—
maybe the toast sitting in front of Bronwyn that she's been
staring at for the past five minutes without touching. It feels
somber in here, like a funeral. I'm exhausted and haven't
slept in days.

Every time I close my eyes, I see Cavin on the floor, blood
pooling around his head, and that massive bastard with the
pipe raising it for another swing. My hands won't stop
shaking.

I force myself to think through the variables again. The
timing of the attack, the placement of his injuries...the fact
that they left him alive. This wasn't random. Someone
wanted to send a message, and they wanted Cavin
conscious enough to receive it.

"Erin, love, you need to eat something," Kyla says softly,
pushing a plate toward me.

She's not the sensitive sort, but all of us have been affected by this beating. She's got dark circles under her eyes too—maybe none of us have slept. Caitlin busies herself by the kettle, switching it on, waiting for it to boil.

"Cup of tea," she says to all of us. We nod quietly.

But when she pours it, she slips and burns herself. She curses and runs her finger under the tap.

Don't think I've ever heard Caitlin McCarthy curse in my life.

Bronwyn looks so fragile. So scared. And she doesn't even know that tonight could be the night she's taken again.

My god, I *have* to stop it. Christ, if she only knew what was really at stake.

"Where is he now?" Bronwyn asks quietly, her voice just above a whisper.

"Still sleeping," I lie.

But he's not sleeping. He's barely conscious, still disoriented and fucked up from the concussion. When I checked on him twenty minutes ago, he didn't even know what day it was.

Bronwyn reaches for my hand and squeezes it. "You were so brave, Erin. I don't know how you did it. How *did* you?"

"I... I love your brother," I say simply. It's the truth.

I tap my fingers on the table. One, two, three, four. But nothing soothes me now. Nothing except... except him.

I want my husband.

Today's the day the doctor's supposed to come. Cavin's supposed to bring him to see Bridget at the hospital. But Cavin can barely stand, let alone drive across the city and coordinate a medical consultation.

What the fuck am I going to do?

"Cavin said Dr. Rosenberg was coming today," Caitlin says. "Your mam talked to me about it."

"Aye," I say. "Cavin was supposed to bring him to see my sister." I clear my throat.

Caitlin looks at me, but nobody asks questions.

"We'll have somebody else bring him, lass."

I nod. "Okay," I whisper.

Kyla gives me a look but doesn't call me on anything. She doesn't trust me. I don't think I can blame her.

The kitchen door swings open, and Declan walks in, looking like he hasn't slept either. The McCarthy family may be brutal, but they love each other, and their loyalty runs something fierce.

Declan's jaw is tight, and there's something in his eyes that makes my stomach drop to my toes.

"Declan," I say, standing up so fast my chair scrapes against the floor. I'm a bit dizzy. "Did you find out who hit him with the pipe?"

I tap my pocket. One, two, three, four.

He glances at Bronwyn and Kyla, then jerks his head toward the hallway.

I follow him out, my heart pounding. Truth be told, I don't trust the McCarthy family unless my husband's in on it. But I have to now.

"Tell me you found something," I say the second we're alone. "Tell me you know who the fuck sent that bastard after my husband."

"I got intel this morning," Declan says, pulling out his phone, his voice taut. "Ran the prints from the pipe. Got a name, location, the whole fuckin' lot."

And then he stops, staring at his phone.

"What?" I demand. "What is it, Declan?"

"It's gone."

"What do you mean, gone?"

"I mean, it's fuckin' gone, Erin. The file, the intel, all of it." He swipes through his phone, his jaw clenching tighter with every passing second. "It was here an hour ago. I had everything, and now... now it's gone."

"How the hell did that happen?"

"Someone deleted it." His eyes snap up to mine, and there's something in them I don't like—suspicion, distrust. "You were the first person to ask me about it, weren't you?"

"Of course I was. I was the one who saw my fuckin' husband get hit with a fuckin' *pipe*."

"Someone with access deleted this, Erin."

My blood runs cold. "Do you think I—"

"I don't know what to think," he says gruffly. "It's a hell of a coincidence, isn't it? You show up, and everything goes sideways. Your da fucked us over."

"My da?" My voice rises. "What the hell are you on about?"

Declan's expression doesn't change. "You don't know? Sure you don't."

"Know what?"

He studies me for a long moment, like he's trying to decide if I'm lying. "Your father. The deal he made with Cavin. He didn't hold up his end. Cost us a shite ton of money."

"*What?*"

"He ghosted us, Erin. Didn't give us the West Coast connections he promised. There *is* no West Coast connection."

The floor drops out from under me. My father? No. He wouldn't.

But even as I think it, I know it's possible. My father would sell his own damn daughter if the price was right.

He sold me, didn't he?

"I didn't know," I say, my voice breaking. "I swear to Christ, I didn't know."

He doesn't look convinced.

"Listen, we need to get Cavin to the hospital. Dr. Rosenberg is coming today for my sister, and Cavin can barely stand. He's disoriented and sick, and if he doesn't get to the doctor, he's not going anywhere—"

"He's not going," Declan says flatly. "Not with you."

"What?"

"You heard me. He's not leaving this house. Not until we figure out what the fuck is going on. Not with that concussion. Doc says he needs to rest."

"But... but today's the day. Dr. Rosenberg's coming," I say, trembling. "This is important—"

"Then we'll reschedule the doctor," he says. "Another day won't kill her."

But the words sit like an anvil in my chest.

Reschedule the doctor. Another day won't kill her.

But it might. It might kill her. Because if Dr. Rosenberg can't see her... and if that tribute doesn't get paid...

But I can't say that. I can't tell them anything. Cavin made me promise.

"You don't understand," I say desperately. "This is important—"

"What I understand," Declan cuts me off, "is that my cousin got his skull cracked open, and you're awful eager to get him out of this house."

"That's not—I'm trying to help."

"Help?" He laughs, but there's no humor in it. "You want to help? Then tell me who the fuck deleted that file. Tell me who you've been talking to."

"I haven't been talking to anyone!"

"Then how the hell do you explain it?"

I can't. I don't have an answer.

Behind Declan, I see Seamus appear in the hallway, his massive frame blocking the way to the stairs. Lorcan's there too, his arms crossed, watching me like I'm a threat. And Christ, they're not going to let me get to Cavin.

But I *know*... it's one of their men. One of the McCarthys deleted that file.

And tonight, if that tribute doesn't get paid, what's going to happen?

"Declan," I say, my voice steady even though my hands are shaking, "I didn't betray Cavin. I would never betray him. My father—whatever he did—it had nothing to do with me."

"Of course that's what you'd say," he says coldly.

"Someone is setting us up," I say. "Someone wanted him dead in that ring. And someone doesn't want us to figure out who."

"Us?" Declan's eyes narrow.

I catch myself. "We need to find out before they try again."

Declan stares at me for a long moment, and I can see him trying to read me. Trying to figure out if I'm lying.

"There is no *we*, Erin," he says coldly. "Not until you prove you're not the one behind this."

And just like that, it's over.

He turns and walks away, leaving me standing in the hallway, with Seamus and the rest of the family blocking my path.

Upstairs, Cavin's alone, barely conscious, with only a vague idea that tonight's the deadline.

I have to get to him. I have to get him out of here. I have to help him pay that tribute.

But how the hell am I going to do it when his own family won't let me near him? When his family thinks *I'm* the one who betrayed them?

I have to do this myself.

Chapter Thirty-Three

Cavin

I WAKE to the smell of antiseptic and the feeling that someone's taken a sledgehammer to my fucking skull. The room tilts and rights itself, then tilts again. I sit up too quickly, and the blood rushes to my head in a sickening wave.

Jesus fucking Christ, am I in a hospital bed? My hand moves before my brain catches up, ripping at the IV in my arm, tearing the heart monitor clip from my finger. Alarms start screaming.

Good, let them fucking scream.

Wait.

This is no hospital. I'm home. I'm in my own home. It's just set up like a hospital room, with nurses on call and machines beeping, the works.

I swing my legs over the side of the bed, and the floor rushes up to meet me. Or maybe I'm falling into it—hard to tell when the whole damn room's doing somersaults.

Doesn't fucking matter. I know what I need to do. I may be fucked up in the head, but I know I need to pay the bastards. Before—

Erin. Jesus Christ, Erin.

The thought slams into me harder than whatever the fuck put me in here in the first place. Where is she?

"Erin!" I call as the sound of feet rushing toward me meets my ears. My brain's scrambled, confusing sounds with sights, but I use the bed rail to haul myself upright.

The room does a sickening barrel roll, and I taste bile. "Erin," I say again. My voice comes out wrecked and rough, like I've been gargling gravel. My head feels twice its normal size, and what the hell happened to my shoulder?

The door bursts open, and two nurses rush in.

"Mr. McCarthy, you need to lie back down."

"Mr. McCarthy—" Someone else is speaking into her phone. "He's out of bed. He's going to hurt himself."

"Where's my wife?" I'm already moving toward them, one hand still braced on the bed because my legs feel as if they're made of jelly.

"Sir, you have a *severe* concussion," one nurse says, stepping closer with her hands up like I'm a spooked horse.

"*Where is she?*" I bellow.

They exchange a look. That's all I need to see. She's not here, and she isn't their concern.

The first nurse reaches for my arm. I don't think… I just move, sidestepping her. I don't want to hurt a woman, but I will if I have to. The second one—a man, thank fuck—grabs me, and I move on instinct. Elbow back, sharp and fast. The crack of cartilage.

He stumbles back with a howl, hands flying to his nose, blood pouring between his fingers.

"Christ!" the woman screams. "Get security!"

The second one tries to grab me from behind, but I drop my weight, twist, and drive my shoulder into his gut. He goes down hard, and then I'm past them both, my hand on the doorframe to keep myself vertical as the hallway stretches and contracts like something out of a fever dream.

Where's my phone? Where's Erin? I dial her number, and it predictably goes to voicemail. I dial Declan's number next. He answers on the first ring.

"Cavin, thank Christ. You alright?"

"Where's Erin?" The words come out slurred. I lean against the wall, pressing my forehead to the cold plaster. It helps a bit.

"We don't know. We've been looking—Cavin, are you out of bed?" He pauses, hearing something in my breathing. "You're in no condition—"

"Where is she?"

Silence. Then, quieter: "Her car's at the house. Her phone's there too. But she's gone. We can't find her."

Can't find her. "What the fuck happened while I was out?"

Declan doesn't respond right away. He knows something.

"Declan," I say, my voice dropping to something deadly. "I'll fucking kill you. *Where is she?*"

"I don't know, brother. I'm telling you the truth." He pauses. "Did you say something to her about her da?"

"I may have mentioned it."

I'm going to bloody kill my cousin. My vision's doubling. I close one eye, and it helps marginally. "What time is it?"

"Half eleven."

"Cavin, listen to me—"

Holy fucking Christ. I've got thirty minutes to pay the second tribute. I can't say it out loud where he can hear me. I push off the wall and start moving down the corridor. Security's coming—heavy footsteps, the crackling of radios.

"Where are you going?" Declan demands.

"I'm not telling you a damn thing. I want you to find my wife."

"Maybe she's betrayed you, brother. Just like her father—"

"I know my wife, Declan." I'm running now, though it's more of a controlled stumble, one hand trailing along the wall to keep me upright. "You tell me everything you know. Now."

Two guards round the corner. One of them is Erin's guard.

"Where the fuck were you, and why weren't you with her?" I grab him by the throat and slam him up against the wall, muscle memory kicking in, even through the haze.

"Sir, I don't know where she's gone—"

"Then you're a shite bodyguard," I snarl. I break his nose with one swift punch. "You fucking arsehole. You were supposed to watch my wife, and now she's not here."

I throw him at the other guard, and they both fall to the ground like dominoes. I don't slow down. The front door's ahead... so close. The floors are undulating like the deck of a ship in a storm, but I have to keep moving.

Wife. In danger. Move.

Someone grabs at my arm, and I spin too fast. My fist connects with something soft.

"Mr. McCarthy, please—"

"Get your fucking hands off me, or I'll break every damn finger."

I eventually crash through the door. The cold air hits me, and I stumble forward and retch. Nothing comes up but acid. Doesn't matter. I'm still moving.

The driveway is a sea of shadows. I blink hard, trying to focus. There—Seamus's Range Rover, parked nearby. Keyless entry. I know the code.

I yank the door open and haul myself into the driver's seat. The steering wheel swims in and out of focus.

This is a bloody *terrible* idea.

I press the start button. The engine roars to life, and I'm moving—down the driveway and onto the street. The headlights blur and streak. I blink hard, gripping the wheel so tight my knuckles go white.

My phone rings. I answer without looking.

"Turn around, you mad fuckin' bastard." Seamus. "You're concussed to shite. You'll kill yourself."

"Then I'll die on the way to her." My voice doesn't sound like mine. "I'm not stopping. She's my wife, Seamus. My fucking wife. And if any cunt has her, if they've fucking—" I can't finish. Can't breathe.

The road tilts, and I overcorrect. The Range Rover swerves.

"Who, brother? Where the fuck are you? Where are you going?" Seamus sounds strained.

"I have somewhere to be."

"What are you not fucking telling me?"

"I need answers, Seamus."

I hang up, then call Declan. He answers on the first ring.

"What the bloody hell are you up to?"

"You listen to me," I growl. "I don't care what the fuck you think you have on Erin. You listening?"

"Aye," he says. "Brother, what the hell—"

"I have something to do, and I need to tell you. I've held it back because Malachy told me if I told any of you, this would all go to shite. War. But guess what?" I sniff. Am I crying? Am I bloody fucking crying? "It's already gone to shite. I've got a damn tribute to pay, Declan. If I don't pay it, Bronwyn's gone. That's why they took her before. I have to do it. We need to put our heads together. But you can't tell anybody except immediate family. Do you hear me?"

"What the hell are you talking about, brother? Listen, you have a head injury, you're not right in the head just now."

"*No.* Listen to me," I say, each word deliberate. "Get Bronwyn. Get her now. Have her brought to the safe house. Do you understand me?"

Someone on the inside.

"Yes, I do. What are you doing, brother?"

"I'm going to rescue my wife. Meet me at the warehouse east of the safe house."

I disconnect and toss the phone into the passenger seat. The warehouse district rises up ahead, all crumbling brick and rusted chain link. I know these streets. I grew up running in them, fighting in them, bleeding in them.

Tonight, I might die in them.

But my wife fucking won't.

The thought is weirdly calming.

This is where I pay the tribute tonight. I *know* that's where she's gone to.

I pull up outside the warehouse I've been instructed to come to, and kill the engine. Tonight, I don't have the damn tribute.

Tonight, the tribute is *me.*

I sit for a second, trying to breathe through the nausea, trying to steady the way the world keeps lurching sideways. The door opens.

"What are you doing here?" Declan's there, stepping out of the shadows. "I don't know what you and Erin are up to, but—"

"I need to find her."

"You look like death, brother."

"Feel worse." I try to stand, but my legs nearly give out. Declan catches my elbow.

"You shouldn't be—"

"Don't." I shake him off and plant my feet. The ground's rolling, but I stay upright through sheer bloody-mindedness. I grab him by the front of his shirt. "You'll fucking get it when it's you. Where *is* she?"

"Don't bloody know," he says. "We tracked her movements. Ciarán says she left her phone at the house. She went back to your house, got something out of the safe."

Fucking hell. She got the money, likely her money from the investments. She's giving it all to them.

"Is she in there?"

"Don't bloody know."

Cars pull up—no lights, no sound. And then I see them. A handful of our best lads, all armed and ready: Seamus, Daire, Ashland, and Colm. Even Da's come. Our best men, tooled up and ready for war.

And there, on the ground at the warehouse entrance, I see a quilted bag. Erin's bag.

I walk over, nearly fall twice, but I make it. I crouch down, and when I do, the world spins faster. Bad fucking idea. I unzip the bag—it's empty.

"Cavin," Seamus says carefully, like he's talking to a man on a ledge. "What's this about?"

I can't hold it back anymore. I need my family to help.

"When Malachy died, he told me I had a tribute to pay," I say, my eyes closed, trying to stop the world from spinning. It doesn't work. "I'm supposed to pay this money every month. I've been paying it. Malachy swore me to secrecy— said if I told you, they'd find out, and we'd have war."

I turn to face the rest of them. "Looks like she's taken her money to pay it—she's the only one I told about it. Malachy said if I told you lads, I'd be fucked. That we all would." I shake my head. "But we are now anyway. If I don't pay it, we're fucked. You see?"

"When do you have to pay it?" Seamus grits out.

"And *who* are we paying?" Da asks.

"Good fucking question," I tell him. "That's exactly what I've been trying to find out. And while I haven't told you lads before, it's time. It's time for me to bring my family in."

Declan frowns as I turn to the warehouse. "I'm going in." I take a step toward the warehouse and stagger. Declan catches me this time, holding me steady.

"Are you sure you're bloody up for this, brother? Jesus—"

I think about Erin. About how she looked when I kissed her the last time—soft and warm and mine. The way her eyes met mine in the darkness, full of trust.

"I've had worse," I say. "Worse than a knock on the head, you gobshite." I straighten and push him off me, then check my gun. "Let's go get my wife."

The warehouse looms ahead, dark and waiting. Someone's dying tonight.

And it sure as hell won't be my wife.

Chapter Thirty-Four

Erin

Behind my back, zip ties cut into my wrists. I can feel blood trickling down my fingers where the plastic digs in.

"You have the money," I say, my voice echoing off the metal walls. The money sits at the masked man's feet like a trophy before he pulls off the damn mask.

Donovan. Of *course* it was fucking Donovan. I knew it was an inside job, and that smarmy smile of his and those lifeless eyes—

"You're the spy," I say, when the realization hits me like ice water.

"Clever girl." He winks at me like I'm a child who's finally solved a puzzle. "Guess you did well in school, didn't you? Took you long enough."

I shake my head. "Why? It's all there. Every cent. Just let me go."

Donovan's leaning against a support beam, his arms crossed, his face twisting into something I don't recognize. Something cruel.

"And you're a fucking traitor," I add, my voice cracking.

"Ah, sure we have the money, darling," he says, his accent thicker than usual, rough around the edges. What's he been playing at all this time? "But that's not really what this is about anymore, is it?"

My heart's hammering so hard I can barely breathe.

"Cavin is going to *kill* you for this."

That makes him actually laugh, like I've told the funniest joke he's ever heard. But when he looks at me again, his eyes are cold.

"Really now? See, that's where you're wrong, love." He pushes off the beam, then walks toward me slowly. "I have far more bargaining chips than you're aware of."

I try to scoot back, but there's nowhere to go. The back of the chair hits the wall. I'm out of options now, completely and utterly fucked.

"You know the best part?" He crouches down in front of me, close enough I can smell the whiskey on his breath. "Cavin doesn't even know who's been playing him this whole time."

"Why?" The word comes out broken. "You're family— you're his cousin. He said you're loyal. Family's supposed to mean something, right?"

He stands abruptly. "Tell me, Erin, what did your family mean to you? What did your da mean to you?"

I flinch at the mention of my father. "Leave him the fuck out of this."

"Can't do that, love. See, your da's the whole reason we're here." He stops pacing and turns to look at me fully. "Did you know he worked for us? For years."

My belly drops. "That's a lie."

"Is it?" Donovan tilts his head. "Padraic Kavanagh. Good man. Loyal man. Well, loyal to the Boston Irish, anyway. Not so much to the McCarthys."

I knew it. I knew there was something with the Americans.

But... Da?

"No." I'm shaking my head, but even as I deny it, the pieces are clicking into place. The money that disappeared. My parents' fights. The late-night meetings. The way my father would go to Boston on "business." How he'd take calls at odd hours—different time zones, I suppose.

"He cheated them, Erin. He had no West Coast connections. And you're the one who'll pull the trigger on this. You're the one who'll make sure we go away, we do what we have to, and your husband will keep paying this damn tribute."

He doesn't know yet that I told the McCarthys. "You know how that's gonna end, don't you, love?"

"Don't you call me that."

He chuckles low. "Was damn fun seeing you and Cavin go mental over the damn posts I made."

"*You* did that? Why?"

He shrugs. "Easy to throw a man like Cavin off. It's simple to know what gets under his skin."

"This was never about what I thought it was, was it? Me and my marriage to Cavin."

"Ah, you're getting there." He laughs and shakes his head. "You were supposed to have access to the doctor, right? Dr. Rosenberg, is it? Where's he now, I wonder?"

Donovan takes out his phone and makes a call. "Padraic. You got him?"

"Aye."

My god. My father?

"Your da destroyed your life for us. He knew that if you got in with the McCarthys, he would too. That you'd have access, right? Me and him—we could take over this fucking McCarthy clan. Work with the Boston Irish. Take over the tribute. It's been going on long before you were around. Malachy was the one who started it all."

"You're lying. You're fucking lying."

"I'm not," he says simply. He crouches again, grabs my chin hard enough to bruise. "This is how it's gonna work. We get tribute every two weeks. Not monthly anymore. And if we don't, you die."

"Cavin's not going to—"

"Cavin will do exactly what we tell him, or he'll be scooping up what's left of you." He releases my chin and stands. "The Boston Irish send their regards, by the way. We've been patient, but our patience is running out. And I'm telling you now, lass—"

The door to the warehouse explodes inward with a crash that makes my ears ring.

Cavin.

He's there, silhouetted in the doorway, looking like death itself. Blood stains his shirt. His face is pale, but his eyes are pure murder. Behind him, I can see his shadows—his family.

He found me.

How? Donovan shows a flash of terror before he schools his features.

"Get away from my wife," Cavin says, his voice deadly calm.

Donovan doesn't move. "Ah, you shouldn't be here, cousin. You should be in the hospital. You're looking like shite."

"Last chance," Cavin says, taking a step forward. He's swaying slightly, and I can see the effort it takes for him to stay upright.

"Or what?" Donovan spreads his hands. "You'll kill me, right? Start a war with the fucking Boston Irish? You can't win. You're in no position to make demands, Cavin."

"Brothers," Cavin says quietly, never taking his eyes off Donovan. "Get her to safety. They need to know what's happening. All of it."

Declan and Seamus move immediately, weapons drawn. But Donovan's not alone. I didn't notice them before, his men in the shadows.

"I don't think so," Donovan says.

Suddenly, there are guns everywhere, armed men I don't recognize.

"Get her the fuck out," Cavin orders. "Now!"

Two of Cavin's men break away, moving toward me. Donovan nods to his own men, and they shift to intercept. The warehouse is a powder keg, ready to explode.

"We'll have to take Erin. Insurance, you understand."

"Over my dead fuckin' body," Cavin snarls.

"That can be arranged." Donovan pulls his gun and aims it directly at Cavin's head. "You're concussed. Barely standing. You really want to do this now?"

"Try me, you treacherous cunt."

Everything happens at once.

Cavin moves impossibly fast for someone who should be barely conscious, launching himself at Donovan. The gun is knocked away, and the two of them crash to the floor. The phone falls to the floor. Somewhere in the house, gunfire barks.

"Cavin!" I scream, while the room erupts into chaos. Gunfire. Shouting. Bodies moving in the darkness.

Two men reaching for me go down hard, bullets in them before they can touch me. *Ciarán.* Another comes from the side. Declan handles him with brutal efficiency, knifework that makes me turn away.

But I can't look away from Cavin and Donovan.

They're animals, tearing into each other with a viciousness that makes my stomach turn. Cavin's clearly hurt—every movement looks like it costs him, but he fights like a man possessed. Fists, elbows, teeth.

I scream and try to get out of my bonds, but the harder I pull, the more I bleed.

Donovan gets on top, grappling for dominance. He rains blows on Cavin's face. I wince. My god, his concussion—

"You should have fucking stayed down!" he screams. "You should have paid your dues!"

Cavin catches his wrists and twists, and I hear something snap. Donovan howls, and Cavin uses the momentum to reverse their positions, slamming Donovan's head against the hardwood. Once. Twice. Three times.

I wince and scream.

Around us, the fight is turning. The McCarthys are outnumbered, but they're better trained, more vicious. Ashland takes down two men with his fists. Seamus is methodical, brutal—one bullet for each target. Declan moves like a dancer, all deadly grace and precise violence. I swear to fuck, I hear him laugh.

"Erin."

Seamus is suddenly there, cutting through my zip ties with his knife. My wrists scream as blood rushes back into my hands.

"Can you walk?"

"Yes. What about Cavin?"

"He's got it. Come with me."

But I can't move, can't look away as Cavin wraps his hands around Donovan's throat and squeezes.

Donovan's face turns purple, his hands scrambling.

"Cavin." Declan's voice cuts through the chaos. "We need him alive. We need information."

"He tried to take her from me," Cavin says, sounding barely human. Blood pours from his nose. His lip is split open. He wobbles on his feet but doesn't let go. He's a shark going in for the kill. "He tried to take my wife."

For a moment, I think Cavin won't stop, that he'll squeeze until Donovan stops moving, until there's nothing left but a corpse. His grip tightens. Donovan's struggles are weakening.

"Cavin, please," I beg. "Don't. We need to know who else is involved. You don't want his blood on your hands, not this way."

Something in my voice reaches him.

"Cavin, it's not worth it. Not your cousin's blood on your hands, love. Cavin. Let them take him."

His hands loosen just slightly, and Donovan gasps, sucking in air. Cavin hauls him up by the throat, dragging him toward the door.

"You're coming with us. And when I'm done with you, you'll wish I'd fucking killed you here."

Around us, Donovan's men are dead. The wooden floor is slick with blood. Seamus keeps a hand on my arm, steadying me.

Outside, the cold air hits us like a blessing. I'm shaking so hard my teeth chatter.

Cavin throws Donovan into the back of a van. The others pile in around him, keeping their weapons trained on the traitor.

Cavin turns to me, his face a mess of blood and bruises. "Are you hurt, love?" he asks, his hands hovering over me like he's afraid to touch me.

"I'm fine. You shouldn't be here. You should be in the hospital."

"Don't fucking care," he says roughly. "I thought I'd lost you. I thought they'd—"

"I'm okay. I'm here."

He kisses me hard and desperate. When he pulls away, he presses his forehead to mine.

"We're going to finish this," he says. "All of it. No more secrets. No more tributes. I'm done playing by their fucking rules."

Behind him, in the van, Donovan is screaming, begging. The sound is cut off abruptly, followed by the wet thud of fist meeting flesh.

"You fucking traitor," Declan snarls from inside.

"Dr. Rosenberg—"

"I know, love."

Cavin's hand finds mine in the darkness and squeezes.

We're not safe yet. Not by a long shot.

But we're together.

And god help anyone who tries to take that away.

Cavin still holds his gun. "You're wrecked, love," I say.

"I know it," he says, shaking his head. "I've had worse. We're headed to your family's house. Let's see what we can find."

When we reach my family's home, the others file out of the van quickly. "Stand behind me. Careful, Erin," Cavin says, slowly leading me to the front door. "We don't know where anyone is."

"Do you hear voices in the kitchen?"

By the time we get to the kitchen, my parents are surrounded by Seamus, Daire, and Ciarán.

"Found them," Seamus says. "Erin, I'm sorry, but they have to go into custody until I have answers."

I nod, even as my eyes go watery and a lump forms in my throat. "Aye. I know."

"Erin!" My mother reaches for me, her eyes wide and terrified. And that's when I see him—Dr. Rosenberg, sitting at the kitchen table, watching all of us placidly.

"Dr. Rosenberg!"

He nods in greeting.

I sink into a chair before my legs give out.

Chapter Thirty-Five

Erin

WE ARE A FUCKING DISASTER. Cavin's sprawled on the bed, blood dried on his knuckles, bruising already blooming across his ribs. There's a cut above his eyebrow—it hurts like hell and probably needs stitches.

I'm not much better with my scraped knees and bruised and cut-up wrists. Everything hurts.

"We need to move," I say quietly.

"Shower, meds, bed." He grunts, but doesn't open his eyes.

"Cavin."

"Five more minutes."

"You're bleeding on your fancy sheets."

"Fuck the sheets." But then he shifts anyway, wincing. "Christ."

I drag myself upright, every muscle screaming. "Come on. Shower first. Then we'll find the pain meds."

The bathroom is all marble and golden fixtures—wealth evident even in the smallest details. I turn on the shower, and steam immediately fills the space.

Cavin leans against the doorframe, watching me with hooded eyes. There's blood on his shoulders and streaked across his jaw.

"Can you stand?" I ask.

"Can you?"

"Fair point."

We strip slowly, carefully. "Jesus, Erin." He glances down at my torso—bruises, lots of them.

We step into the shower together. The hot water feels glorious, soothing sore muscles even while stinging every cut and scrape. Cavin hisses through his teeth.

"Steady," I murmur.

"I'm grand."

"Oh, you liar."

I get him under the spray, letting the water wash away the worst of the blood. "I talked to Bridget," I say quietly. "She's doing alright. I only told her a little—just a wee bit." I steady him with a hand on his shoulder. "Lean on me. I don't want you falling and hitting your head again."

He does, his weight settling against my shoulder. We stand there, letting the water wash away the evidence of tonight's violence.

I reach for the soap and start cleaning him gently. The cuts look raw and angry. He winces, but he's been through worse.

"You are *not allowed* to fight anyone, protect anyone, or go into the ring for like... *forever*."

"That right, lass?" he asks with a smirk. "You're the boss of me now?"

"I'm your wife."

My hands move to his chest, careful around the worst of it. He flinches when I touch his ribs.

"Bruised or broken?"

"Bruised, probably."

"We should get you checked out."

"Later." He leans on me and lets me keep washing.

When I'm done, he takes the soap from my hands. "My turn."

His touch is gentler, reverent almost, like he's afraid I'll shatter. I feel like maybe I will.

When we're both clean, or as clean as we're getting, I turn off the water. We dry in silence, but he cups my jaw, rubbing his thumb over my lips. Then he leans down and presses his mouth to mine.

"My love, it's going to be alright. It's all going to be alright. No more tribute. No more debts. No more blackmail."

"Aye. But my parents..."

He sighs. "I don't suspect your mother was in on this. Your father was. You know the rules."

I nod. I do.

"Exile or death. I'll make sure it's the first option. I'd bet anything your father's selfish and desperate, not dangerous." He kisses my cheek. "He doesn't have an heir to his throne, so his only option would be a power move, like this."

"Please, Cavin. Exile," I whisper. "My father and I have never been close, but I can't imagine what—what it would do to Bridget."

"You have my word, love."

He frowns when he gets a text. He turns his phone to show me. "It's Kyla."

> **Kyla**
> You told me to find out who was posting to the St. Albert's account. Bronwyn and I have been on it. And it's strange, Cav, but we discovered who. It's the photographer from the wedding, brother. Him, and Donovan

He shakes his head. "Of *course*. God. The photographer? The one my cousin Donovan just *happened* to defend for no reason."

"Oh god."

Cavin shakes his head. "He was there the night my car was bombed, there the day Bronwyn was taken, there the day she came back, and we had no security feed." He sighs. "You were right. I didn't want to believe you, but you were right."

I kiss his cheek. "Shh. Put it down now. It's over."

The pain medication is in his nightstand. I grab water from the bathroom and shake out pills for both of us.

"Here."

We swallow them, then collapse back onto the bed. The sheets are ruined with blood, but neither of us cares.

He pulls me against his chest, careful of our injuries, and his arm comes around me. I rest my head on his chest, on the one spot that doesn't seem to hurt.

"Cavin."

"Hmm?"

"I love you. And I'm sorry. So fucking sorry for everything that happened. For my father, the debt—"

"Stop." His hand comes up, his fingers threading through my damp hair. "You've shown loyalty to me and to my family. You've nothing to apologize for."

"He used me," I say, my voice shaking. "Here I was, thinking my mam was the villain."

"He did use you, and your father made his choices. He'll answer for them."

I sigh.

"Your father will be leaving Dublin for good."

The words should hurt more than they do, but all I feel is relief, and then... shame for feeling relieved.

"Where?"

"Don't know. And he won't get to tell you." His thumb brushes my cheekbone. "He won't get to hurt you again."

"Cavin—"

"Sleep, love. We've got a long day tomorrow."

Tomorrow, we meet with Dr. Rosenberg at St. Vincent's.

Morning comes too soon, gray light filtering through the windows of Ballyhock. I'm moving like I'm fucking ninety years old. Everything hurts.

"I've arranged something," Cavin says over a cup of tea. "For Bridget."

"What's that?"

"Dr. Rosenberg's waiting to see us at St. Vincent's, with Bridget."

"Is she okay?"

"She's grand, but the hospital is a better place for her to see him."

"Right." I squeeze his hand. "*Thank* you."

We take Cavin's car to St. Vincent's. Every bump in the road is agony, and the pain meds barely touch it, but neither of us complains. It's worse for him than for me.

The hospital is busy—morning rounds, visiting hours just starting. A nurse directs us to a private room where Bridget's been moved.

There, standing beside her bed, is Dr. Rosenberg.

"Miss Kavanagh—ah, excuse me," he says with a smile. "Mrs. McCarthy. Pleased to see you again." He takes a look at Cavin. "Seems like you may need some medical attention as well."

"I'm fine."

"Hmm. You sure about that?"

"He's not, sir," I say. "But I think he'll listen to reason after you see my sister."

Cavin's hand squeezes mine. It hurts, but I welcome it.

"Take care of Bridget," Cavin says. "Please."

Dr. Rosenberg studies him for a moment. "Very well. Family first. I respect that."

Bridget looks worse than I remembered. Her skin's got that translucent quality, with purple shadows under her eyes. But when she sees me, she smiles.

"Erin."

"Hey, Bridget." I cross to her, take her hand. It feels so small, so fragile. "How are you feeling, love?"

"Like shite," she says weakly. "But better now that you're here. Christ, what happened to you two?"

"Oh, it's a fucking long story," Cavin says. "Bridget, meet Dr. Rosenberg."

The doctor clears his throat and smiles kindly. "Pleased to meet you. I specialize in cases like yours. Your sister's gone to considerable trouble to arrange this consultation, and I'm here to help. If you'll permit me, I'd like to review your case and determine the best course of treatment."

Bridget's eyes widen. "You're the doctor from Glasgow?"

"The same." He pulls up a chair beside her bed, then opens a tablet. "Now then, let's see what we're up against, shall we?"

I watch from the corner as Dr. Rosenberg starts his examination, asking questions in that calm, clinical voice. Bridget answers as best she can, though she's clearly exhausted.

"I'm sorry about all the... drama," I say to the doctor.

He waves a hand. "Been friends with the McCarthys for years. I know how things go."

I nod. "If there's anything I can do—"

The doctor smiles up at me. "As a matter of fact, there is."

I wait expectantly as he tips his head at me. "I hear you knit these bulletproof hats..."

Chapter Thirty-Six

Cavin

ERIN HASN'T LEFT her sister's side. She's holding Bridget's hand like it's the only thing anchoring her to earth.

"The disease is aggressive," Dr. Rosenberg says after reviewing her charts.

"Can you help her?" Erin's voice is small. Desperate.

He looks up and smiles. "Oh, yes. I believe I can."

The relief on Erin's face nearly breaks me.

"It won't be easy," he continues. "The treatment I'm proposing is experimental. Aggressive. We have a long road ahead of us, and it will make her feel worse before she feels better. But the success rate for cases like hers is encouraging. Approximately seventy percent achieve full remission."

"Seventy percent..." Bridget breathes.

"Those are good odds, given where we're starting." Dr. Rosenberg closes his tablet. "I'll need to run additional tests today. Bloodwork and the like. Then we can begin treatment tomorrow, if you're willing."

"I'm willing," Bridget says immediately.

"Eager, good." Dr. Rosenberg stands and winks at her. "That fighting spirit will serve you well. Now, let me coordinate with the hospital staff. I'll need specific equipment brought in." He pauses at the door. "Oh, and Mr. McCarthy?"

"Aye?"

"After I'm done here, you're getting those ribs wrapped, that cut stitched, and your bloody head looked at again. No arguments."

"Aye."

He leaves before I can protest.

Erin giggles, and Bridget follows suit.

"Bloody hell," I mutter, which only makes them laugh harder. I smile and shake my head. I'm outnumbered, and I wouldn't have it any other way.

Chapter Thirty-Seven

Erin

WHEN WE'RE ALONE—JUST me, Bridget, and Cavin—Bridget turns to look at me properly.

"You did this," she says softly. "You made this happen."

"Cavin did it. He—"

"Because of you." Bridget's grip tightens on my hand. "I know what you sacrificed, Erin. I know what Da did. What he made you do."

My throat closes.

"Bronwyn told me everything after you left. After Da..." She swallows. "You sold yourself for this family. For me."

"Bridge—"

"Let me finish." Tears stream down her pale cheeks. "You gave up everything. Your innocence. Your future. Maybe your soul. All so I could have a chance." Her eyes shift to

Cavin, then back to me. "I won't forget that. Ever. And whatever happens, whatever you need, I'm with you. Always."

I lean forward, pressing my forehead to hers. "You just focus on getting better, yeah?"

"I will." She manages a weak smile. "And Erin? For what it's worth? I think he loves you too."

I glance back at Cavin. He's watching us with an expression I can't quite read.

"He does," I whisper. "I know he does."

Two hours later, Dr. Rosenberg returns with a team of nurses. They whisk Bridget away for tests, leaving me and Cavin alone in the room.

"Your turn," I tell him.

"I'm fine."

"Dr. Rosenberg said—"

"I know what he said."

But he lets me lead him to the emergency department anyway. A young doctor stitches his eyebrow, wraps his ribs, inspects his head, and does some tests, then prescribes stronger pain medication. The whole time, Cavin doesn't flinch.

"You're stubborn," I observe.

"Pot. Kettle."

When we're finally done, both of us properly patched up, we head back to Bridget's room. She's already there, looking exhausted but hopeful.

Dr. Rosenberg stands beside her bed, reviewing results on his tablet.

"Well?" I ask.

He looks up, and his smile is genuine. "We start tomorrow. Erin? This looks very promising, very promising indeed. Your sister's ill, yes, and the prognosis without proper treatment is fatal." He sighs, taps the papers together and smiles. "But I'm confident we're going to save your sister's life."

For the first time in months, I let myself believe it.

I turn to Cavin, bury my face in his chest, and finally let myself cry.

Chapter Thirty-Eight

Erin

THAT NIGHT, Cavin and I lie in bed, the room dark except for the dying fire casting shadows across the walls.

We're in our house.

Our. House.

Da's been locked away, still up for questioning. Mam's been released. And Bridget's... here, with us, in the guest room, sleeping.

"Tell me something," I say softly. "What do you see when you look at the future?"

It's quiet for a moment, his breathing steady against my hair.

"I never did think of the future until you, but now..." He pauses, his thumb tracing circles on my hip. "I see us here at Ballyhock. I see Bridget healthy and thriving. Maybe you knitting, bookkeeping. Whatever makes you happy." He winks. "And keeps you safe."

"Right then. So no undercover operations or shooting guns in rings."

He slaps my arse playfully, then his hand finds mine under the covers, lacing our fingers together. "I see you with your knitting, making things—beautiful things. I see us growing old together, navigating whatever comes our way. Even the dangerous bits."

His voice drops lower, more serious. "I won't lie to you, Erin. This life, our life—it's not easy. There'll be threats and rivals, people who want what we have. But we'll face it together."

"Together," I echo.

"Aye." He kisses me softly. "You and me against the world, love."

And I think about that. About the Boston connection that Declan's investigating. All the unknowns still lurking on the edges of our happiness. There will be more challenges, more danger. This isn't a fairy tale with a perfect ending.

But it's our ending. A hard one, honest and real.

"I can live with that," I say.

"Good. Because I'm not letting you go."

"You possessive Irish bastard," I murmur against his mouth.

"*Your* possessive Irish bastard," he growls, and I seal it with a kiss.

Epilogue

Cavin

THE HOUSE IS full of laughter and music, not the forced politeness of a formal gathering, but something real and warm.

Family.

Bridget's dancing with Declan, both of them laughing at something like an inside joke. Seamus is in deep conversation with Dr. Rosenberg, probably discussing medical innovations or some such shite. Mam's talking with Da, who's looking more relaxed than I've seen him in months. Erin's mam declined the invite, and I understand.

Tara Kavanagh found out about Padraic's betrayal the same way Erin did. She swears she didn't know—that he'd been lying to her for months about where the money was going, what deals he was making. Erin believes her, which is good enough for me. Erin says her da was always good at compartmentalizing his shite, keeping the women in the dark.

Whether my family believes her is another matter entirely. We agreed to let them both live, let Tara keep the house, but there's a price for that mercy—exile for her father, and Tara Kavanagh doesn't show her face at McCarthy events. Keeps her head down and her mouth shut.

It's likely why she declined tonight, though I suspect the conditions I've made—for the way she treats Erin and now having to ask for my permission—had something to do with it too. Maybe she needs to find another whipping boy or girl, as it were.

Erin and I sneak away onto the terrace, where the night is clear and the stars are out in force.

"Happy?" she asks.

"Deliriously." I lean into her warmth. "Never thought I'd have this," I say quietly. "A proper marriage. Love. Someone who chose me." I tug a lock of her hair. "You? You once told me you didn't believe in marriage."

She shrugs. "Mmm. That was a lie."

I chuckle. "Well, hope you do now."

She turns to face me, her eyes fierce in the moonlight. "I suppose. And you're stuck with me."

I kiss her, slow and sweet, and I taste forever in it.

Behind us, someone clears their throat. We break apart to see Seamus grinning at us like a cat with cream.

"Sorry to interrupt the moment," he says, sounding not sorry at all, "but there's something you should know."

Erin tenses beside me. "What's that?"

"That Boston connection Declan's been watching? Wants a meeting."

"When?" My voice has gone cold, professional.

"Next week." Seamus's expression is serious now. "Could be nothing. Could be everything. Either way, we need to be ready."

Erin looks at me, and there's a question in her eyes. *Are you ready for this?*

She straightens her shoulders and lifts her chin.

That's my girl.

"I'm Erin McCarthy now. Wife to Cavin. Sister to Bridget. Part of this family." She meets my brother's gaze steadily. "We'll handle it. Together."

Seamus grins, approval gleaming in his eyes. "That's what I like to hear. Welcome, Erin."

"Thank you." She pauses. "We don't bring to the table what I thought I would. I'm sorry about that. My family—they don't have—"

"No." I cut her off, my voice firm. "You bring *you* to the table, and that's all I need." I kiss her temple, possessive and tender. "You're my family now."

Erin McCarthy is fearless when the ones she loves are threatened, not to mention her skill at turning pocket change into gold. She told me she'll let them know that when the time is right.

I lean in, my lips brushing hers, my voice dropping to a wicked whisper. "Are you ready to do the devil's work, Mrs. McCarthy?"

She grins. "With you by my side, *Mr.* McCarthy."

THE END

Preview

Wicked Sanctuary A Dark
Irish Mafia Stalker Romance

CHAPTER ONE

SIX YEARS EARLIER...

Ashland

I LOVE THE TASTE of blood in my mouth during a fight. It tastes like victory.

I spit it on the concrete floor of the ring, and red splatters across grey.

My ribs ache from where The Cork bastard caught me early, a hit I'll feel tomorrow, but when he comes in with a right hook, confident, thinking he's got me figured out, I duck. I drive my fist into his kidney, Once. Twice. Three times in rapid succession, each hit precise and targeted. I feel something give under my knuckles.

And I love this. God help me, I fucking love this.

He grunts and tries to pivot away, but I'm too fast for him. He swings wild, desperate now, and clips my jaw. Blood floods my mouth, the familiar coppery taste sweet and satisfying.

Beautiful.

He grins, breathing hard, and his guard's dropped.

"Come on, then," I say, my voice rough. I tap my jaw where he hit me. "That all you got?"

He charges.

I sidestep and hammer my elbow into the base of his skull as he goes by. Not hard enough to do permanent damage— I'm not trying to kill the fucker—but hard enough.

He staggers. Knees buckle.

I'm on him before he can recover. Left jab to the temple, right cross to the cheekbone. I feel the satisfying crack under my knuckles. Another shot to his fucked up ribs, and this time something cracks.

"Finish him, Ash!" Tiernan shouts from somewhere behind me, and it's all the encouragement I need.

I drive my knee into his stomach. The air leaves his lungs in a sick *whoosh.*

He drops face first on the canvas. The ref's beside him instantly, checking him, and I step back. My chest heaves. My hands throb. There's blood on my knuckles, and I can't tell if it's his or mine.

His crew screams for him to get up, but he won't, not after what I did to his ribs. Wouldn't be wise, would it?

"Time," the ref's voice echoes through the warehouse, and the crowd erupts.

I don't hear them when I'm playing, don't hear them when I'm fighting, but I do after I win a damn fight.

McCarthy! McCarthy! McCarthy!

The McCarthy family's name is one of their favorite cheers, and I fucking love it. I love being a part of something bigger, of knowing I stand in solidarity with my brother and cousins.

Today, I don't move or raise my arms, don't celebrate. I just stand there, knuckles split and bleeding, waiting for the roar to fade. It doesn't, really.

I've found that violence sits in my chest like a living thing, coiling tighter and tighter until the next fight. I've come to welcome it.

"Ash." Tiernan's voice cuts through the roar of the crowd. "Get out of the fuckin' ring, lad, will you?"

I turn and find him at the ropes. Tiernan's my uncle. My mom's younger brother, though he was nearly an adult himself when my parents married. He has a family of his own now, but he's always been my mentor.

"Y'alright?" he asks as I duck through the ropes.

"Aye. Grand."

"That wasn't *grand*, Ash," he says, giving me the look of pride mixed with worry I've come to recognize. "That was fuckin' brutal." He leans closer, and I can see the gray mixed with ginger in his hair, the lines around his eyes, and the way his brow creases. I remember when I thought he was invincible, the day I saw *him* in this ring and decided it would be me, one day. Tiernan was a bit of a legend in Ballyhock. Still is.

He tosses me a towel. I wipe away sweat and blood and ball it up in my fist. I shrug. "You're acting like I tried to kill the fucking bastard. If I wanted him dead, he'd be dead."

I wink at him as I lift the ropes and exit the ring. He stands beside me, my bodyguard by habit even though I haven't actually needed one for some time now.

Tiernan huffs a laugh, but there's truth in it. We both know what I'm capable of, what I've been taught, what the family's made me.

I'm the weapon they bring out when negotiations fail.

I'm fucking good at it, too.

I like to think the ring's like sharpening a blade—necessary maintenance for what I am.

"Your Da wants you to ease up, you know," Tiernan says, falling into step beside me as we head toward the back exit. "He says you're fighting too hard, too often. People are starting to talk."

I shrug. "Let 'em talk."

I drag the towel across my face again, tasting copper and sweat. I know what I'm doing. I don't like to think about what would happen if the coil of violence inside me didn't have an outlet, but I know better than to say that out loud.

Tiernan sighs, but doesn't push it. He knows better. We've been doing this dance for years now—him trying to keep me from going too far off the edge, me pretending I'm not already halfway there.

The ring's a few blocks from The Craic, the McCarthy family bar and exclusive club, so means the crowd largely favors us.

I nod to people who cheer and absorb the congratulatory slaps to my back.

This is home.

But sometimes, every once in a while, I fantasize about getting on a plane and flying far, far away. Somewhere nobody knows my name or what the ink carved into my skin symbolizes. A place where I don't have to be who I've been trained to be.

"Fancy a drink at the club?" Tiernan asks, hands shoved in his pockets. He doesn't go much now that his family needs him. Still, he likes to grab a pint with the lads, just like I do. "I heard Cavin's there. Declan, too."

I shake my head. Cavin runs the place and Declan's a frequent flyer, but I'm not in the mood to see my cousins tonight.

"Nah, I'm good."

"Honestly, brother," he says, giving me a look. "I know things have never been the same since Donovan—"

"I *don't* want to talk about Donovan."

I interrupt him before he can go further. My older brother betrayed the McCarthy family and paid the ultimate price. When I go to The Craic, I still fancy I can see him there sometimes with his pale blue eyes, smirk, and sharp tongue.

His punishment was justified, but I won't ever forget. Ever.

"Not tonight," I say, my voice husky. "I might—"

I freeze when I hear a scream just outside.

"Did you hear that?"

Tiernan concentrates and listens, then shakes his head. Sometimes my ears ring a bit after a fight. "Aye, but doesn't sound serious, is it?"

Laughter follows the scream, and I reckon it's just some drunk eejits having a go at each other.

"Go home, lad," he says. "Take care of yourself, will you? I'll supper with you at the weekend. See you?"

I shrug. Maybe.

Maybe not. I like my quiet.

"All right, then," he says. "Watch your back. Don't think that lad from Cork has anybody who's gonna shiv you in the alley, but you never know, eh?" He says it with a wink, but it's only half a joke. We've all learned to have eyes in the back of our heads.

He cuffs my jaw gently. "You did well there, lad. Proud of you."

Something like warmth blooms in my chest.

I cuff his shoulder back. "Thanks. Could still best you, eh?" He fakes me out, and lands a solid but playful jab to the stomach before I block and retaliate. We jokingly spar before he gets into his car and leaves.

But before I'm a few paces into my walk, I hear it *again*.

A scream. Sharp and sudden and cut off too quick. I wait, breath caught.

This time, there's no laughter that follows.

Every instinct I have flares to life. I stand up straighter, my hands balled into fists.

I'm already reaching for the knife tucked in my waistband before I realize I left it in the fucking locker.

Jesus.

The scream came from the alley behind the ring, the one that runs parallel to the main street. It's dark back there with only one flickering streetlight at the far end.

I turn the corner, and my eyes adjust instantly, scanning for threats.

I see it all in seconds.

Two men. Masked. Vaguely familiar, though I can't place them.

One holding a struggling figure who's fighting with every-thing he's got, the other pulling a black bag over his head. They work in sync, wasting no time. Professionals.

They haven't seen me yet. *Good.*

The figure they're trying to kidnap is slight, small enough to be a teenager, but I can't see their face with the bag half over their head.

"For fuck's sake, *hurry*," one growls. "The goddamn McCarthy fight got out."

"Thought it'd be easier!" the other snarls.

We're in McCarthy family territory. This is *my* turf. Could be anyone, someone I fuckin' know for Christ's sake.

The first man doesn't even see me coming. I hit him full force, shoulder to his ribs, and he goes down like a sack of shite.

The second one drops his victim and reaches for something, but I'm faster. I grab his wrist, twist it until I hear the snap, and drag my fist into his face.

Once. Twice. Three times.

He crumples.

The adrenaline from the fight still pumps through my veins, sharper now, hotter. These fuckers tried to *take* somebody. In *our* territory. Tried to hurt somebody younger, smaller, innocent.

Big fucking mistake.

I grab the first man by his collar and haul him up. He's conscious but barely, blood pouring from his nose. In my peripheral vision, the hooded kid scrambles to his feet.

Who sent you? Who the fuck are you?

I don't recognize the bastard. He spits blood at me.

Wrong answer.

I hold him up by the shoulders and slam him against the brick wall hard enough that his head cracks and bounces.

"I asked you a *fucking* question."

"Fuck you," he wheezes.

I'm about to hit him again when I remember the victim. I glance over my shoulder and freeze.

It's a kid dressed all in black, backed up against the opposite wall with wide, terrified eyes.

I turn back to the arsehole. I want to slit his throat right here, right now, in front of somebody who could report me.

The man in my grip tries to twist away while I'm distracted, but instinct takes over. I drive my knee into his stomach and let him drop.

He stays down.

Behind me, one of the men groans. I glance back and see him trying to crawl away.

Without thinking, I step on his hand, grinding his fingers into the pavement until he screams.

When I look back, the boy's has pressed himself flat against the wall.

Fuck. I'm not helping the situation. Haven't given these arseholes half of what they deserve, but the lad's seen enough.

"Go," I tell him. "Get out of here. Find somewhere with people. Somewhere bright." He shouldn't be out here fucking alone at night.

He doesn't move. *Of course* he doesn't. Probably terrified.

In the sky overhead, clouds shift. Moonlight spills down into the alley, landing on the kid beside me.

I stifle a gasp.

Fuck.

It's not...a boy.

She's about fifteen or sixteen, with wide blue eyes staring straight at me. Her thick, black hair falling loose from her braid. There's a scrape on her cheek where they must have hit her.

And she's staring at me like *I'm* the monster.

To be fair, I probably look like one. covered in blood—some mine, most not. Knuckles split. Shaved head. Scars. Ink.

And I've got some bastard slammed against the wall.

She's too young to be here. Too young to be caught up in whatever the fuck this is. Too young to be *alone.*

You alright? I ask, my voice rough.

She doesn't answer, just stares. Still in shock, maybe. Can't blame her.

Still holding the bastard, I take a step toward her, and she flinches.

Fuck.

"I'm not gonna hurt you," I say, keeping my hands where she can see them. "Those men—did they do anything to you? Do you know who they are?"

Over my shoulder, I hear an engine. *Christ.* They've got backup. Course they fuckin' do.

I'm instantly on alert, wishing for a weapons, when an unfamiliar black car screeches to a halt on the curb.

"Hey—" I growl.

Gunshots ring out, loud and fatal. *Jesus.*

I release the arsehole and lunge for the girl, slamming us both to the ground. My body covers hers, a shield of muscle and bone. Bullets spark off the brick above us. The two men scramble into the car, tires squealing as they tear off into the night.

Fuck.

I push myself up slightly, still shielding her. "Those men," I growl. "You sure you don't know them?"

I didn't get fucking anything on them.

She shakes her head slowly, dark blue eyes as deep and endless as the ocean locked on mine.

"What's your name?" I ask her.

She opens her mouth, closes it. Her lips are trembling. She doesn't trust me.

Of course she doesn't.

"It's alright," I say, gentle now. "You're safe. They're not going to hurt you."

Then I realize what this could look like.

Me with a fucking *minor,* alone in an alley, standing too damn close. Everybody knows who I am. Can't be seen like this.

Jesus, the rumors.

I leap back from her as if she's lit me on fire.

"Go," I bark this time, angrier, sterner. "You've got no god-damn business being here alone. Get the fuck out of here!"

Finally, she jolts into motion.

"And don't you fucking go out here alone again!" I scream after her retreating figure.

I watch her disappear around the corner, footsteps echoing in the alley. Something in my chest twists when she looks back once just before she turns the corner.

Then she's gone.

She could have been one of my younger cousins. Something terrible could have happened right here in Ballyhock.

The air's too quiet after everything that went down tonight. But once again... I'm alone.

I shove my hands in my pockets and head home. It's too quiet after what just happened.

I think about telling my family what I did, what I saw. But something stops me, something I don't want to name.

We're not in the business of *saving* people.

Christ.

I'm Ashland fucking McCarthy. Feared across Ireland.

I'm no *hero.*

But I can't shake the image of her backed against that wall. Those wide, terrified eyes. The way she looked at me like *I* was the monster instead of them.

Little does she know... I am.

Pre-order the next book in the Jane's new McCarthy Family Legacy series "Wicked Sanctuary: A Dark Irish Mafia Stalker Romance" by scanning the QR code below. Available May 1, 2026!

Fueled by dark chocolate and even darker coffee, USA Today bestselling author Jane Henry writes what she loves to read – character-driven, unputdownable romance featuring dominant alpha males and the powerful heroines who bring them to their knees. She's believed in the power of love and romance since Belle won over the beast, and finally decided to write love stories of her own.

Scan the QR Code below to receive Jane's Newsletter & be notified of upcoming new releases & special offers!

Be sure to visit me at www.janehenryromance.com, too!

www.ingramcontent.com/pod-product-compliance
Lightning Source LLC
Chambersburg PA
CBHW020335010826
48970CB00012B/834